THE SILVER STAIN

THE SILVER STAIN

An Alex Mavros Mystery

Paul Johnston

CRÈME de la CRIME

This first world edition published 2012
in Great Britain and the USA by
Crème de la Crime, an imprint of
SEVERN HOUSE PUBLISHERS LTD of
9–15 High Street, Sutton, Surrey, England, SM1 1DF.
Trade paperback edition first published
in Great Britain and the USA 2012.

British Library Cataloguing in Publication Data

Johnston, Paul, 1957–
    The silver stain. – (Alex Mavros novels)
    1. Mavros, Alex (Fictitious character) – Fiction.
    2. Private investigators – Greece – Fiction. 3. Suspense
    fiction.
    I. Title II. Series
    823.9′2-dc23

ISBN-13: 978-1-78029-018-8 (cased)
ISBN-13: 978-1-78029-523-7 (trade paper)

All Severn House titles are printed on acid-free paper.

Severn House Publishers support The Forest Stewardship Council [FSC],
the leading international forest certification organisation. All our titles that
are printed on Greenpeace-approved FSC-certified paper carry the FSC logo.

Typeset by Palimpsest Book Production Ltd.,
Falkirk, Stirlingshire, Scotland.
Printed and bound in Great Britain by
MPG Books Ltd., Bodmin, Cornwall.

To
John Connolly
in friendship and gratitude

AUTHOR'S NOTE

Mavros has been confined to a wooden box (file) for the last seven years. I didn't want to him to age so much and, accordingly, the action of this novel takes place in 2003, the year after his last outing, *The Golden Silence*. Anyone wanting depictions of life during the Greek economic crisis that started to bite hard in 2010 should look elsewhere – or wait for future volumes in the series. On the other hand, the roots of the catastrophe were already deep in 2003 and the 2004 Olympic Games fertilized them copiously.

Greek is a much less difficult language than many think, but readers should note the following:

1) Masculine names ending in –is, –os, and –as lose the final –s in the vocative case – 'Mikis, Yiorgos and Nondas are drinking your health'; but, 'Drink the readers' health, Miki, Yiorgo and Nonda!'
2) Feminine surnames end differently from masculine ones: Alex Mavros, but Anna Mavrou; Haris Tsifakis, but Eleni Tsifaki.
3) The consonant transliterated as 'dh' (e.g. An*dh*roniki, Fe*dh*ra, *Dh*rakakis) is pronounced 'th' as in English 'these'.
4) Chania is pronounced 'Chan*yah*' with the stress on the final syllable; likewise, Kornaria is pronounced 'Kornar*yah*'.

School's out.

ONE

Mavros was sitting on the large, plant-festooned balcony of his mother's flat with the orange juice he had just squeezed. Normally a late-riser – the boon of being self-employed – he had woken before dawn, for no apparent reason, and been unable to get back to sleep. The early sun had appeared over Mount Imittos and was casting tentative rays over the grey-white apartment blocks of the Athenian sprawl. To the south, the Aegean still retained the last of its dawn darkness, stretching away towards the islands and the Peloponnesian peaks. A northerly wind ensured that the air was relatively clear, and the sound of traffic and drivers quick on their horns was already ascending the slopes of Lykavittos. The view, taking in the Acropolis and its scaffolding-clad temples, was glorious, but Mavros was struggling to come to terms with it.

Bare arms slipped round his shoulders. 'Still missing the old flat, Alex?' Andhroniki Glezou's soft cheek rubbed against his stubble and then her lips sought his. Their tongues briefly touched. 'Oh no.' Niki said firmly. 'I was just saying good morning. I've got an eight o'clock meeting.'

Mavros smiled. 'I don't know what you mean. I was just saying good morning too.'

'Uh-huh. And what's that?' Niki pointed to his groin.

'Don't take it personally, my love. Morning glory answers to no woman.'

Niki slapped him on the arm. 'Charming. You haven't answered my question.'

Mavros looked back over the city. The flat on Pikilis, just north of the Acropolis, had become too expensive for him to continue renting at the end of 2002. That coincided with his mother suffering a stroke that had made her frail, so she had left the large flat in Kolonaki, the most exclusive area in central Athens, and moved in with Mavros's sister in Anna in the northern suburbs.

'If only you charged reasonable fees,' Niki said, 'instead of waiving them half the time.'

Mavros frowned. 'Now you're running my business too, are you?' He knew as soon as he said the words that he was in trouble. Although he and Niki were closer than they had ever been, her extravagant temper was never caged for long.

'Don't take that tone with me,' she said, glaring. With her dark eyes and tousled hair, she had the look of the mythical Gorgon that dealt stony death, though no part of Mavros's body was hard any more. 'You don't let me run anything, never mind your business, Alex. And what kind of a business is it, exactly, tracing missing people?'

'I seem to remember finding a girl you managed to mislay,' he muttered.

The reference to the daughter of a Russian-Greek immigrant family that Niki had looked after as a social worker shut her up, but not for long. 'You didn't even charge the Tratsous the going rate.'

'They aren't exactly the Onassises.'

'No, but you . . . oh, what's the point, Alex? You don't even tell me about most of your jobs.'

Mavros shook his head. Niki's ability to overlook the dangers his work entailed and the damaging secrets he uncovered never failed to irritate him. 'You nearly got shot in the Tratsou case. You were in hospital with a police guard, remember?'

'And you nearly got killed several times on that case,' she riposted. She was leaning over him, her long legs visible to the residents of the block across the street and her shapely breasts fully in evidence to him down the neck of her T-shirt.

He laughed, never the sensible option. To his surprise, and after a pause long enough to move his hands down to protect his crotch, Niki laughed back.

'Why do we do this?' she murmured, cheek against his again. 'I love you.'

'And I love you,' he replied. 'We just have—'

'Different ways of showing it.' She kissed him on the lips. 'I know. I'm going for a shower.' She raised a finger. 'And no following. Wait till tonight.'

'So stern,' he said, as she turned away. 'And so desirable.'

Niki swung her hips seductively as she disappeared inside.

She was right, Mavros thought, looking back out across the city. Although his mother's flat was large and well-appointed, he still hankered after the rundown single-bedroom place in Plaka, the rock wall of the Acropolis louring over it like a stone tsunami. He had been there for five years, but he always knew that his days were numbered. With the Olympic Games little more than a year away, owners had been taking advantage of grants to upgrade their properties and, of course, raise the rents.

He went inside. That wasn't the only reason he had come to Kleomenous, despite his dislike for the gilded but acid-tongued neighbours. His mother Dorothy, the Scottish side of his dual heritage, was still running a successful publishing business, and owned the flat, meaning he didn't have to pay a single Euro of rent. Not that he felt at home. He insisted on sleeping in the larger of the two guest rooms, feeling that taking over the master bedroom would make his residence permanent. That irritated Niki, despite the fact that the guest room was larger than both his old bedroom in Pikilis and the bedroom in her flat in the southern suburb of Palaio Faliro. And it was true that the exclusive address had impressed the kind of clients that he would have preferred not to work for, except he needed their money. But there was still another, more important reason.

'Ta-dah,' Niki said, taking a twirl in a short, well-cut skirt.

Mavros looked down at his groin. 'No, sorry, nothing doing.'

She came at him with her bag, a large, file-filled object that he had been hit with before. He sidestepped her and grabbed her arms.

'Tonight,' she said, keeping her freshly painted lips out of range. 'Tonight I'll show you a really—'

The sound of a key turning in the front door made Niki's eyes widen and her smile depart quicker than a bribe slipped to a tax inspector.

'Your obese friend,' she groaned. 'I thought I'd seen the last of him when you moved here.'

Not for the first time, Mavros regretted having given Yiorgos Pandazopoulos a full set of keys. Then again, if he'd done what he'd often urged his mother to do and put the chain on, Niki's tantalizing farewell wouldn't have been so rapidly terminated.

'Morning, Alex,' Yiorgos said, taking in Niki's presence. 'Morning, Andhroniki.' This was a recent tactic, calling her by her full Christian name. Designed to wind her up, it was highly effective.

'Morning, Fat Man,' Niki responded, even though Mavros had frequently told her that the nickname was for his use alone. 'Have a busy day, the pair of you.' She strode towards the door, her head high.

The Fat Man waited till it closed behind her. 'What got up her—'

Mavros gave him a full-on glare.

'Nose?' Yiorgos completed.

'You wouldn't understand,' Mavros said, wondering if Niki would now follow through on her interrupted promise.

From *The Descent of Icarus,* an unpublished memoir by Rudolf Kersten:

May 20th 1941 has lived with me all the days of my life since.

We were drenched in sweat, having been fully kitted up since 2 a.m. – padded parachutist helmets, flying service blouses, jump smocks over combat trousers, knee pads, machine-pistols, grenades, Lugers, bayonets and gravity knives, as well as the bulky RZ16 parachutes. I wasn't the only one who slipped a hand inside my smock to finger the jump badge with its silvered wreath of acorn and oak leaves beneath the gilt diving eagle that was the *Fallschirmjägers'* talisman. I also repeated under my breath the commandments written for us by the Führer – 'You are the elite of the Wehrmacht, for you combat shall be fulfillment . . . be nimble as a greyhound, tough as leather, hard as Krupp steel . . .'

The Ju52s' three engines started at six and we heaved ourselves on board, each of the twelve with the end of his slip cord between his teeth, like giant pirates pulling captured ships – so empowered did we feel. The canisters containing our rifles, machine guns and ammunition made the interior of the affectionately nicknamed Auntie Ju with her corrugated metal skin even more cramped. Thick red dust rose from the untreated runways and there were delays between flights, but eventually the pilot gunned the engines and we moved sluggishly away. I was seated opposite one of the windows in the fuselage, but Peter Wachter's tall frame blocked it effectively until we were airborne and the juddering made him shake. I saw the first rays of the sun come over the mountains to the east of Athens. I may have imagined it, but I thought I caught a glimpse of the Acropolis as we climbed over the island of Salamis. It seemed like a good omen, ancient Greek civilization and its triumph of arms soon to be emulated by the spearpoint of the modern world's greatest fighting force.

Broken-nosed Max Zielinski next to me started to sing the para-chutists' song and soon we were all bellowing it out: 'Red shines the sun, be prepared, it may not shine for us tomorrow . . .' None of us believed that, of course – young men going into battle are as naïve as the most closeted virgin. Besides, we had reason to be optimistic. The enemy forces in Crete were inadequate and had been subject to intense bombardment and strafing by our Luftwaffe comrades for many days, and the RAF had been swept from the skies. The Cretan people were said to be avidly awaiting our arrival to liberate them from the dissolute imperialism of the British. And, though we would have wished to be first on the island, glider troops had been sent ahead to secure the airfield at Maleme. No matter – there would be plenty of Churchill's rabble left for us.

Squeezed between Max and thick-lipped Bernie Necker, and thankfully cooler at last, I saw images cascade before my eyes: my mother, filed with pride despite her damp eyes on the day I gained my jump badge, wishing that my father had survived his Western Front wound a little longer to see me in my dark-blue uniform; my old Classics teacher, Herr Feldmann, who encour-aged my love of the ancient world and gave me a sad smile when I visited him after I had joined the service; slim Martha Nussbaum, kissing me for the last time before we boarded the train for the Balkans. They were all part of another less brilliant world now. I had become one with the myths that had made me strong, taken me through the Hitler Youth, driven me to undertake the hardest training in Germany's armed forces. I had become a modern-day Icarus, one whose flight would not be interrupted by melting wax, one who would never die.

I saw the sea beyond Peter's shoulder, the water changing from grey to pale blue. There were Auntie Jus all around and, craning forward, I saw the fine lines of Messerschmitt 109s, our fighter protection, higher in the cloudless sky. If there had been any Royal Navy ships in the area, they would have been bombed to the depths, titans defenceless beneath German firepower.

Lieutenant Bruno Schmidt, handsome as a film star, caught my eye and nodded slowly. He knew my tendency to lose concen-tration and had spoken to me about it before the successful drop at the Corinth Canal. I smiled and nodded back. I knew what I had to do and had shown that by saving our beloved section commander before the bridge was blown up by the British – a futile action as our engineers soon replaced it.

The engines changed pitch as the plane made a sharp left turn. Now I could see the great wall of the White Mountains, still crowned with shining snow. It was an incredible sight, but I soon forgot it as the Auntie Ju's fuselage was pitted with holes, some of them only a few centimetres above the window. Wachter ducked his head, then I felt Zielinski's helmet knock against mine. There was blood on his jump smock where rounds had gone right through his body.

The klaxon sounded. We hooked our jump chords to the line above us and the dispatcher pulled open the door. Lieutenant Schmidt moved forwards and shouted a few inaudible words of encouragement, before throwing himself into the air. As I moved towards the door, I saw the black blasts of anti-aircraft fire and felt the plane judder. The man before me leapt out and it was my turn to grip the vertical rails, before jumping out in the crucifix position we had practised so often. We were low, I estimated under a hundred metres from the ground, when my parachute opened with a jerk like a kick from an elephant. Then my descent slowed and I was able to take in the scene.

To my right, an Auntie Ju was diving earthwards, smoke billowing from the fuselage. No men emerged from the door. Another aircraft's unit was jumping, but one of its number's parachute had snared on the tailplane. 109s were swooping over the anti-aircraft positions, machine guns rattling, but the defensive fire remained heavy. Looking around, I saw several parachutists slumped forward and motionless. Others were firing their MP40s and pistols. I struggled to bring my own weapon to bear, but the ground was approaching fast and I had to get my body into position for the forward roll on landing.

The dried up bed of the Tavronitis River, our target area, was to my right. I watched our men cutting themselves free of their chutes and racing for the weapon canisters. Many of them dropped lifeless before they made it.

And then I saw them, the Cretans who were supposed to be welcoming us as honoured guests. They were on my side of the river and they had already done for several of my comrades. There were old men with pitchforks and axes, women with heavy frying pans, and a priest who had made a spear from a long knife tied to a broom handle.

I thought the descent of Icarus was about to reach a premature end, but in fact that Cretan morning was only the beginning.

The Fat Man brought two cups of unsweetened Greek coffee on a tray to the balcony and delved into a paper bag.

'It's not the same,' Mavros said, suspiciously eyeing the pastry he had just been handed.

'So what do you want me to do?' the Fat Man demanded. 'Bring the old woman back from the dead?'

That terminated conversation for as long as it took Yiorgos to wolf down his double helping of *galaktoboureko*. His mother, Kyra Fedhra, had daily produced pastries that were the mainstay of the café run by the Fat Man until he too had been forced out by a ridiculous rent rise. Kyra Fedhra had expressed annoyance that her sixty-year-old son would be permanently under her feet and died of heart failure shortly afterwards – leaving the Fat Man with a valuable property on the other side of Lykavettos and nothing whatsoever to do. Although he had been a foot soldier in the Communist Party since his teens, he was no longer on good terms with the comrades after they had told him his duty was to sell the house and donate half the profits to the party.

That was the other reason Mavros had moved to his mother's flat. Without the Fat Man's café down the road, his old flat was substantially less appealing. He had used it as an office, judging potential clients by their reaction to such a downmarket place in the heart of tourist-land. And while the much-missed Kyra Fedhra had made the best pastries in Athens, Yiorgos made the best coffee, without which Mavros struggled to start the day.

Mavros finished his shop-bought *galakotoboureko* – which was actually not bad – and washed it down with cold water.

'Heard anything from that cop?' the Fat Man asked.

'That cop who has a name?'

Yiorgos sank his chin into the soft flesh of his neck. 'I forget . . . Damis?'

'You forget, my arse. No, I haven't. Calm down. What you fondly imagine is your job is safe.'

Mavros swallowed a smile. Damis Ganas had been his

partner for a few months the previous year, but he had returned to the island of Evia when his heroin addict girlfriend was released from psychiatric care. In the meantime, the Fat Man had combined his daily visits to provide breakfast with acting as Mavros's unofficial secretary and office manager. Years of grinding through the Communist Party's multiple layers of bureaucracy had made Yiorgos a remarkably competent record keeper. The fact that – with off-white shirts stretching over his paunch and threadbare trousers – he was hardly presentable to clients was a way of controlling his involvement in cases.

The Fat Man looked out over the opulent blocks around the park of Dhexameni. 'What would your father have thought about you ending up in this platinum-coated sewer?'

'Oh, thanks,' Mavros replied, going back inside. 'What would he have thought about you avoiding the comrades and coming here every day?' He looked at the photographs of his family on the display table by the fireplace. His mother had taken most of them with her, but there were still portraits of his father, Spyros, with his thick black hair, hooked nose and piercing gaze: and of his brother, Andonis, a bright-faced version of the older man, who had been popular with the opposite sex from his early teens.

'Let them go,' the Fat Man said softly, going towards the kitchen with his tray.

Mavros thought about that. His father, a lawyer who was also a high-ranking official of the then illegal Communist Party, had died when he was five and he had few memories, mainly of a serious, prematurely aged man whose smile had been tinged with sadness, but who always greeted him with a tight hug. His brother Andonis, who disappeared during the Dictatorship aged twenty-one, had played a much larger part in his life, and was the reason he had become a missing persons specialist. But Andonis was the only failure in his career – every trace of his brother had led to dead ends and desolation.

'I *have* let them go, Yiorgo,' Mavros called. And it was true. Spyros, despite being a hero of the Party, had never been close enough to inspire him – whence his essentially apolitical stance – while Andonis had gradually ceased to influence him. Besides, he had sworn to his mother that he would concentrate on his own life and on Niki rather than his lost male relatives. 'I have, believe me.'

The problem was, he didn't always believe it himself.

Mavros was showered, his shoulder-length and still black hair damp on the shoulders of his denim shirt, and shaved, an activity he undertook once a week at most, when the landline rang.

'You know who this is,' said a gruff voice.

'Do I?' Mavros replied. 'The Prime Minister? The ghost of Maria Callas with a bad cold?'

'As funny as ever – you think.' Nikos Kriaras, head of the Athens police organized crime division, was a man with no humour in his soul. 'I have little time for this, so listen carefully. You will shortly have visitors. It would be a very good idea to take the job you will be offered. A very good idea indeed.'

'I've had bad experience of your good ideas,' Mavros said, immediately antagonistic to anything suggested by the well connected but less than straight cop.

'Tell me why I should do what you say.'

Kriaras sighed. 'Why are things never easy with you? All right, this is nothing to do with my current portfolio.' The commander was terrified of phone taps and habitually spoke in a clipped mode he thought would be incomprehensible to outsiders. 'My friends at the Concert Hall would like your input on this.' A child could have broken that codename. Next to the main Athens music venue was the American embassy.

'Oh, great,' Mavros said, remembering a case involving the Americans and a terrorist that had nearly cost him his life. 'I think I'd rather take in the May sunshine on my balcony, thanks.'

'Don't screw with me, smart-arse,' Kriaras said. 'Take the job. It'll be well paid, it's not dangerous and you'll meet interesting people.'

The truth was that Mavros hadn't had a case in two weeks and was as bored as a shark in the overfished Aegean. Not that he was going to tell the cop that.

'Well, I'll think about it,' he said languorously. 'That sun, you know, it's very—'

'Take the fucking job, all right?' yelled Kriaras, slamming down the old-style phone that Mavros had seen in his office.

'Who was that?' the Fat Man asked, his heavy face creased with curiosity.

'Just one of my many admirers.'

'That wanker Kriaras.'

Mavros laughed. 'Very good, Yiorgo. He says I'm about to be offered a job. A good one.'

The Fat Man flicked his dish-towel at a fly with surprising dexterity. 'Don't take it. You can't trust that murderous organ of the state further than you can—'

'Toss him? Jesus, Yiorgo, lighten up with the Party terminology. Besides, we could do with some income.'

'Income? Profit, you mean. You're as bad as everyone else in this benighted country. Take what you can and deprive the needy.'

Mavros led the Fat Man to one of his mother's antique armchairs. 'Now, now, don't get overexcited. You might burst – I don't know – a belly?'

The doorbell rang, meaning that Mavros escaped verbal and possibly physical abuse. He looked at the miniature screen and saw a man in his late thirties, his thinning hair in a ponytail, and a young woman. Both were dressed in high-end casual clothes and the latter was carrying a laptop case. Although the man could have passed for Greek, the woman's red hair and pale skin gave her away as a foreigner. Mavros decided to speak English.

'Can I help you?'

'Mr Mavros? We were told to contact you by a Mr Kriaras.' The man mangled the stress on the cop's name – it should have been on the final syllable – and his accent was American.

'Come up to the sixth floor.'

Mavros turned to the Fat Man. 'You'd better make yourself scarce. Sit in the kitchen and take notes if that turns you on.'

'What if they want coffee?'

'I'll give you the order like you're a Filipina and collect it myself. All right, Georgia?'

The Fat Man gave him a less than threatening glare – there were few things he liked better than overhearing Mavros's clients – and withdrew.

Mavros went to the door, wondering what kind of fine mess he was about get himself into.

The young woman was now standing in front of the man.

'Alex Mavros?' she asked, with an accent that was East Coast, unlike the man's Californian tones. 'My name's Alice Quincy. It's my privilege and pleasure to introduce you to Mr Luke Jannet.'

The second name rang a faint bell, but Mavros played dumb. 'Right,' he said, extending a hand to the man, who had now pushed himself to the front, and then to the woman. 'Come in.'

'Cool place,' Jannet said, walking into the open living area. 'Kinda old-style furnishings, though.'

Mavros shrugged. 'Care to park your backsides on that antique sofa?' He'd never liked being talked down to and he wasn't going to make an exception for this hotshot. There were spots of red on Alice Quincy's high cheekbones, which made him perversely happy. She was one of those tall women with flat chests known to Greeks as 'ironing-boards', but her face was attractive enough.

'Would you like something to drink?' Mavros asked, watching Luke Jannet. He hadn't shown any sign of being affronted, but there was a watchfulness in his green eyes that suggested he didn't miss much.

'Coffee for us both,' Jannet said. 'Alice can make it.'

'That won't be necessary. Georgia?'

The Fat Men squeaked from behind the partially open kitchen door.

'Coffee for two, please.' Mavros looked at the Americans. 'Cappuccino?'

They both nodded.

Mavros repeated the order, aware that Yiorgos would be swearing under his breath – his mother had bought a machine and the Fat Man knew how to operate it, but he regarded the frothy concoction as an abomination.

'So, what can I do for you?' Mavros asked, deliberately directing his gaze at the young woman.

'See, here's the problem,' Jannet said, leaning forwards. Pointed cowboy boots made of some exotic skin extended from his dark-blue chinos. 'I'm directing a movie down in Crete.'

The bell rang louder in Mavros's head, but he kept silent.

Alice Quincy couldn't contain herself any longer. 'Surely you've heard of Mr Jannet and the film? It's been all over the media.'

'I don't really follow the film world,' Mavros lied. He was a big fan of classic noir and modern crime movies, but he suspected Jannet didn't direct that kind of thing.

'*Freedom or Death*?' the young woman persisted. 'About the Battle of Crete in 1941?'

'*Captain Corelli* meets *Zorba the Greek*, with a touch of *Cross of Iron*,' Luke Jannet interposed. 'It'll be out in time for the Olympics and it'll make a mint.'

Mavros had read about the production without paying attention to who was directing it. The Greek Ministry of Culture had been prominent in its efforts to attract a big budget American movie that would put Greece even more in the global eye in 2004. The fact that 'Freedom or Death' was the motto of the modern Greek state hadn't put off any politicians except extreme nationalists from licensing it to Hollywood.

'Kind of a new version of *Ill Met by Moonlight*?' Mavros said, remembering the Dirk Bogarde movie about the kidnapping of a German general on Crete.

'What?' Jannet asked, his expression blank.

'Mr Mavro?' came a high voice from the kitchen.

He went to collect the coffees. 'I hope you didn't spit in them,' he whispered.

The Fat Man was a dogged anti-American, as were all the comrades, and he regarded film-makers as the cream on the cake of worker exploitation.

'No, but that can be arranged,' Yiorgos riposted.

'Let's wait and see what the job is,' Mavros said, grabbing the tray.

The Americans watched curiously as he handed over their cups and saucers.

'My maid's a bit shy,' he said. 'She was abused in her last position.'

'How awful,' Alice said, glancing towards the kitchen.

'Here's the thing,' Jannet said, ignoring her. 'I've got an actress – in fact, the female lead – who's giving me the runaround. Cara Parks? Don't tell me you haven't heard of her?'

Mavros wasn't going to play that dumb. Cara Parks was the

next big thing in Hollywood, combining the physical allure of Kate Winslet with the smouldering looks of Sharon Stone.

'Sure,' he said. 'I saw her in *Spring Surprise*.' The low-budget horror movie set in a machine factory had given the actress plenty of opportunities to exercise both her vocal chords and her stunning body.

'That was nothing,' Jannet said scathingly. '*Freedom or Death* is going to make her into a global star.'

'OK,' Mavros said. 'And what's her problem?'

'Tell him, Alice,' the director said, as if the details were beneath him.

'Yes, Mr Jannet.' The young woman looked at Mavros. 'Like all actors in major roles, Ms Parks has a personal assistant, in her case a woman called Maria Kondos.'

'A Greek-American?' Mavros asked. The surname for a female would have been Kondou if she'd been a Greek native.

Alice Quincy nodded. 'The problem is, Maria disappeared yesterday and no one has any idea where she is.'

Jannet put his empty cup down with a crack. 'And Cara Parks, the self-centred bitch, won't do anything until she's found. She won't even come out of her suite.'

Mavros wasn't attracted to the case. The Greek-American had probably had a row with the star and gone voluntarily AWOL. Kriaras obviously wanted him on the job because of the production's significance to the country and the Culture Ministry, not necessarily in that order.

'We're prepared to pay you two thousand euros per day plus expenses,' Alice Quincy said.

Mavros heard a stifled exclamation from the kitchen. Years of extracting money from unsuspecting tourists who had wandered into the café had given the Fat Man a good command of numbers in English, and Mavros's standard rate was 500 euros a day.

'What's more,' Luke Jannet said, 'we've got a limo waiting in the street and a Learjet at the airport.' He caught Mavros's eye. 'You coming? We gotta haul ass.'

Mavros thought about it for a couple of seconds. Niki would be pissed off, but she'd approve of the money. The Fat Man would sulk because he wasn't coming along. Tough.

'Sure,' he said. 'Give me a few seconds to toss some things in a bag.'

TWO

From *The Descent of Icarus*:

I hit a piece of rough open ground very hard. It was the worst landing I'd ever made, but I hadn't broken anything and I told myself to keep calm. Small arms fire came at me from the east and I could hear shouts from my comrades across the dry river-bed. I used the gravity knife to cut away my parachute and then the first of the Cretans was on me. He wasn't much more than a boy and he came at me with a rock held in both hands. I twisted out of the way, still on my knees, then a spray of blood came from his forehead and he crashed to the flower-dotted earth.

'Over here, Rudi!'

I saw Peter Wachter crouching behind an olive tree, replacing the magazine of his MP40. The motionless bodies of the Cretans I had seen from the air were between us. I looked to my right. A weapons canister was dangling from an olive tree about fifty metres away, the lower end close to the ground. I pointed at it.

'No!' Peter yelled. 'You'll never make it!'

Bullets flew past me, proving his point. Although the sky was full of Luftwaffe aircraft – Auntie Jus dropping men, 109s strafing gun emplacements – I was on my own, caught in clear ground. I wouldn't last long with only my short-range machine-pistol and my Luger. I started crawling towards the tree, the first of a row. Earth and stones were flung into my face by gunfire, pinging against my helmet. Already my throat was parched and my stomach filled with acid. My training drove me on – the often-repeated words about sacrificing everything for the unit's greater good, the insignificance of my own life compared with the paratroopers' ultimate victory. Then I saw two of my comrades. One had landed in the tree beyond the canister, a line of large, bloody holes almost cutting him in half. The other was lying face down on the ground, arms still outstretched and parachute in rags, obviously hit by an anti-aircraft shell not long after it opened.

I stopped behind a low furrow in the earth to catch my breath. Fire was still being directed at me from the heights above the airfield and I had to press on. Then I caught a glimpse of rapid movement to my left. I rolled on to my right side, levelling the MP40. What I saw made my heart stop. A young woman dressed in black was running towards me, her long skirt flapping and her raven hair streaming behind her. She was screaming like a banshee, an old-fashioned rifle raised to her shoulder. There was a puff of smoke then a loud report and a heavy round smashed into the earth a few centimetres in front of my chest. Reloading was obviously not an option for her, but she kept charging, the rifle now reversed with the butt towards me.

I knew I had to kill her, but I couldn't. For all the savagery in her expression and her glaring eyes, she was beautiful and so young. I loosed off a blast above her head, which did nothing to stop her. The sound of firing all around had disappeared and all I could hear was her gasping breath and the words – clearly full of hatred – that she was shrieking at me. I fired again. She was so close that I couldn't fail to hit her. The ancient rifle flew from her grip and she crashed to the earth, clutching her shoulder. I crept over to her and she spat in my face. That was enough. I turned my attention back to the weapons canister. Just before I reached it, a grenade exploded in the tree and I was showered by branches, which reduced the force of the shrapnel.

Stretching up, I cut the shrouds from the canister and it dropped to the ground. It had been damaged and wouldn't open. I heard a burst of MP40 fire and turned to see another group of Cretans – old men in black jodhpurs and tasselled headscarves, and boys in shorts – crash to the earth. I pulled out my bayonet and inserted the blade in the canister catch. At last it sprang open and I found what I wanted – an air-cooled MG34 with a bipod and plenty of ammunition. I took a good position behind a tree trunk and set up the weapon facing the open ground. Another group of Cretans was advancing towards me, but that wasn't the first of my problems – it wasn't even the second.

The young woman I had shot was on her feet again and charging me, the rifle raised with her good arm, while behind me I saw heavily-built figures slipping through the rows of trees, wearing battledress and slope hats. They were the enemy I least wanted to face. They were the New Zealand Maoris.

Mavros managed a whispered conversation with the Fat Man in the kitchen, asking him to keep the plants watered if he was delayed.

'What about your girlfriend?' Yiorgos asked, smiling slackly.

'Call her and tell her I've left her for a willowy American.' Mavros shook his head. 'Don't even think about it. I'll talk to her. And she's not my girlfriend, she's the woman of my life.'

The Fat Man looked like he was going to vomit. 'Keep in touch, young Alex,' he said. 'Maybe you'll need a sidekick down there. You know how nasty the Cretans can be.'

In your dreams, Mavros thought. The last time Yiorgos had got involved in a case, he nearly ended up dead.

'Let's go, fella,' Luke Jannet called from the *saloni*. 'I've got a scene to shoot this afternoon.'

Mavros picked up the small bag he'd filled. Travelling light was essential to him, even if it meant buying clothes – they could always be put on expenses. He made sure he had his laptop and his phone charger. Niki had a tendency to punish him severely if he was out of touch for more than a day.

'So what's your story, man?' Jannet asked, after they had crowded into the small lift.

Mavros looked at him. He was pretty sure Kriaras had passed over the salient details, but for 2000 Euros a day, his client deserved a mini-biography.

'Father Greek, mother Scottish. Degree in law and criminology from Edinburgh, worked in the Ministry of Justice here, set myself up as a missing persons investigator nine years ago. Never failed to find a misper.'

Jannet raised an eyebrow. 'Never failed, huh? That's what your cop friend said. How d'you do that? Keep away from the real hard cases?'

Mavros had already decided that the director was a dick – the kind of powerful man who got a kick out of needling his minions. 'I can't talk about previous cases – client confidentiality. You got that in the States?'

Alice Quincy's eyes sprang open, then she looked down in embarrassment.

'Yeah, we got that. We got smart-arses too and I don't like them. Watch yourself, Alex Mavros.'

They went out into the sunlight. A long black Mercedes was blocking the street, a chauffeur in a grey suit standing by the rear door.

A leather-clad man on a powerful motorbike tried to squeeze past the car unsuccessfully. He flipped up his visor and started cursing; something along the lines of rich masturbators being the ruin of Greece.

'Excuse me,' Mavros said, stepping towards him. On the long list of Athenian pains in the arse, he placed motorbike riders near the top. 'Have you any idea who you're yelling at?'

'Should I?' the biker demanded, his belligerence undiluted. 'Looks like a pimp with his latest tart to me.'

Mavros laughed. 'I'll be decent and not pass that on. No, that's Luke Jannet, the director of *Freedom or Death*.' It was immediately obvious that leather man had heard about the film. 'He was telling me he needed experienced bikers as extras to ride replica German machines.' He smiled tightly. 'Looks like you've completely blown that gig.'

'What did you say to him?' Jannet asked, after Mavros had got into the front seat.

'Don't worry, your name didn't come up,' Mavros lied. He saw no reason to keep his client informed about anything not directly related to Maria Kondos.

The driver knew his job and soon they were heading out of the centre on Mesogeion Avenue. Jannet and Alice Quincy were on their mobiles, talking intently, so Mavros decided to make his own calls.

'Hello, Mother.'

'Alex, dear.' Dorothy Cochrane-Mavrou's voice was weaker than it had been, but she was still in full command of her intellect. 'Are you coming to Kifissia?'

'Afraid not. I'm off to Crete on a case.'

There was a pause.

'Mother?'

'Yes, dear. Sorry, I was thinking . . .'

Mavros knew that tone. She had come to terms with the losses of her husband and elder son long ago, but she still had vivid memories.

'Thinking what?'

'Your father . . . he was in Crete during the war. He hardly ever spoke of it, but . . . but I think he saw some terrible things.'

Mavros was surprised. He had never heard that Spyros had been on the Great Island, as it was known. In fact, he knew very little about his father's wartime activities and the Party had hidden away the relevant papers in its archive.

'Tell me more, Mother.'

'I can't, Alex. That's all I know.'

Mavros felt instantly deflated. The moment he thought he might find out more about his old man, the hope turned out to be illusory.

'All right, I'll talk to you soon,' he said. 'Is Anna there?'

His sister wrote features for several glossy magazines, but was spending more time at home now their mother was in residence.

'Yes, dear, I'll call her. Take care.'

'Yes, Mother,' he said dutifully. 'Hi, Anna.' He spoke Greek for privacy, even though they normally used English. 'I'm going to Crete on a case.'

'Oh, lucky you. Whereabouts?'

'Good question.' Mavros raised a hand to interrupt Alice Quincy. 'Where are we going exactly?'

'The shoot's in the vicinity of Chania,' the young woman answered, stressing the first syllable rather than the last.

'I heard that,' Anna said. 'Do you want to use the flat?'

His sister's husband Nondas was from Chania and had a family property in the old city.

'Let me think about that,' he replied, suspecting that a hideaway might be useful – clients, especially rich ones, often became unacceptably demanding.

'Well, you know where to get the keys. Barba-Yannis is still looking after the place.'

Mavros remembered the old man – he still wore the traditional baggy trousers and high boots. He lived in the same street and had known Nondas since he was a baby.

'OK, thanks. I'll be in touch.'

'Very likely.' Anna rang off. She was five years older and was often curt with him, regarding his work as less than respectable.

The fact that she and her family had been involved in the terrorism case that had almost cost the Fat Man his life hadn't made her change that view.

The Mercedes joined the Attica motorway and Mavros summoned up the strength to call Niki. She wasn't particularly bothered by the fact that he was going to Crete, having passed an unhappy holiday there when she was young. But when he said that he was going to be involved with the film, she became animated.

'But Cara Parks is starring. She's very . . . very attractive.'

Mavros was using his hands-free, so Jannet and his assistant couldn't hear what Niki was saying. He had to be careful, though, after what he'd said about client confidentiality.

'So?'

'What do you mean "so"?' Niki demanded. 'Every man on the planet wants to get inside her knickers. And her bra. She's known as Twin Peaks.'

'Really, my love? I doubt she'll have the slightest interest in me.' He wasn't going to tell her that he'd been hired to find the actress's beloved assistant.

'What about if I come over at the weekend? We could have fun in your time off.'

'Today's Tuesday. You know how good I am. I'll probably have things wrapped by tomorrow.'

'All right,' Niki said reluctantly. 'But no playing around, promise?'

'Promise. Got to go.'

'I love you,' she said, the stark declaration taking his breath away.

'Ditto.'

'That better be because you can't speak openly.'

'Of course it is. Bye.' He cut the connection and looked out over the green slopes of Imittos and the spring flowers nearer the highway. He did love Niki, he had no doubts about that, but she wasn't the kind of woman who made her man's life easy. Then again, considering the shit storms he got into with his work, he was hardly one to complain.

The airport's control tower rose up ahead and Mavros suddenly realized what he was about to get into – a small aircraft. The last time he had boarded one of those, he had nearly fainted.

Fear of flying wasn't something he put on his curriculum vitae.

As it turned out, the Learjet was a lot less terrifying than the propeller plane he had taken to a small island on a case a few years back. Being ushered through the VIP gate and across the tarmac was neat too. A bronzed pilot in an immaculate uniform saluted Jannet, who was then led to his seat by an impossibly attractive stewardess. Mavros didn't get a salute, but the middle-aged fly-boy did give him an avuncular nod.

Alice Quincy sat opposite him at the front of the plane, while Jannet had the rear to himself. As soon as the door was closed and they had belted up, she handed him a red plastic folder.

'That contains everything you should need to acquaint yourself with the movie and the people you'll need to talk to.'

Mavros concentrated on extracting his blue worry beads from the back pocket of his jeans. He had given up smoking several years ago and found the *komboloï* a helpful distraction at times of stress. A couple of red beads among the blue ones were supposed to guarantee good health, while a silver hand pointed to good fortune. Not that they had always been a huge help.

He looked up as the plane began to taxi towards the runway, surprised by how little noise the engines made. The seat was plush leather and there was no shortage of legroom. Glancing at Alice Quincy, he saw that she was looking at his left eye. Most women did.

'David Bowie,' he said.

She smiled. 'Almost – except it's the size of his irises that's different, not the colour.'

'Uh-huh. It's some sort of genetic defect. My father's eyes were dark-blue, but some of my mother's brown got into one of them.'

Alice smiled. 'Weird.'

'You ain't seen nothing yet.'

She pursed her lips. 'No, I mean your father, the Greek, having blue eyes and your Scottish mother having brown.'

'Scots are more Mediterranean than the natives.'

That seemed to be beyond her. 'You'd better start reading,' she said. 'The flight's only half an hour.'

So he read. Fortunately he was quick at taking in facts and, even more fortunately, the Learjet flew like a dream. In fifteen minutes, after drinking a cup of coffee that could have come from the Ritz, he had mastered the file, at least with regards to what would be of significance in tracing the missing woman.

Maria Kondos was a third generation Greek-American, but the photo showed she could have passed for a Greek of the dark-haired and rings-beneath-the-eyes variety – presumably the family had made sure her father married a woman of Greek heritage. She was thirty-five, born in Queens, New York, but had moved to Los Angeles after college. She'd worked her way up the ladder as a personal assistant with actresses – most of whom Mavros had never heard of – until striking lucky with Cara Parks. She had been with her since *Spring Surprise* and was an integral part of her team.

'OK,' Mavros said, leaning towards Alice Quincy. 'Tell me what isn't in the file.'

She pressed herself back in her seat. 'What do you mean?'

'Oh, come on, Alice. You're the director's number one girl. You know what goes on behind the scenes, so to speak.'

Spots of red appeared on her cheeks. 'Well, it would be fair to say that Ms Kondos isn't the most popular person in the crew.'

She stopped, making Mavros give her an encouraging smile.

'Her job is to look after Ms Parks and she does it very effec-tively – but sometimes with a distinct lack of diplomacy.'

'Tell me more.'

'She can be very blunt, even to Mr Jannet and the producers. And there are rumours that she provides certain special services for Ms Parks.'

Mavros raised an eyebrow. 'What are we talking about here? Middle of the night omelettes? Drugs? Sexual favours?'

Alice Quincy looked queasy. 'I wouldn't know about the first and second, but perhaps the third. I repeat, these are rumours.'

'Any particular quarrels that might have driven someone on the crew to get violent with her?'

The American woman's doe eyes widened. 'Good Lord, that's ridiculous. Film shoots are full of clashing egos.'

Mavros wondered how Alice survived in such an atmosphere – there must have been steel beneath the soft exterior.

'Have the local police been involved?'

She nodded. 'An Inspector Margaritis came to the shoot hotel and expressed concern, but Mr Jannet thought he was just going through the motions.' She gave a tight smile. 'Which is where you come in.'

'Hey, Al!' Jannet's voice sounded from the rear of the plane.

'Excuse me,' Alice said, adapting into slave mode, though Mavros noticed she wasn't keen on that form of her name.

He looked out of the window and saw a lengthy mass of rock topped by snow. The White Mountains were as striking as ever. He remembered staying with Anna and Nondas one summer and snow-covered areas still being visible. As the Learjet lost height on its way to the private airport at Maleme, a conversation he'd had with Nondas came back to him.

'The Germans should never have been allowed to capture the airfield,' his brother-in-law said. 'The Allies made so many mistakes. As it was, the invaders only made it by the skin of their Nazi teeth.'

They had been looking around the battlefield sites and memorials. Thousands of paratroopers had been killed in the first days of the assault, Nondas had told him, but still they came. If Freyburg, the Allied commander, had armed the gendarmerie or taken on the locals as irregulars, the result could have been very different.

The model/hostess checked that he had his safety belt on with a stunningly fake smile. Alice Quincy did not return, presumably now nailed to a seat opposite her boss. As the plane slowed, three things struck Mavros. The first was that he was out of his comfort zone on an island whose inhabitants, apart from Nondas, had always seemed to him very unlike other Greeks. The second was that Hollywood film people were unlike any other human beings. And the last was a question – why had a major director broken into his schedule to spend a morning flying to and from Athens when Alice Quincy could easily have done the job on her own?

THREE

Mavros followed Luke Jannet off the plane and was hit by a blast of heat – Crete was hotter than Athens had been. Then he got a surprise.

'Neat, aren't they?' Jannet said, following the direction of his gaze.

'Something like that,' Mavros muttered. His Greek heritage had asserted itself and the World War Two German aircraft with swastikas on their tails did not impress him.

'A Ju 52 transport aircraft – they dropped paratroopers – and an Me109 fighter,' the director said proudly. 'We'll be filming more aerial shots tomorrow.' He shrugged. 'But you'll be busy finding that fuckin' dyke.'

'Unless I find her today.'

Jannet gave him a thoughtful look. 'Don't get overambitious, my man. This is a big island.' He grinned. 'But if you do, you're welcome to see the planes in action.'

Mavros followed him towards a pair of cars. The director got into the first, a large dark-blue BMW, while Alice hung back.

'The Jeep will take you to the shoot hotel. Ms Parks has been told to expect you. An account has been opened in your name for meals, car hire and so on, and you'll find a cash advance in the safe in your room. We should exchange cell numbers.' They did so. 'I'll be available to help you, subject to Mr Jannet's needs. If you run into any difficulties with crew members, let me know. Will there be anything else?'

'Sounds like you've thought of most things.'

She smiled. 'Mr Jannet will be expecting regular reports.'

'Hey, Ali, shake your tail feather.'

Mavros watched as her slim form inserted itself into the BMW. He'd have liked to know what Alice Quincy really thought about her boss, but she was almost as inscrutable as a jade Buddha. Even more, he'd have liked to know what else she knew about Maria Kondos and Cara Parks.

The Jeep, with a parachute-festooned *Freedom or Death* logo on the door, was driven by a young man with a moustache Nietzsche would have been proud of.

'First time in Crete?' he asked, revealing a lower line of gleaming teeth.

Mavros considered sticking to English, but decided he'd find out more by speaking Greek. He introduced himself, saying he was a writer from Athens.

'Mikis Tsifakis,' the driver replied. 'You writing about the film?'

Mavros nodded vaguely. 'How about you? Contracted by the production company?'

Mikis nodded happily. 'My old man has hired out most of our fleet. That was him in the BMW.'

'Good work?'

'Ah, good enough. These Americans, they know how to keep their costs down.'

'So, tell me, have you driven anyone famous?'

The young man beamed. 'You bet. When the old man's busy, I drive Cara Parks.'

'Wow, what's she like in the flesh?' Mavros asked, playing the part of the lust-driven fan.

Mikis laughed. 'Even more luscious than on screen. She's nice, as well. She doesn't have any airs. What I wouldn't give for five minutes alone with that woman.'

Mavros spotted another interesting angle. 'I suppose she always has an entourage in tow.'

'Not really. A couple of security guys and a stuck-up woman called Maria, who I've heard speak Greek, but she never bothers with me. She acts like Cara's personal Cerberus.'

'She's got three heads?'

Mikis glanced at him, grinning. 'A tongue that's three times more cutting than my grandmother's.'

Mavros looked at the citrus groves to his right and the almost constant line of hotels and villas on the left, before getting to the point. 'I hear this Maria's gone missing.'

The driver's face tightened. 'Really? I didn't know that.'

Mavros wasn't sure he was telling the truth, but he let it go. The Jeep took a left turn and stopped in front of an elaborate, barred gate. There was a column of TV vans and men with cameras on the roadside, a police officer watching them. A man dressed in traditional Cretan garb – high boots, baggy trousers, the *vraka*, and a tight headscarf, the *mandili* – came out of a hut and nodded at Mikis before admitting the vehicle.

'The Heavenly Blue Resort,' Mavros read on a gilt sign. 'I've heard of this place.'

'You should have,' the young man said proudly. 'Biggest and best hotel on the island. Mr Kersten brought in architects and designers from all over the world to upgrade it ten years ago.'

Although he habitually binned the travel, property and design sections of the Sunday newspapers with little more than a glance, Mavros had read about the resort and its German owner. It had been one of the few European-class hotels in Greece when it first opened for business in the 60s and it maintained that status. Suddenly he found himself wishing that the search for Maria Kondos would take weeks.

Mikis drove the Jeep along a tree-lined avenue to a large expanse of well-watered lawn, beyond which stood an imposing six-storey concrete building whose modernist brutalism was diluted by the flowers on every balcony. To its left and right were complexes of villas, along with more swimming pools than Mavros had ever seen in one location, even though the sea was only a few hundred metres away.

'Amazing, eh?' the driver said.

Mavros agreed, though the fact that all the staff seemed to be in Cretan costumes struck him as excessively kitschy.

'Here you are.' Mikis handed him a card. 'Give me a call if you need a ride. It makes a change to have a Greek-speaking passenger.'

Mavros accepted it and extended a hand with a tip.

'Not necessary,' Mikis said, with a smile. 'In fact, forbidden under the terms of our contract.'

Mavros stuck the banknote in the young man's shirt pocket. 'Not my contract. See you, my friend.' He got out, sure that he would be making use of Mikis in the near future.

'Good day, sir,' said a young woman weighed down with a colourful but less than practical full-length costume. 'Welcome to the Heavenly Blue Resort. Follow me to reception.'

Mavros did so, taking in the tastefully minimalist décor – pale grey marble floor, replicas – he presumed – of Minoan, Classical and Venetian art works on the walls, a high ceiling with lights hanging from wires entwined by convincing fake vines. The German owner definitely had better taste than the average hotelier in Greece.

'Yes, Mr Mavros, we're expecting you,' said the receptionist, a svelte young man, in English, imagining the new arrival was a Greek-American. He looked momentarily confused when he saw Mavros's Greek ID card.

'Don't worry, English is fine,' Mavros said. 'But don't go talking about me in Greek when I turn my back.'

The receptionist looked horrified at the idea. 'Here's your key card, sir. You're on the first floor, lifts over there. Do you need help with—'

'No,' Mavros said, lifting his small bag. 'Long live Hollywood.'

A smile flickered across the receptionist's face.

Mavros took the stairs to the first floor and walked down a long corridor to his room. The trek, which, along with the low level, showed that he wasn't a major player, was worth it. The room was actually a small suite, the bedroom looking towards the sea and the sitting-room towards the mountains of the Rodhopou peninsula to the west. The air con was running and a television greeted him in sibilant tones. He turned both off and opened the balcony windows. People in shorts were walking to and from the villas, while others drove golf buggies to more distant locations. Even searching the grounds for Maria Kondos would take plenty of man hours.

He found the safe in one of the wardrobes and punched in the number supplied in an envelope, before changing it to the day and month of Niki's birthday. There were two thousand Euros inside, along with a receipt, which he signed. Maybe his employers really did believe he could solve the case in a day. In any case, he wasn't going to have many living expenses.

After a shower and change of shirt, Mavros picked up the phone and asked to be connected to Cara Parks' suite. A harsh female voice answered in English.

'The name's Mavros. Ms Parks is expecting me.' He heard muffled voices and then the woman came back on the line.

'Come now,' she said curtly. '501.'

Mavros climbed the stairs, all four flights, assuming it was the done thing to arrive at a Hollywood starlet's suite panting.

*　　*　　*

From *The Descent of Icarus*:

It was a simple choice. I turned the MG34 towards the New Zealanders and emptied a drum of ammunition at them. The trees took many of the rounds, but there was no shortage of men yelling, falling and soon lying motionless. Then I looked round, the woman's scream louder than all the shooting in the area.

I twisted aside just before the heavy butt of the antediluvian rifle crashed into the earth. There wasn't time to fit another drum, so I swung the machine gun at her and swept her legs from beneath her. She didn't stop coming at me, pulling herself forward despite the blood that was pouring from her shoulder. To my amazement, she laced her fingers round my neck and started to apply pressure.

Back then, I was ninety kilos of muscle and I broke her grip easily enough. Then she smashed her head into my face, breaking my nose. Where had she learned to fight like this? A Cretan cathouse? Again, I pushed her off me, wiping my sleeve across my streaming nose.

'Rudi!'

I looked beyond the woman and saw Peter Wachter and a small group of comrades approach across the open ground. She tried to headbutt me again and I finally lost patience, landing a right that Max Schmeling, former world heavyweight champion and now also a paratrooper somewhere in Crete, would have been proud of. She hit the dirt and lay still.

'Fuck's sake, Rudi,' Peter said, as he crouched down beside me. 'You take out a section of Maoris and then get your nose crushed by a woman?'

'Defensive positions, boys,' Lieutenant Schmidt ordered. 'Well done, Kersten, at least with the New Zealanders.' He smiled grimly. 'But that wasn't all of them.'

A 109 shrieked past overhead, its machine guns blasting, and then we heard an unknown sound that got all our hackles up. It was a chant, voiced loudly and in perfect unison, by numerous voices in a language none of us had ever heard. But we got the message clearly enough. It was a more terrifying war cry than anything our instructors had come up with, a challenge that made clear mercy would not be forthcoming. When it stopped, there was the sound of heavy men crashing through the trees.

Schmidt looked at the five of us and shook his head. 'Screw this, we need to get back across the open ground. On your feet.'

We got up, Wachter fitting a drum and handing the MG34 to me. The rest of them loaded up with as many weapons and as much ammo as they could carry.

'What about her?' I asked the lieutenant. The woman was rolling her head from side to side, her jaw already swelling.

He shrugged. 'She attacked a *Fallschirmjäger*. Shoot her.'

The Maoris were still shouting and we could see their shapes approaching.

I aimed the machine gun at her, waiting till the others were looking in the opposite direction. Then I let off a blast, tearing up grass and stones from the soil. Some of the debris hit her face, but she was alive when I followed my comrades into the open.

Only Peter Wachter and I made it, the others picked off by the Maoris as their jump boots kicked up pollen from the yellow and white flowers. I never expected to see the woman again but in that, as in so many things, I was completely wrong.

There was a security guard outside 501, so he got the benefit of Mavros's heavy breathing rather than the actress. He wasn't a clown in Cretan costume, but a heavy-duty steroid-cruncher – shaved head nearly reaching the top of the door and biceps flexing beneath the sleeves of a black suit.

'ID,' he demanded, in English.

Mavros decided against saying, 'It speaks', and handed over his card. Then he froze as hands with home-made sausage fingers patted him down without any attempt at delicacy. Then the gorilla knocked twice on the door.

Things got no better. Mavros was confronted by a short but heavily built woman in her thirties, her bottle-blonde hair cut short. She was wearing something akin to an ancient Greek chiton. It wasn't flattering.

'Rosie Yellenberg,' she said, not offering her hand. 'Producer. Follow me, Mr Mavros.'

The hall was about the size of a cricket pitch, leading on to a living area that could have accommodated two teams and their extended families comfortably. It was sparsely furnished but, to Mavros's untutored eye, every piece looked top of the range. Sitting in the corner of a red leather sofa was an unexpectedly small figure in jeans, her hair in a turban. To his surprise, Cara

Parks got up and extended a hand. Close up, her famously curva-
ceous figure was unavoidable, even though the presence she had
on the screen was diminished.

'Sit down here, won't you?' she said, patting the sofa about
a metre away from her. 'Can we offer you some refreshment?'
The actress's voice was soft and her dark eyes were on his.

'No, thanks.' Mavros looked across at Rosie Yellenberg, who
was hovering by the large glass coffee table. 'Do you think I
could talk to Ms Parks alone?' he asked, in a tone he hoped
would brook no opposition.

The producer's jaw jutted forward but, before she could speak,
the actress cut in.

'Sure, I'd prefer that too. Close the door after you, Rosie dear.'

The look that passed between the two women would have
melted an asteroid.

'You always do that?' Cara Parks asked, when they were alone.
'I mean, lay down the law at the start of meetings.'

Mavros smiled. 'Only when I get the feeling people are surplus
to requirements.'

The actress laughed, but he noticed there were lines round her
unmade-up eyes. 'Well, you got that right. Ms Yellenberg's taken
it upon herself to be my nursemaid since Maria . . . Maria left.
Every five minutes I've been getting a lecture about how important
it is not to delay the schedule, how much money's at stake, you
can guess the kind of thing.'

Mavros nodded. 'Why's she dressed up like an ancient Greek
goddess?'

'Who knows? She certainly isn't Aphrodite.'

He noted the familiarity with Greek myth, which seemed
unlikely to be a standard feature of major movie actors. 'So, Ms
Parks—'

'Call me Cara.' She gave him a tight smile. 'Until I tell you
different. And I'll call *you*?'

'Alex.'

'Your English is perfect.'

He gave her a rundown of his background.

'You certainly sound like the man for the job. So what do you
think's happened to my Maria?' The actress frowned. 'That didn't
come across right. Just to be perfectly clear about this – no matter
what anyone tells you, I haven't got the hots for her. She has for

me, but she doesn't let that get in the way of being an excellent assistant.'

'To be honest, since that's what we're being here, it's a bit early to say.'

'What have they told you? That she's a rude bitch with plenty of enemies in the crew?'

'Something like that.'

'Well, it's true enough. You've got to understand, people like me need protection. Not just the man-mountain on the door, but people with brains – people who take the heat and let you get on with your job.' She gave him a penetrating look. 'Which, whatever you might think, Mr Private Eye, isn't just a question of looking sexy in front of the cameras.'

Mavros raised his hands. 'Not guilty. I saw *Spring Surprise*. You needed to be much more than sexy in that film. Though you were that too, of course.' He put a brake on the babbling that the star's powerful presence was causing. 'Tell me about Maria, please.'

Cara Parks leaned back on the arm of the sofa. 'Tell you about her? She's been with me for over five years. We hit it off straightaway. I wasn't sure about doing a dumb scream movie – believe it or not, my background is in off-Broadway theatre – but my agent was keen and so was Maria. Turned out to be the best move I ever made. And I couldn't have done it without her. The crews on those movies can be pretty gross, but Maria licked them into shape and even the nude scenes were OK.'

Mavros tried hard to put those from his mind. 'So you'd say you were friends beyond the work level?'

'Friends, no. For a start, there isn't anything beyond work in Hollywood. Even going for a drink means bonding with people who have some professional interest. Put it this way – I've never been to Maria's house. But I can call her any time and she's there for me. I guess what I'm saying is that as well as needing her, I respect her. Any good?'

Mavros nodded. 'When and where did you last see her?'

'Right here, on this piece of furniture. It must have been about nine in the evening on Sunday. I was looking over my lines and Maria was telling that asshole Jannet to keep his comments till the morning.'

'You and the director don't get on?'

Cara raised her shoulders. 'It's no biggie. He's good at his job and I don't have any fundamental problems with what he wants.'

'But you don't like him?' Mavros persisted, probing her unwillingness to come clean.

'No, I don't,' the actress replied, after a pause. 'He's a loudmouth and a bully, though that applies to plenty of his kind. Is this relevant?'

Mavros didn't answer. 'When did you realize Maria was missing?'

'She always comes to the suite at least an hour before I'm due to leave for a shoot. But on Monday she didn't. I called her, both in her room and on her cell. She didn't answer either. It turned out that no one in the hotel had seen her since Sunday evening. Nobody else seemed to care. If I hadn't started shouting, the assholes wouldn't even have called the cops – and they were worse than useless.' She paused. 'I hope you aren't.'

'No,' he replied, 'I'm not.' He reckoned displaying his battle scars was de rigueur. 'I've found everyone I've gone looking for professionally. But I'm not surprised the police weren't interested. It still isn't much more than thirty-six hours since Maria disappeared and she's an adult. If there are no suspicious circumstances, all the police in any country will do is add her name to a list.'

'Well, I guess that's why you've been brought in. Tell me, Alex, what do you usually do when a woman goes missing?'

'The same as I do when a man or a child goes missing. Follow up on the people in their immediate circle. It hardly ever happens that people disappear without a trace.'

Cara Parks' expression was grim. 'You'll be earning your corn, Alex. Maria's immediate circle comprises the residents of this resort complex.'

'I'm sure you can narrow them down a bit,' Mavros said, taking out his notebook. 'Who did she spend time with on set?'

'Apart from me and the other people who look after me, no one that I know of.'

'Give me their names.' He noted her personal hairdresser, dialogue coach, costume designer and various others. 'What about in her free time?'

The actress laughed. 'Free time? You don't get much of that on location. For all I know, Maria might have spent every evening in the hotel bar or disco – though I doubt it – but she was always fresh at six a.m.'

'No significant other?'

Cara looked blank. 'Oh, you mean lover. Never heard of one. Sorry.'

'That's OK. I'll take it from here.'

'And you'll find her.' She raised her hand. 'I know you've never failed, Alex, but this is important to me. I care about Maria, I really do.'

Mavros watched her carefully. Her eyes were damp and her lips had trembled. For all her acting skills, she looked sincere.

'Where was she staying?'

The star held up an envelope. '243. There's a duplicate key card here. The hotel's been asked to leave the room untouched.'

'Thanks.' Mavros got up.

'No, thank you,' Cara Parks said, rising and shaking his hand again. 'I know you'll help us out.'

'I don't suppose Maria's ever done this kind of thing before?'

'Nope.'

'By the way, what role are you playing in the film?'

The actress took a moment to refocus. 'Oh, I'm Eleni Panakaki. The village girl-next-door who becomes a heroine and nearly gets herself shot. It's a good part, plus I get it on with a Maori officer – except he's white, not one of the tattooed hunks you see walking around here.'

'Hugh Rook,' Mavros said, remembering the actor from a magazine article. He was a former pretty boy trying to extend his range.

'Yeah,' Cara said, without enthusiasm. 'Spends most of his time talking to his parents. They're in the hotel too. Apparently his grandfather fought in the battle.'

Interesting, Mavros thought, but hardly significant. He headed for the door.

'*Ade yeia*,' the actress hazarded.

He raised a hand without turning round as he repeated the second word of the farewell phrase. The dialogue coach had been doing a good job.

FOUR

Mavros went down to the second floor and found the missing woman's room. There was a 'Do Not Disturb' sign on the door and he made a note to ask housekeeping if it had been there since Monday morning. Then he pulled on the latex gloves he kept in his back pocket. The place had a similar lay out to his own but it was in a considerable state of chaos, with files all over the floor and clothes draped across the furniture. It took him a few minutes to satisfy himself that this was the way Maria Kondos lived, not least when he found the bathroom messier than a teenage boy's. If someone had turned the place over, it had been done very subtly – which didn't mean that someone hadn't been through it and covered his or her steps. But he doubted it. The open tubes of make-up and the heaps of unwashed clothes suggested a life with time only to think about the important things, and there was no obvious sign of a struggle.

The question was, where to start? There was a desk in the living area, on which Maria Kondos seemed to have maintained a modicum of order. On the left side was a pile of papers, some bound together. They turned out to be the script for *Freedom or Death*, with additional dialogue on separate sheets. Cara Parks' lines were highlighted. In the centre was a mobile phone, the battery discharged, an American passport in the missing woman's name, a wallet containing credit cards and a California driving licence in her name, as well as over five hundred euros, and a small leather clutch bag with mascara, lipstick and the like. There were also two condoms.

After plugging the phone into its charger, Mavros sat back in the velvet-covered chair. The condoms suggested that Maria Kondos had a least some interest in the male sex, while the lack of a key card for the room gave the impression that she'd left willingly, expecting to return. On the other hand, she had taken no ID or means of payment. Had she expected not to need any? That could have meant she wasn't going outside the resort area, or that she had left with someone who would pay on her behalf.

But would a woman go anywhere without the other items in the clutch bag?

He turned to the right side of the desk. There were several small framed photos, showing a very Greek-looking elderly couple and some small children. Then it struck Mavros what he hadn't seen – any form of computer. He checked the desk drawer and the rest of the suite. Under the bed, he found a charger for a laptop, but no sign anywhere of the machine itself. There were no diskettes or external memory devices to be seen either. Which left him with the suspicion that Maria Kondos had gone somewhere in the hotel with her laptop – perhaps leaving her phone behind by mistake. Searching a hotel the size of this one would be a hell of a job, especially with all its outbuildings.

The buzz of the doorbell interrupted his thoughts. He moved as quietly as he could across the marble floor and looked through the spyhole. A tall but stooping elderly man with a walking stick was in the corridor. He definitely wasn't from housekeeping.

Mavros opened the door.

'So sorry to bother you,' the man said in Greek, his voice surprisingly strong and his accent only slightly foreign. His nose was misshapen. 'I take it you are Mr Mavros?'

'Em, yes . . . and you are?'

The old man handed him a card. 'Rudolf Kersten,' he said. 'I created the Heavenly Blue.' The way he put it almost made Mavros laugh: as if he was an Eastern potentate – or the proprietor of a Chinese restaurant. 'Ms Cara Parks just called me. I wondered if I might be of assistance.'

'Ah, right.' Mavros looked over his shoulder, reluctant to invite the man into what might be of interest to the authorities if the woman never returned. 'Actually, there are some things you could help me with. Could we go down to my room?'

'No, no, come to my residence,' Kersten said, turning away. 'I insist. It isn't far.'

They went down to the ground floor in the lift, the old man asking a couple of exhausted guys in high-visibility jackets and shorts if everything was satisfactory. They looked at Kersten sullenly and nodded.

'I see it as my duty to talk to all my guests,' Kersten said, leading Mavros to a door beside reception. The staff nodded to the owner punctiliously. 'Even the less than polite technicians on the film crew.'

The mixture of conscientiousness and condescension silenced Mavros for a few seconds. The old man's residence was literally behind the shop. A short corridor led to a large living area with a view across the grounds to the sea.

'Please be seated. I will arrange coffee.'

'No, I . . .' Mavros tried to stop him, not being a fan of that beverage in the afternoon, but Kersten headed away without paying attention.

'There,' he said, returning almost immediately. 'Hildegard will be with us shortly.' He sat down in what was obviously a favourite armchair, his walking stick fitting into a groove on the side. 'Ms Parks is most distressed about her friend Maria, Mr Mavro. I understand you have undertaken to find her.'

'I have.' Mavros looked at his notebook. 'Actually, there are some specifics you could pass on to your people.' He paused, wondering if the old man would call a secretary or take notes of his own.

'Fear not, my memory is still excellent,' Kersten said, with a smile. His face was leathery and his hair sparse, but the sparkle in his pale blue eyes gave him the look of a younger man.

'All right. Could you find out from housekeeping when the "Do Not Disturb" sign was first noticed on room 243?'

'That is easy. I have already ascertained that the sign has been on the door since Ms Kondos arrived nearly two weeks ago. It seems the lady likes to look after herself.'

Or not, Mavros thought. 'Right. Did any of your people see Ms Kondos on Sunday evening?'

'As far as I have been able to ascertain – and I have been working on this since Ms Parks first called me yesterday morning – none of them did.' He looked down briefly. 'That isn't to say that one or more of them might not have been paid for their silence. It is my experience that people in the film business, especially Americans, can demonstrate remarkable largesse when the mood takes them.'

Mavros sensed the wisdom in the old man's words – he had clearly seen much in his years as host to the rich and powerful. 'Do you have CCTV?'

'Outside the perimeter, yes, but not inside. I am not enamoured of today's surveillance society.' He looked across at Mavros. 'I came of age in Hitler's Germany.'

'Rudi?'

Mavros looked round to see a short woman in an unseasonably thick skirt coming towards them with a tray between her hands. Although she must have been in her seventies, her hair was pale gold and plaited elaborately at the back of her head. He stood up to help, but she tutted him away, putting the coffee pot and cups on the mahogany table.

'This is Mr Mavros,' Kersten said, continuing in Greek. 'My dear wife, Hildegard.'

Mavros shook hands with her and watched as the old couple kissed each other on the lips.

'How do you take your coffee?' the woman asked.

'White, no sugar,' Mavros replied, wanting to dilute the caffeine hit.

'Mr Mavros has come to find Maria Kondos, Hildegard,' Kersten said. 'I'm giving him all the help I can.'

'I'm sure you are. It's a shame the people making the film haven't shown more interest.'

The hotel owner looked surprised. 'But they brought Mr Mavros from Athens. He's the best in the business.'

Hildegard Kersten turned her eyes back on Mavros. 'Is that so? Well, I wish you luck. They are all crazy, those people. It's only Ms Parks who really wants her friend back.'

'Why do you say that?' Mavros asked. He had seen that Rudolf Kersten gave his guests a more personalized service than that of most hotel-keepers, but he didn't want him and his wife to retreat behind the shield of confidentiality. He had also picked up a hint of tension as the old woman had come in – when her husband had mentioned Hitler's Germany.

'I've seen them together,' Hildegard replied. 'They have a high level of dependency on each other.'

'But you haven't seen Maria since . . .?'

'Sunday afternoon,' she replied instantly. 'When the limousine brought them back from the shoot.'

'We were in the car behind,' Rudolf Kersten added.

'My husband is the film's official consultant regarding the *Fallschirmjäger* – the German paratroops.'

Something had stirred in Mavros's memory, a newspaper article with photographs from a previous May when the Battle of Crete memorial was attended by veterans from all sides.

'You were one of them, weren't you?'

The old man nodded slowly. 'Yes, I was,' he said, his voice weaker. 'It was the worst experience of my life – and later I fought on the Eastern Front.'

'Hush,' Hildegard said, going to her husband and taking his hand. 'I told you the film would bring back too many painful memories.'

Kersten smiled sadly. 'But that is precisely the point, my dear. The film will lay the memories that have been tormenting me at last. The film will make me free.'

Mavros felt like a child that had strayed into a room where the big people were doings things far beyond his ken.

From *The Descent of Icarus*:

Allied resistance around the Tavronitis river-bed had been subdued, at least for the time being, by bombing and strafing. Peter Wachter and I made our way across the rock-strewn watercourse, keeping our heads down as the 109s streaked overhead. One of our gliders had crashed into the west bank, the aircraft's flimsy frame crumpled like a dirty handkerchief. Bodies were strewn around it, limbs at crazy angles and faces already swollen in the heat.

'What now?' I asked, after gulping from a water flask I'd picked up from a dead man.

Peter was peering through the trees that lined the dry river. 'I reckon Maleme airfield's a couple of kilometres to the north.' He pointed. 'See the bridge? It's beyond that, on the other side.'

I took in the fragile metal structure. 'You'd have thought the Brits would have blown it.'

'You would. And you'd have thought they'd be defending it on both sides, but we seem to be in the clear here.'

I caught the unmistakable low rumble of Auntie Jus, coming toward us from the sea. One of the leading aircraft was hit in the port wing and dropped to the ground like a lead weight before anyone could jump. The others ploughed on through the storm of fire and parachutes started to appear.

'They're going to come down ahead of us,' Wachter said,

clutching my arm. I saw that he'd been badly scared by what he'd been through. I hadn't had time to be afraid. 'Come on.'

I followed him through the trees and we came upon a comrade cutting away his parachute lines. We exchanged unit numbers with him as more men came down, most of them escaping the machine-gun fire from the hill across the Tavronitis.

'You'd better come with us,' a gnarled sergeant said, handing Peter drums of MG ammo from a canister. 'Our officers have made it.'

I recognized the leaders of the company. Lieutenant Kurt Horsmann was a decent enough type, but Captain Horst Blatter, his face marked by duelling scars, was the kind of stiff-necked Prussian who led by instilling terror in his men. He glared at Wachter and me as if we were deserters.

'You say you're the only survivors of your unit?' he demanded. 'That's impossible.'

Wachter nodded to the hill. 'We came down in open ground to the rear of that, sir. There are New Zealanders all over it. And that's not all.' He stopped and looked at me, expecting me to continue the story.

'There are civilians, sir,' I said. 'Armed civilians.'

Blatter removed his helmet and put on his peaked cap – he was even more of a crazed Prussian than I'd imagined, showing no fear of the bullets that were cutting through the trees.

'Civilians?' he barked. 'Armed with what?'

'Rifles that looked at least a hundred years old,' I replied.

'And axes,' Wachter put in animatedly. 'And knives, frying pans, spades, whatever you like.'

The captain glanced at Lieutenant Horsmann, who had sensibly kept his helmet on. 'Did these savages account for any of our men, Private?' he asked, his eyes boring into Wachter's.

'They certainly did, sir. I saw two old women cut Heini Stentzler's throat and a priest with a long white beard ran Wolf Dietrich through with a knife tied to a broom handle.'

'*Franc-tireurs*,' Blatter said in a voice that combined hatred and disgust. I found out later that his father had been shot by a Belgian irregular at the beginning of the Great War. 'Men, gather round,' he shouted. 'I hear the civilians of this benighted island have allied themselves with Churchill's minions. You remember what our commandments have to say about that?'

'Fight with chivalry against an honest foe,' bellowed the sergeant. 'Armed irregulars deserve no quarter.'

'Indeed,' Blatter said, turning back to us. 'I take it you dispatched these scum.'

'Yes, sir,' Wachter said proudly, and at that moment any comradely feeling I'd ever had for him vanished. 'Kersten here shot a young woman.'

I felt my hollow belly somersault – not because I'd spared the woman, but because the idea of killing civilians, even those opposing us, was utterly repellent to me. Having been led to understand that the Cretans would welcome us with open arms, I had never thought that I might have to kill them. Wachter wouldn't have either, but for him it didn't matter. His fellow soldiers were in danger, so the opposition merited the magazines he had emptied into them.

'Did you, Private?' Blatter asked, his grey eyes locking on to mine.

I hesitated, and then nodded. 'Yes, Captain.'

He slapped me hard on the back. 'Good man! You set a fine example.'

Then he turned away and started talking about tactics with Lieutenant Horsmann and the sergeant.

Wachter and I drank deeply. He ate some bread, but I couldn't have forced anything solid down. I was thinking about the woman who charged me – the hatred and harshness in her eyes and expression, even when she was on the ground and helpless. She reminded me of the woman in Delacroix's painting *Liberty Leading the People*, which had been a favourite of my history teacher, even though her black clothes had not slipped down her shoulders. I suppose there was something sexual in the way I thought of her, despite her clear abhorrence of me and all I stood for, but I could no more have raped her than I could have killed her. I knew she was a worthier human being than I was, a better person than all the men around me.

'Very well, paratroopers,' Captain Blatter called. 'We move on the airfield. Radio contact has not been established, but I hope to join up with other units on the way. Even if not, there are enough of us to clear the skulking British out of their positions.' He looked around us, his eyes bright in the early summer sun. 'Remember, the landing strip at Maleme is the key to this part of the assault on Crete. Take it and there will be thousands of our comrades on the island in hours.'

We made ready to move off, heavily laden with weapons and ammunition, but the captain hadn't finished.

'Remember this also,' he said firmly. 'This is a battle. There is no place for mercy when the stakes are so high. Until further orders, no prisoners will be taken. Scouts, move out!'

I watched as lightly armed men headed towards the bridge. Glancing around, I saw that none of the others seemed unduly affected by Blatter's penultimate order. Was I the only one who found the sudden cancellation of one of our commandments sickening?

As it turned out, I wasn't, but that made no difference at all.

Mavros was walking across the wide reception area when another elderly man accosted him. Unlike Kersten, he was of scarcely medium height and heavily built, walking at a brisk pace over the marble.

'David Waggoner,' he said, extending a hand. The accent was Queen's English and the words clipped.

Mavros took it, feeling strong pressure, and introduced himself.

'You're wondering who I am, old chap. Come over to that sofa and all will be revealed.' Waggoner smiled beneath a tidy pepper-and-salt moustache. His hair, which was considerably whiter, was short at the back and sides.

Mavros followed him, noting perfectly polished brown shoes, cream cavalry twill trousers and a dark-blue jacket. The old man had obviously been in the services.

'I hear you're looking for Maria Kondos,' Waggoner said, after they'd sat down together. 'Gin and tonic,' he called to a passing waiter. 'Join me?'

Mavros shook his head. 'Too early for me. Water, please.' He paused. 'If you don't mind my asking, how do you know what I'm doing?'

'My dear boy, everyone on the crew knows why you're here.'

Great, thought Mavros – though maybe he could turn that to his advantage. 'So you're on the crew?'

'Indeed I am,' the old man said proudly. 'Allied forces consultant. I was in the Hussars here during the battle, and then came back with SOE. The Special—'

'Operations Executive,' Mavros completed.

'Smart fellow. Do you have British blood?'

The tone of the question irritated Mavros and he was tempted to play the well-educated Greek. He restrained himself, needing to keep Waggoner cooperative.

Perhaps he had information about the missing woman to pass on.

'My mother,' he said.

'Ah, I see.' The former military man's eyes were slightly clouded, perhaps from incipient cataracts. Their softness was in marked contrast to his hand movements, which were rapid and percussive. 'Thank you, my man,' he said, signing the bill and rewarding the waiter with a five-euro tip before taking a heavy pull from his drink. 'I can use the film production's tab,' he explained.

'I take it you know Mr Kersten,' Mavros said, before he had finished drinking. That provoked the abrupt removal of the glass from Waggoner's lips.

'*Oberleutnant* Rudolf Kersten? Winner of the Iron Cross, First Class? Indeed I do, Mr Mavros. In fact, he's the reason I wanted to have this little chat.'

'Really?' Mavros tried to keep the pricking up of his ears metaphorical. 'How so?'

'Don't trust him,' David Waggoner said, the words a clear order.

Mavros's glanced down at the old soldier's tie, regimental with a very tight knot, before rising again to meet the hazy blue eyes. 'What do you mean by that?'

'Exactly what I say.' Waggoner took another slug of gin and tonic.

'Would you care to elaborate?' Mavros asked, suddenly aware that he was unintentionally copying his interlocutor's formal English. 'Does this have anything to do with Maria Kondos's disappearance?'

'Oh, I don't think so, but anything's possible.'

'Did you know Ms Kondos?'

'By sight, yes. I deal with the production assistants and the scriptwriters most of the time, but I saw her on location with the big star.'

Mavros picked up on the sarcasm. 'You don't like Cara Parks?'

'Fine-looking young woman, but not my idea of a Cretan peasant girl.' Waggoner twitched his head. 'Then again, this film doesn't greatly concern itself with historical accuracy.'

'That must be frustrating for a veteran like you,' Mavros said. 'And for Mr Kersten.'

David Waggoner's lips twisted. 'That old fraud has never cared for historical accuracy, I can assure you. He's never cared for anything or anyone except himself.'

Mavros waited for more, but the volcano seemed to have exhausted itself.

'Anyway, I wanted to make your acquaintance,' the old soldier said, getting up and handing over a card. 'Feel free to ring me if you need any help on the island. I gather you're an Athenian. You'll find things are rather different down here. I built up a lot of contacts during the war and I live here year round.'

Mavros watched David Waggoner march away across the hall – another one to be checked out.

FIVE

After eating a sandwich in one of the Heavenly Blue's numerous bars, Mavros spent the afternoon following up leads. He was called by the hotel's security manager, one Renzo Capaldi, and told that Maria Kondos had not left in any of the hire car company's vehicles. He went back to room 243 and checked the mobile phone. Although it was an advanced model, the messaging service hadn't been activated, which seemed odd – unless she never turned it off and answered every call. There were no texts in either the in- or out-box, which also struck Mavros as unusual, though, again, maybe she always spoke rather than wrote. The possibility that someone – perhaps the missing woman herself – had deleted texts couldn't be discounted, though the fact that none had been received recently suggested it wasn't a mode she employed much.

Then he got somewhere. There was a missed call, timed at 9.21 on Sunday evening. He checked the code with the switch-board – it was that of a village called Kornaria, about thirty kilometres away in the foothills of the White Mountains, he was told. He came up with a cover story and pressed 'Call Back' on Maria Kondos's mobile.

'Yes?' answered a deep male voice in Greek.

'I'm a friend of Maria's. Is she there?'

'A friend of whose?' the man asked, but the pause before he spoke gave Mavros the firm impression that he was prevaricating.

'Don't mess me around, friend,' he said brusquely. 'Maria Kondos gave me this number. Tell her to come to the phone.'

There was more hesitation. 'Who are you?' the man demanded, his tone also more aggressive. 'I don't know any Maria Kondos.'

You don't know any Maria Kondos, Mavros thought, but you repeat her name in its ungrammatical form without hesitation. 'Do I have to come over and drag her out of there?' he shouted. 'She owes me money and I need it now!'

The gears in his interlocutor's mind were grinding almost

audibly. The sensible thing for him to have done would have
been to cut the connection, but his Cretan machismo wouldn't
permit that.

'She owes you money? I don't believe you! I'll find you and
cut your balls off!'

'Not if I find you first,' Mavros countered, wondering how to
get Maria to the phone.

'Fuck your mother and your sister,' the man said.

The line went dead. When he tried again, it was engaged.
Someone had stepped in before the Cretan bull had said too
much, or perhaps he'd come to his senses. Mavros had seen
a map of the island on top of one of the piles of papers on
the floor. He scanned it and found Kornaria. It was isolated
and at the end of a very windy, unsurfaced road, and seemed
like an improbable place for a Greek-American to be. The
impression that the man knew her didn't mean she was in the
village, and setting out on a long and tricky drive on the off-
chance didn't seem like the best use of his time at that
juncture.

Besides, he still had a suspicion that Maria had never left the
hotel. There was one way to confirm that, at least in terms of
the land side of the resort – he would check later if boats came
and went from the beach. He went down to reception and asked
where the security office was. A young lad in Cretan costume
led him, his high boots squeaking on the marble.

A large man in a suit whose tenor voice Mavros recognized
opened the door.

'Mr Capaldi,' he said, smiling.

'Ah, hello.' The door stayed only half-open. 'You need something else?'

'I want to see the CCTV recordings from Sunday evening.'

The Italian stood motionless. 'You have authorization for this?'

Mavros shrugged. 'Call Mr Kersten.' He took out his mobile.
'Better still, I'll call him.'

Capaldi's hand came up quickly. 'Not necessary. Come inside.'

They went down a passage and into a small room. The Italian
squeezed into a desk chair and waved Mavros to a battered
armchair.

'No, thanks. Tell me, did you check the Sunday evening traffic
recorded at the main gate?'

Renzo Capaldi suddenly looked like a schoolboy caught with his hand down his trousers. 'No. I was not told to.'

'It didn't occur to you that Ms Kondos might have left on foot?'

The Italian laughed dismissively. 'People do not walk out of the Heavenly Blue, especially not the film crew. There is the press, the photographers.'

'So you won't mind if I check?'

Capaldi accepted that without enthusiasm and installed Mavros at a screen connected to a large server. He showed him which keys to use to stop and restart the sequence of images, and to speed up or slow them down. Mavros decided to start from nine thirty on Sunday evening, shortly after Cara Parks had last seen the missing woman. At first he found the pixelated images hard to make out, but soon he became accustomed to them. There were regular processions of cars turning in and out of the gate. Those entering mainly came from the west, presumably film personnel coming back from the airfield at Maleme. Those leaving mostly turned east, probably heading for the bars and restaurants of Chania.

Then, when the timer at the top right of the screen showed 22.17:23, he caught sight of a female form in a knee-length black dress approaching the gate. Her face wasn't visible, but her hair was similar to Maria Kondos's. She waited until a van came in and left on the opposite side of it from the camera, speeding up to remain obscured. She disappeared into the darkness beyond the furthest light just over a minute later. Mavros spoke Capaldi's name as he went back to the first sight of the missing woman.

'See this?' he asked.

'Yes,' the Italian said apprehensively.

'Is it her?'

'Could be. Can't see face.'

'"Could be" will do for me,' Mavros said. 'I want you to do the following – take the number of every car that turned east for an hour after she left. If you have a record of the driver or regis-tered owner, I need that too. All right? Call me on 171 as soon as you can.'

'Yes, sir,' Renzo Capaldi said, without irony. He seemed to have realized the seriousness of the situation.

Back in his room, Mavros booted up his laptop and went on

to the Internet, accessing a site that illicitly provided a reverse phone directory. The number he had called in Kornaria was registered to a Vasilios Dhrakakis, farmer. Then he entered the missing woman's name in a search engine. There were plenty of references, but as he went through them it became clear they were all articles about Cara Parks that referred to her assistant en passant – which made Mavros wonder. He was no connoisseur of glossy magazine-style journalism, but he was pretty sure that the hired help didn't often get namechecked. Then, on the third page of listings, he found something much more interesting.

'Actress PA in Youth Auto Death' was the headline in a Los Angeles newspaper, dated August 9th 2000. It seemed that Maria Kondos, aged 32, assistant to 'rising star' Cara Parks, hit and killed Michael 'Zee-Boy' Timmins, a seventeen-year-old African American boy, while driving Cara Parks' Mercedes late at night. The case against her fell apart when the defence produced witnesses, who saw Timmins stumbling down Mulholland Drive on what the post-mortem proved to be a crack cocaine high. He also had a police record as a member of a major drugs gang, the Letter-Men.

Mavros sat back and thought about that. It seemed unlikely to have any connection with Maria Kondos's disappearance after three years, but he wondered how she'd been affected by the ordeal. That was a question he could ask Cara Parks.

There was a knock at the door. Renzo Capaldi was standing there with some printed papers.

'Here's what you wanted, Mr Mavros,' he said, eager to please. 'Seventy-one cars turned towards Chania in that hour. Twenty-eight of them were taxis.' He handed over a sheet with licence plate numbers. 'Do you want me to find out the drivers' names and where they took their passengers, if they weren't dropping off?'

Mavros nodded and saw the big man's shoulders slump.

'And the other forty-three were either vehicles belonging to the hire company of the film crew or were used by individual guests or visitors.' He gave Mavros the second sheet, which showed licence numbers and names.

'Thanks,' Mavros said, running his eyes down the names. He recognized Tsifakis, the company owned by the driver Mikis's father, on nineteen of the cars. Of the remaining twenty-four, only one name stuck out – that of David Waggoner. He mentioned it to Capaldi.

'Oh, the old British colonel. He doesn't stay here, but he's in and out every day seeing people on the production. He's got one of those Range Rovers – as big as a tank.'

'And the others?'

'Guests who have long-lease villas in the resort. They're the only people here this month apart from the film crew.'

'OK,' Mavros said. 'Concentrate on the taxi drivers – I'll need a contact number, preferably a mobile, for each one.'

Capaldi went off down the corridor, surprisingly light on his feet for such a hulking figure.

Back in the room, Mavros highlighted the hired vehicles used by the production team – Rosie Yellenberg would probably be able to link each of them to particular members of the crew.

His phone rang.

'Alex, is it nice down there?'

'Hi, Niki. All right, I suppose. I haven't had a chance to see anything of the island except from the Learjet.'

There was a sigh. 'I wish I'd been on a Learjet.'

'OK, I'll get them to send it for you tomorrow morning.'

'Ha-ha. I miss you. Is there something wrong with that?' Niki's voice was wistful.

'Er, no. I miss you too,' he said, hurriedly. He did miss her, it was just that he hadn't had a chance to think of her since he'd arrived.

'Making any progress?'

'It's too early to say. I—' He heard the bleep that indicated he had another call. 'Shit, I've got to go. Sleep tight, my love.' He pressed the button. 'Hello?'

'Mr Mavros, we'd be grateful if you could some to Ms Parks' suite.' Rosie Yellenberg's voice was as hard-edged as before. 'Immediately.'

Wonderful, Mavros thought. Then again, there were things he needed from his employers.

He suddenly had a vision of the old-fashioned record player his father had insisted on keeping for his Beethoven and Mahler. It had a great trumpet for a speaker and a label showing a dog listening to a picture of the same. His Master's Voice, he remembered: except, in his case, it was His Mistresses' Voices.

As he left the room, he realized how unimpressed Niki would have been by that thought.

This time the gorilla opened the door to Ms Parks' accommodation without comment. Mavros walked into the living area to be confronted by more people than he had expected. Luke Jannet was sprawled in an armchair, a glass of some dark spirit in his hand. Behind him, perched on a dining chair sat Alice Quincy, an open laptop on her knees and a hands-free connection leading from her phone to her right ear. Cara Parks was at the end of the sofa where she had been sitting earlier, while Rosie Yellenberg was at the other. The atmosphere was icy, and not just because the air con was working hard.

'It's Philip Marlowe,' the director said, proving that he wasn't completely illiterate culturally. 'Pull up a chair, man.' It sounded like the drink wasn't his first.

Mavros nodded to him, and then to the others. He sat down in an excessively comfortable armchair and immediately felt his presence, such as it was, diminished. He should have remained standing.

'Hello, Alex,' Cara Parks said hopefully. She looked like she'd been crying.

'Give us a progress report, Mr Mavros,' Rosie Yellenberg said, her lips hardly opening as she spoke. 'This time we're all staying to hear it.'

Mavros smiled and ran through what he had been doing. The producer said he would have the names of the crew members who had been driving the vehicles he had highlighted the next morning.

'One of them was me,' Jannet said, slurring his words. 'Took some of the extras out for a night on the town.'

'Young, female extras,' Cara said, in a low voice.

The director raised his glass to her. 'At least they've been doing what their contracts say – working.'

'Have you spoken to the resort owner?' Yellenberg asked.

'Yes, he's been helpful.'

'Should be, considering what we're paying,' the producer said acidly. 'What did he give you?'

It was time to draw a line in the sand, Mavros decided. 'This isn't how I work, Ms Yellenberg,' he said. 'Most of the information

I dig up turns out to be useless. I'd be wasting your time and mine if I went through it all.'

She accepted that with ill grace.

'You do what you have to do,' Jannet said, his eyes hardening. 'We're giving you another two days.'

Mavros shrugged. 'That's up to you. In the meantime, what can you tell me about David Waggoner?'

'That old—'

Yellenberg raised a hand to cut the director off. 'Alice, give Mr Mavros a summary of the appropriate file.'

The director's assistant's fingers flew over her keyboard. 'David Waggoner, Colonel, the Hussars, retired. Commanded a tank during the Battle of Crete, awarded the Military Cross. Escaped to Chora Sfakion and evacuated to Alexandria. Trained with SOE and landed by submarine near Treis Ekkliseies, November 4th 1941. Officer in command of Chania and environs until April 17th 1943, when he was sent back to Egypt with a shoulder wound. Returned by parachute—'

'That isn't what I want,' Mavros interrupted – he could find the old soldier's history easily in an online encyclopedia. 'I meant, what impression do you have of him? He told me that he knows Ms Kondos by sight.'

Luke Jannet laughed loudly. 'You think that pompous Brit got the hots for Maria and kidnapped her?'

'No,' Mavros answered bluntly, seeing Cara Parks smile out of the corner of his eye. 'There seems to be some animosity between him and Mr Kersten. Could that have any bearing on the case?'

'I don't see how,' Rosie Yellenberg said, turning to the actress. 'Do you?'

Cara shook her head. 'I've only spoken to Mr – what is it? Waggoner? – a couple of times. He told me about the Cretan women who got involved in the fighting. I don't remember Maria ever saying more than "hello" or "goodbye" to him.'

'If I might add something,' Alice Quincy said, her cheeks reddening. 'I did see Mr Waggoner and Maria next to each other in the queue for coffee and doughnuts on set one morning.'

'Were they talking?' Mavros asked.

'I couldn't say for sure,' Alice answered. 'I think they might have been.'

Mavros smiled at her. 'Thank you.'

'Anything else?' Jannet said, getting to his feet unsteadily.

'Not at this stage,' Mavros said.

'Well, I'm off for an early one,' the director said. 'Tomorrow we're doing some aerial shots so don't hit the dirt if a Messerschmitt comes over at head height.' He headed for the door. Alice Quincy followed him with her head bowed, making Mavros wonder exactly what her duties included.

'If you wouldn't mind, Rosie,' Cara Parks said, holding her gaze on the producer until she too withdrew. 'Come and sit a bit closer, Alex.'

He did so. 'Are they giving you a hard time?'

She nodded. 'And my agent and my lawyer and . . . oh, forget it. All I want is Maria back. I appreciate what you're doing. Are there any other angles you could follow up on?'

'I'd recommend that laminated posters with a recent photo of Maria are put up both in the resort and on the roads and villages in the surrounding area.'

'Good idea. The technical guys can fix that. We should give a description and say when and where she was last seen, shouldn't we? In Greek and English?'

Mavros was impressed by the speed of her thinking. 'Yes. I'd advise offering a reward for information leading directly to her return as well. We'll get a lot of scam artists, but they shouldn't be too hard to rumble. There might be one person who saw or heard something important.'

'How much?' the actress asked.

'Five thousand euros?'

'Make it ten.'

'OK.'

They spent five minutes constructing the text, Mavros translating it into Greek.

'The photo?' he asked.

'I've got some in my laptop. I'll find the best. Rosie can hand over all the material to the geeks.'

'The hotel will be able to find people to put the posters up.'

'Right.' Cara Parks smiled, this time less tentatively. 'You know your job, don't you?'

He raised a hand. 'You might not like what I'm about to ask you.'

'Try me.'

'The night of August 9th 2000, Mulholland Drive.' Mavros watched her face. Her eyes widened, but she held his gaze.

'You *have* been busy.'

'Wonderful thing, the Internet.'

'If you can sort the truth from the lies. What do you want to know?'

'Was it usual for Maria to be driving your car?'

Cara was silent for a few moments. 'Not exactly usual, no. It happened occasionally, still does.'

'Would you care to tell me why she was driving it that particular night?'

The actress pursed her lips. 'Sure. If you care to tell me what it has to do with Maria going missing on Crete. You think the dead boy's gang hired an international assassin?'

'I don't know enough about the Letter-Men.'

'Believe me, they were assholes. Most of them were wiped out in a gun battle with a Mexican outfit last year.'

Mavros poured himself a glass of wine from the bottle in a silver stand.

'I'm sorry,' Cara said, 'I should have offered.'

'I'm sorry, I should have asked.'

She laughed. 'I like your style, mister.' Her expression grew serious again. 'OK, here's what happened. Confidentially.' He nodded. 'I was going to see this guy up on the Drive – a producer I'd got entangled with. Thing was, there was another man I was seeing, an actor. He used to get real jealous, would drive past my house and check if my car was at the front.'

'I thought you people lived on estates with high walls.'

She smiled. 'High railings and thorny plants in my case. You can see through if you try hard enough and I'd told the security guys to leave him alone. So Maria was driving the Merc back. She'd left her car at my place so she could get home. It had worked before. I'd given her a wig so she looked like me from a distance.'

The lives of the rich and famous, Mavros thought – just a scuzzy as anyone else's.

'Then that kid came out of nowhere, stumbled straight into

the car. Maria wasn't even going fast, but he flew through the air and hit the road head first.'

Mavros was still watching her closely. 'I don't know much about the Californian legal system. Was it an easy case to defend?'

'The best lawyers can do anything,' Cara said.

'So you paid?'

'Of course,' she said, looking shocked. 'It was my fault that Maria was driving back so late.'

He nodded. 'Imagine the scandal if it had been you at the wheel.'

Cara Parks looked away, her face suddenly pale. 'Yeah,' she said softly.

Mavros left a few minutes later. He hadn't learned much about Maria Kondos, but he knew more about the star. Cara Parks was convincing on the big screen, there was no doubt of that. Close up, on the sofa, things were harder to hide. He was almost certain *she* had been driving her Mercedes when it hit and killed Michael 'Zee-Boy' Timmins.

SIX

From *The Descent of Icarus*:

The sky was still full of our aircraft when we reached clear ground about three hundred yards from the Tavronitis bridge. There was sporadic fire from the trees on the other side of the river-bed and heavier weapons loosing off from the hill, but our scouts had done a good job. It seemed there was a gap between a pair of defensive positions. Captain Blatter arranged for covering fire at both, while the rest of us picked our way back across the stony watercourse and, to our amazement, reached the other side unscathed.

By now the sun was high in the sky and we were sweating like packhorses in our jumpsuits, the flies hovering around as if we were already dead. I was still carrying the MG34, with Wachter as my loader. He had seen something in my expression and was keeping behind me – or, more likely, he was using me as a shield against enemy fire. Lieutenant Horsmann moved from unit to unit, outlining the plan of attack on the RAF camp south of the airfield. It was unclear how many men were arrayed against us, so maximum force was to be used.

'Including killing prisoners?' I asked.

The lieutenant, a young man with little more than peach fuzz on his chin, avoided my eyes. 'You heard Captain Blatter's orders. We are the spearhead of the Wehrmacht. We cut through the enemy without mercy.'

I was going to raise the commandments, but I knew I'd be wasting my breath. My comrades were ready for action, their brows furrowed and their breath coming fast. They'd seen the dead men floating down under their parachutes and the planes taking flak. Now was their chance to blood themselves. Most of them were no older than Horsmann and hadn't experienced the assaults in Belgium and Norway early in the war.

The idea was to probe the camp to see how well it was guarded. Several MGs were set up to cover the first wave, though I was told to go forward with the lighter-armed men.

I caught sight of Blatter at the head of a group to my right. He was still wearing his cap, something which would earn him a stern reprimand from his senior officers if he survived. It was then I understood how his mind worked. He didn't expect to survive and he instilled this in his men. That made them an almost invincible fighting unit, caring nothing for personal survival. I was thankful that my own lieutenant, now rotting in the spring flowers, had never been so harsh.

Rifle shots rang out from the camp boundary, immediately answered by machine-gun fire from our men. I saw enemy soldiers drop down, while others remained in their slit trenches. Blatter's unit was already at the edge of the camp and we were urged forward by Lieutenant Horsmann. I held the MG34 levelled in both hands, but I didn't intend to fire it at another man. I had decided that my part in the war was over. My so-called comrades were savages and our invasion of foreign territory made us no better than the Mongol hordes that piled high the severed heads of the enemies they defeated.

'Shoot them!' I heard Captain Blatter scream, watching as men in Allied helmets with their arms high in surrender clambered out of the trenches. They collapsed as the paratroopers opened up on them.

'Look out!' Peter Wachter yelled.

I turned to my right and saw a group of huge men in tattered battledress charging us. Maoris. Although some of them fell as machine-pistols and rifles were directed at them, plenty more came on. I shivered when I saw that they had fixed bayonets. High-pitched screams came from those of our men who received the cold steel.

'Fire, damn you, Rudi!' Wachter screamed from the ground, where he was struggling to fit a new magazine to his MP40. 'Fire!'

The New Zealanders were only a few yards away. I blasted away over their heads, making some of them dive to the earth. Others kept up the charge and I leapt to my right to avoid a bayonet that was directed at my chest. Then Wachter got his weapon going and the big men tumbled like children at play, though none of them got up again.

'What the hell's the matter with you?' Wachter shouted, ducking his head as a grenade thrown by the next wave of Maoris exploded some yards in front of us.

I was still standing upright, gripping the MG34 loosely. I was smashed to the ground by a weight I realized was my loader.

'Give me that, you fucking lunatic!' He tugged the machine gun away and was soon emptying a drum of ammunition into the advancing foe. Then there was a diversion as some RAF men made a dash from Blatter's murderers, the New Zealanders kneeling down to give them covering fire. A few of them made it to the the treeline at the base of the hill.

'Come on,' Wachter said, getting to his feet. 'Horsmann's waving us towards the airfield. What's the matter with you? Take these drums.'

I loped after him, as careless as the killers about my own safety. I knew I wasn't going to die that day, not because I had some crazed notion of Aryan supremacy but because I had been chosen as a witness by some higher power. No matter what I did, I would survive while my comrades would not. I knew even then that I would die old, and only after I recorded my part in the events of the battle for Crete.

Because I had spared the woman, because I had shown mercy, I was no longer a proper paratrooper. I was the scribe, the sole recorder of my comrades' butchery.

The stench of cordite, aircraft fuel, shit and rapidly decomposing flesh washed over me as I looked out to the heavenly blue of the sea. Above it was the sky's darker and less pure blue, discoloured with the blotches of anti-aircraft bursts and smoke from doomed Auntie Jus.

There was a burst of machine-gun fire as a line of trembling aircraftmen were flung backwards into the dust by the men I had seen as brothers only a few hours ago.

Mavros went out of the main hotel building, his leather jacket over his shoulder. He had eaten a hurried room service meal and now wanted to have a look round the grounds. After a few minutes, he pulled on his jacket – the night air still had a bite from the snow-capped mountains to the south. The resort estate was lit up like an airport, pathways illuminated at knee height and different coloured lights on the villas, bars and swimming pools that filled the large expanse of ground. The lines of trees were decorated with white lights, giving a weird feeling of

Christmas. He had Maria Kondos's passport in his pocket and he intended to show it to as many out-of-the-way barmen and guests as he could.

Which he did over two hours, with nothing concrete to show for the effort.

Members of the film crew chilling out knew her, of course, but few of the resort staff did – it seemed she spent time with the actress or on her own. Seeing the lights of a last drinking hole down by the shore, Mavros headed towards it. The sea was running softly up the beach and the almost-full moon illuminated the shape of a small island not far out.

'Ayii Theodhori,' came a voice from behind him.

He turned to see David Waggoner, his face set in an expression that was probably the closest he got to good humour.

'It's a reserve for *kri-kri* – mountain goats, as you no doubt know.'

'I do, actually,' Mavros confirmed, though he had only the vaguest recollection of the beasts.

'They found Minoan votive objects in a cave that was supposed in one myth to be the jaws of a petrified sea monster. Of course, the Venetians – inveterate empire-builders – turned the island into a fortress.' The old soldier shook his head. 'I remember the Ju52s and the bombers coming over it in '41. We got a few, but the rest sailed through.'

Mavros kept walking, hoping to ask Waggoner some questions. 'A nightcap?' he suggested.

'I shouldn't. Got to drive back to Chania. But why not? The police don't stop me.'

Mavros didn't rise to that, but the arrogance of the man was grating. He was a war hero, so he thought he could do anything he liked.

'You live there, do you?'

'I have a pied-à-terre in the old town, yes, but I spend most of my time up in the foothills of the *Lefka Ori*.'

That got Mavros's attention, remembering the phone call he had made to Kornaria. 'In noble solitude or in a village?'

Waggoner glanced at him curiously. 'Outside a village,' he said, without offering further information.

Mavros let that go for the time being. They went into the bar, an almost deserted open-air affair covered by bamboo. The old soldier didn't seem to notice the chill, but Mavros zipped up his leather jacket.

'Carafe of *raki*,' Waggoner ordered in Greek. 'Have you tried the local spirit?'

Mavros remembered headaches after nights drinking with his brother-in-law, but decided to play the dumb Athenian. 'No,' he said. 'Is it fiery?'

'The stuff Kersten sells isn't,' the Englishman said scathingly. 'The real thing is.'

Mavros diluted his drink with water to keep up the act and ate some peanuts. He wanted to ask Waggoner about his apparent feud with the German, but that wasn't his priority.

'On Sunday night, you drove out of the Heavenly Blue at . . .' He consulted his notebook. 'Ten nineteen.'

One of David Waggoner's untrimmed eyebrows curved upwards. 'How do you know that?'

Mavros ignored the question, watching him closely. 'Were you on your own?'

'Certainly.'

'And you didn't pick anyone up on the road?'

'What do you think I am? Some kind of pervert? I don't touch those foreign whores.'

Mavros kept quiet, a technique he often found productive.

'Oh, I see. You think I had something to do with Maria Kondos's disappearance?' Waggoner didn't seem unduly concerned. 'Well, I didn't see her.'

'All right,' Mavros said, changing tack. 'Surely it would be more convenient for your consultation work if you stayed in the hotel.'

'Not bloody likely. I spend enough time in the bloody German's place without giving him the satisfaction of acting as mine host.' The old man looked away and took a hit of undiluted spirit.

'Why did you warn me off Mr Kersten?'

'Because he's a liar and a hypocrite.' Waggoner's eyes were narrowed now. 'He participated in the worst atrocities the *Fallschirmjäger* perpetrated against our men and the local people, but he's managed to worm his way into a position of respectability'

'Building the resort and staffing it must have brought plenty of jobs to the area,' Mavros commented.

'And unfortunately that's all some Cretans care about. Let me tell you, it's different up in the mountains.'

'In Kornaria?' Mavros slipped the words in smoothly.

'How did you—' The old soldier's eyes were less unwavering now. 'I suppose you've read one of my books.'

Mavros kept silent, satisfied that his guess had been confirmed. He certainly would be looking at Waggoner's memoirs if the case dragged on.

'Well, anyway,' the Englishman continued after a pause, 'the point is that Rudolf Kersten should have been tried and convicted of war crimes. He shot men who had surrendered and he took part in one of the worst massacres of men, women and – God help us – boys.'

'Where was that?'

'Makrymari, June 3rd 1941. It's only about ten kilometres from here. Fifty-eight souls slaughtered without trial in front of their families.'

Mavros heard the outrage in his voice, still strong despite the passage of over sixty years.

'Kersten claims he was taken ill before the executions,' Waggoner added. 'And that he shot over the heads of our men at Maleme. If you believe that . . .'

Mavros felt the need of a stronger drink, but he confined himself to several gulps of the watered down *raki*. 'He'd never have been given permission to build this place with that sort of record.'

Waggoner stared at him as if he were a small child. 'Money is all that counts down here on the coastal strip. The locals have made a Faustian pact. They take the German tourists' money and forget the past.' He slapped the bar hard. 'Well, not all of us have forgotten.'

Mavros noted the old man's passion, but held back from asking more about Kornaria and its connection with Maria Kondos. He had the strong feeling that he wouldn't get anything useful until he had more information to use as leverage.

'Better be off,' Waggoner said, getting to his feet. 'Mark my words. Kersten might look like a harmless type in his dotage, but he's killed women before. Maybe you should be looking more closely at him when it comes to your search for Maria Kondos.'

Mavros watched him march up the pathway, his heels ringing. The former SOE man had crept up on him effectively enough before, so he still possessed some of his wartime skills.

Draining his glass, he poured in more *raki*, diluting it with only a dash of water. There was more to this case than met the eye: the uneasy relationships between Cara Parks and the rest of the senior crew, Maria Kondos's telephone link with Kornaria, and now the old soldier's blatant attempt to put Kersten in the frame. He needed to consider his options.

He signed for the drinks and showed the barman Maria's photo. As he'd expected, he showed no recognition of her.

On the way back to the main hotel building, Mavros texted Cara Parks and suggested she arrange for the missing woman's photo, name and mention of the reward to be placed in the local newspapers. He suspected the correct procedure would have been to contact Alice Quincy or Rosie Yellenberg, but the actress had taken a major interest in the search.

Coming round the side of the hotel, he saw the flashing lights of police cars and quickened his pace. Had Maria Kondos been found? He went into the expansive reception area, in which people were milling around, and looked for Cara Parks. There was no sign of her. Renzo Capaldi, the security chief, was hanging around like a large spare part. Then he saw Hildegard Kersten, her face white with shock and a blanket around her shoulders, being tended to by two of the hotel staff. She stared at him as if unsure who he was and then beckoned him over.

'Mr Mavros,' she said, 'thank God you're here. It's . . . it's Rudi.'

'What's happened?' He looked around again, wondering if David Waggoner was in the vicinity. He couldn't see him.

'We've been burgled,' Hildegard said. 'The police are here, but I don't have any faith in them. Please help.'

Mavros held back for a moment, then decided that this was a good opportunity to get close to Rudolf Kersten.

'What happened to your husband?' he asked. 'Is he hurt?'

'No, no. It's just that he's being questioned by that idiot Inspector Margaritis and I know his blood pressure will be rocketing upwards. Come with me.' Hildegard dismissed the hotel staff with a movement of her wrinkled hand and pushed past the policeman who was standing at the door to their apartment.

'My husband needs me,' she said firmly.

There were more policemen in the living area, but they were powerless to impede the old woman's progress. Mavros saw Kersten at the dining table, facing a slim officer in plain clothes.

'Haven't you finished yet?' Mrs Kersten demanded. 'My husband is exhausted.'

'A few more questions, if you please.' Margaritis was unshaven and his shirt was unironed. 'Who is this?' he asked, giving Mavros a sharp look.

'A family friend,' Hildegard said, offering no further information.

The inspector shook his head and looked at his notes. 'Let me run through this, Mr Kersten. You and your wife had dinner in the hotel's Minos restaurant between approximately eight and ten. When you returned here, you noticed no damage to the external door. You had left none of the veranda windows open, while one in the bedroom appears to have been forced. You noticed that the wardrobe door was open and clothes had been disturbed.'

'We told you all this nearly an hour ago,' Hildegard protested.

'Please allow me to finish,' the inspector said, displaying discoloured teeth.

Mavros looked at his fingers – on his right hand, two bore yellow nicotine stains, though he had not dared to smoke in the Kerstens' apartment. 'Mr Rudolf, you went to the safe inside the wardrobe and immediately ascertained that your collection of coins had been disturbed.'

Kersten nodded wearily. 'A preliminary inspection showed that thirty coins are missing – the majority of them Hellenistic, but some Roman, Byzantine, Arabic and Venetian.'

'As soon as you can give me precise information and descriptions . . .'

'First thing in the morning,' the German said.

'What is the value of these coins?' Margaritis asked.

'Some of them are very rare. I would estimate at least fifty thousand euros.'

'All right, Inspector, that will have to suffice.' Hildegard Kersten starting shooing the policemen out of the room. 'My husband is not well. You will have your information tomorrow.'

Margaritis got up and walked slowly towards the door, his shoes scuffed and unpolished. 'Family friend, my ass,' he said to Mavros in a low voice, as he passed. 'I know exactly who you are. Keep out of my hair.'

'Delighted,' Mavros said, eyeing the greasy strands that only partially covered the inspector's cranium.

'Mr Mavro – Alex – thank you for coming,' Rudolf Kersten said, waving him to the table. He suddenly seemed much less tired. 'I would like to hire you to get my coins back.'

'That's not the kind of work I do,' Mavros said, sitting next to the old man. 'Besides, I'm already working a case.'

'Can't you handle the matters side by side?' Hildegard asked, sitting at the head of the table.

Mavros shrugged. 'Possibly, but you must understand that I am contracted by the production company, so I've got to give the search for Maria Kondos priority.'

'That's quite all right,' Kersten said, smiling loosely. 'You see, we know who took the coins.'

'You . . .' Mavros broke off. 'Did you tell the inspector?'

The elderly couple exchanged glances.

'No,' Kersten said. 'We cannot do that. You see, the thief is our . . . is our grandson.'

Mavros sat back in his chair. He was used to dealing with family feuds, but till now they had always been between Greeks. Maybe the Kerstens were more naturalized than he'd realized.

'His name is Oskar Mesner,' Hildegard said. 'He was always the black sheep of the family. Our daughter Franziska married a most unsuitable man, a tiler, if you please, a drunkard and a leech. Oskar has taken after him in all senses.'

'And you suspect he's in Crete?'

'We know he's in Crete,' Rudolf Kersten said. 'He's in Chania with an unsavoury group of individuals.' He scribbled an address on a piece of paper. 'Will you go here and ask him for the coins, please? You may offer him ten thousand euros in recompense.'

Mavros looked at each of them. 'Three questions. What proportion of your collection are the missing coins?'

'Numerically, about five per cent. In terms of value, rather less. I should keep them in a safety deposit box, but I like to look at them on a daily basis.'

The rich man and his foibles, Mavros thought. 'Why don't you go and talk to Oskar yourselves?'

'Because he hates his grandfather,' Hildegard said. 'He thinks he betrayed his country by coming to live here.'

Mavros intended to come back to that. 'If you want to pay Oskar off, why did you involve the police?'

'Ah, that was unfortunate,' Kersten said. 'One of our gardeners saw someone coming out of the rear window. He gave chase, but the individual ran to the gate and got away in a waiting car.'

'Which will be on the gate's CCTV.'

'No doubt,' the resort owner said. 'But I won't be giving that to the police.'

'Ah. Tell me, what should I know about this Oskar? Is he, for instance, two metres tall and a hundred and thirty kilos of muscle?'

Hildegard got up from the table and returned with a photograph, showing a thin man in his late twenties, his blond hair cut short and tattoos on his puny forearms.

'And the unsavoury group he hangs out with?' Mavros asked.

'Some of them came here once with Oskar,' Kersten said. 'Skinheads, layabouts. I gave them food and beer and they left quietly enough.'

'You could go now,' Hildegard said. 'You can't do anything to find the Kondos woman at this time of night.'

'I could sleep so I'm in good shape to carry on the search for her tomorrow.'

Rudolf Kersten stood up stiffly. 'Alex, if you do this small thing for us, I will pay you a thousand euros.'

Mavros looked at them and then nodded. He'd been made another offer he couldn't refuse.

SEVEN

The Kerstens gave Mavros a money-belt filled from with cash from their safe. It made him look like he had a pot belly.

'Are you sure you trust me with this?'

Rudolf looked at him unwaveringly. 'I'm sure. I can't send anyone from the hotel staff with you in case they recognize my grandson. We do have a standing on the island.'

Mavros nodded, wondering if now was a good time to ask about the wartime atrocities he'd heard about from Waggoner. He decided against it, not fully trusting the former SOE agent.

'I'll think of something,' he said, wondering if he would.

'Oskar often goes to that bar, the Black Eagle, behind the old harbour,' Hildegard said.

Mavros had a feeling he'd been there with his brother-in-law. In any case, it was only a few minutes' walk from Anna and Nondas's flat. He wondered if Barba-Yannis would still be awake – it would be an opportunity to get the keys.

'Anything else I should know?' he asked.

The Kerstens exchanged a glance. 'Well,' Rudolf said, 'Oskar got involved with a far-right group back in Germany after he left school. It's possible some might be out here with him. He . . . he also has contacts with a group of extremist Greeks.'

Whence the skinheads, Mavros thought. Neo-Nazis and bonkers Greek hyper-patriots. Were they worth it for a thousand euros? Definitely not, though there was no harm in checking Oskar Mesner out. Maybe he'd be on his own in the corner of the bar nursing a small bottle of lager.

'I have . . . I have weapons,' Kersten said.

'World War Two relics or something more modern?' Mavros asked, unable to restrain himself.

'I have nothing from the war,' the old man said in a low voice.

'No, thanks,' Mavros said firmly. Like his father and brother, he was opposed to violence in all forms except verbal. It was said on the Left that both Spyros and Andonis would have risen even higher than they did in the resistance movements they were engaged in if they had sanctioned the use of armed revolution.

'Here,' Kersten said, giving him a folded piece of paper. 'This note tells Oskar that this is the last money he will receive from me. Please give it to him after you get the coins back.'

'One of us will be awake all night,' Kersten said, with a soft smile. 'We have great faith in you, young man.'

Mavros wished them goodnight, inordinately happy to be called 'young' when he was forty-one. Maybe it was the long hair.

Renzo Capaldi was hovering outside the private door, looking like a giant who was about to be thrown out of his castle for eating the furniture.

'Mr Mavros, is there anything I can do?'

'I don't know. Dance *Swan Lake*?'

It was as he approached the main door that the thought struck him. He looked in his pocket and found the car-hire company card, then pressed out the number on his mobile.

'Is Mikis around?' he asked the woman who answered. 'I'm with the film crew at the Heavenly Blue and I'd like him to pick me up?'

'Now?'

'Would that be a problem?'

'Not unless he's hitting the beers, which he better not be.' The woman laughed. 'I'm his mother.'

Mavros wondered if Mrs Tsifaki had biceps like her son's.

'No, it's all right,' she said after a pause. 'He was watching the basketball. He'll be with you in under ten minutes, Mr . . . ?'

'Mavros.'

'Black by name, not black by nature, I hope?'

'Only occasionally.'

Mikis turned up in the same Jeep.

'Where are we going?' he said, after greeting his passenger.

'Centre of Chania. Sorry to drag you away from the basketball.'

'Nah, it's rubbish. Opium of the people.'

Mavros turned to him. 'That's not exactly what I expected to hear from a guy who spends his time servicing Hollywood capitalists.'

Mikis laughed. 'I'm not a member of the party or anything, but I like some of the things Marx said.'

'Yeah, so do I,' Mavros agreed. He'd never had any interest in joining the Communists or any other party, despite his father's decades of underground service. He'd never been sure why, but it was probably because he didn't like authoritarian structures. According to the Fat Man, it was because he didn't care about his fellow men and women, something he tried to disprove in his work. It was an ideology of sorts.

'I've got to pick up some keys and then deliver something,' he said to Mikis. 'You're not rushing off anywhere?' It had occurred to him that having the burly Cretan at his side might be useful if Oskar was with his friends.

'Whatever you want. It's the production company's bill.'

Driving around the old town of Chania at night, even during the early part of the tourist season, was less than straightforward. Mikis dropped Mavros as near Barba-Yannis's place as he could; they'd arranged to meet outside the Black Eagle twenty minutes later.

Mavros knocked on a neatly painted blue door, encouraged by the sound of a television inside. The door opened and a wizened old man with a spectacular moustache looked up at him. Even at night he was wearing the *vraka*, though he had taken off his high boots.

'Is that you, young Alex?' he asked, squinting.

Twice in one night, Mavros thought. Once more and I'll turn back into a student. He shook the old man's hand and asked him how he was.

'Better than I ought to be. I was ninety last month, you know.'

Mavros passed on greetings from Nondas and Anna, then said he was in a hurry – he'd call back to see the caretaker at a more civilized time.

'Civilized?' the old man cackled. 'This is the best time of the day. The TV's full of girls in their underwear. Have you ever called one of those numbers?'

Swallowing laughter and taking the keys, Mavros headed down the narrow street to the flat. It was on the second and third floors of one of the Venetian houses that had escaped the German bombing before and during the Battle of Crete. Inside it was cool, the furniture covered in sheets. There were cockroach traps all over the place. He considered taking a knife from the kitchen or leaving the money there, but decided the presence of Mikis would be enough to keep things calm.

He locked up after himself and stowed the heavy keys in his jacket pocket. The Black Eagle was round a couple of corners and a hundred paces nearer the harbour. Although it was past midnight, music was playing from all directions and the yells of drunks rang out regularly. Mavros remembered what David Waggoner had said about the Cretan deal with the devil – it sounded like the demons were loose tonight, and it was still only May.

He saw Mikis in a doorway about ten metres from the tables outside the bar.

'What's up?' he asked.

'I don't think you want to go in there,' the Cretan said. 'It's full of shaven-headed shitheads, the kind who think Hitler was a god. There are Germans and Greeks. The latter call themselves the Cretan Renaissance.' He laughed harshly. 'They wouldn't know a renaissance if it performed colonic irrigation on them.'

Mavros laughed, then went closer and glanced inside. The back of the bar was full of shouting yobs, one of whom was Oskar Mesner. The question was, how to lure him out on his own?

From *The Descent of Icarus*:

We got our toe in the door at Maleme and over the next couple of days the Auntie Jus landed mountain troops in large numbers. There were plenty of planes hit as they came in to land or took off at their excruciatingly slow speed, but our forces were mustering. Captain Blatter had several RAF men shot for refusing to assist in shifting damaged aircraft from the runway. I felt sick the whole time, going about my duties like a machine. Wachter kept away from me and I was sure he had told the other men about my failure to fire. Cowards were not countenanced in the ranks of paratroopers, so I was left alone.

Until it was time to advance. Surprisingly, the New Zealanders had not pressed us when our position at Maleme was critical – I later learned that the Allies' communications were almost non-existent and their commanders had failed to realize how vulnerable we were. That's what days of bombing and strafing will do to men in inadequate defensive positions. Units were sent forward to probe locations to the east, many of them making good progress despite dogged defence from the Maoris and Greek irregulars. Captain Blatter dispatched Lieutenant Horsmann's company – including

Peter Wachter and me – towards a village called Galatsi. The 109s were still shrieking over our heads, their machine guns shredding trees and anyone beneath them. I had been ordered to the front of the line by Blatter before we left. It was clear that he hoped I would stop at least one bullet. Horsmann gave me a sympathetic glance, but was powerless to contradict his superior.

It was a hot morning and we passed several German corpses. Their faces were blackened and flyblown, their bellies swollen to bursting point except for those who had been hit in the abdomen. Soon the word went round that our men had been mutilated. This caused anger and a burning desire for revenge amongst the others, but I was only saddened by the waste of young lives.

The outskirts of Galatsi – less a village than a hamlet – were deserted, the walls of the simple peasant houses wrecked by strafing and the roofs of most of them collapsed. There was the occasional burst of firing on the higher ground to the south, but little of it came our way – Blatter's men were clearing out the enemy.

We assembled in the small square around an ancient tree, most of its leaves blown to the dusty ground. There was a gap in the aerial activity and I heard birds singing from the small gardens behind the shattered buildings. And then came a combination of sounds that, first, set our nerves on edge and, second, sent us scurrying for cover.

Two British light tanks came into view at the other end of the street and started firing at us. They accelerated, our return fire ringing off their armoured fronts and sides. But they were only the start of our travails. Behind them came the New Zealanders, bellowing war cries and carrying rifles with long bayonets. They were followed in turn by Greek troops, some of them armed with nothing more than pistols and knives. They were also shouting a battle cry, a single word repeated over and over again. Later I learned it was '*aera*', meaning that the fighters should fall on the enemy like a great wind. And then came members of the local population, whose homes we had destroyed and were now taking refuge in.

We were the elite, so inevitably my comrades dealt death to many of the attackers, but they were not discouraged. The tanks ran to a stop, their crews killed – at least so we thought, until a stocky officer with fair hair leapt from the turret and emptied his pistol into a paratrooper who had foolishly gone forward. He then seized the dead man's weapons and took cover behind the vehicle, waiting for the charge to reach him.

Machine-gun fire rang out from all around the square. I saw Wachter, his face set hard, discharge drum after drum. That didn't save him. He was skewered by a pair of burly Maoris, one of whose bayonets broke off when it pinned him to the ground.

'Direct your fire!' Lieutenant Horsmann yelled, but it was too late.

The wave of attackers dashed over us, New Zealanders trampling paratroopers with their heavy boots, the Greeks, who I later found were gendarmes, cutting throats and smashing heads open with the butts of German rifles they had taken from the dead. Then came the locals, old men throwing rocks at downed men, boys handing them more, and women . . . it was then that I saw her, the woman I had left on the ground before we retreated to the Tavronitis. There was a bloodied bandage over her shoulders, but she was firing an MP40 from the hip. Her hair was tangled and raised by the wind – she could have been a Gorgon or a Fury, come to claim our bodies for the death god.

Fire from my comrades was minimal now. The lieutenant charged forward with an MG34, but was cut down by a blow from a curved sword wielded by a bearded man in baggy trousers. His head was almost severed.

Panicked, I tried to fire, but my machine-pistol jammed. I took out my bayonet and pistol, ready to face what was coming to me as the last of the unit. I hit a gendarme in the leg and a hail of fire was directed at me. By some miracle, I escaped injury. Then a Maori leapt on me and knocked the weapons from my hands. He heaved me up and threw me against the wall, pulling back his rifle with its awful bayonet.

'No!' came a scream from the window.

I looked past the New Zealander and saw the woman I had spared, her face spattered with blood.

'This man, mine!' she said in a crude English accent, coming through the window frame. Beyond her I saw the fair-haired British officer. He was shooting our wounded in the head with the Luger he had plundered.

The Maori shrugged and strode away, while the woman raised

the MP40 at me. The irony of being executed with a German weapon didn't escape me, but I wasn't afraid. I wanted to leave this world of fire and slaughter.

She fired above my head, pieces of plaster falling past my eyes. Then she stepped up, eyes burning into mine all the while, and beckoned me to take off my helmet. She swung back the machine-pistol and smashed the butt into the side of my head.

Before I went into the darkness I saw her lips form into a smile that wasn't completely full of hate.

There was no alternative, Mavros realized, to going into the Black Eagle and asking Oskar Mesner to come outside with no more than one sidekick. Tempting him financially seemed the most likely method to work, so he fumbled with the money-belt and took out a thousand euros.

The bar was smoky and the music ear-shredding metal – it was making many of the customers nod their shaven heads like demented puppets. Mesner was at a table with three men, two of whom had bare skulls and the other a crew cut that the US Marine Corps would have approved. Mavros wondered how the Kerstens' grandson, with his unshaved head and sparse moustache, fitted in.

Moving slowly closer, he held up the money and slipped it into the German's shirt pocket. That obtained him a degree of interest.

He leant close. 'There's more waiting for you outside, Oskar,' he said in English, having been told Mesner spoke the language. 'You don't have to come on your own, but a tough guy like you doesn't need more than one bodyguard, does he?'

The German looked at him with a mixture of curiosity and disgust – he no doubt disapproved of shoulder-length hair. 'Karl,' he said, angling his head to the front of the bar.

One of the skinheads got up, banging his large backside into a young man wearing a Greek national football shirt. Words – probably incomprehensible to each of them – were exchanged, before he pushed his way out of the place. Mavros beckoned Mesner to follow and took up the rear.

'What's this about?' the German demanded, as soon as they hit fresh air.

'You know what it's about, Oskar,' Mavros replied, leading the incongruous pair towards the doorway where Mikis was concealed and stopping a few paces away from it. 'You have something your grandfather wants.'

'Oh, that old *arschloch*,' Mesner said, his voice unnaturally high. 'He can go fuck himself.'

'Except that he's authorized me to pay you another nine thousand euros,' Mavros said, with a smile.

'Who are you? His *schoassniessen*?'

The skinhead guffawed.

'Which means?' Mavros asked politely.

'How you say in this fucking language . . . ? Person who sneezes shit.'

'No, I'm his person who sneezes euros.'

Mesner looked around – the street was deserted.

'You have this money with you?' he asked.

'Do you think I'm crazy?' Mavros had considered leaving the funds in Nondas's place, but had decided he could handle it, especially with Mikis in reserve. 'You give me the coins, I'll take you to the cash.'

'Fuck that,' the German said, then his face froze. 'What coins?'

Mavros laughed. 'Too late. Besides, you were seen. You should be thankful your grandfather didn't tell the police.'

'He'd never do that,' Oskar Mesner bragged.

'Yes, he will. This is the last time you get let off. Look on the bright side – you've just made ten grand.'

The German glared at him. 'Do you know how much the . . . the merchandise is worth?'

Mavros nodded. 'But twenty per cent is better than nothing.'

'What if we make you take us to where you've got the money?' Mesner said, glancing at his bulky comrade.

'Go ahead and try,' Mavros said.

Mikis, whose English was clearly as good as he'd said it was, stepped into the street, his arms crossed to demonstrate the size of his biceps.

'Of course, you can also call your friends in the bar,' Mavros said, 'but I'm not sure how much cash you'll be left with once they get a sniff of it.'

The look on Mesner's face suggested he wasn't convinced of that either.

'All right,' the German said. 'I've got the coins. Where's the money?'

Mavros disguised his surprise. He hadn't imagined Oskar would be as stupid as to carry the coins on him. Then again, they weren't bulky. He handed over the note Rudolf Kersten had given him. Mesner looked at it, scoffed and dropped it to the ground. That made Mavros's mind up for him – the arsehole would never leave his grandparents alone.

He raised the shirt to show the belt, opening a pocket stuffed with banknotes.

'You lied,' the German said, his voice even higher than before.

'It happens.' Mavros undid the belt, aware that the skinhead's eyes were locked on it. He raised an eyebrow at Mikis, whose face remained as impassive as a statue's. Meanwhile, Mesner had taken a crumpled plastic bag from the pocket of his jeans. 'Let me see.'

Mavros didn't know anything about ancient coins, but he didn't think the German was smart enough to substitute thirty worthless coins when he'd had no idea an exchange was on the cards. Not that it mattered, considering what he now had in mind.

'Thirty of them because your grandfather's a Judas, eh?'

Mesner nodded. 'For a Greek, you're unusually smart.'

Mavros let that go – for the moment. 'One,' he counted. Out of the corner of his eye, he saw Mikis move closer to the skinhead.

'Two.' Oskar Mesner licked his lips.

'Three.' Mavros held out the money-belt – then grabbed the bag of coins, pulled back the belt and kneed Mesner in the groin.

'Smart and nasty,' he said, with a grin.

Mikis had his fingers round the sidekick's throat.

'I think it's time this pair went for a short flight,' Mavros said, nodding towards the bar.

They dragged the Germans over to the entrance. Mikis flung the big man towards the Greek nationalists, then Mavros launched Mesner at the barman.

'Time to go,' he said, turning on his heel.

They stopped briefly at the end of the street. The music had stopped and had been replaced by yelling and the sound of breaking furniture.

'Thanks,' he said to the Cretan.

'My pleasure. I hate those bastard Nazis.'

It was only after they got back to the Jeep and were heading for the resort that Mavros had a disturbing thought. What if Oskar Mesner wasn't the weak-minded scumbag his body suggested he was? What if he took other steps against his grandfather?

As they drove out into the sweet-smelling night beyond the city, he reckoned that was unlikely. He had saved Rudolf Kersten nine thousand Euros, got his precious coins back and made himself a grand.

Result.

EIGHT

Mavros woke up at eight, his head and body heavy. He had to report back to the Kerstens before he continued the search for Maria Kondos, although he had called after he got back to confirm that he had the coins. After a shower, a couple of excellent croissants and a Greek coffee that wasn't a complete disgrace, he called the Fat Man's flat in Athens.

'Oh, boss, I was so worried about you.'

'Cut the crap, Yiorgo. I've been away for under twenty-four hours.'

'And suddenly you find you need me.'

Mavros laughed. 'As it happens, yes. I want you to do an Internet search on some people.'

'Great,' the Fat Man groaned. 'You know how much I adore modern technology.'

'You fool no one. Ever since your blessed mother departed this life of sorrows, you've hardly been off that laptop you bought.'

'One word,' Yiorgos said. 'Girls.'

'And the odd, I mean huge number of conspiracy theories.'

'Are you saying the CIA doesn't run the world?'

Mavros sighed. 'Check out the following please: Rudolf Kersten and David Waggoner.'

'Waggoner?' the Fat Man repeated. 'Wasn't he one of those British agents who screwed up the patriotic struggle in Crete?'

'Try to keep an open mind till after the search, will you? Email me whatever you get asap.'

'Yes, sir. Certainly, sir.'

'Long live the revolution,' Mavros replied, then cut the connection. He picked up the bag containing the coins and the money-belt and headed for the stairs.

Downstairs, Renzo Capaldi was again hovering around the door to the Kerstens' apartment.

'Still here?' Mavros asked cheerfully, as he knocked.

'How is Mr Kersten?' the security chief asked, keeping his distance.

'Ask me when I come out.' Mavros followed a maid in a black dress into the living area. 'Good morning,' he said to the elderly couple, who rose politely from their places on the sofa.

'Good . . .' Rudolf Kersten broke off, his eyes on the objects in Mavros's hands. 'What have you there?'

Mavros opened the plastic bag and let the German pour the coins on to the glass table. Then he laid the money-belt down beside them.

'I gave a thousand to your grandson,' he said, 'and I've taken a thousand for myself, as agreed.' Although Mikis Tsifakis had refused to accept any payment for his part in the previous night's events, Mavros was going to give him some cash. 'I take it those are the missing coins.'

Kersten nodded slowly, then glanced at his wife. 'What happened with the money? I can't imagine Oskar turned it down.'

'He didn't.'

Hildegard leaned forward. 'Did you hurt him, Mr Mavros?'

'Not more than he would have hurt me. He may try to get in here again, though. I recommend you tell Mr Capaldi to check the shutters and doors, and to set up a patrol outside.'

'Quite remarkable,' Kersten said, his voice low. 'We have much to thank you for.'

Mavros shook his head. 'It was no problem and I've been very well recompensed. If you'll excuse me, I must get back to my original job.' He glanced at the glistening coins. 'I'd also recommend you put those and the rest of your collection in the hotel safe or – better – a bank's. Presumably your grandson won't be here for too much longer.'

'We're not sure about that,' Hildegard said. 'He's fascinated by the film and the anniversary of the battle next week. The last we heard, he had no work back in Germany.'

'If you want him to leave, you're right not to give him any more money. That thousand should get him home. Now, I have to get back to my original case.'

Rudolf Kersten got up and followed him towards the door. 'Dine with us tonight, Alex,' he said. 'I'm more grateful than I can say.'

'Let me see how my schedule pans out.' Mavros found himself touched by the old man's gratitude – though the Fat Man would have said it was no more than relief that he'd got his ill-gotten possessions back.

Outside, he nodded to the bulky Italian. 'Don't go away. I think you're about to be called in.' He grinned. 'Don't panic. I put in a good word for you.'

One case down, another harder one to go, he thought, as he walked to the stairs. This time he was going to arrive panting whether Cara Parks liked it or not.

As it happened, the actress was breathing more heavily than Mavros when he was let into her suite. She was in a leopard skin leotard that left little to the imagination, performing high kicks. He was relieved to see that Rosie Yellenberg wasn't present.

'Sit down,' Cara said. 'Let me get a towel.' She reappeared with one over her shoulders.

Mavros tried not to stare at her well-toned thighs, but found himself looking at her breasts before he glanced away. 'I need you to set something up.'

'Shoot.' The actress poured herself a glass of water and drained it in one.

'There's a driver from the company servicing the crew—'

Cara Parks let out a peal of laughter.

'Let me rephrase that,' Mavros said, wondering if she was flirting with him. She certainly seemed less uptight.

'It's OK,' she said. 'What about him? Or is it her?'

'The former. I need him today.'

'That handsome, huh?'

Mavros flashed her a look that gave her to understand, if she hadn't already, that he wasn't interested in men.

'Consider it done.' She wrote down the name when he said it. 'Where are you going?'

'Various places.'

'Not saying, huh? Good. Make sure you don't tell any of the others, especially dear Rosie.'

The actress's tone was corrosive. Mavros realized the strength of character she had needed to attain the position she occupied on the Hollywood pecking order. He wouldn't have liked her to be an enemy.

'Have a good time last night?' she asked, in a way that suggested she knew he'd left the resort.

'Following some leads.'

'Jesus, how much do we have to pay you to get some answers?' she demanded, the tension back in her voice.

Mavros raised his hands to placate her, though she was still glaring at him. 'I'm being paid to answer one question only,' he replied stolidly. 'Where's Maria Kondos? At the moment, all I can say is, "I don't know".'

Cara Parks relaxed slightly. 'You'd better hurry up. This is your penultimate day, according to Luke.'

He shrugged. 'I've got Matthew, Mark and John in reserve.'

Another peal of laughter rang out as he headed for the door.

'Hey, Scottish-Greek?'

He looked over his shoulder.

'Get yourself across to the set this afternoon. They're flying the old planes, remember?'

He didn't commit himself, but wondered whether that was why Rudolf Kersten had looked so apprehensive, even after he'd got his coins and money back.

Mikis was on another job, but would be at the hotel in an hour. In the meantime, Mavros went back to his room and called Niki on her work line.

'Morning, pretty woman.'

'Ah, the prodigal lover,' she said, with only mild irony. 'How's living it up with the cream of Hollywood? Did you have dinner with the stars?'

He decided against telling her he'd just had a private audience with Cara Parks. Or that he'd started a bar fight in Chania old town last night.

'Pretty dull, really. Still haven't found the woman.'

'Keep it that way. I'm flying over if you're not back by Friday night.'

That would be an enormous distraction. Besides, he'd be off the job by then if Luke Jannet had his way – which was pretty strange, considering the director had flown all the way to Athens to hire him. Maybe he liked turning the screw for the sake of it.

'Alex?'

'Oh, sorry. Yeah, well, I'll see how things go.'

'Is she as stunning as the photos suggest? And don't say "who?".'

'The delectable Cara? There you are – I've answered the question already.'

'With another one. Don't even think of touching those Twin Peaks.'

'Sorry, I'm being waved at by an irate producer,' he lied. 'Talk to you later.' He loved Niki dearly, but her constant fear that he would be unfaithful got him down. There were times when he'd been tempted, but so far he hadn't let her down. That didn't mean he liked being reminded of his duty.

He rang the Fat Man.

'Christ and the Holy Mother,' the communist said – the comrades were surprisingly unconcerned about swearing by things they didn't believe in. 'I haven't got much yet.'

'Quick question. Have you ever heard of a village called Kornaria down here?'

'Isn't that the place where the locals grow cannabis, and fought the cops off?

Hold on, I'm accessing a search engine. Yes, that's right. It was last autumn. The forces of public order – it says here – attempted to reach the cultivation sheds, but they came under severe attack from the Kornariates, who loosed off anything from Second World War machine-pistols to hunting rifles at them, wounding four and driving the rest – nearly a hundred of them – back down the mountain road. There's been an enquiry going on ever since, but it won't get anywhere. The local MPs and other officials know all about the drug production and are doing everything they can to obstruct external interference in Cretan affairs. Fucking hypocrites!'

'Yeah.' Mavros was turning pages in his notebook. 'Do a search on Dhrakakis, Vasilios,' he said, finding the name registered to the number he had called from Maria Kondos's phone.

'Bingo,' Yiorgos said, after a few seconds. 'He's the mayor of Kornaria. Doesn't say much else, only that his family is the biggest in the village.'

'That'll do for now. Thanks, Fat Man.' He rang off before he heard more than a couple of words of complaint.

A few minutes later, Mikis pulled up at the front of the hotel. 'Apparently I'm your private chauffeur until further notice,' he said, grinning widely. 'More neo-Nazi baiting?'

'Possibly.' Mavros climbed into the Jeep and stuffed two

hundred Euros into the driver's shirt pocket. 'Special request from Mr Kersten,' he said. 'You wouldn't want to offend such an important local figure.'

Mikis didn't look happy, but left the notes where they were. 'Where are we going, then?'

Mavros was looking at the map he had bought. 'Get us to Karies and then I'll direct you.'

'Karies? There's not much up there.' He turned to Mavros. 'Except the track to Kornaria. You wouldn't by any chance be wanting to go to that crazy end-of-the-road place, would you?'

'Erm, maybe.'

Mikis stopped the Jeep. 'You need to be straight with me, Alex. I know this island. There are places you can't go asking questions.'

'You're right.' He recounted the story of his call to Dhrakakis and his idea that Maria Kondos might be in the village.

'Sounds pretty thin to me,' the Cretan said.

'I'm sure he knew her,' Mavros countered. 'In my business you learn to tell when people are lying.'

'That may be,' Mikis said, 'but Kornaria is bandit country – always has been. Not that I've ever been near the dump. It's up in the middle of nowhere for a reason, you know. The Venetians never got it, the Turks steered clear, even the Germans left the locals to themselves. The headbangers from Sphakia like to think they're Crete's bad boys, but they've got nothing on the Kornariates.'

'Wonderful,' Mavros muttered. 'Couldn't I just pretend to be a dumb foreigner on a personal tour?'

'Need to take these off,' Mikis said, slapping the outside of his door.

Mavros remembered the stickers for *Freedom or Death*. 'Yeah, maybe you should.' He didn't mention that David Waggoner, one of the film's consultants, had a place near the village. He presumed he'd be on location today, watching the planes and remembering the days of death and defeat.

Mikis jumped out and peeled the decals off. 'Plenty of these back in the depot,' he said, getting back behind the wheel. 'OK, let's play it your way. You speak only English and I'll see if we can pick up any hint of the missing woman.'

They drove out of the resort and headed east, before turning south on a road that bisected lush groves of fruit and olive trees. The sun was already high in the sky, but they were shaded from its heat and the first half-hour of the trip was a pleasure. Then the road started to climb and the foliage thinned, until soon all that confronted them were the sheer bare flanks of the White Mountains, their summits capped in glinting silvery white. Although they weren't far from Chania as the crow flies, it was a different world.

'Don't be fooled,' Mikis said, as he slipped into third gear. 'There are plenty of watercourses that you can't see from here and villages were built around them, even in ancient times. There's one of those Mycenaean beehive tombs not far from here. A lot of the villages are deserted now, the people down on the coast fleecing the tourists.' He laughed. 'Like my family. Our village is further to the west. There are twelve people in it now, all of them over seventy-five.'

Mavros nodded. It was a common tale in the mountainous parts of Greece. Signs pointed to villages that weren't on his map. The road was asphalt, the result of European Union grants, but it was badly potholed.

At Karies, Mikis turned to him. 'Are you sure you want to go through with this?'

'Yes. Here's what we'll do. I'll claim that my British grandfather was here during the war with the SOE.' That way, he might also find out more about Waggoner. 'Let's say he was known as Panos, that's common enough. If we get anywhere with that, we'll ask if there are any Kondos's in the village.'

Mikis shrugged. 'It's not a very Cretan name.' He was concentrating on the much rougher track they were now grinding up. The bushes on either side were thick and thorny, but the trees were leafless and bent.

'True. Maybe her family shortened it when they got to the States – lots of them did.'

'Kondakis?' the driver suggested. 'Kondhylakis?'

'No, let's stick to Kondos. If she had relatives in the village, they'd know the family's new name, wouldn't they?'

Mikis didn't look convinced. 'Wasn't it some Hollywood guy who said nobody knows anything?' He swerved as a goat walked across the track with its head held high.

'Impressive,' Mavros said, meaning both the driving and the quotation. 'William Goldman. Have you read him?'

'No, one of the guys on the crew told me.' Mikis laughed. 'I'm a driver. I don't read.'

Mavros had noticed the corner of a book under tissues and torches in the open glove compartment. 'So you use this for wiping your arse, do you?' He held up a new-looking copy of Nikos Kazantzakis's *Kapetan Michalis*, remembering that it had been translated into English as *Freedom and Death*.

The Cretan crossed himself. 'How can you say such a thing about a book by the greatest modern Greek writer?'

'I could argue the toss about that for hours.' Mavros was not a fan of the great man's work, finding it overblown and under-edited, though this book – the story of a freedom fighter and family patriarch who dies in a final skirmish against the Turks – was better than most; certainly more powerful than *Zorba the Greek*, which largely owed its popularity to the film. Give him a poet of few words like Cavafy or Seferis any day.

'Actually, I was only messing with you. I have a literature degree from the University of Crete,' Mikis admitted. He stared ahead. 'And now the fun starts.'

Mavros followed his gaze. A pickup truck with massive chrome bull bars was parked across the road, completely blocking it. Two men in high boots, *vraka*, and *mandili*, stood in the back, each carrying a shotgun, while another one in the cab spoke into a walkie-talkie.

'Shit,' Mikis said, under his breath. 'You sure you want to go through with this?'

Mavros looked over his shoulder. Another pickup was drawing up behind them. 'I don't think we have much choice, my friend.'

'Play dumb and British,' said the driver. 'If that isn't a tautology.'

From *The Descent of Icarus*:

It was dusk when I came round, unaware of where I was until I managed with great difficulty to pull myself up from the floor of the ruined house. I stumbled over to the shattered window and looked out on to the small square. What I saw was a scene of unbelievable horror.

The bodies of my fellow paratroopers were now almost completely covered by those of the New Zealanders, gendarmes and local people who had defeated them. I was unable to focus and struggled to walk, so hard had the blow to my head been. But at least I was still alive – not that I took any comfort from that. I could only imagine that either 109s had strafed the enemy to destruction or that our troops on the higher ground to the rear had fired down on them. The place smelled like the slaughterhouse in my grandparents' Bavarian town in August – iron blood, rotting guts and lacerated flesh.

Leaning on a rifle, I staggered out into the square and started looking for the woman. I was drawn to her and, if she had been killed, I wanted to lay her out and place her arms across her chest as a mark of respect. But there was no sign of her, even though there were several other women in black among the dead. Then I heard a groan from what turned out to be the sole survivor.

It was the squat British tank officer I had seen giving our men the coup de grâce – an action I was fairly sure was not within the bounds of the Geneva Convention. Not that we had been observing that either. He was at the side of the street, his legs covered in blood and his face peppered with shrapnel. I dropped to my knees and lifted his head, then poured some water from my canteen into his mouth. He stared at me in amazement.

It wasn't long before paratroopers began to trickle into Galatsi, initially observing the drills for taking possession of disputed territory and then showing themselves as it became clear there was no danger from the enemy.

'Identify yourself!' came a raised voice I recognized instantly.

I slowly hauled myself upright and gave my name and unit.

Captain Blatter came closer, limping from a wound above his right knee. 'Where are the others?' he demanded.

I nodded to the square. 'Underneath.' I said, provoking a glare. 'Sir.'

Troops were pulling enemy bodies off their comrades and swearing.

'Herman! Throat cut!'

'My God, the lieutenant's head's nearly off!'

'Two men stuck by the same Maori!' I watched as the sergeant drew his own bayonet and stabbed it repeatedly into the dead New Zealander's back.

Blatter ignored that. 'What have we here? A British survivor?'

The wounded man stared up at him. 'Waggoner, Captain David.' He stated his regiment and serial number.

'How many of my men did you kill, Captain?' Blatter placed one of his jump boots on the Britisher's legs and pressed down hard. 'How many?'

'My Captain,' I said. 'You—'

'Silence!' he roared. 'You hid yourself away while your comrades were massacred. Do not think I will forget that!'

Captain Waggoner looked at me, his eyes dull, then turned back to Blatter. 'Fuck you!' he shouted. Blatter kicked him hard and he lost consciousness.

The regimental doctor came up to me and examined the side of my head. 'He couldn't have done this himself, if that's what you're thinking,' he said to the captain. He was taking a risk, but the medics were a law to themselves after they proved themselves in battle, as this one had in Belgium.

'They will pay for this,' Blatter said, limping over to an old woman who had been nearly cut in two by machine-gun fire. 'Your children and grandchildren will burn in hell!' he yelled, his spittle flecking the dead woman's swollen features.

Without being ordered, the paratroopers set about removing our dead from the heaps in the square, treating the bodies of the enemy without the slightest respect. I was glad the woman who saved me had escaped, fearing that her corpse would have been mutilated because of her great beauty.

'With a head wound like that, you should be in hospital,' the doctor said to me in a low voice.

'No,' I replied. 'I should be beneath the ground.'

He didn't understand my meaning. Why should he? We were the spearhead of the German armed forces, we did not crumble after a few days' fighting. But it wasn't the fighting that had undone me, hard and ghastly though that had been. It was the dauntless courage and nobility of the Cretan woman. I realized that if I'd found her body in the square, I would have plunged one of the long Maori bayonets into my own heart.

NINE

'Leave this to me,' Mikis said, opening his door.

'No,' Mavros said, doing the same with his. 'Time for me to play the blundering Brit.' He walked forward slowly, waving his hand. 'Hello!' he said, in English. 'Is the road closed?'

Mikis swiftly overtook him. The men in the pickup had levelled their shotguns at them.

'The gentleman is British,' he said, in Greek. 'He asks if we can visit the village.'

'Why?' demanded one of the men, beetle-browed and bearded. 'Don't you know better than to bring tourists here?'

Mikis let his shoulders slump. 'I'm sorry, but he insisted. He says his grandfather was here when the Germans held the island.'

The men's expressions remained stony, but they exchanged a glance.

'Was he sent by someone?' the bearded villager asked.

Mavros was playing dumb, but the question put him in a dilemma. Should he lie about Waggoner providing an invitation? And if so, how could he get that across to Mikis?

The Cretan wasn't thrown. 'I think so,' he replied. 'I can't understand the name he says.'

'Ask him again.'

Mikis went through the process of asking Mavros in halting English for the name of the man whose writings had led him to visit Kornaria.

'Waggoner,' Mavros said.

'O Lambis,' hissed the bearded man to his sidekick.

Mavros presumed that was the cover-name Waggoner had used when he was on Crete during the war. He cursed himself for not asking the Fat Man to do those searches overnight. Outwitting Oskar Mesner had distracted him from the main case.

He nodded. 'Lambis, that's right,' he said, in English.

There was a hurried conversation between the men in the first pickup and another who had come up from the one behind the Jeep.

'All right,' the bearded man said to Mikis. 'You can go up to the village.' He frowned. 'Keep your tourist under control and don't go beyond the houses.'

Mikis raised his shoulders. 'It's a dead end anyway, isn't it?'

'It's certainly been that for all the invaders who tried to take us,' the other man said, his eyes unwavering.

The pickup was manoeuvred out of the way and Mikis drove on.

'I hope you enjoyed that demonstration of mountain hospitality,' he said.

Mavros grunted. 'Friendly types, aren't they?'

'Still sure you want to go through with this? I won't be able to step in like I did last night. There are dozens of guys like those ones in Kornaria.'

'I'll keep my questions to a minimum.'

The track led down into a wide valley and ahead of them lay a surprisingly large patch of flat land covered in sheds, with a cluster of white houses in the centre. The air was clear and tinged by the chill of the snow on the peaks. It struck Mavros that this would be a very harsh place in winter.

'See those sheds?' Mikis asked.

'Not for mushrooms?'

'Correct. Don't even think of taking photographs.'

'Never crossed my mind.' The only camera he had with him was in his mobile and it wouldn't pick up much from such a distance. 'Anyway, I don't give a shit about them growing dope.'

Mikis glanced at him, then steered round a large pothole. 'You say that, but it isn't the way things work. Everything that goes on in Kornaria has some connection to the core business. And that business extends far beyond the village.'

Mavros thought about that. David Waggoner had a house up here – could the old soldier have anything to do with the narcotics trade? The mayor, Vasilios Dhrakakis, would obviously be in the business up to his neck. And what about Maria Kondos? Was the missing woman linked to it in some way too? Had she been driving Cara Parks' car after all when the drugs gang member was killed?

They drove past a few abandoned buildings and into the village proper. It was spotless, the white houses on each side of the concrete road gleaming in the sunlight, their wooden shutters and fences freshly painted. There was obviously no shortage of water, as the bougainvilleas and oleanders were tall and healthy. Old women in black peered at the Jeep and its occupants curiously, while young women in jeans played with chubby children.

The road ended in a wide square with a large tree in the centre. It was very quiet – the men presumably in the cultivation sheds or playing cowboy in their pickups. Metal tables and chairs with wicker seats were arrayed outside a solitary *kafeneion*.

'Give them a few moments,' Mikis said. 'They'll have been told we were on the way.'

Sure enough, a trio of barrel-chested men in traditional garb and boots came towards the Jeep. They weren't armed, but they hardly needed to be. Mavros had the feeling that they were being closely watched from the open windows of surrounding houses, each of which no doubt had a well-stocked gun cabinet.

'Welcome,' the man in the middle said, in Greek. He wore a moustache that extended horizontally across his cheeks. 'I am the mayor, Dhrakakis is my name.'

Mikis introduced himself – he had no choice about using his real name since 'Tsifakis' was all over the Jeep. 'I have brought an Englishman whose grandfather was here in the war.'

Mavros bowed extravagantly. 'Arthur Smith,' he said, with a tentative smile. 'Very pleased to meet you.'

Dhrakakis eyed him diffidently and then extended a horny hand. 'Kornaria welcomes the offspring of the brave man who fought for Crete's freedom.'

Mikis translated for form's sake.

The mayor turned on his heel and walked over to the *kafeneion*. He stopped at the most shaded table and extended his arms. 'Please, accept our hospitality.'

Mavros nodded and smiled frequently, trying to look as foreign as possible. As he sat down, he realized what a dangerous game he was playing. These men had their code of honour and it wasn't long since the vendetta had become less common – for all he knew, it might still be flourishing in Kornaria. Deceiving them might be very costly. Then again, he'd be off the island as soon as he found Maria Kondos and he didn't think their reach would extend to Athens.

After glasses of *raki* had been consumed – Mavros pretending to choke – and coffee provided, along with slices of a dark, nutty cake, the mayor turned to him.

'Your grandfather, what did he tell you about Kornaria?'

Mavros explained via Mikis that Ralph Smith had been a wireless operator in the mountains, spending weeks with only a pair of guards, but that he had always spoken with great pleasure of the days when they came down to Kornaria to replenish their food supplies. The villagers had been most generous, slaughtering sheep and chickens and opening casks of aged wine.

Dhrakakis nodded throughout Mikis's presentation, a slack smile on his lips.

'And he was part of Lambis's group?' he asked.

Mavros smiled broadly.

'Ou-anggoner,' Dhrakakis said, struggling with the English 'w' and 'gg' sounds.

'David Waggoner,' Mavros said, nodding vigorously. 'I have read about him, but my grandfather didn't say if he was attached to his unit.'

The mayor raised a shaggy eyebrow. 'Lambis was in command of all the British in this area,' he said firmly.

'Well, then, my grandfather was with him,' Mavros relayed back.

'How was he called, your grandfather? He still lives?'

Mavros shook his head. 'He died last year.'

Mikis's translation brought exclamations of grief and sympathy. Again, Mavros felt bad about deceiving them. Then he remembered Dhrakakis's voice on the telephone – he definitely knew Maria Kondos and had been concerned by mention of her name.

'How was he called?' the mayor repeated.

Mavros looked confused and then gave the impression of understanding. 'Ah, you mean his cover-name? Yes, he told me it was Panos.'

Dhrakakis, who looked like he was in his late fifties, shook his head. 'I have learned from the old ones of all the British and New Zealand fighters. No one ever mentioned any Panos.'

A heavy silence fell. Mavros considered and then decided to take another risk.

'My grandfather mentioned a family he stayed with, they were very good to him. I can't quite remember the name . . . Kond . . . there were more letters . . . Kondo-something . . .'

Mikis translated, with a dubious look on his face.

The three men in black leaned together and started talking in low voices. Mavros glanced at Mikis and then looked around the square, as if enchanted by the picture of rustic simplicity.

'There was the Kondoyannis family,' the *kafeneion* owner said, from the doorway. 'They moved to America in the Fifties. There are none of them left here.' He was given very heavy stares from his co-villagers.

'How sad,' Mavros said, realizing a hot piece of information had dropped into his lap and dissembling as best he could. 'Do none of them ever come back?' The return of Greeks who had made good abroad was a feature of Greek popular culture – they made elementary mistakes with the language, wore expensive clothes and threw money at their dirt-poor relatives as if it were feeding time at the zoo.

Dhrakakis was staring at him. Mavros had done what he could to change his voice from the one that the mayor had heard on the phone, but even if he had succeeded in fooling him on that count, all bets were off now he had heard what could be the vital name.

'Perhaps I made a mistake,' he said, looking at Mikis. 'Are there any villages with a similar name?'

It wasn't much of an escape plan, but Mikis did what he could.

'Well, there's Koulouridhiana and . . . Kambanos and Koudhouriana . . .'

Mavros asked for the last one to be repeated. 'I don't know, maybe that was what Grandpa said. He was quite vague in his last years.'

Mikis got up and extended his hand. 'I'm very sorry to have brought this man to your village under false pretences.' He was being deliberately over-respectful, which impressed Mavros. The young Cretan was turning out to be a useful associate.

Dhrakakis regarded Mavros with ill-disguised contempt. 'The English today have become women,' he said. 'Take him to a barber, young Tsifaki.'

Mikis smiled. 'I will.'

The appropriate farewells were made and they made it back to the Jeep. One of the mayor's henchmen was already speaking on a walkie-talkie, alerting the guards to let them pass, Mavros hoped.

'I hope you think that was worth it,' Mikis said, as he drove out of the village.

'It was. I have a name I can work with – Kondoyannis.'

'May it bring you much joy.' Mikis waved at the men in the pickup. 'Christ and the Holy Mother, that was nerve-wracking. And it's all right for you, back in Athens shortly. They can find me easily enough.'

'Sorry about that. Anyway, there's no reason they should come after you.'

'Is that right? What if Dhrakakis describes the English visitor to David Waggoner?'

Mavros looked out at the sparsely covered terrain. The sea and the thick tranche of cultivated land alongside it were visible in the distance.

'You're right,' he agreed. 'That would not be ideal. Let's hope that Waggoner's too busy with the film to come up to the village for a while.'

'It only takes a phone call.'

Mavros was getting irritated by Mikis being right all the time. 'For your information, I'm not an Englishman. I'm half-Scottish.'

Mikis shook his head. 'As if that makes any difference.'

In the context of heavily armed Cretan dope-producers, Mavros had to admit he was right. Now didn't seem the right time to ask how often vendettas occurred on the Great Island these days.

About ten minutes out of the village, the track took a bend round a large rock. There was a line of ancient olive trees, their trunks as wrinkled as a dinosaur's legs and their pale leaves almost touching the ground. It was then that Mavros saw the woman, stepping quickly down the hill.

'Stop!' he shouted, opening his door before Mikis brought the Jeep to a halt. He ran through the treeline and towards the woman, whose black hair flew out behind her as she started to stumble on more quickly. 'Stop!' he repeated, in English.

As he got closer, he realized her feet were bare and bleeding. She was wearing a soiled white blouse and a pair of black jeans that were badly stained with earth or something worse. Although he had caught only glimpses of her face, he was sure who she was.

'My name's Mavros, Maria,' he called. 'Cara Parks sent me to look for you.'

The woman slowed and then stopped completely, dropping to her knees and starting to sob.

Mavros reduced his own pace and approached with caution. 'Cara's been very worried about you.'

She turned to him, her face soaked with tears and her eyes wide. There was no doubt about her identity from the photograph he had been given, but she was thinner and there were heavy lines on her forehead and around her eyes. He managed to catch her before she toppled forward.

'Steady,' he said, holding her head to his chest. 'You're safe now.' He glanced over his shoulder and saw that Mikis had driven the Jeep as close as he could. They needed to get Maria into the car and away from the stony hillside at speed.

'Come on,' he said, 'there's transport waiting.'

She tried to pull away from him, whimpering.

'Don't worry, we're not going back to Kornaria,' he said. 'Is that where you've come from?'

The woman's entire body was shaking and she didn't seem to be able to speak.

Mikis arrived. 'Is it her?' he said, in Greek.

Mavros nodded, unsure whether she understood the language. 'She's in a bad way. Where's the nearest hospital?'

'There are clinics in the larger villages, but the best thing would be to get her to Chania.'

'OK. You realize that we may be pursued. It looks like she's been held captive – she has no shoes or belt – and somehow got free. Dhrakakis had her after all.'

'Whatever you say. We need to move.'

They got the woman into the Jeep, Mavros keeping his arm round her when they were inside. She was shivering, but she seemed to be less terrified. She wouldn't answer any of his questions, only gulping water from a bottle and chewing biscuits that the Cretan produced from beneath his seat.

Mavros was looking at the map. 'There seems to be a choice of three roads at Karies.'

'One of them's only fit for goats and suicidal bikers.'

'So which one's quicker?'

'The right turn that takes us down below Theriso.' Mikis glanced at him. 'The sensible thing to do would be to hole up somewhere and see if any tough guys come past.'

Mavros looked at Maria Kondos. She was shaking violently again and her breath was coming in rapid gasps. 'No, this woman needs medical care. You'll have to drive like the wind.'

The driver grinned. 'That can happen. You'd better put your belts on.' He did the same and then upped the revs substantially. He also made a call on his mobile phone.

'Reinforcements?' Mavros asked when he'd finished.

'My cousin and a couple of his mates. We work out together. One of them's the All-Crete heavyweight wrestling champion. They'll come to meet us.'

'Wrestling won't be much help against shotguns.'

'Don't be too sure. Those arseholes won't fire at us in broad daylight when we're down in the populated areas.' He laughed hollowly. 'They'll wait till dark.'

'Great.' Mavros looked at the woman. Her tears had soaked his shirt and were running like an in-car waterfall off the leather jacket he'd put around her. 'Maria? Tell me what happened. It might make things easier when it comes to keeping you safe.'

She gave him a brief glance and then looked away. Ahead, there were more trees and the hillside was less bleak. They had passed a couple of villages. Mikis was driving as if he was in a rally, cornering with skill and accelerating past slow-moving farm vehicles when the road allowed.

'Under half an hour now,' he said, casting an eye in the mirror. 'Oh-oh, we've got company,' he said, in Greek. 'The pickup with the two hard men in the back.'

Maria Kondos clearly understood as she shrank down in the seat, her upper body jerking back and forward so rapidly that Mavros thought she was having a fit. After a few minutes, when it became clear that the Kornariates weren't gaining on the Jeep, she began to calm down.

'You got any weapons?' Mavros asked, in a low voice.

Mikis felt under his seat again. 'A hunting knife.' He handed over a sheathed blade not much smaller than a machete. 'And a Colt 45 automatic.' He kept that hidden.

'You're kidding,' Mavros said, in amazement. 'What if the cops caught you with that?'

The Cretan shrugged. 'My old man knows people. It's not like I ever use it, except on deserted beaches for practice.'

Mavros clung on to Maria with one arm and clutched the side

of his seat with the other hand as the Jeep took a bend at high speed. 'I don't suppose your friends have similar arsenals?'

Mikis smiled. 'I told them to bring what they could.' He glanced in the mirror. 'We should be all right. Those dope-heads can't drive for shit.'

Then the nearside front tyre burst and they slewed all over the road, finally coming to a stop centimetres from a low stone wall. There was no sign of habitation nearby.

'Oh shit,' said Mikis, with surprising equanimity. 'Everyone out.'

They opened the doors and clambered over the drystone wall, Maria Kondos wailing hopelessly. Mavros got her to lie down and put his jacket over her head and shoulders, then asked her to be quiet. Mikis handed him the knife, having slipped off the sheath.

'You ever used one of these?' he asked.

'I've never even seen one like that. Maybe it's better if I have the pistol. I've occasionally fired one of those.'

'Occasionally isn't going to get us far. Listen, you stay here. I'm going to work my way back up the road. The villagers are bound to stop some distance away and advance on foot, after splitting up. That'll give me some chance to pick them off.'

'You're going to shoot to kill?' Mavros asked, his stomach clenching.

'If necessary. You think they won't? They want the woman, though, not us. Stay next to her with the knife hidden. That way you might take one of them with you when they get close – if I don't manage to deal with them all.' He squeezed Mavros's knee and headed up the slope, keeping below the wall.

'Keep calm, Maria,' Mavros said, in a low voice. 'It'll be all right, you'll see.'

He couldn't imagine a situation further from 'all right', but at least Mikis was looking out for them. He wondered how long it would take his friends to show up.

In the distance, he heard the sound of brakes being applied hard, then words which he didn't catch. Then there was a shout and the sound of a shotgun being discharged. It was rapidly followed by the thunderous boom of Mikis's pistol.

Mavros kept Maria Kondos's head shielded by his arms.

A few minutes later he heard heavy steps and then Mikis appeared further up the wall, carrying a shotgun as well as his Colt. He was with them in seconds.

'You didn't kill him?' Mavros said.

'Didn't even hit him. He dropped his weapon and took off up the hillside. The problem now is his two friends. They split up and disappeared into the vegetation.'

He looked around. 'I'm going to stalk the one on this side of the road. The other, we'll have to take our chances with.' He crawled off under the trees.

Mavros had rarely felt so helpless. He had to stay with Maria – there was no knowing what she'd do if he left her – and all he had was a king-size carving knife. It was too large to throw, not that he had any experience of that. He rubbed his back where the sharp-edged stones were jagging into it, and suddenly had a thought. He had never been much use at sport, finding team discipline hard to handle. The only exercise he'd done when he was growing up in Athens was track and field. He'd been a decent long jumper and a passable discus thrower, but his best event – oddly, given his slim build – had been the shot putt. He carefully extracted several stones from the upper part of the wall and heaped them by his leg. If he heard anyone approaching across the road, they'd get an unwelcome surprise – assuming they didn't manage to fire first.

There was a double shotgun discharge over in the middle distance and then a single shot from the Colt. His immediately felt his spirits rise. Two down and one to go. Maybe he'd take the hint and slip away like his friend. Then he realized how unlikely that was. A Cretan villager was unlikely to leave his comrades in arms and they would regroup. Besides, the mayor of Kornaria had probably sent backup.

There was the scrape of a boot on the other side of the road. Mavros got to his knees, selecting the most rounded of the stones he'd piled up. He heard cautious steps approaching the Jeep. After a few seconds, they moved closer.

Mavros knew he would have only one chance – if he was quick, he would succeed in dropping behind the wall after he let loose. Then, if the mountain man kept coming, he'd have time to grab the knife – not that he expected it to save them.

Maria Kondos had realized how dangerous the situation was and was lying mute beneath the leather jacket. He wondered where Mikis was. Maybe he'd only got the shot off after being hit by one or both shotgun blasts. This was down to Mavros.

Niki and the Fat Man came into this mind unexpectedly and he found himself wishing he was with them in the safety of his mother's apartment.

Then the sound of leather-soled boots came much closer. He took a deep breath as he took a firm grip on the stone, fitting it between his chest and shoulder and spreading his feet in a squat. There would be no chance of a swivel. Then he stood up as quickly as he could, taking a mark on the startled villager's head and cast the stone.

It was a direct hit on the man's forehead and he collapsed like Goliath before David.

'Sweet move,' said Mikis, from behind him. The Colt was in his belt and he was holding a fancy over-and-under shotgun and a pair of almost full bandoliers in his hands. 'The second one fell over after I fired and will soon wake up with a very sore head. What about yours?'

Mavros hurdled the wall and grabbed the man's wrist, after kicking away the shotgun. It was slow but regular. There was a lot of blood coming from the hairline.

'No, just knocked—'

The sound of screeching brakes rendered his words inaudible. He watched as a trio of heavily armed men got out of a Range Rover.

Mikis waved to them. 'You're too late, but let's get that tyre changed before the rest of the fuckers arrive.'

Mavros watched as that feat was accomplished in a few minutes. Then he escorted Maria Kondos to the Jeep. She was still silent, but more in control of herself.

He looked over his shoulder as Mikis drove on. The Range Rover was behind them and he didn't think any men from Kornaria would get past Mikis's friends.

He looked at his watch. It was only one p.m., even though the day seemed to have been going on forever. He'd still have time to watch the old planes being filmed at Maleme, though now he'd had his own experience of battle in Crete he wasn't too excited by that prospect.

Maria Kondos had fallen asleep.

TEN

'You need to decide which hospital we're taking her to,' Mikis said, as they entered the heavily cultivated area south of the coast. 'There are several private clinics, as well as the general hospital at Mournies.'

'It isn't up to me,' Mavros replied. He should have called Cara Parks earlier, but his heart had only recently returned to normal pace. She answered immediately and he told her about Maria.

'That's fantastic, Alex. You're a genius.'

'I get that a lot. Listen, she needs medical care. Her feet are lacerated and I can't tell what else might have been done to her.'

'What do you mean?'

'She's in shock and she isn't speaking.'

'Oh.' There was a pause. 'OK. Rosie's got a local fixer. I'll get her to call you asap. I'll come over myself.' She rang off.

Mavros looked in the wing mirror. Mikis's friends were close behind and there were no suspicious pickups further back.

'So, this vendetta thing,' he said. 'Does it still go on?'

'Oh yes,' the driver said solemnly. 'Especially in the mountain villages.'

'Which means what, exactly?'

'Well, I embarrassed one Kornariate and knocked another out, while you rearranged the third guy's brains.'

'Yeah, what about the injured men? Shouldn't we send out an ambulance?'

Mikis looked at him as if he were slow. 'You want to make things worse? Don't worry about it. Those lunatics look after their own.' He smiled weakly. 'And they don't take kindly either to being bested or to having their weapons confiscated.'

Mavros wasn't feeling proud. 'I've landed you in a very deep cesspit, haven't I? I'm sorry, my friend.'

'Forget it. That village is a bad place and the shit-heads up there obviously did something nasty to the woman. Besides, we know how to look after ourselves.'

'I noticed.'

The Cretan smiled. 'These things usually get sorted out eventually, but there's no chance we'll bribe them to lay off us. My old man doesn't give money to wankers like them.'

Mavros's phone rang. Rosie Yellenberg told him that a private room had been booked at the West Crete Clinic. He relayed that to Mikis, who nodded.

'You've done well, Mr Mavros,' the producer continued. 'Would you like to go back to Athens on the Learjet tonight?'

He dismissed that without much thought. 'No, thanks. Tomorrow will be OK. I take it I can stay at the Heavenly Blue tonight?'

Rosie Yellenberg gave a throaty laugh. 'If Cara Parks goes back to work, you can stay as long as you like.'

As far as Mavros was concerned, the case wasn't over. He wanted to know how Maria Kondos had got to the village – it seemed clear that someone had taken her there against her will – and he wanted to know why she had seemingly been kept in captivity.

Mikis pulled up in front of a new building on the outskirts of Chania. A lot of money had been spent on the façade, combining multicoloured concrete sections with traditional wooden balconies. No doubt the film company's insurance would cover everything.

Maria Kondos, who stirred when the engine was switched off, was put in a wheelchair by a pair of keen orderlies and taken quickly inside.

'What now?' Mikis called.

Mavros had got out and was watching the patient disappear down a corridor. 'I'm staying,' he said. 'You can split if you want.'

'Let me sort out my friends. Don't tell the film people, but it would be a good idea to have a guard outside here.' He glanced across the road, which was wide. 'They can take up position over there and do shifts.'

'What about payment?'

'The woman's been harmed by Cretans. That goes against our code of hospitality.' Mikis grinned. 'Plus, my mother will find a way of putting it through the books. These Americans have far too much money.'

Mavros laughed. Not only was the driver smart and useful in a fight, he had the kind of contradictory character that Cretans were famous for.

A large Mercedes pulled up. Mavros saw the chauffeur open

the door for the actress and went over. She was wearing a rose-pattern dress and dark glasses.

'No paparazzi here,' he said.

'Just as well,' Cara replied. 'I didn't even bring my security guys. Where is she?'

They went inside and Mavros asked at reception. They were told Maria was undergoing tests and that they couldn't see her yet. The secretary directed them to a private lounge on the third floor and said they'd be advised when the patient could have visitors.

The empty room was comfortable and Cara sat down in a leather armchair.

Mavros went to the fridge and poured them glasses of water. He had suddenly realized that his throat was parched.

The actress eyed him as he sat down opposite. 'What have you been doing, Alex? There's dirt all over your pants.'

He looked down. 'Ah. We ran into a bit of trouble.'

'Details,' Cara said imperiously.

He gave her them, without censoring.

'Jeez,' she said, when he'd finished, 'this place is worse than Tombstone in its glory days.'

Mavros shrugged. 'Not exactly. It's just that there are some out-of-the-way villages – Kornaria being one – that have never submitted to other people's laws.'

'And you think Maria was kidnapped?'

'She was obviously held there. It's possible she went under her own volition, but I doubt it.'

The actress, who had taken off her shades, opened her eyes wide. Mavros noticed that she hadn't put on any make-up and there were dark rings around her eyes. Blonde hair aside, she could have been a Mediterranean.

'I don't understand. Why would they have imprisoned her? Are you sure that's what happened?'

'No. She hasn't said a word. But she was very frightened when we found her and the lack of footwear suggests they weren't keen on her leaving.'

Cara Parks sighed and dabbed her eyes with a tissue from her Hermès bag.

'It's terrible, I can't take it in.'

'She was running too, like a hunted beast.' He grimaced.

'Which is what it turned out she was.' He watched the actress carefully. 'Have you ever heard the name Kondoyannis?'

She caught his gaze and held it. 'No, I don't think so. Should I have?'

'No,' he replied, summoning up the nerve to ask her about the death of the young gang member in LA and who had really been driving her car.

Then a tall man in a white coat and slicked back hair walked in.

'Good afternoon,' he said in English, his accent excellent. 'My name is Stavrakakis. I'm the neurologist here.'

The actress got up and offered her hand. 'Cara Parks. Maria – Ms Kondos – is my assistant and friend.'

If Stavrakakis knew who Cara was, he didn't show it as he outlined Maria's injuries. The wounds on her feet had been dressed by the surgical team – they were fairly severe and she wouldn't be able to walk for several days. A full set of tests was also being carried out.

'I would like to ask how your assistant, friend, got into this state.'

'Mr Mavros here found her.' Cara stopped speaking abruptly, passing the baton to him.

He described Maria's disappearance and her downhill flight, but said nothing about the location or the clash with the villagers.

'You see,' the neurologist said, 'I've examined the patient closely and can see no sign of a head wound – though obviously an MRI scan will confirm that. Do you know of any reason for her silence? She has not said a word to anyone and we have tried both English and Greek. I take it from her name that she has Greek heritage.'

Cara nodded. 'But, as far as I know, she doesn't know the language and this is her first time in Greece.'

'I'll ensure that English is the sole language used. I understand you are filming out at Maleme.'

So he had recognized the actress, Mavros thought.

'Maleme and neighbouring areas, yes.'

'And it's a war film. I wonder if anything could have shocked her into this condition. Has she been near explosions or suchlike?'

Cara shook her head. 'Nothing like that. We've been doing pre-invasion scenes so far. It's only today that the aircraft are flying for the first time.'

'Did she seem normal before she disappeared?' the doctor asked. 'And why did she disappear?'

'She was completely all right,' the actress said. 'Busy, as we always are on a shoot, but not unduly pressured.' She didn't offer any more information.

Stavrakakis turned to Mavros. 'So we don't know why she disappeared?'

'She was seen walking out of the Heavenly Blue resort on Sunday evening. We don't know where she was until I picked her up today.'

'And you are . . . ?'

'Alex Mavros, a member of the production team,' Cara put in.

The doctor nodded. 'Very well. I will let you know when I have news.' He left the room.

Mavros looked at the actress. 'A member of the production team?' he asked, with a smile. 'Rosie Yellenberg wanted me on the plane back to Athens tonight.'

'Rosie's a coin-counter,' Cara scoffed. 'Do you think this case is over?'

Mavros shook his head.

'Good,' she agreed. 'I need to know what happened to Maria. Until she comes back to herself, I want you to keep on it.'

'OK,' he said, not sounding over-enthusiastic. 'Ms Yellenberg did say that I could stay as long as I like since I found Maria.'

'I'll bet she did,' Cara said sharply. 'She wants me back at work.'

'Are you going to oblige?'

'Can't really say no now, can I? But I'll stay here for the rest of today. I want to see Maria and assure her that everything's all right.'

Mavros looked out of the window. Mikis and his friends were crowded round the Range Rover across the road.

'I don't think you should stay here alone,' he said.

Then the door opened and Rosie Yellenberg walked in.

'Go get 'em, tiger,' Cara Parks said, with a surprisingly warm smile.

He left the women to it.

'Shit!'

Mavros ducked as a Messerschmitt 109 with Luftwaffe markings screamed overhead, only a few metres above the electricity poles. He watched as it streaked towards the airfield, where a Junkers 52 troop carrier was manoeuvring in a cloud of dust.

Mikis had left him at the entrance to Maleme aerodrome and gone back to the resort to talk to his father. The security guys on the gate let him through when he showed the plastic-covered card he'd been given by Alice Quincy.

'Where's Mr Jennet?' he shouted, as the fighter came back to make a second pass.

The guard pointed to a group of people at the far end of the runway from the modern buildings. 'You can wait for a lift or take a *papaki*.' He indicated a row of 'little ducks' – Honda 50s.

Mavros hated all forms of mechanized two-wheel transport, but in this case he was prepared to make an exception. It was hot and he didn't want to wait in the sunlight. Mounting the contraption, he was pleasantly surprised to find that he remembered how to start it and even change gear – like every Greek boy, he had messed around with them before becoming heartily sick of the racket from shot exhausts.

He made it to the crowd in a few minutes. There was a large amount of equipment spread around – not only cameras, but generators, screens and numerous other things he didn't know the name or purpose of. Then he saw a line of chairs under sunshades, as if an impromptu café had been set up. Rudolf and Hildegard Kersten were at one end, while David Waggoner was at the other. Between them were members of the film crew, some working on laptops and others arranging equipment. Alice Quincy saw him and came over.

'Hello, Mr Mavros,' she said, struggling to make herself heard above the sound of the taxiing Ju52.

'Alex,' he shouted back. The noise reduced as the plane headed away.

'Can I help you?' The young woman was in jeans and a long-sleeved black shirt that must have made her uncomfortably hot.

'I want to talk to Mr Jennet. Is he available?'

'If it's about Maria Kondos, he knows you found her.' She shaded her eyes as dust gathered around them. 'The runway's concrete, but we're throwing up dust to make it look like it was back in the war.'

'Art's all about the little things,' he said.

Alice Quincy wasn't sure how to take that, which was his intention.

'If you don't mind, I need to sign off with Mr Jannet. He was the one who hired me, after all.'

Irritation flashed across her face, then she nodded. 'You'll have to wait. He's arranging the next shots.'

Mavros shrugged and went over to the Kerstens.

'May I join you?' He signalled to the old man to remain seated. Hildegard gave him a soft smile.

'Of course,' Rudolf said. 'I hear you found Maria Kondos, Alex. I'm so glad.'

There were bottles of water on the table and Mavros helped himself after offering the others. He was still plagued by thirst. He wondered what it must have been like for the soldiers.

'Did you have enough water during the battle?' he asked.

Kersten was watching the Ju52. '*Tante* Jus, we called them,' he said. 'Auntie Jus. I don't know why they had that affectionate nickname. They were slow, cramped and highly vulnerable to anti-aircraft fire. To answer your question, no, we never had enough to drink. Most of us drained our bottles within minutes of landing.' He looked over his shoulder to the trees in the distance. 'It may look well irrigated now, but I can assure you that back then there was very little water on the ground. We survived by taking dead men's bottles.'

Hildegard had turned away, as if mention of the fighting was abhorrent to her.

'Look at that,' Rudolf said, pointing to the group of men in wartime jumpsuits and parachutes outside the now stationary Ju52. 'I've told them several times that they should hold the end of their cords between their teeth as they climb the ladder. Only one of them paid attention.'

'Did they use Maleme for jumps after it was captured?' Mavros asked, puzzled.

'No, they're pretending this is an airfield outside Athens. I boarded during the night, but it's true there were later waves. The producers didn't see any need to film on the mainland as well.'

Mavros watched as the men finished clambering on board and the plane taxied to the other end of the runway. He noticed that there were cameras mounted on pickup trucks all around, presumably to give many different angles to the flight.

'This morning they filmed inside the *Tante* Ju,' the old man said. 'They could only fit six men in with the cameras and other equipment. Now they're going to record the drop, both from inside the plane and from the ground.'

There was an increasing roar as the plane's three engines were gunned and it started down the runway, dust rising in its wake. Pickups kept up with it, the cameras pointing at the dun-green fuselage. The black crosses on the side and swastika on the tail gave Mavros a bad feeling, but he told himself to get a grip. It was only a movie.

The Ju52 moved sluggishly down the runway, eventually pulling into the air not far in front of the hangars. It headed out to sea, followed by a pair of smaller and more modern planes that filmed it from above, below and alongside. Eventually the troop carrier turned and came back towards them, the engines pulsing more powerfully now. Mavros felt hairs raise all over his body. From what he remembered, there had been dozens of planes in each wave. It must have been the most incredible sight for the defenders – awe-inspiring and terrifying. He leaned forward and looked over at David Waggoner. He was watching through binoculars, his jaw set firm. What memories was this bringing back to him?

The Messerschmitt made another pass, diving over the airfield. Lights flashed from its machine-gun slits – Mavros assumed that the sound of firing would be added at the editing stage. Then the *Tante* Ju came over the land, only a few hundred feet above them. Cameras all around were trained on it, as the door was pulled back and a man appeared.

'They are Greek paratroopers,' Kersten said. 'I have spent many days instructing them in the jump and landing positions that we used. Now we will see if I was successful.' He gave a rueful smile.

Mavros watched as the man launched himself into the air with his arms and legs extended in the shape of an 'X'. A few seconds later, another man dived out, then another and another. Their parachutes sprouted into inverted white cups at what seemed far too close to the ground. Mavros felt his palms sweating as the men came down fast. They hit the ground and rolled forward, then started pulling in their chutes. The last man shook in his harness and then hung limp for as long as he could before making a different kind of landing.

'They didn't shoot so many of us in the air,' Kersten said. 'That was Allied propaganda. A man falling at that speed is not an easy target. But they certainly did kill hundreds in the trees and on the ground before they reached the weapons canisters.' His eyes clouded and he turned away.

Hildegard was immediately on her feet and at her husband's side. She spoke to him in German, before turning to Mavros.

'I told him this would be too much for him. He didn't need to be here today. His work has already been done.'

'No,' the old man said, his eyes damp. 'It is good that I saw it. Now I understand what it was like for the Cretans, seeing the invader come in with all his hubris and conceit.' His wife wiped his face with a tissue. 'We had no right,' he said, his voice wavering. 'No country has the right to invade another. But the Cretans had every right to fight us with everything they had.'

Mavros looked up as a shadow fell over them.

'Not weeping for your lost comrades, are you, Kersten?' David Waggoner said callously. 'The ones who were shot to pieces in the olive groves and slaughtered in the open ground?'

Mavros stood up and put his hand on Waggoner's arm. 'You're wrong,' he said bluntly. 'Leave him alone.'

'No, Alex,' Rudolf said, getting to his feet slowly. 'Mr Waggoner is right. The *Fallschirmjäger* met their match on this island, there's no doubt of that.'

'And you've made a fortune with your fake remorse, your blood money to the victims and your rich man's resort.' The Englishman stared up at the taller German. 'Just remember this. I know what you did. I know you were at Makrymari.' The ex-SOE man executed a parade-ground turn and marched away, the sun glinting off the regimental badge on his blazer.

Rudolf Kersten sat down again. His wife spoke to him in German. Mavros wanted to ask what Waggoner had meant, but he could see it wasn't the right time. He moved away and saw Luke Jannet and Alice Quincy coming towards him in a golf cart.

'What'd'ya think of that?' the director said triumphantly, as the vehicle drew up. 'We got enough material for the whole drop in one afternoon. We can edit it so the single planes look like dozens.'

'It was certainly spectacular,' Mavros agreed.

'And you found pouting Cara's dyke too. Quite a day it's turned out to be.'

'She's been badly treated,' Mavros said, his eyes on Jannet's. 'And she isn't speaking.'

The director stared back at him. 'Some rapist pick her up?'

Mavros was angry with himself for not thinking of that. It would certainly explain Maria's condition – but Jannet hadn't seen her. It was quite a thing to suggest, unless he'd heard something from the clinic.

'Has Rosie Yellenberg been on the phone?' he asked.

'Rosie? Nah, she knows better than to bother me when I'm shooting.'

Mavros glanced at Alice Quincy. She looked uncomfortable, but that was her default mode.

'We'll be having a drink tonight,' Jannet said. 'Alice will tell you where and when. Guess you'll be leaving tomorrow.'

'Maybe,' Mavros said, turning away. He wasn't sure about Luke Jannet – either he was nothing but a coarse Hollywood operator, or he was more concerned about Maria Kondos than he was letting on – his eyes had been hard to read when he was talking about her. Either way, he could probe again later.

Riding the *papaki* back to the gate, Mavros saw Mikis leaning on the Jeep outside.

'Good timing,' he said, as he was let through on foot.

'That's what you think. My old man thinks you should get off the island immediately.'

Mavros's heart missed a beat. 'Why?'

'We had a call from Kornaria – that wanker Dhrakakis. He made all kinds of threats to us and to you, including one about your kidneys.'

'Great.'

'There's only one thing you can do if you want to stay,' Mikis said, a smile hovering on his lips.

'Take up pistol shooting?'

'Wouldn't hurt. No, you need to take heed of what the mayor of Kornaria said.'

Mavros stared at him uncomprehendingly.

The Cretan laughed. 'Seriously consider getting your hair cut.'

'Screw you, Miki. I'd rather take my chances with the dope-growers.'

'Oh, that's on the cards,' the driver replied, his expression darkening. 'That is definitely on the cards.'

ELEVEN

B ack in his room in the hotel, Mavros booted up his laptop and checked his emails. The Fat Man had forwarded a large number of files in English – the old communist had never learned many words of the former imperial power's language on principle. He had learned other things, which he asked Mavros to call him about.

'How goes it, Yiorgo?'

'Ah, the arse-licker of Hollywood. Still alive?'

Mavros told him about the dust-up with the men from Kornaria and the vendetta that had been proclaimed.

'Marx, Engels and Lenin,' the Fat Man said, with a groan, 'you've been on the Great Island less than two days and already there's a price on your head?'

'Just doing my job. What about yours?'

'Oh, I'm getting paid for this, am I? That'll make a change.'

Mavros rolled his eyes. 'As a matter of fact, the money is the only good part of this case. Make out an invoice. And talk.'

'"Make out an invoice," he says,' Yiorgos said caustically. 'Where do you think you are? Germany?'

The Fat Man wasn't far from the truth, Mavros thought. The Heavenly Blue was an oasis of German order and calm, despite the staff in local costumes. Outside the perimeter fence, things were rather more fraught.

'All right, let's have it, Fat Man,' he said, opening his notebook.

'Who do you want first? There's more on the Greek sites about Rudolf Kersten than the others. And – get this – he's really popular for a German.'

As his friend spoke, Mavros was scrolling down the pages he'd been forwarded about the former paratrooper.

'He made a fortune in the building trade in the Ruhr valley after the war,' Yiorgos said, 'starting off as a bricklayer and ending up as chief executive of the company.' He grunted. 'What we'd call a class traitor.'

Mavros ignored that, his eye having been caught by Kersten's later war record. 'He served on the Eastern Front,' he noted, 'wounded three times, twice seriously, and was both decorated and promoted several times.'

'So he was an enemy of the Soviet motherland too,' the Fat Man said sourly.

'He passed through the denazification programme in 1947 and, having made his fortune, moved to Crete in 1964 to build the Heavenly Blue. He used only Greek architects, designers and labour, as well as donating large sums of money to villages that had suffered during the Axis occupation.' He remembered what David Waggoner had said about blood money. That seemed a pretty uncharitable view.

'He was in with the bastard Colonels, of course,' Yiorgos said. 'They were very happy to sell him permits to develop the hotel.'

'Not sure if you can blame him for that,' Mavros countered. 'How many Greeks did the same thing?'

'Greeks of the thieving, collaborating class.'

Yeah, yeah, Mavros thought. There was some truth in what the Fat Man said, but life wasn't that simple. The dictatorship had lasted seven years and people had to feed their families somehow. He had a brief glimpse of his brother Andonis – long lost and a likely victim of the brutal regime – but, unlike in the past, the smiling face faded quickly.

'Your problem, Yiorgo,' he said, scrolling down more attachments, 'is that Rudolf Kersten seems to be a genuinely good man, even though he's a capitalist.'

'And former Nazi. You should see what David Waggoner has to say about him.'

'I've already heard him on the subject.' Mavros found a file bearing the Briton's name. There was a newspaper report of the sixtieth memorial of the Battle of Crete in 1941, when there had been tension between Allied and German veterans. A group of former SOE men, including Waggoner, had rounded on paratroop survivors and berated them for singing Nazi songs in the cemetery near Maleme. From what he could gather, Rudolf Kersten had stood apart with Hildegard and remained silent.

'You see that story in the *Free News*?' the Fat Man asked.

Waggoner had been interviewed following the death of one of his SOE comrades in Crete. He said that several Nazi war criminals, including one who had taken part in a massacre on the island, were still at large and had never been brought to justice – and one was even the head of a large enterprise near Chania.

'Did you find anything else on that?' Mavros asked.

'Not even in *Rizospastis*,' Yiorgos replied, naming the Communist Party organ. 'It wouldn't surprise me if Kersten is friends with the capitalist press barons. Maybe he put his lawyers on our people.'

'Or maybe they reckoned he was clean.'

'What is he?' the Fat Man demanded 'Your new best friend?'

Mavros held back from mentioning the money he'd earned from the German.

'No, but I've met him and he doesn't strike me as a hypocrite, never mind the type that has his nose up the press magnates' arses. There's a look in his eyes—'

'Oh, there's a look in his eyes,' Yiorgos said snidely. 'A look that your hypersensitive antennae picked up, suggesting he never did anything wrong in his life. Despite being on the Eastern Front for over three years.'

'You finished? Did you get anything else on Waggoner?'

The Fat Man paused. 'I did actually,' he said dramatically, like a magician pulling a halibut out of a hat. 'I talked to one of the old comrades who was on Crete during the occupation. He said that Waggoner was a crazy man, always pushing for the most dangerous sabotage raids. It seems he was wounded during the original battle. The Germans took him to Athens for surgery – strangely decent of them – and some months later he escaped from a train in Yugoslavia, before getting himself sent back to Crete.'

'A man on a mission.'

'Looks that way. He was a hard-line anti-Communist as well, like most of the British agents, and our people suspected him of "disappearing" several EAM operatives.' EAM had been the National Liberation Front, which was largely under Communist control. 'Of course, we never had much influence in Crete. They have their own ideology down there.'

'I've noticed. What's this about Cyprus?'

'I found that on one of the far-right sites so I don't know how accurate it is, but they say he was in charge of a British undercover execution squad in the late Fifties, before independence. Several innocent citizens, including a young lad of seventeen, were left in the street with their brains blown out. Eventually Waggoner got thrown out for being too much of a headcase even for the occupiers.'

Mavros wondered about that. Could it be that the former SOE man had a worse past than the German he'd accused?

'OK, Yiorgo, I'll go through what you've sent. Thanks.'

'Oh, it's "thanks" now, is it? Well get this, weird eye. I made a *galaktoboureko* and it's even better than the old woman's.'

Mavros had a saliva rush. 'Save me a couple of pieces.'

The Fat Man laughed. 'What makes you think there are any pieces left?'

Mavros cut the connection and continued scrolling down the attachments. There was an article from one of the Chania provincial papers about the house Waggoner had built outside Kornaria – it had dark stone floors and was very Spartan, which wasn't a major surprise. There were also several pieces saying how popular the ex-soldier was, acting as godfather to numerous villagers' children. His exploits during the war were described in heroic terms – Waggoner had led plenty of ambushes on German patrols and was said to have personally killed over thirty of the enemy.

Mavros was interrupted by his phone.

'This is Cara. I need you.' The words were simple, but the tone less so. Mavros picked up more than a hint of flirtation. 'I'm in my suite.'

'And I'm in the middle of something,' he said. 'Give me a few minutes, please.'

'All right,' the actress replied, less silkily.

Mavros called Niki. He had to wait for her to answer.

'Hello?'

'Oh, shit, were you asleep?'

'It has been known to happen at this time of day.'

'Sorry.' Niki didn't often take a siesta, but she was never delighted to be woken from one. 'I'm not sure what I'll be up to later in the evening.'

There was a rapid intake of breath. 'If you go near any Hollywood actresses, your dick is doomed.'

'Don't worry, I've found the missing woman. I should be home soon.'

'Oh. Well done. Are they appropriately grateful?'
'I'm supposed to be going out with the director and his people.'
'Would they include one Cara Parks?' Niki asked.
'Don't know. Look, her assistant is in a bit of a state. She's
not talking and she may have been mistreated. I think Cara . . .
I mean, Ms Parks has got other things on her mind.'
Niki instantly picked up on the vagueness in his voice.
'I'm so sorry to hear that. I hope she's not too upset.' Her
voice hardened and rose in volume. 'And doesn't need
consoling, especially from a man she only met the day before
yesterday.'
'Love you, dearest,' Mavros said. 'Got to go.' She wouldn't
like that rapid exit, but he had a lot on his mind – not least, the
growing sense that finding Maria Kondos had opened several
large and evil-smelling Pandora's Boxes.

'How is Maria?'
Cara Parks, seated in her usual place on the sofa and wearing
a short denim skirt and multicoloured silk blouse, looked at him
uncertainly. 'To tell you the truth, I'm not sure,' she replied,
beckoning him to join her and pointing to the tray of drinks on
the table. 'Give me a vodka tonic, will you? Two of the former
to one of the latter, a single rock.'
Mavros obliged and poured himself a shot of Wild Turkey.
'The doctor . . . how do you pronounce his name?'
'Stavrakakis,' he said, raising his glass.
'Cheers, and thanks, Alex. I really appreciate what you've
done. Anyway, the doctor says the tests are all clear. She hasn't
sustained any head or internal injuries. She hasn't been raped or
anything like that.'
'Great.'
'Yeah, but she's obviously suffered some pretty major psycho-
logical damage.'
'She still isn't talking? Not even to you?'
Cara Parks looked down. 'No. I'm just back from the clinic.
She turned her head to the wall. The last person I saw do that
was my grandfather. He'd had chemotherapy too many times and
he wanted it all to end.'
'I'm sorry.' Mavros watched her eyes. 'Do you know anything
about Kornaria, the village she escaped from?'

'Only what you told me earlier.' The reply was quick. 'Why? Is it a nest of perverts as well as being Dopeville, Crete?'

'Not that I know of. Stavrakakis seems like a competent type. I'm sure they'll have English-speaking shrinks on hand.'

Cara nodded. 'They do. But—'

There was the sound of voices in the hall. Luke Jannet came in unsteadily, followed by Alice Quincy and Rosie Yellenberg. Presumably the gorilla had admitted them.

'Two little love birds . . . how does that song go?' the director said, heading for the drinks tray.

Alice and Rosie exchanged a glance and shook their heads.

'So, Mavros,' Jannet said, raising a highball glass full of Glenfiddich, 'whatcha think of the airplanes?'

'They were cool. Glad I wasn't on the ground when the 109s' bullets were real.'

The director laughed. 'That's what the old Brit said.'

'Waggoner? He was wounded during the battle.'

'Is that right? I heard he took plenty of Krauts out later.'

Mavros sipped his drink. 'Still, making a film's not the same as being in a war.'

There was a prolonged silence, broken by Cara Parks.

'Luke, Maria's still not talking.'

'I heard that from Rosie. She'll come round.' Jannet's face tightened. 'You telling me you're not going to show up tomorrow? Jesus, Cara, it's the fucking massacre scene.'

Rosie Yellenberg, who had confined herself to a small glass of red wine, intervened. 'I've spoken to Cara, Luke. She will be on set tomorrow.'

'Well, thank Christ for that,' the director said, emptying his glass. 'Come on, we're all going into Chania. There's a restaurant on the harbour-front that does ace lobster.'

Mavros glanced at Cara.

'I want to talk to Alex,' the actress said. 'We'll find you later.'

Jannet raised an eye and grinned. 'OK, you two do what ya gotta do. Come on, ladies. I get the feeling we're cramping their style.'

'Asshole,' Cara said, after the trio had left.

Mavros raised his shoulders. 'I've worked for worse.'

The actress held her glass out. 'Same again, bartender. Have a refill yourself.'

'Thank you, ma'am.'

She laughed and then a shadow fell over her face.

'Maria will be OK,' Mavros said, 'I'm sure of that.'

'How can you be sure?' Cara demanded. 'You aren't a fucking brain doctor.'

'Em, no, I'm not,' he replied, taken aback by her venom.

'Oh, shit.' She bent forward, resting her forehead on her upper arm, and started to sob.

Mavros put her refilled glass on the table. He considered comforting her by word or touch, but decided against it. She was, in effect, his client, and besides, there was something he didn't fully trust about her – he couldn't always clearly see the line between her acting persona and her real one.

Cara sat up after a few minutes and wiped her face with a tissue. 'I'm sorry. It's just . . . I rely on Maria so much. I can't function without her.'

'Can I ask a personal question?'

She took a pull of her drink. 'As long as the answer won't appear in some showbiz rag.'

He smiled. 'I take client confidentiality seriously.'

'Shoot.'

'Were there any problems between you and Maria before she left?'

Cara stared at him. 'Problems? What do you mean?'

He was almost convinced, but he needed to be sure. 'The young man who was killed by your car back in LA. You were driving, weren't you?'

The surprise on the actress's face was genuine, but was that because the question was out of the blue or because the accusation was well founded, Mavros wondered. For a time, it looked as if she was summoning up the strength to bawl him out, but then her shoulders slumped.

'How did you know?' she asked hoarsely.

'I didn't, till now.' He sipped Wild Turkey. 'But I had my suspicions when we spoke about it before.'

'Like you say, client confidentiality. You can't tell anyone.'

He nodded. 'Wasn't thinking of doing so. But I would like to get to the bottom of the case I was hired to handle. Was Maria kidnapped or did she go to Kornaria willingly? What happened to her when she was there? Why isn't she talking, even to you?'

Cara stood up quickly. 'I can't answer any of those questions. Come on, I need some fresh air.'

'The front in Chania is pollution-free.'

'Screw that,' she said, picking up a denim jacket from the chair opposite. 'I've had enough of Luke and Rosie and the crowd. There's a bar here down by the sea. Come with me?'

The look on her face was that of a little girl asking her father to accompany her. Mavros thought about their ages – she was twenty-four and he was forty-one. At a stretch, he could be her father.

He decided against holding her hand.

From *The Descent of Icarus*:

In the days that followed the slaughter at Galatsi, everything passed in a blur – perhaps because of my head wound, but more likely because my spirit, my soul, whatever you might call it, was trying to withdraw into a safer, more childlike world.

I must have collapsed, because I came round in what had been an enemy hospital encampment, the British flags in shreds and the swastika on its white and red background flapping in the strong wind.

Although my head was aching, I picked up information from the men around me. Some were silent – either in exhausted sleep or drug-induced oblivion – but others were chattering excitedly.

'The Tommies are running,' one wheezed, his chest completely covered in bloodstained bandages. 'Our fly boys will pick them off on the road south.'

Another one spat noisily. 'The New Zealanders fought well. I wouldn't like to face those Maoris again.'

'They did a lot of bayonet work,' a loudmouth at the end of the open tent said. 'But we did more with our MG34s. The crows are eating the black bastards now.'

'And the peasants who cut our boys up,' said the first man. 'Savages! One of them stuck a fork in my friend Willi's neck.'

'I hope you executed him on the spot, Private.'

There was a brief silence as the men realized who had spoken. I recognized Captain Blatter's voice immediately.

'Yes, sir! Except it was an old woman, sir, and I took her head off with my MP40.'

'Good man!' Blatter moved down the passage between the camp beds. I tried to shrink into my bed, but it was no good. 'Ah, Private Kersten. The hero of Galatsi.' His tone was ironic in the extreme. 'Men, let's have a round of applause for the sole survivor of that disaster.' He began to clap slowly and the wounded men who were able joined in, fully aware that I was being humiliated.

I saw the doctor standing at the end of the tent. His face was expressionless, but I felt his disapproval of Blatter.

'So, my hero, are you ready for some more of Reichsmarshall Göring's work?' The captain leaned over me, inspecting my bandage with a curled lip. 'You seem well enough.' He looked over his shoulder. 'Doctor, can I have this man?'

I saw the medic raise his shoulders. 'If you feel it's completely necessary, Captain.'

'Indeed I do.' Blatter seized my arm and pulled me up. 'Boots on and outside in one minute, Private,' he ordered, turning on his heel.

I fumbled with the laces of my jump boots and tugged on my jacket.

The captain was waiting for me outside, surrounded by a group of under-officers and sergeants. 'Gentlemen,' he said, 'this is Private Kersten, the heroic survivor of Galatsi. Fortunately, his head wound isn't severe enough to have prevented him from volunteering for this afternoon's mission.'

The others regarded me with contempt bordering on revulsion. It was clear that Blatter had told them I was a coward, who had inflicted the head wound on myself. None spoke as we marched out to a line of vehicles, the smaller of which must have been landed by the Luftwaffe. The absence of gunfire confirmed what I had heard in the hospital tent – the battle was over and the enemy absent from the area around Maleme.

I was told to climb up into a captured British lorry full of paratroopers. They were all armed with rifles or machine-pistols, while I didn't even have my gravity knife. It must have been stolen when I was unconscious – or perhaps the doctor thought I might be suicidal. We drove for about half an hour, but it was impossible to see anything out of the uncovered rear because of the dust raised by the lorry's large wheels.

'Out!' shouted a sergeant.

The men jumped down, brushing past me. Whatever the operation was, they were avid for it. Most of them were wearing shorts – supplies of equipment and weapons were abundant now.

I climbed down slowly, my head spinning. When it cleared, I saw that we had pulled up in an olive grove outside a village. Paratroopers were already breaking down doors and pushing people out into the single unpaved street – old men, women in black, children.

'Kersten!' Blatter roared. 'Over here, now!'

I went, a black curtain descending over my eyes as I tried to keep a regular pace. I blinked, but still could only see fleeting visions of my surroundings.

'What's the matter with you, man?' the captain demanded. 'Give him an MP40, sergeant.'

The weapon was shoved into my hands and ammunition clips stuffed into my pockets.

'Follow me, at the double.'

By the time Blatter and I got to the three-sided square in the centre of the village, a large crowd had gathered. I saw wizened elderly faces and the smooth cheeks of boys. There were no young men – they would have been conscripted when the Italians invaded mainland Greece. But there were young women. And she was one of them.

I closed my eyes for a long moment, nausea flooding through me, and then opened them again. Her dark hair was matted and unwashed, and her black dress looked like it had been pulled through a thorn bush, but her eyes were as haughty as ever. She saw me and gave me a look of such untamed courage that I had to lower my eyes.

'Every tenth man over there!' Blatter ordered, pointing to the open field on the square's fourth side. It was lined with eucalyptus trees, presumably watered by a stream to the rear.

Paratroopers started grabbing men from the crowd and sending them stumbling across the tall grass. I couldn't make out any system in the count – whoever the soldiers wanted was chosen.

'Now the women!' Blatter screamed. 'Check them for recoil marks.'

There was uproar from the villagers as paratroopers tore down the dresses of the women, some of them obviously grandmothers. When one of my comrades came to my saviour, he slapped her face when she held her eyes on his, and then ripped the top of her dress away. I saw her firm breasts and then my heart stopped. While the wound on her right shoulder was covered by a blood-stained bandage, her left shoulder was heavily bruised. She had managed to use a weapon even on the wrong side.

'Over there!' the captain ordered, pushing her towards the line of men in the meadow.

Twenty of our men had already formed a firing squad.

'What is this?' I stuttered. 'These are civilians.'

'The Reichsmarshall has ordered that exemplary measures be taken against all who dared to resist us.' Blatter gave a tight smile. 'Without any further process of law. Makrymari is home to many murderers and *francs-tireurs*. Private, join the execution detail. Immediately!'

I tried to keep my balance as I walked over. I had it in my mind to give the woman a quick death, but the order came too soon for my befuddled mind and the firing started before I could even pull back the slide on my weapon.

She was already on her back, her arms flung wide and her head an explosion of crimson.

Darkness came over me and I collapsed.

TWELVE

Mavros and Cara Parks walked out of the hotel and followed the lit path towards the beach. The actress walked close, her shoulder brushing against his.

'The night's beautiful here,' she said, stopping and looking up. 'You can see every star sprinkled across the dome of the heavens.'

'Don't you get that in LA?'

She laughed softly. 'You obviously haven't been. The city's lit up like an operating theatre. You can't see anything of the night sky.'

'Not even on Mulholland Drive?'

'You don't give up, do you?' she said, turning to him and then walking on.

'I thought you brought me out here to talk about the accident,' he said, catching up with her. 'Rather than warble poetically about the sky at night.'

'Perils of an English major,' she said, looking at him thoughtfully. 'Besides, I grew up in Arizona. You really think that old story has something to do with what happened to Maria here?'

'I don't know, but something strange is going on. It seems like a good place to start.'

They had reached the beginning of the beach. Cara led him to a table at the extent of the bar area. A waiter in boots, *vraka* and embroidered cummerbund appeared instantly, and she ordered fizzy water. Mavros went along with that to keep sharp.

'What do you want to know?' the actress asked, after the drinks had arrived.

'The accident and the boy's death don't interest me as much as the substitution of drivers.'

Cara stared at him. 'Are you kidding? What do you think being a killer driver would have done to my career? Back then I wasn't where I am now.'

'But, as far as I've seen, Maria escaped punishment because the victim was out of his head.'

'Yeah, but we didn't know that at the time, did we? Christ, he came out of nowhere. He could have been a kid on a midnight ramble.'

Mavros wasn't sure if she was being straight with him. If not, her professional skills were even better than he'd given her credit for.

'So, what? You called Maria and told her to get out there as quickly as she could?'

Cara nodded.

'And when did you tell her to take the rap?'

'I didn't.' The actress's eyes met his. 'As a matter of fact, it was her idea. Dear Maria, she'd do anything for me. She told me to go home and leave her car in the drive – when the cops asked, I was to say I'd given Maria permission to drive the Merc. I was in shock and I had trouble driving, but I managed it. She called me from police headquarters and I went in a taxi to bail her out.'

'You went yourself? Don't you have people to do your dirty work?' Mavros chose the last words carefully.

'Dirty work? Maria stood up for me and I'm supposed to send – who? My agent? – to get her out of that stinking holding pen?'

'I imagine most of your fellow actors would send a lawyer.'

'Yeah, well, I must be weird, then. Besides, like I told you, Maria isn't just my assistant, she's my friend.'

Mavros thought about that. Was it possible that Maria Kondos was the one who was covering up? Could she be taking advantage of Cara in some way? That still didn't explain why she left the resort under her own steam, or why she had ended up in Kornaria.

'Good evening, Alex, Ms Parks.'

Mavros stood up as Rudolf Kersten and his wife approached the table from behind.

'Please, don't let us disturb you,' the old man said, in good English. 'We often take a turn down here in the evening.'

Mavros glanced at Cara. She was smiling at the resort owner.

'Join us, please,' she said, apparently relieved that their private conversation had been ended. 'We're enjoying the night sky.'

Rudolf looked up at the stars and the great swathe of the Milky Way – the lights at the bar were not intrusive. 'Yes,' he said, 'it is magnificent, indeed. And the scent of the trees passing over the water.' There was sadness in his voice.

'Come now,' Hildegard said, 'you have been here a thousand times. It's a place of joy, Rudi.'

The resort owner shook his head slowly. 'Only in part, my dear.'

His wife gave him an exasperated look. 'I told you to have nothing to do with that . . . that damned film. It has been bad for you, all these memories coming back to life.' Then she glanced across at Cara. 'I am sorry, Ms Parks, but it is the truth.'

'Don't apologize,' the actress said graciously. 'Acting in this movie has made me realize how terrible the war was for everyone involved in it. How terrible any war must be.'

'Thank you, my dear,' Rudolf said, smiling. 'It is important that the message gets across to the young. That is another reason for my involvement in *Freedom or Death*.'

The waiter arrived again, beaming as he greeted the owner and his wife. He was dispatched for more water and a bottle of *raki*.

'I'm not supposed to drink alcohol any more,' Rudolf said, 'but sometimes I feel the need.' He smiled softly at Hildegard. 'Don't worry, I won't overindulge.'

When the drinks arrived, he poured shots of the spirit into three glasses.

'My dear wife is teetotal,' he said, 'but I hope you young people will join me.'

Mavros, flattered at being linked in that way with the actress, nodded. She did the same and soon they were raising their glasses.

'To . . . to peace,' Rudolf said, his eyes suddenly damp.

'This is good stuff,' Mavros said, as the old man blinked away his tears.

'Yes, indeed,' Rudolf said. 'It's from a village to the west.' He looked across to the barman. 'Angelos comes from there.'

Mavros remembered David Waggoner's accusations. The waiter's attitude to his boss was hardly suggestive of blood money having been paid.

'You have a lot of staff from the area?' he asked.

'Oh yes,' Hildegard replied, her hand on her husband's. 'Rudi has always made sure the local people get jobs in the Heavenly Blue.'

'Especially those whose villages suffered under my country's rule of terror,' the old man said, his voice low. 'I have been accused of buying favours, I have been accused of using my wealth to absolve myself from sins committed during the war – as you heard this afternoon, Alex.'

Cara Parks looked on in bewilderment.

'But what I and my countrymen did during the war,' Rudolf continued, 'cannot be forgiven by financial offerings, even though the vendetta tradition on this island allows for such a solution. What we did was a crime for which there is no atonement.'

'Come, dearest,' Hildegard said, getting to her feet. 'You are tired. Leave the young ones to their contemplation of the night's beauty.'

Rudolf Kersten stood up slowly, his shoulders slumped. 'And tomorrow, Ms Parks, you film the massacre, I understand.'

Cara nodded, her expression sombre. 'I'm not looking forward to it.'

'Ah, but you must give of your best,' the old man said, his face animated. 'You will give hope to all oppressed people, you will inspire the cause of freedom around the world.'

The actress, now also on her feet, looked humbled. 'I will try,' she said.

'Goodnight, Alex,' Rudolf said. 'Come to see us before you leave.'

Mavros nodded, finding himself almost moved to bow before the old man's nobility of spirit.

'You won't be on set tomorrow?' Cara asked.

'He most certainly will not,' Hildegard said, her chin jutting. 'There are some memories he cannot live through again.'

Mavros was reluctant, but there was a question he had to ask.

'The *raki* and the waiter, which village do they come from?'

Rudolf Kersten gave him a direct look. 'Makrymari,' he replied. 'Where the massacre the film is recreating took place.'

Mavros and Cara watched the old couple move slowly up the path towards the hotel. Neither of them had anything to say.

Shortly afterwards, Mavros's phone rang.

'Hey, private eye, where the fuck are you?' Luke Jannet sounded like he'd consumed a barrel of Crete's finest. 'You gettin' it on with Twin Peaks?'

'No.'

'Well, get your asses over here. I've kept you a couple of

creatures with claws.' He guffawed. 'And I don't mean Rosie and Alice.'

Mavros put his hand over the phone and looked at Cara. 'Jannet wants us to join them in Chania.' ·

She rolled her eyes. 'Tell him I'm learning my lines.'

He relayed the message, then had a thought. 'Mr Jannet, would it be possible for me to postpone my departure for a day or two?'

There was a long pause. 'And why would you want to do that, my man?'

'A couple of things to tie up. Besides, I'd like to see the massacre shoot that everyone's talking about.'

As he'd suspected, that appealed to the director's self-importance. 'Well, if that's the case, why not? We should be finished the run-throughs by lunchtime, so get yourself to the set by two p.m.'

'The set in Makrymari?'

Jannet laughed. 'Shit, no. We built our own village. The locals weren't too keen on going through another mass shooting, even a staged one. All the drivers know where it is.' The director rang off.

'Let's go,' Cara said, getting up. 'I really do have to look over my lines.'

Mavros signalled to the waiter, but he said that everything was on Mr Kersten.

As they walked back up the path, the actress took Mavros's arm. 'You don't like me very much, do you, Alex?'

He turned to her. 'No, I don't. I mean, yes, I do. Shit. It's irrelevant what I think. You're one of my clients.'

She laughed. 'Who said anything about thinking?' She squeezed his arm. 'Don't you do feeling in this country? I thought Greeks were demonstrative and led by their emotions.'

'I'm only half Greek, remember. The other part is a cold Scottish loch.'

'A what?'

'Loch. As in the Loch Ness Monster?'

'Oh, a *lock*.' She giggled. 'Didn't that *raki* warm you up?' She managed to mispronounce the spirit too.

'Oh yeah,' he replied. 'But the massacre talk froze me to the core.'

'So why are you coming to the shoot?'

'Good question. Maybe I just want to see you play a freedom fighter in a black dress.'

'Is that right?' They had reached the hotel entrance. 'How about a nightcap?'

Mavros was tempted, but he had things to do and Niki to consider.

'No, thanks. I'll see you tomorrow.'

Cara took the rejection in her stride. 'Goodnight, then.' She kissed him on the cheek and headed for the stairs. Apparently he wasn't the only resident who kept fit that way.

He was outside his room when his phone rang again.

'Hey, Alex, it's Mikis.' The driver's voice was rushed.

'What's up?'

'We've had an episode with the bullies from Kornaria.'

'Any casualties?'

'Only on their side.'

'You sure they didn't get into the clinic?'

'As sure as I am that two of them will wake up with broken ribs.'

Mavros glanced at his watch. It was nearly ten and his stomach was rumbling. 'I'm coming over,' he said. 'Fancy something to eat?'

'Any neo-Nazi baiting tonight?'

'I don't think so.'

'Pity. OK, take one of our vehicles – get the driver to call me before you set off.'

'Can't be too careful, eh?'

'Not in vendetta-land, no.'

Mavros went into his room and put his laptop and Nondas's keys in his bag. He decided he'd spend the night in his brother-in-law's place and try speaking to Maria Kondos in the morning.

After he'd gone through the procedure with the driver, a late-middle-aged man named Yerasimos, the car – a high-end saloon – swung out of the resort gate and headed east.

'How do you find the film crew?' he asked. Not having a car in Athens, he always talked to taxi drivers. Although some were morons, many had informed views about life and he often picked up useful information from them.

'West Coast Americans,' Yerasimos replied, as if that was sufficient explanation.

'Loud, overconfident?' Mavros encouraged.

'Put it this way. I spent thirty years driving a cab in New York City. Californians are pussycats compared with the customers there. But I don't think they're very serious people.'

'Hollywood doesn't exactly have a reputation for encouraging intellectuals,' Mavros said, realizing that Yerasimos would know plenty about the film crew. 'Have you driven Cara Parks?'

'Occasionally. She seems like a nice person. I don't like her assistant, though. She's got a tongue in her head.'

'You heard she went missing?'

'I did. Can't say I was sorry. She'd have got on all right. She could tell anyone what she thought of them in the coarsest Greek, Cretan pronunciation and expressions included.'

That was interesting. No one had said that Maria spoke good Greek, let alone the local dialect. What might that add to the issue of her disappearance?

'How about the director, Luke Jannet?'

Yerasimos overtook an ancient tractor smoothly. 'Jannet? I've only had him a couple of times. What was that you said about loud and overconfident? I won't be going to see his film, I can tell you that.'

'You reckon it'll be another *Captain Corelli*?'

'Full of inaccuracies and unconvincing love affairs? Probably. But not just that. It's an exercise in bloodsucking.'

'Striking phrase. What does it mean, exactly?'

The driver smiled tightly. 'You're from Athens, right? I know that plenty of people there died during the Axis occupation, maybe you've even got relatives among them. But here it was different. People haven't forgotten on Crete.'

'You mean the massacres?'

'Those, and the burning of villages and the torture and the beatings. It may look like everyone's welcoming German tourists with open arms – and they are, for their money – but deep down there's a hatred, especially among the older generation and in the villages that don't have income from tourism.'

'What about Rudolf Kersten?' Mavros asked. 'He was a para-trooper during the invasion.'

'Ah, Mr Kersten is the exception that proves the truth of what

I'm saying. He's done so much for this part of Crete that it would take days to list everything. He's rebuilt villages, he's given thousands of people jobs over the decades, he's set up scholarships for poor kids to study abroad . . . he's that rare thing, a genuinely good man.'

Mavros thought of David Waggoner. 'But still there are some who hate him.'

'There will always be dissenters, jealous people who got less than others.'

The lights of Chania's suburbs were shining ahead.

'I heard Mr Kersten was involved in the massacre at Makrymari.'

Yerasimos didn't speak for some time, his hands tight on the wheel.

'There are people who say that, usually inspired by that piece of shit Waggoner. The British think he was a hero, but all he did was bring down more Nazi reprisals on the heads of innocent Cretans. We didn't need the British. If they'd dropped us the weapons, we'd have done the job ourselves but, of course, they never trusted us enough.'

That was a different angle to those Mavros had heard before. He thanked the driver when they pulled up outside the clinic. Mikis was at his door before he could open it.

'Interesting guy, Yerasimos,' Mavros said, after the saloon had departed.

'Yeah,' Mikis said, with a grin. 'Hidden depths. Did he tell you he was in New York for years?'

'Yes.'

'But he didn't tell you why he went, did he? He was involved in a vendetta. He pushed a guy who betrayed his father to the Germans off a cliff.'

A tremor of unease ran through Mavros. 'How was it resolved?'

'Eventually the major players died of old age and agreement was reached.'

'Thirty years,' Mavros said ruefully.

'Yeah, encouraging, isn't it?'

Mavros looked around at the men on the street – some of them he recognized, other not. The Range Rover was where it had been in the afternoon, baseball bats visible through the windows.

'The influence of American culture,' Mikis said, following the direction of his gaze. 'They're useful weapons because they aren't lethal unless you really want them to be.'

'As long as you don't bore out the middle and fill it with molten lead.'

Mikis laughed. 'Now there's a thought.'

'Are your boys all right for an hour or two while we go and eat?'

'They're organized for the whole night and I'm only a phone call away.'

He went over and spoke to the young men and then beckoned Mavros to the Jeep.

'I'll take you to a good place,' the Cretan said, heading for the city centre.

'On the harbour front?' Mavros asked, not wanting to run into the well-lubricated Luke Jannet.

'No, this is a family taverna in the backstreets. If you're lucky, they might have snails.'

Mavros made no comment. Cretan snails were a delicacy he had no desire for, having had a disastrous encounter with them in the past.

Mikis parked near the cathedral and led the way down a narrow street. The taverna was under a huge spray of pink bougainvillea blooms. There were only a few tables outside and the nearest was occupied by two men, one stocky and one lanky, both of whom Mavros recognized immediately. He put his hand on Mikis's shoulder and retreated behind him.

'We've got to go back the way we came,' he said in his ear. 'I don't want those guys to see me.'

Mikis stared at him and then turned, keeping himself between Mavros and the taverna. 'Start walking,' he said, 'single file like in the army.'

After they were round the corner, Mikis spoke. 'So you didn't want to see David Waggoner. I can understand that – he's a nasty piece of work. But the tall streak of piss?'

'That was Tryfon Roufos, the owner of Hellas History SA and the most bent antiquities dealer in Athens, probably the whole of Greece.' Mavros shook his head. 'He's also a suspected child abuser and blackmailer of the rich and famous.'

'Charming. Do you want me to bring him in for questioning?'

'No! What I would like to know is what he's doing in a huddle with the British war hero David Waggoner.'

'Want me to tail them when they've finished?'

Mavros smiled. 'Did you get rejected by the police academy?'

'You think I'd work for those bullies? No, I'm trying to learn from you. It might help me stay alive.'

'It might help *us* stay alive,' Mavros corrected. 'No, let's leave them to it. At least that asshole Oskar Mesner wasn't with them. If he had been, I'd have been straight on the phone to Rudolf Kersten about his coin collection.'

'Speaking of which,' Mikis said, leading him down another narrow street. 'I've got something to tell you about that.' He smiled. 'But let's wait till we've had something to eat and drink. I could put a donkey away.'

Mavros followed him reluctantly. It wasn't beyond the realms of possibility that the taverna they were en route to offered stewed beast of burden as a speciality.

THIRTEEN

As it turned out, the food in the small taverna Mikis knew was excellent, the lamb succulent and the mountain greens a subtle blend of sweet and bitter. The owner's casked wine had a faint taste of flowers to it and they got through a kilo quickly.

'OK,' Mavros said. 'Time to talk.'

Mikis grinned and discarded a toothpick. 'If I wasn't such a pushover, I'd be charging you for this.'

Mavros had a vision of the fight on the way back from Kornaria. '"Pushover" isn't the word that immediately comes to mind. Anyway, I can pay you, as I did before. One thing you can say for the production is that there's plenty of cash around.'

'Except this doesn't directly concern the film people,' Mikis said.

'Really?'

'But it may have something to do with that mismatched pair we saw round the corner.'

'Roufos and Waggoner? I'm all donkey's ears.'

'I was going to ask you about that,' the Cretan said, laughing. 'All right, here it is. I got this from my old man, among others. The story goes that during the war, in late 1943 after the Italians had surrendered and the Germans got even more jumpy, a group of resistance fighters found a hoard of silver – ancient stuff, coins and other things – in a cave up in the White Mountains.'

'Has this got something to do with Rudolf Kersten?'

Mikis held up his hand. 'I'll get to that. And before you ask, it wasn't near Kornaria.'

Mavros let him continue, taking notes.

'The *andartes* wanted to rebury it and split it up after the war was over – at least, that was what their leaders ordered them to do. They were from different villages, so there was some dispute.'

Mavros imagined the half-starved mountain men, few of whom would have possessed more than a coin or two after years of fighting, coming to blows over this sudden source of wealth.

'And then other people got to hear of the find.' Mikis raised an eyebrow suggestively.

'David Waggoner.'

'One out of two. It wasn't his area, but the British commander there had been sent back to Egypt after being wounded and Waggoner – Lambis – was temporarily in charge.'

Mavros nodded. 'And the other guy?'

'A Communist, one of the few EAM people with any influence in western Crete. He was known as Kanellos. Maybe he had cinnamon-coloured hair.' Mikis drained his glass. 'As you can imagine, he was keen on the silver being used for the good of the people.'

'Meaning, not divided amongst the *andartes*.'

'Correct.'

'So then what happened?'

'You should ask Waggoner.'

Mavros gave him a stony look. 'Maybe I will. But he's not the one sitting opposite me.'

'All right, all right. What I heard was that Lambis wanted to send the hoard to Alexandria on a submarine. He ordered it to be brought to a monastery called St Athanasios that's in the middle of nowhere on the south coast, just a few hundred metres from a small beach that had been used for landings more than once.'

'And?'

'The Germans were waiting for them. Over twenty *andartes* were killed, while Waggoner managed to get away with a bullet in his shoulder. The silver was taken to the German headquarters building in Chania and that was the last anyone heard of it. The rumour was that Kanellos had betrayed the mountain men and Waggoner rather than lose the silver to the British imperialists.'

Mavros knew there had been such betrayals during the occupation. He looked at Mikis. 'There's more?'

The Cretan nodded. 'In the Sixties, workers found a safe in the foundations of a building scheduled for demolition near the harbour front.'

'The German headquarters?'

Mikis raised his head in denial. 'That had been thoroughly checked years before. No, this was a private house. The owners had been Jews, but there weren't many left after the Germans had finished with them.'

'And the silver was in the safe?'

Mikis shrugged. 'So some people said. The problem was, it disappeared a week after it was found.'

Mavros sat back in his chair, unsure where this information left him.

'You mentioned Mr Kersten,' Mikis said, waving for the bill. 'Some people, the few around here who don't like him – maybe egged on by Waggoner – say he got hold of the safe's contents and that his collection of silver came from it.'

'And what does your father think about that? What do you think?'

The Cretan counted out banknotes, brushing away Mavros's attempt to pay. 'I'll tell you what I know. After he came to live here, Rudolf Kersten spent a lot of his own money buying up silver ritual objects and ornaments that had belonged to the Chania Jews. He contributed towards a museum to their memory – it's only a couple of streets from here – and he donated the pieces he'd bought.'

They walked up the quiet lanes. Mikis' story had been fascinating, though it hadn't added anything to the Maria Kondos case. But it had provided more background to the curious relationship between Rudolf Kersten and David Waggoner, as had the meeting between the former SOE man and the dubious antiquities trader.

After parting from Mikis, Mavros looked up into the star-dotted night between the balconies. He had the distinct feeling that he was on the verge of a momentous discovery, not necessarily one that would do anything for his peace of mind.

He tried to sleep in Nondas' and Anna's wide bed but, after rolling about for what seemed like hours, he gave up. Booting up his laptop, he checked his emails. There were some more attachments from The Fat Man, but they didn't tell him anything else suggestive about Kersten or Waggoner. He sent a message asking for information about the EAM operative known as Kanellos. The Communist Party archives were hard to access, even for a long-standing member like Yiorgos, but he had no option. Pandelis Pikros, the disaffected old comrade he used to tap as a source, had died a few months ago.

Mavros went on to the Internet and typed 'Kersten Jewish Museum Chania' into a search engine. All he found was short reference in a local newspaper article about the opening of the museum in 1987. Rudolf Kersten had been present at the ceremony as a major donor, but had declined to comment. That squared with Mavros's take on the former *Fallschirmjäger's* character – he wasn't the type to go courting praise.

He tried to find more details about the silver hoard in the mountains, but there was nothing. He wasn't surprised – stories like that tended not to be written down. Then he tried 'Waggoner Silver Hoard' and was directed to an extract from David Waggoner's *Where the Eagle Flies*, his memoir of the war in Crete.

'. . . on November 1st 1943. With great difficulty, I had convinced Captain Dhiavolos that the silver would cause nothing but internecine strife if it remained on the island. Runners were sent out to the Abbot of St Athanasios and to the men guarding the cave, while radio contact with Cairo resulted in a submarine being dispatched four nights later – when the moon was only two days beyond new.

Although I had studied Cretan archaeology at Cambridge, much of the silver was beyond my ken. There were around fifty Hellenistic coins and over a hundred Roman, the former ranging from Armenia to Sicily and the latter mainly from the late Empire. But the majority of pieces were even later – ranging from the Arab occupation of Crete in the ninth and tenth centuries, to the Byzantine reconquest of the island, to the Venetian period of rule, to the Ottoman domination that followed. I had no idea of the coins' value, but it must have been considerable. There was no question of the hoard being split up amongst uneducated mountain villagers, even if the leaders of the *andartes* permitted that.

Although I found the coins interesting, it was the prehistoric pieces that caught my imagination most. They comprised thirty-two double-headed axes, the primary symbol of the Minoans. I had visited Knossos several times before the war and was aware that the *labrys* had great religious significance. The Minoans seem to have worshipped a mother goddess, the religion being largely administered by females, and it was said that the priestesses used the axes to sacrifice animals. Some of the pieces were about six inches across, while others were much smaller, presumably votary objects. I have since learned that gold *labrys* were prevalent in other areas, but for some reason no doubt lost in history, our hoard had only silver examples. According to some scholars, the curved shape of the opposed blades represented the waxing and waning moon, which doubtless was one manifestation of the deity's power. Less inspiring had been the use of the *labrys* by the pre-war Greek dictator Metaxas as a symbol of his regime's integrity. For that reason, the *andartes* had no interest in the axes.

I reached the rendezvous with my men in the late afternoon. The Abbot, Father Christodhoulos, was his usual charming self, plying us with bread, olives, goat's cheese and *raki*. Shortly after dark, the sound of muffled hooves could be heard on the steep path leading down the gorge. Captain Dhiavolos burst into the monastery, bellowing for food and drink, his men apparently unaffected by the long and dangerous trip.

The submarine was expected at midnight, but such operations rarely went according to plan, the southern coast of Crete being a perilous place even in daylight. At last, one of the lookouts spotted the brief flashing of a red light out to sea and we prepared to greet the crew in their inflatable dinghy.

The German is a patient hunter. They waited until we were all on the narrow, stony beach before the lights from the patrol boat came on and the machine guns on it and on dry land opened up. I later learned that HMS *Whale Shark* tried unsuccessfully to torpedo the enemy craft before turning back to Alex. *Andartes* fell all around me, Captain Dhiavolos's chest riddled with bullets. I was knocked to the ground by a round in my left shoulder, but two of my surviving men managed to drag me out of the lights and up a steep defile. I later heard that Father Christodhoulos and his six monks had been shot against the wall of St Athanasios.

I have no doubt that the ambush was a result of treachery by the EAM man known as Kanellos. I first met him during the Battle of Crete, when he tried to dissuade Greek gendarmes and local people from taking part in the attack on Galatsi. At the time, I thought he was a coward and denounced him as such to the people. From then he worked tirelessly to undermine both my efforts and those of my fellow SOE officers. He had the deluded idea that passive resistance would be more effective and less costly in terms of Cretan lives. Fortunately, the islanders left him in no doubt as to their feelings on that issue. After the Germans slaughtered us on the beach and took their savage revenge on the churchmen, Kanellos disappeared from Crete. No doubt he returned to the mainland and continued to sow the seeds of dissension that led the country to civil war after the Nazis had been defeated. Such men are dangerous beyond their station – the one known as Kanellos was of scarcely medium height, with a great hook for a nose and unnaturally bright blue eyes. May the earth lie heavy on his bones and those of his vicious, misguided comrades. As for the silver, it was lost to the occupier and probably ended up in the cellars of the arch-thief Göring.'

Mavros noted the date of the book – it had been published in 1957. Waggoner wouldn't have known about the discovery of the safe in the Jewish home at that time, and Kersten's donations to the museum were still far in the future. Which didn't mean that he wasn't in full possession of those facts now.

His eyes getting heavy, Mavros logged off and lay back on the bed. He was uneasier than he had been before going on the Internet, but this time he was repressing thoughts that were trying to break through, even though he knew there was no future in that. The vendetta wasn't exactly helping, either.

He fell into the sleep of the anxious, thinking before he went under that he was only the latest in the long line of intruders into Cretan history to be wondering if he'd leave the island in one piece.

Mavros was woken by the sound of a key in the lock. He had left his own in there, so the door would not open. Still semi-submerged in sleep, he stumbled out of the bedroom,

'Who is it?'

'Ah, Mr Alex, it is you?'

Barba-Yannis stood on the landing, a tattered straw hat on the back of his head. 'I always come on Thursdays to water the plants on the back balconies. I wasn't sure if . . .'

'Don't worry,' Mavros said, admitting the old man. 'It's time I was up anyway. Would you like coffee?'

'I should be making you coffee, Mr Alex.'

'No, no. You do your watering and I'll make the coffee. How do you take it?'

'*Varyglyko*, my child. I always had a sweet tooth.'

Mavros had a quick shower, then found the *briki*. He made the old man's sugar-laden brew in the long-handled metal pot first, followed by his own unsweetened cup. He found Barba-Yannis sitting at a small table on the balcony to the rear of the living room, water dripping off the marble floor to the unused space below.

'Thank you, my child,' the old man said, drinking from the glass of water Mavros had brought with the coffee. 'I can hardly walk down the street now without needing to sit down.'

'You look very well.'

Barba-Yannis threw up his wrinkled arms. 'I am on my own, like many of my generation. My wife died last year and my children and grandchildren are in Germany. They have done very well. They say I will soon be a great-grandfather.'

'May they live for you,' Mavros said, calculating that the old man would have been in his early twenties during the war. 'Tell me, why did they go to that country?'

'I went there first myself,' Barba-Yannis said. 'In the Fifties things were not good here and I had a record – I was in EAM during the war. I wasn't a communist, mind – I never liked the party's hard-line stance. But it was better to be absent for some years, especially since there were jobs in the factories up there.'

Mavros looked into the rheumy brown eyes. 'But didn't you feel bad after everything the Germans did here?'

'Of course I felt bad!' the old man said, slapping the balcony rail. 'I lost relatives and friends – comrades . . .' His voice failed.

'I'm sorry. I didn't mean to upset you.'

Barba-Yannis drew his forearm across his eyes. 'No, my child, it is good to remember the past. The younger generations do not like to – they prefer to make money rather than honour our sacrifices. Besides, there is no benefit in hating. The German soldiers paid a heavy price too.'

'One of them even put back a lot into the local economy.'

'You mean Rudolf Kersten? Yes, he is greatly admired.'

Mavros caught a hint of disapproval. 'But?'

The old Cretan rubbed his thinning hair. 'But some people say he took part in one of the massacres. Even though he denies it,

I've never been able to see him as the repentant do-gooder most
people do.'

'Makrymari,' Mavros said, in a low voice.

'You've been doing your homework, my boy,' Barba-Yannis
said, nodding in approval.

'I'm trying,' Mavros smiled. 'I hear there was a Jewish population in Chania.'

'Ach, the Jews. They kept themselves to themselves, but we
didn't mind them.' The old man lowered his head. 'You can
imagine what happened to them.'

'Sent to the camps?' Mavros said, aware that many thousands
of mainland Greek Jews had been gassed.

'Worse. They were loaded on a ship in Iraklio with Italian
soldiers who had surrendered. For years, it was thought that the
Germans had sunk it themselves, but not long ago I heard it was
torpedoed by a British submarine. No survivors.'

A chill ran through Mavros. War really was hell, not only
because of the slaughter of combatants and non-combatants,
but because of the ghastly twists of fate leading to 'accidents'
that destroyed the lives of countless families – including those
left to mourn.

He roused himself. Barba-Yannis was a potentially useful
source about resistance activities.

'Did you know an EAM man called Kanellos?'

'Did I know Kanellos?' the old man asked, with a gap-toothed
smile.

'Kanellos was that rare thing – a hero who cared about other
people. After the first days of the invasion, he swore he would
never fire a gun again.'

'What happened?'

'I wasn't here – I'd been sent with a message to the EAM
commander in Rethymno the day before the landings started and
got caught up in the fighting there. But what we heard was that
Kanellos was in the killing grounds outside the city with a band
of fighters. They slaughtered the paratroopers with knives when
they landed and then took their own weapons to fire on them. I
still don't understand how the airfield at Maleme was lost. The
British generals were fools.'

Barba-Yannis emptied his water glass, and Mavros passed his
across.

'Thank you, my son. And then Kanellos was at the village of Galatsi. Almost all his men had been killed. The British – well, most of the fighting men were those big New Zealanders – decided to charge the Germans up the main street, with a couple of tin-can tanks at the front.'

Waggoner, Mavros thought. There was mention of his role in the battle on the Internet sites he'd trawled and in extracts from his books.

'Kanellos realized from the start that it was a suicide mission, because the Germans had landed thousands of men by then. He tried to talk the gendarmes and the local citizens out of taking part, saying their efforts and their lives would be much more valuable in the future.' The old Cretan blinked away tears. 'He was right about that. The initial charge was a success, but within an hour they had all been cut down by Germans on the higher ground. Apart from a few wounded British at the rear, there were hardly any survivors. It was a tragedy and it is to Kanellos's honour that he tried to avert it.'

'Presumably Kanellos wasn't his real name,' Mavros said, his voice unsteady.

'Of course not. The senior men all used aliases, even before the war.'

Mavros nodded. 'And after that? Kanellos stayed throughout the occupation?'

'Till the German surrender in Chania.'

Mavros looked across the space to the flat opposite, trying to keep calm. An old woman in a nightgown was playing listlessly with an overweight cat.

'Did you ever hear of a hoard of silver that was found in a cave up in the mountains?'

Barba-Yannis gave him a sharp look. 'How do you know about that, Mr Alex?'

Mavros gave him a shortened version of the story in Waggoner's memoir.

'Kanellos betrayed them?' the old man said, his voice breaking. 'Ridiculous. He would never have done a thing like that. He worked by persuasion, not betrayal. Some of those British agents were madmen,' he continued. 'Lambis – Waggoner – was one of the worst. He used to come down from the mountains and shoot Germans with the *andartes*. There were many reprisals.'

'I thought the Cretans generally were prepared to make the ultimate sacrifice to get rid of the Germans?'

Barba-Yannis looked at him thoughtfully. 'You know, that's the kind of bravado the mountain men still come out with. Of course, people were prepared to die for the cause of freedom. But not everyone agreed with old men and boys being put against a wall. That was Kanellos's message: no sabotage unless it was a major target – most of those were so well guarded that you couldn't get near them – and no civilian lives to be put at risk. Some of the British – Waggoner, especially – had different priorities.'

Mavros looked down. 'Kanellos – describe him, will you?'

'Medium height, thick black hair brushed back from his forehead, a hooked nose and a thick moustache.' The old man raised a hand. 'But most striking of all were his eyes – they were dark-blue and penetrating. You felt they could see all the way inside your soul. He was a wonderful man. I never saw him again after he left the island.'

Mavros's phone chirruped. There was a message from the Fat Man asking him to call urgently. Mavros didn't need to. He already knew Kanellos's real name.

FOURTEEN

After the old caretaker had gone, Mavros called the Fat Man. 'Kanellos was my father,' he said, without any preamble. 'How the hell did you . . .' Yiorgos broke off. 'Oh, I get it. You do the work and get me to confirm it. That's typ—'

'Shut up!' Mavros yelled. 'Have you . . . have you any idea what this means to me? I hardly knew my father before he died, none of us knew anything about what he did in the war . . . or did you, Yiorgo?'

'I swear on my mother's grave I didn't, Alex.' The Fat Man's tone was sombre now. 'You know what the Party's like about past operations. I only got a steer on Kanellos because someone owed me a very big favour.'

Mavros sat back in the armchair by the phone, his heart rate gradually slowing. He had been speaking to a man who had worked with his father, who had seen him when he was in his prime and who admired him. It was as if a familiar ghost that always kept its distance had suddenly come up behind him and whispered in his ear. The problem was, he couldn't understand the words.

'Alex? Are you all right?'

'What do you think? My mind's doing a passable imitation of a washing machine on spin cycle.'

'What? Oh, I see. Look, I can try to find out more if you—'

'Not now, Yiorgo. I've got enough to think about. I should really phone my mother, but that'll have to wait. I need to talk to her in person.'

'It isn't bad news, Alex. From what I heard, Spyros did great work for the movement, like he did before and after the war. Your father was a hero, I've always told you that.'

'A hero I didn't know,' Mavros muttered, 'like my brother.'

'Well, it seems you know him better now. Isn't that a good thing?'

'I need time to think about that. I'll talk to you later.' Mavros cut the connection and called Niki.

'Hello, how are you?' he asked.

She heard immediately that something had got to him. 'What's happened, Alex? Are you all right?'

'Of course,' he replied. He still wasn't going to tell her anything about the men from Kornaria and the vendetta. 'Tired, though. Listen, I might have to stay on a bit longer here. There are some more things I have to check out.'

Although Niki could be self-centred, she was good at picking up other people's moods. 'I thought you'd found the woman, Alex. Why don't you come home? I'll look after you, my love, I promise.'

Mavros was touched. 'It won't be long, I promise. Listen, I have to dash now. I'll talk to you later.'

'I love you,' she said.

He repeated the words, with enough feeling to reassure her. He did love her, but he'd loved his father – the sad-eyed phantom – for much longer.

His mobile rang.

'Do you want me to pick you up?' Mikis asked. 'I'm in the area.'

They arranged to meet at the corner of the street.

'Christ and the Holy Mother, what's happened to you?' the young Cretan asked, as Mavros got into the Jeep.

'Must have been something I ate.'

Mikis glanced at him dubiously before driving on. 'Anything you feel like sharing?'

'Not right now. Can you take me to the clinic?'

'I'm heading there to check on the boys. I've talked the old man into letting me stick with you today. The film people are mostly over at the fake village they've built anyway.'

Mavros remembered the massacre scene that was due to be filmed. 'Thanks. Maybe we'll go there later.' He kept silent for the rest of the short trip, trying to get his mind back on the Maria Kondos case.

There was a black Mercedes outside the clinic, with two bulky, besuited men inside, while the watchers' Range Rover was in its usual place across the street. Mikis went over to talk to his friends.

Going up the stairs, Mavros knocked on the door of the private room. It was opened by Cara Parks.

'Good morning, Alex,' she said, the smile freezing on her lips. 'What is it?'

'Erm, some family news. Don't worry, it won't get in the way of anything.'

'Well, you're finished here, anyway,' the actress said, extending an arm towards the patient, who was in a wheelchair. 'Maria's talking again and Dr Stavra . . . Stavra . . .'

'Stavrakakis,' he completed, with a weak smile.

'Yes, he says that Maria can come back with me to the Heavenly Blue.' Cara leaned over her assistant and kissed her on the forehead. 'Not that she's going to work, of course.' She introduced Mavros and explained his role.

Maria Kondos nodded her thanks, though it was unclear if she recognized him, then turned to the actress. 'I *will* work,' she said, her voice surprisingly strong. 'The only thing that's wrong with me is my feet.'

'Hold on a moment,' Mavros said, stepping forwards. 'What did the doctor say about your temporary inability to speak?'

Maria looked at Cara. 'That it was shock-induced. Can we go now?'

Mavros was beginning to understand why the woman was disliked among the crew. She was haughty and brusque, clearly regarding him as a low-level servant.

He turned to the actress. 'I'd like to ask your assistant some questions. I'm still unclear about what happened in the village.'

'I can't remember,' Maria Kondos said firmly. 'The police inspector was here this morning. He didn't ask many questions.'

'Margaritis?'

Cara Parks nodded.

Mavros wondered about that. Then again, the police hadn't been told about the fight on the road, so his interest in a forbidding woman who remembered nothing about her disappearance wouldn't have been huge.

'Do you speak Greek?' he asked, trying another angle.

'A bit,' Maria replied. 'My parents spoke it at home, but I lost most of it when I went to the West Coast. Why?'

'I was wondering if you'd heard anything when you were in Kornaria.'

'I told you, I can't remember a thing.'

'Even why you walked out of the resort on your own on Sunday evening?'

'I imagine I wanted some fresh air.'

Mavros kept on at her. 'Someone called your mobile from a phone registered to Vasilios Dhrakakis in Kornaria on Sunday evening, not long before you left the Heavenly Blue. Have you no recollection of that?'

'The name means nothing to me,' Maria replied, her eyes meeting his.

Mistake, he thought. She thought she could take him on, but he had too much experience of liars. He let it go for the time being and turned the heat up another way.

'Are you aware that the driver who helped me get you away from the men who were pursuing you is now involved in a vendetta? As am I.'

'Alex!' the actress said, shocked. 'Why didn't you tell me?'

'Not your problem. Besides, what could you do?'

She glared at him. 'Get the production's lawyers involved, the American consul.'

'Yeah, that's going to help.'

'All right, if it's money you need, I'll give you it.' She glanced at the other woman. 'After all, you saved my precious Maria.'

'Don't worry, I'll sort it out,' Mavros said, with considerably more bluster than he felt. 'Aren't you supposed to be on set?'

'This afternoon,' Cara said. 'Now I'm going to take Maria back to the hotel.'

'Let me escort you down.'

'No, that's not your job,' the actress said, calling her body-guards on her phone.

Mavros looked at Maria Kondos. Why wasn't she talking? Was she protecting someone in Kornaria? Or could it be that she was less of a victim than she appeared?

He didn't have a clue.

Mavros watched as one of the gorillas loaded the wheelchair into the boot of the Mercedes, while the other helped Maria into the back seat.

As Mikis was on the way across the street, Mavros's mobile rang.

'This is Hildegard Kersten, Alex. I really need your help.' The old woman sounded close to panic.

'What's happened?'

'It's Rudi. He's slipped away from the resort. Don't worry,

it's not like that woman. I know where he's heading – to that
damned massacre set. But he won't answer his phone and I don't
know who's driving him.'

Mavros moved to the Jeep, beckoning to Mikis to follow.

'I'll check with the car-hire company while we're on our way
to the set. I'll let you know as soon as I see him.'

'Thank you,' Hildegard said. 'I'm going over there now
myself.'

'Are you sure that's a good idea? Your husband presumably
wants to be there without you.'

There was a pause. 'Very well. You are correct. I will stay in
the apartment. Goodbye.'

Mavros addressed Mikis. 'Can you ask your old man if any
of your drivers is taking Rudolf Kersten to the massacre set?'

'My mother's in charge of dispatch,' Mikis said. It took him
under a minute to confirm that Yerasimos had been hailed by
Kersten outside the hotel. He had advised that they were at the
Black Bird.

'The Black Bird?' Mavros said. 'What's that?'

'The German paratroopers' memorial on the way to Maleme.
It was put up during the war.'

'And it's still there?' Mavros asked, amazed.

'Yes. People left it as a memorial of Cretan suffering, I think,
even though some call it the Evil Bird. The only thing they did
was knock off the swastika the bird was holding.'

Mikis answered his phone and spoke briefly. 'That was
Yerasimos. They're on the move again, heading west.'

Mavros considered calling Kersten, but he had the feeling the
old man had reasons of his own for attending the filming and
he didn't think it was his place to interfere. He wanted to see
the shoot himself, and he was also interested to see if David
Waggoner would be present. He wasn't going to tell him that
Kanellos was his father, but he might be able to get more information about Spyros's activities on Crete, even from a biased
participant. He rang Hildegard Kersten and said that her husband
was in a Tsifakis company car and being well looked after. She
didn't sound happy, but she was grateful for the news.

Mikis's phone rang again several minutes later.

'Yerasimos again,' he said, after cutting the connection. 'Mr
Kersten is at Makrymari.'

'The real massacre village?'

'Correct. Do you want me to head there?'

'If you can get us there without him seeing me.'

'Done.' Mikis took the next left off the main road and followed a narrow track through the orange trees. 'This takes us round the back of the village.'

The leaves filtered the bright sunlight and the temperature was suddenly lower. It was a bucolic scene, the plump oranges weighing down the branches and the ground beneath covered with dark-red dust. Mavros thought of the early days of the war, when the paratroopers had been caught in the foliage and killed before they could untangle themselves. In the midst of beauty had been death. And his father . . .

Makrymari was a small village, the white houses shaded by vines and oleanders. The buildings were all in good condition. A few hens clucked to their chicks.

'There isn't much to see here,' Mikis said, pulling in behind a bulky pickup. 'Only the memorial.'

Mavros walked forward slowly, taking in a curved wall in the middle of the fourth, open side of the square. Rudolf Kersten was on his knees in front of it, his head bowed. Mavros retreated behind a eucalyptus tree and waited until the old man had got up unsteadily and left a small bunch of wild flowers on the ground in front of the wall. The German then went back to the Mercedes at the far end of the square and got in, Yerasimos holding the rear door open.

When the car had turned and disappeared, Mavros walked through the uncut grass, past the spot where Kersten's knees had crushed it, to the rough stone wall. Looking along, he realized what it represented. There were names at chest height every metre or so. Beneath them were dates of birth and death, the latter all being June 3rd 1941.

'It's the line of the executed,' Mikis said.

'I got that.' Mavros looked at the name above the flowers – poppies that were already wilting, crown daisies and a couple of gladioli – and got a shock. 'Aikaterini tou Pavlou Alivizaki,' he read. A woman.

'Black Katina, they call her,' Mikis said. 'Her father died before the war and she was in mourning. She also killed over twenty Germans and was one of the few who survived the Battle of Galatsi. They found recoil marks on her shoulder.'

Mavros put a hand out and touched the wall. He wondered if his father had met her when he was trying to dissuade the Cretans from the charge. He felt closer to him by thinking that he had.

'Who carried out the massacre?' he asked.

'Paratroopers. There was a Captain Blatter who hated civilians who resisted. Not only that, but Göring had authorized summary executions.'

'Do you think Kersten was here?'

'He's never confirmed or denied it, but he paid for the memorial wall and gave plenty of money to the families of the fallen – to the whole village, in fact.'

'Jesus,' Mavros said. Maybe Waggoner had been right – maybe Rudolf Kersten really had paid blood money.

Mikis's phone rang.

'That was Yerasimos,' he said, after he'd finished. 'They're at the shoot.'

Mavros followed him back to the Jeep, wondering what kind of man could go straight from the place where he'd witnessed a massacre to a film set?

A large parking lot had been set up in a dusty field. After showing their passes, Mavros and the Cretan were admitted through the chain gate that marked off the shoot area. There were trailers, generators and cameras all over the place, men and women in caps and shorts running between them. Beyond, there were old buildings that had been supplemented with painted wooden facades and plants in pots.

'They filmed some combat scenes here last week,' Mikis said. 'I guess they're getting their money's worth by staging the massacre in the same place.'

Mavros caught sight of Luke Jannet, surrounded by technicians at a large camera on a track. A raised platform under a sunshade had been set up behind the machines. Rosie Yellenberg was standing on it, wearing headphones and speaking constantly into a mouthpiece. David Waggoner was a few seats along, in blazer and dark glasses, while Rudolf Kersten was sitting outside a caravan with a security guy on the door. Mavros watched as Cara Parks appeared in a shabby but well-cut black dress, a black wig covering her blonde locks. She had been made up to have unnaturally rosy cheeks, though her arms were dirty and there was a fake bloodstain on her right shoulder. As she came out, Kersten got to his feet and spoke to her, an urgent look on his face. The actress nodded and then patted his arm. She was led by a production assistant to the edge of the set. There was no sign of Maria Kondos, though she may have been in the trailer.

A woman with a stentorian voice started bellowing instructions through a megaphone. Men in *Fallschirmjäger* uniforms, several wearing shorts, started pushing extras dressed in Cretan costume and peasant clothing towards an open space in front of the trees. Before they got there, a heavily-built officer raised his hand and strode to Cara. He ripped her dress down from the neck, uncovering a bloody bandage on the right side and what was supposed to be heavy bruising on the left. No doubt deliberately, the costume had been sewn so that both her heavy breasts became visible. She crossed her arms over them and walked to the line that the old men and boys had already formed. She stood in the centre and then shouted in a clear voice, 'Freedom or Death!'

Just before the machine-pistols started to rattle blanks, Cara stepped backwards and the men in the line joined up to cover her. Cameras on rails and pickups followed her as she sprinted to the trees and disappeared behind them, by which time the men were spurting fake blood and twitching on the ground. Paratroopers ran after her, the officer screaming orders impotently.

'Cut!' the women with the megaphone yelled.

Mavros watched as Luke Jannet went into a huddle with his sidekicks. Shortly afterwards, the woman started ordering people around again – the scene with the victims being chosen and sent to the line-up was to be shot again, which involved a long delay as their clothes were changed and new blood packets and squibs attached. During that time, Cara Parks ran to the trees several times as she was filmed from different angles. Mavros began to get bored with the process and moved away.

He heard his name called from the raised platform. David Waggoner was waving to him.

'What did you think of that?' the former SOE man asked, when Mavros had joined him.

'Pretty powerful, I suppose.'

'Nothing like the real thing, of course.' Waggoner wiped his brow. He looked rather unwell.

'You witnessed one?'

'In a way of speaking.' The old man looked into Mavros's eyes.

'You took part in one.'

'Not as large as this, but we had to dispose of Germans and traitors.'

Mavros held his gaze. 'You killed enemy soldiers in cold blood?'

Waggoner looked back at the set. 'Cold blood, hot blood – those distinctions don't exist in war. As you just saw, they certainly didn't exist for the Krauts.'

His use of the term showed how little the passage of time had changed old prejudices, though Mavros doubted Rudolf Kersten would have used equivalent language about his war-time enemies.

'Anyway, my point was that the real massacre at Makrymari didn't happen as in the film.'

Mavros nodded. 'Black Katina didn't make it to the trees.'

The old soldier raised an eyebrow. 'You *have* been digging.'

'You met her, didn't you?'

'Indeed I did. At Galatsi. There was a charge and she led the locals.' The wrinkled face slackened for a few moments. 'My God, she was magnificent. We were under heavy fire from the *Fallschirmjägers*. My tank was knocked out and I found myself fighting alongside her. She led a charmed life – although she'd been wounded in the shoulder previously – and she was merciless. We killed the lot of them.'

'So how did she end up in the execution line?'

'I'm not sure. I was wounded when the enemy started firing from the higher ground – they cut down almost all the survivors. I presume Katina was captured at some point. You should ask that bastard Kersten. He was at Galatsi and he was in the firing squad at Makrymari.'

If what Waggoner said was true, how could Kersten bear to watch the reconstruction of the massacre? That he was plagued by guilt had been shown by his kneeling in front of the memorial wall at the village, but attending the shoot was incredible. Mavros's Greek side, reinforced by the involvement of his father in the battle, was overwhelming the reserve he had inherited from his mother.

Leaving Waggoner without a word, he went in search of the German. He was no longer outside Cara Parks' trailer. Mavros asked the security guard if he'd seen him.

'He went over there,' the big man said, pointing towards a grove of orange trees.

'How long ago?'

'About half an hour, I guess.'

So Kersten hadn't witnessed the execution scene, Mavros thought, his anger still raging. He'd gone to hide; but he would have heard the sound of the machine-pistols. Served the bastard right.

'Kersten?' Mavros shouted, running through the first line of trees. 'Where are you? Ker—' He broke off and slowed down, but his heart continued to pump hard.

The old man was hanging from a branch, his belt round his neck. His knees were partially bent and the points of his shoes touched the earth, his trousers having slipped down his thin hips. His eyes were bulging, but his face was its normal tanned colour.

Mavros knew he shouldn't interfere with the scene, but there was a chance Rudolf Kersten was still alive – hanging yourself that way took a lot longer than the clean break of a gallows. He turned to the left and approached the body from the rear. Putting his arms under the old man's, he lifted him up, then struggled to open the belt enough to slip the head through the noose. He dragged Kersten to the rear and laid him down, ripping open his shirt and putting his ear to his chest. There was no heart beat. He was about to start artificial respiration when the old man's head flopped to the side slackly.

Rudolf Kersten had managed to break his neck even though the tips of his feet were still on the ground.

FIFTEEN

Inspector Margaritis was not pleased with Mavros. It had taken the police nearly an hour to reach the set, during which time Mavros had informed Luke Jannet and Rosie Yellenberg, arranging with the latter for a cordon to be set up by members of the crew between Cara Parks' trailer and the place where Rudolf Kersten lay. He had put a clean handkerchief over the old man's face to protect it from the flies that were already gathering.

The actress returned from the shoot with a shawl over her shoulders. She was tearful and accepted that she couldn't use her trailer until the police had checked it. In the event, Maria Kondos had stayed at the Heavenly Blue to rest.

'What did he say to you when you came out?' Mavros asked.

'He . . . he told me to give . . . to give my all,' she replied, sobbing. 'That she – my character – deserved . . . deserved the best.'

Mavros thought about that. Guilt, or was there something more behind the words? Had he chosen to kill himself or, more likely, been killed when the massacre was being filmed?

'Oh, Alex, he was such a sweet old man. How could he have done that?'

He squeezed her arm and went to meet the inspector. There were several cars, marked and unmarked, in his procession, along with an ambulance.

'What the hell were you doing, Mavro?' Margaritis demanded, after he'd seen the body laid out in the orange grove.

'Hoping I could save his life. His face wasn't distended and he might have still been alive.'

Margaritis watched the technicians as they examined the ground in front of the tree. There weren't any obvious marks among the dusty dead leaves, even from the dead man's feet.

'You realize you're my prime suspect,' the inspector said.

Mavros shrugged. 'Ask around. I was watching the shoot and plenty of people must have seen me. Then I spoke to David

Waggoner and the security man outside the trailer. Kersten had left half an hour before, according to him.'

'Don't worry, I will be asking around. In the meantime, you'll be sitting in a police car with this pair of beauties.'

Two uniformed officers stepped forward.

'Phone,' Margaritis demanded, extending a hand.

Knowing that cooperation was the only way to go, Mavros gave him his mobile.

'Search him.'

The older and more corpulent policeman subjected him to a less than subtle body search, handing the inspector his notebook and wallet.

Mavros watched as a doctor knelt down by Rudolf Kersten. He was about to point out his broken neck, but decided anything he said might count against him. The cops took his arms and walked him to a squad car, where he was put in the back seat with the windows closed. In the sultry heat, he tried to make sense of what was going on.

He was almost certain that Kersten had been murdered – that his neck had been broken before he'd been strung up – but he had doubts the police would see it that way, even if they cleared him. So who could be in the frame? David Waggoner, although highly antagonistic to the dead man, had been on the platform throughout the shoot – Mavros had glanced round and seen him several times, including once when he was speaking on his mobile. Two possibilities struck him – either some local, maybe encouraged by Waggoner and enraged, as Mavros himself had been, by the film's stirring up of old horrors, had taken a long-standing vendetta to its conclusion; or, that the killing had nothing to do with the film or the war, but rather was connected to Kersten's silver collection. Did Oskar Mesner, the old man's grandson, have the balls to kill him? That thought didn't make Mavros feel good, considering he had been the one to humiliate the young German and take the coins back from him. But, despite Mesner's involvement with the far-right in Germany and Greece, he doubted that murder was in his repertoire – not even getting some other skin-headed bastard to do it.

Then he thought of Waggoner's dinner companion Tryfon Roufos, the extremely bent antiquities dealer cum thief. He had never heard rumours of Roufos using violence, though he certainly used common criminals to steal ancient objects and icons. It didn't seem likely that a robbery would have happened in the orange grove, unless blackmail had been involved. Had Waggoner fed Roufos information about the German's role in the war, forcing the old man to bring pocketfuls of coins to the set, and the exchange accidentally turned to murder? If it had, Mavros found it less than likely that the men involved would have wasted time faking Kersten's suicide.

He heard shrieks from behind the car and looked round. He had phoned Hildegard Kersten before Margaritis arrived, but hadn't told her that her husband was dead. Some insensitive bastard must have broken the news when she arrived. He watched her run past, her hair loose and her feet kicking up dust.

'Let me out,' he said to the cops in front. 'That's the widow. I'm working for her.' Strictly speaking, it was an untruth, but he wanted to help the old woman cope with her husband's death, even though he knew that would be no easy task.

'Tough shit,' the bulky sergeant said. 'You're here to sweat like the rest of us.'

A few minutes later, the radio crackled into activity.

'Bring the dick to the scene,' said Margaritis. 'Hands off him.'

Obviously Hildegard Kersten had applied her husband's considerable standing in the community to bring the inspector round. The cops glared at him as he got out of the car. Fortunately the T-shirt he'd borrowed from his brother-in-law was extra large, so it didn't stick to him as much as one of his own would have.

The widow was standing a few yards in front of her husband – the crime scene team having already given up on trying to find footprints. At least the doctor had put the handkerchief back on the dead man's face.

'I'm terribly sorry,' Mavros said, standing behind Hildegard.

'Ah, there you are, Alex,' she said, in English. 'This ridiculous man says you're a suspect. I told him . . .' Suddenly she started to sob loudly again, though that quickly became silent weeping. Mavros put his arm around her and she huddled against him. 'I want . . . I want you to find out who . . . who killed Rudi,' she said, looking up at him with tear-filmed blue eyes. 'They say . . . they say he probably committed suicide. He would . . . he would never do . . . that to me.'

Mavros looked over her grey head to Margaritis, who was looking at him with undisguised hostility.

'You're saying it's suicide?'

The inspector looked down. 'The forensic surgeon will carry out a post-mortem, but our initial feeling is that Mr Kersten hanged himself, yes.'

'Which means I'm a free man,' Mavros said, extending his hand. 'My things, please.'

Margaritis couldn't argue with that. 'Over here, please, Mr Mavro,' he said.

'Excuse me a moment,' Mavros said to the widow.

'This is not over,' the inspector said. 'We'll be checking your movements very carefully, you Athenian scumbag. And, by the way, I understand English. If you get in the way of my investigation or step out of line by a millimetre, you're dog food.'

'My things, please.' Mavros got back his phone, wallet and notebook.

'By the way,' Margaritis said, with a sharp smile. 'You should be careful. I hear the Kornariates want to drink your blood.'

Mavros raised his shoulders. 'If you people had done your job, Kornaria would be a normal, law-abiding village.'

The inspector's eyes opened wide, but he managed to keep his mouth shut. Mavros went back to the widow.

'Come, I'll take you home,' he said softly.

'No, I'm going . . . I'm going with Rudi,' she protested, but eventually allowed herself to be steered out of the trees.

Mikis was standing with Yerasimos beside the Mercedes that had brought Rudolf Kersten to his place of ending. Hildegard headed for the big car, dismissing the driver who had brought her.

'Follow us,' Mavros said to Mikis. 'I think I'm going to need you.'

In the limousine, Hildegard sank back in the leather and inhaled. 'I can smell my Rudi,' she said, then steeled herself. 'Whatever the police and their idiot doctors say, I know Rudi was murdered. You will help me, Alex?'

'It's rather out of my area of expertise.' He was still troubled by his anger against the dead man but, even if he had taken part in the massacre, Hildegard was in no way to blame.

'If money is the problem . . .'

'No, no, you've already shown how generous you can be.' Mavros looked through the tinted glass at the villas alongside the road, then turned back to her. 'I'll need to ask some difficult questions.'

The widow looked at him unwaveringly. 'I have no secrets from you, Alex.'

'Did your husband keep any secrets from you?'

'No,' she said emphatically. 'What do you want to know?'

Mavros took out his notebook, and then closed it. After its recent confiscation by Margaritis, he didn't want to put anything potentially incriminating in it.

'All right,' he said, 'assuming it is murder, who do you think could have done it and why?'

'David Waggoner,' she said, without hesitation. 'He has always hated Rudi.'

'Why?'

Hildegard gave him a sharp look. 'Because of the war, of course.'

'Yes, but specifically?'

'Oh, because of the massacre at Makrymari. You know about it?'

Mavros nodded. 'Your husband took part in it.'

'No!' she cried, causing Yerasimos to look in the mirror. 'I'm sorry. No, Alex, that isn't true. He was forced by a vile captain to stand in the firing squad, but he had suffered a serious head wound and he collapsed when the execution started.'

'He told you that?'

'Yes, but he also wrote it down as a kind of memoir. It's in the safe back at the hotel. It's in German.'

They had already established that he didn't speak the language.

'Is there anything about Waggoner in it?'

'Yes,' she said. 'That's just the point. Rudi was in the battle at Galatsi and he describes a fair-haired and stocky British officer in a tank. He later saw the same man shooting wounded Germans in the head.'

Jesus, Mavros thought. The Battle of Crete was like a tumour in the island's entrails, a stain on its history that contaminated the present.

'How did your husband survive the fighting?'

'He was saved by that woman, the one known as Black Katina. On the day he landed, he had avoided killing her.'

Now Mavros understood Rudolf Kersten's actions at the memorial wall and his words to Cara Parks before the recreation of the massacre. He felt ashamed of his anger.

'Why would Waggoner wait for so many years?' he asked.

'Because he'd been blackmailing Rudi since we came to Crete. How do you think he could afford that house up in the mountains? He hasn't worked since he was drummed out of the British Army. Now we have little except the apartment, which is on a lifelong peppercorn lease. The resort has been sold and all our property in Germany liquidated. Rudi told him there would be no more money last month.'

'Not quite everything,' Mavros said. 'There's the coin collection.'

'Yes, there is. Rudi's precious silver. I never liked his collecting those objects. He should have given them all to museums.'

'As he did with the Jewish relics.'

Hildegard looked at him. 'You already know much about us.'

'Not enough, apparently.' He told her about Waggoner's location during the film shoot.

'Ach, that is nothing. He would have used the grandson of one of his *andartes* in the war.'

'Maybe. Have you considered that your own grandson might be involved?'

She stared at him with undisguised horror, as the Mercedes stopped at the gate of the Heavenly Blue. 'Oskar? No . . . it's impossible. He doesn't have the nerve to do something so awful.'

'He has some unpleasant friends.'

'Those fools with the shaven heads and the big boots? Straw men, all of them. They wouldn't dare.'

'Your grandson did steal those thirty coins.'

'He's lazy – a leech. His father died when he was three and his mother spoiled him, not that she ever had much. He grew up in the East after reunification – she found some man there, a spendthrift who tried to get money from Rudi. He was always strict with Franziska, so they never got more than the minimum to supplement their benefits. And before you ask, both our daughter and he are dead, in a car crash ten years ago.'

'I'm sorry,' Mavros said, getting out of the car. Yerasimos held the door open for Hildegard. 'Is there someone you can call to sit with you?'

'We have many friends on Crete, but I prefer to be on my own now.' The widow gave him a brief smile. 'Don't worry, I'm not what the police doctors would call suicidal. Knock on the door or call if you need anything.' She kissed his cheek.

'Thank you, Alex. You don't know how much this means to me.'

Mavros watched her go, the weight of her sorrow pressing down on him. Then he remembered something and ran after her.

'One more thing,' he said. 'Do you know a Tryfon Roufos?'

'Horrible man!' Hildegard exclaimed. 'He's been badgering Rudi for months about the silver collection. Only a few days ago, they had words on the telephone.' She walked towards the apartment door, the staff bowing to her, their faces tear-stained.

Mikis appeared at his shoulder. 'This is terrible. I can't believe Mr Kersten killed himself.'

'He didn't. Let's go and find the fuckers who made it look like he did.'

'So, left or right?' Mikis asked, as they went past the resort gate in the Jeep.

'Left for Chania,' Mavros replied. 'Now that Maria Kondos is out of the clinic, what are your pals up to?'

'Their jobs. Why? Do you need them again?'

'Maybe later. I've found out some interesting things.' He told the Cretan about Waggoner's blackmailing of the Kerstens and Roufos's attempts to buy his silver collection.

'I always thought the Englishman was a piece of shit,' Mikis said, accelerating past a tractor. 'I've seen plenty of those guys at the battle celebrations and they're friendly enough – even the Germans. But Waggoner always seemed to be on his own, as if even his former comrades didn't like his smell.'

'You know anything about the communists on Crete during the war?' Mavros asked, wondering again about his father's role.

'Not much. There weren't many of them to start with and those that stayed were pretty well boxed in by the resistance leaders and the British.'

'Waggoner claimed he was betrayed by one of them.'

'That cache of silver was to be shipped to Egypt. According to my grandfather, who was a shepherd in Selino, with contacts in the resistance, the Germans killed most of the *andartes*, as well as the monks at Ayios Athanasios, and grabbed the loot.'

'That's right. According to Waggoner, an EAM operative known as Kanellos tipped off the occupiers.'

'No, that's rubbish,' the driver said, slowing as they reached the city limits. 'The informer was one of Waggoner's own Cretans. He killed the man himself after he came back from Egypt. My grandfather knew the guy – he'd been tortured by the Germans and his family had been threatened. Standard occupiers' tactics.'

Mavros blinked away the sudden film of tears that had covered his eyes. So his father hadn't been a rat. He'd never really believed he was, but the confirmation made him feel much better. It also showed that David Waggoner had lied in his memoir. Was he embarrassed about shooting one of his own men – his admission to such an act earlier made that unlikely – or by his lack of judgement in trusting the man?

'Shit, I've just remembered something.' Mikis pulled to the side without warning, provoking a blast on the horn from the driver behind, and took out his phone. 'Hey, Dad,' he said, after speed-dialling. He ran through the story and then asked where the traitor had come from. 'OK, thanks, see you later,' he signed off, turning to Mavros. 'Thought as much. The traitor was from Kornaria.'

'What a surprise,' Mavros said, with a wry smile.

'Yeah. Achilleas Kondoyannis was his name.'

'Kondoyannis? What the hell?'

Mikis nodded. 'The name the guy in the *kafeneion* gave us.'

'A relative? People called Kondoyannis emigrating to the USA might easily have shortened their name to Kondos.'

'Right,' the Cretan said, smiling at the pun – 'kondos' was Greek for 'short'. 'Maria Kondos. You think that's why she was up there? Some kind of payback for the disgrace some relative brought on the village?'

'The village where, as we know, vendettas are a speciality. It certainly needs to be checked out. Let's get back to the Heavenly Blue and talk to the less-than-talkative Maria.'

'I thought she'd started speaking again.'

'Not much.'

Mikis applied full lock and turned the Jeep back the way they'd come.

In the hotel, Mavros ran up to his room and booted up his laptop. A search for 'Kondoyannis USA' brought up numerous references, though not as many as 'Kondos USA'. Cross-referencing them would be a long job. He was about to give up and go in search of Maria when a newspaper headline caught his eye – 'Florida Mobster Kondoyannis Jailed'. Maybe the surname hadn't been changed, after all. The article was dated January 17th 2003 and described the end of the trial of Michael 'the Bat' Kondoyannis, fifty-seven, boss of one of northern Florida's 'most vicious' criminal organizations. Born in Tallahassee, 'the Bat', so named for his use of a metal alloy baseball bat to deal with his enemies, had risen to the top of a gang run by Greek immigrants, originally from the island of Crete. Initially, they had been involved in illegal gambling and robberies, but in the last twenty years had controlled a significant part of the drugs trade in the South. Scrolling down, Mavros found a photograph of the mobster, a bull-chested man with short black curly hair. His features, including heavy rings beneath the eyes, were certainly Greek. He had been convicted of heroin, marijuana and hashish trafficking, using shipping containers supposedly full of olive oil, and of two murders. It was suspected he had links with organized crime in Sicily and other parts of the Mediterranean. Then there was another photo, this time of 'the Bat' with his family before his arrest. Next to a short, plump woman stood a figure with long black hair – his daughter Maria. There was no doubt that she was Cara Parks' assistant. Presumably she had changed her name when she went to Hollywood. That was one of several things he needed urgently to ask her.

Before he could get out of the door, his phone rang.

'Alex, it's Cara.'

'Oh, hi. Is your assistant with you?'

'That's just it. I expected she'd be in my suite when I came back from the shoot – she stayed there to handle the backlog of fan mail – but she wasn't. I still have a card to her suite, so I checked. She isn't there. I've asked at reception and no one has seen her, even though she's still in that wheelchair. Apparently the shift changed. They're contacting the people who were on duty, but no news yet.'

'Here we go again. Tell me, did you know that Maria's father is a recently jailed Florida mobster of Cretan stock?'

'What? You must be joking.' The actress sounded genuinely surprised.

'No, I'm not. The question is, was she involved in the family business?'

'That's ridiculous, Alex. She wouldn't have time . . .'

'Really? Might only take a few phone calls a day to ensure the drugs were running into LA smoothly.'

There was a pause. 'And that mountain village she was in grows dope, doesn't it?'

'Kornaria? Oh, yes, in a big way. And guess what – David Waggoner's got a house up there. Are you sure you never saw them in conversation?'

This time there was a longer silence. 'I don't know. Maybe when we were preparing for the Galatsi battle scenes.'

'Any raised voices?'

'I . . . I don't know. I don't remember.'

'All right.'

'Alex, you will find Maria, won't you? You will finish the case?'

He said he would try and hung up. It looked like all roads led to Kornaria, where the locals would shoot him before saying '*Kali mera*'.

SIXTEEN

Before going any further, Mavros called Niki. She sounded tired.

'What is it, my love?'

'The job, of course,' she said sharply, then, 'I'm sorry, Alex. Sometimes it's too much, the endless stream of people coming to Greece, thinking their lives will improve overnight. There's a limit to the jobs I can find them.' She took a deep breath. 'Anyway, when are you coming home?'

He'd been expecting the question. 'You're not going to believe this – the woman I found has disappeared again.'

'And there I was thinking you'd got yourself involved in the Rudolf Kersten death. Some of the news bulletins are hinting there was foul play.'

Mavros had been hoping Niki wouldn't have seen the news – she didn't always watch it as she thought most journalists were liars.

'I don't know,' he said. 'The cops here are saying it was probably suicide.'

'So you *are* involved?'

'Well, the widow has asked me to help find the killer – if there was one.'

There was a pause as she filled her lungs. 'Get back here, Alex Mavro. You know how these cases end – with you facing death and your bill unpaid. Come back tomorrow. Tonight, if they'll give you their stupid Learjet.'

'That's not going to happen, Niki,' he said firmly. 'You've got to let me do my job.'

'Oh, fine. And what am I supposed to do? Sit here waiting to hear that some lunatic Cretan villagers have chopped you to pieces?'

He gave a weak laugh. 'Don't be ridiculous. It's not like that down here on the coastal strip.'

'Alex, please. Come back home. I miss you.'

'I'll get back as soon as I can. Promise. I've got to run now.

Love you.' He cut the connection, disturbed by how close Niki's imagination was to reality. All he'd done was buy himself some time – she'd be back on his case tomorrow.

He rang the Fat Man.

'I see the German's dead,' Yiorgos said, after they'd exchanged unpleasantries. 'You wouldn't happen to be involved in that case too, would you?'

Mavros filled him in.

'Sounds to me like you've got too much on your plate. Maybe I should come down.'

The idea of the Fat Man stomping around antagonizing people in the luxury resort wasn't appealing, though he might have been useful in Kornaria.

'No, thanks.' He told him about Michael 'the Bat' Kondoyannis. 'See if you can dig up anything about him and Crete. His family came from Kornaria.'

'He was a drug dealer and he came from Afghanistan, Crete? It wouldn't take a genius to work out where he got his supplies.'

'Some of them, at least. But I want more than deductions, Fat Man. See if you can dig up something concrete about him.'

'Concrete, as in the stuff the mob puts on people's feet before chucking them overboard?'

'Very funny. I found out something else.' He told Yiorgos what Mikis had told him about his father when he had been known as Kanellos, and the lie told by Waggoner.

'So an agent of the imperial power sets up a Communist. How unusual. I take it you'll be having words with the shit-head.'

'Soon enough. In the meantime, I've got a rendezvous with a Hollywood starlet.'

'Screw you,' the Fat Man said harshly. 'Then again, if *she* does that, Niki will hang your intestines from your mother's balcony.'

'Over and out,' Mavros said, heading for the door.

The man on the other side was wearing black clothes and a matching balaclava. Only the long knife in his right hand provided any contrast. Its point pierced Mavros's T-shirt before he walked rapidly backwards into his room.

From *The Descent of Icarus*:

I came round in another field hospital, this one in the grounds of a Cretan prison. The inmates were all gone, most of them, I learned, killed when they joined the locals in the battles against the mountain troops who had flooded the west of the island from Maleme. My head was pounding and every movement provoked worse pain. I slid my hand up slowly and felt a bandage swathing my skull.

'Ah, the brave paratrooper has woken up,' said a sardonic voice.

I looked up at the doctor who was standing by my bed. His white hair was cut short at the sides and he wore a moustache like Himmler's – clearly the kind of martinet who wished he was in the SS but had been deemed too old. The army was less choosy.

'How long have I been out?' My voice sounded tinny, as if it came from outside my body.

'Your three-day coma has apparently rendered you unable to use the customary terms of address.'

'I'm sorry, sir,' I mumbled, my interest in military discipline long gone.

'Your captain – what's his name?'

I didn't know if it was a test, but I found that my memory was working adequately.

'Blatter.'

'Indeed. Captain Blatter, who, you'll be pleased to learn, has been awarded the Iron Cross Class One by General Student, thinks you're a coward and a malingerer.' The doctor gave me a tight smile. 'I have no opinion about the former, but I seriously doubt you've been faking the comas you've been in. Here's my difficulty. We are unable to treat head injuries such as yours on Crete. We therefore will have to send you to Athens, from where I would hazard that you'll be returned to the Fatherland and discharged from the parachute division – meaning you'll spend the rest of the war stamping papers or fire-watching. Meanwhile, your unit has been ordered to leave the island tomorrow to take part in a major operation elsewhere.' He glanced at my chart. 'So how do you feel today, Private?'

I didn't know what he was trying to do – maybe he felt a trained paratrooper shouldn't be wasted even if he had a potentially catastrophic head injury, or maybe he wanted to see if Blatter was right about me being a coward. In any case, after what I'd seen at Makrymari, I had a single imperative – I was going to prove myself to the captain and then I was going to kill him. For myself? For the executed woman? I've never been able to decide. Maybe it was for both of us, victims of the war in our different ways.

Blatter welcomed me back to the unit with an ironic smile and a sarcastic remark, but he had more important things to think about. A month later we were storming into the Soviet Union, but as ground forces. After the Pyrrhic victory on Crete, Hitler had decreed there would be no more airborne assaults, so we fought alongside the ordinary army troops and the cold-eyed bastards of the Waffen-SS. Blatter's zeal began to waver after two months of the winter, but I bided my time. I wanted him to be in full disarray before I ended his life.

That happened in early spring, when the birds on the great Ukrainian plain had started to sing again and the first shoots of grass had begun to appear under our ragged boots. We were ordered to attack a Red Army stronghold by a small river, and Blatter's nerve finally went. I stepped up and said to his second-in-command, a Bavarian lieutenant named Wanner, that I'd look after the captain, taking my Luger from its holster and putting the muzzle against Blatter's back.

We moved forward in an extended line, taking heavy machine-gun fire at several points. We had artillery support and that eventually pounded the enemy into disarray, not that they surrendered. After the last of them had been mopped up, I pushed the captain into a command post filled with shattered bodies and took out my service bayonet.

'This is for the woman in Crete,' I said. 'And for me.'

He started to beg, dropping to his knees, which made it easier for me to slide the blade slowly into his mouth and upwards into his brain.

That was the end of the real war for me. I fought on, robot-like, but I remember few details. I was always the first to charge forward, the first to volunteer for suicidal missions, the last to turn tail when the great Soviet advance commenced. I expected every day to be my last, but I survived. It was as if I was under the protection of some jealous god. Eventually I could refuse promotions no longer and did what I could to protect the ever-younger, doe-eyed recruits from the inevitable. I was even given medals, which I accepted on behalf of my men. My unit was finally cut to pieces in western Poland and I dropped my decorations into the River Oder as the last of the great expedition staggered back into our homeland.

After the war I was still in some parallel world, passing through camps and offices until I was declared clean of the stain of Nazism and free to remake my life. Which I did, after I met Hildegard.

But my heart had never left Crete and I returned as soon as I could to live out my days near the places where the dark-haired woman and I had saved each other's lives; and where I had failed to give her death from a compassionate hand.

When Mavros got further into the room, he saw there were two more balaclava-clad men behind the one with the knife. The latter pushed him backwards so he landed on the sofa. Then he went behind it and held the edge of the knife against Mavros's throat. The shorter of the others sat down in the armchair on the other side of the coffee table, while the third stood alongside him. None of them were wearing Cretan boots or other garb.

'You move, you lose your Adam's apple,' said the seated man, in Greek.

Mavros didn't recognize the voice, but the accent was definitely Cretan.

He decided that moving his tongue and lips was an unnecessary risk.

'You're in luck, you know,' the man opposite continued. The bared teeth in the balaclava's slit suggested he was smiling. 'I mean, you could already be dead. A vendetta isn't something you Athenian ponces should take lightly. So we're here to teach you a lesson.' He paused for effect. 'Cut his throat.'

Mavros was instantly drenched in cold sweat, his heart thundering. The knife blade was moved round his throat, nicking the skin. Then he felt warm drops on his forearms. He was about to duck out of the position, even though he knew such a movement would only bring death more quickly, when he thought of his father. Spyros was looking at him steadily, dark-blue eyes willing him to hold his nerve. Mavros stayed still and got his breathing under control, as the knife continued its light pressure round his neck.

'Enough,' the man in the armchair ordered, a hint of

disappointment in his voice. 'You're a cool one, Mavro. But this
is your last warning. Go back to Athens by tonight or next time
you'll be drinking your own blood.' He came over, then took a
wide roll of duct tape from his pocket, pulled off a length and
held it up for the man with the knife to cut. A moment later, the
tape was over Mavros's mouth. Then the rest of the roll was
wrapped round his body, binding his arms to his sides and pressing
his legs together.

'You'd better hope you never see us again,' the leader said, as
one of the others checked the corridor through the spyhole in
the door.

They left, closing the door softly behind them.

Spyros had faded from view and now Mavros did begin to
panic, unaware how deep the cut in his throat was but feeling
pain. How long would it take for him to bleed out?

Mikis was standing by the Jeep in the hotel car park. Mavros
had asked him to hang around while he made some calls. The
sun was sinking over the high ground to the west and bats were
flitting about the oleanders and palm trees. Despite the Kornaria
vendetta, Mikis was at peace with the world. His father would
sort those idiot mountain men out one way or another and, if it
came to another fight, he was ready. He hadn't told Mavros that
this wasn't the first vendetta his family had been involved in,
even though they were much rarer than they used to be. An uncle
on his mother's side had been accused of stealing the woman
who became his wife from a village on Mount Psiloritis. Shots
had been fired, including some by the seventeen-year-old Mikis;
nobody had been badly hurt and money had exchanged hands.
He didn't think the Kornariates would be so open to
compromise.

Mikis thought about Mavros. He was different, to put it mildly,
and not just because of his long hair and weird eye. He was
subtle and understated, perhaps from his Scottish genes, but he
didn't give up, and he was decisive when he had to be – as when
he'd hit the shotgun-wielding hard man on the head with that
rock. But he was secretive as well, something which wasn't a
good idea when armed men were after you. Mikis knew there
were aspects to the Maria Kondos case the detective hadn't shared,
and he suspected the same applied to Rudolf Kersten.

Then he saw them – three men in black shirts and trousers coming out of the hotel. Their pockets were bulging and one of them had failed to conceal the haft of a knife up his sleeve. All three had hair cut almost to their scalps and he recognized the shortest of them. He took out his mobile and called Mavros. No answer. Looking over his shoulder, he saw the large red pickup they were getting into and noted its registration number. Then he ran like hell for the hotel.

Mavros heard the pounding on his door from the floor, where he had managed to slide from the sofa. He tried to shout through the duct tape, but all that came out was a stifled moan.

Then he heard Mikis's voice, saying he was going to get help. While he was waiting, he tried to wriggle across the floor, but the blood on the tiles scared him and he rolled on to his back to reduce the flow.

Eventually – though it couldn't have been long – he heard voices in the hall and a key card slip into the slot above the handle. Mikis pushed past the hulking figure of Renzo Capaldi and knelt down beside him.

'Jesus Christ, Alex,' he said, bending over. 'Are you all right? This is going to hurt.' He picked off a corner of the tape and then ripped it from Mavros's mouth.

'Fuck!'

'Told you.' Mikis looked over his shoulder. 'Find a knife or some scissors.' Capaldi went to the desk against the wall and came back with a pair of the latter.

'You've lost a lot of blood,' the Cretan said.

Capaldi, who was cutting through the tape on Mavros's chest, shook his head. 'Throat wounds look worse than they are, as long as the jugular veins aren't affected, and his are OK.'

'And you know this how?' Mikis asked, easing Mavros into a sitting position.

'Ten years in the Fifth Alpini.' The Italian smiled. 'Elite mountain regiment.'

'Really?' Mikis said, unimpressed. 'How do you feel, Alex?'

'I'm . . . I'm all right apart from my throat. Can you get a cloth or something?'

Mikis came back from the bathroom with a pile of luxurious white towels. Capaldi raised an eyebrow but didn't comment.

'We're going to the clinic,' Mikis said, helping Mavros to his feet.

Capaldi followed them out and closed the room door. 'Anything else I can do?'

'Yes,' Mavros said. 'Call Rosie Yellenberg and get her to advise the West Crete Clinic to expect us.' He had an afterthought. 'And don't tell Mrs Kersten about this.'

'Didn't you see three men in black come in?' Mikis demanded, as they reached the lift. 'Three arseholes with "bad man" written all over their shaven heads?'

Capaldi shook his head. 'I can check the gate cameras.'

'Forget it,' the Cretan said. 'I'll handle it.'

'So masterful,' Mavros said, as they went out into the evening.

'Don't talk,' Mikis ordered, getting him into the Jeep and then heading for the gate at speed. 'Here's what I saw.' He told Mavros about the three men as they pulled away past a line of cars – the press pack was present in even greater strength. 'Unfortunately I didn't see them go in or I'd have been on their tails in a flash.'

'They had a knife,' Mavros croaked.

'I noticed. I've got their pickup's number, but I already know who the short guy was.'

'The leader.'

'Yeah.' Mikis glanced at him. 'Keep that towel tight on the wound or you'll have a nasty scar.'

'Who is he?'

'Petros Lagoudhakis. A far-right scumbag who runs his own band of crazies. They call themselves the Cretan Renaissance, but they're too dumb to do anything other than shout insults outside the Jewish Museum and goose-step around the back-streets. He was in the Black Eagle the night we created mayhem.'

Mavros told him about the threat that he leave Crete that night.

'It doesn't sound like the kind of thing they'd do themselves. Someone's paying them.'

Mavros thought about that. Oskar Mesner was into neo-Nazi shit, but why would he want him off the island? Did he think his grandfather's coin collection would be an easier target now the old man was dead? Or could Tryfon Roufos, the bent antiquities trader, be using local muscle? If that was the case, was David Waggoner involved too, given their close huddle at dinner in the taverna? And Waggoner was a link back to Kornaria, with his house up there.

'You don't think our friends in the mountains might have subcontracted the work?'

'If they had, I doubt you'd be talking to me now. Keep quiet!'

He pulled up to the clinic entrance. A few minutes later, Mavros was under the lights, having been sprayed with a local anaesthetic, while stitches were skilfully applied. One thing he was sure of – no way was he leaving the island. This was all getting far too personal.

Mavros emerged from the room where he'd been treated half an hour later.

'Christ and the Holy Mother,' Mikis said, crossing himself. 'If they'd put a couple of bolts on, you'd be a dead ringer for Boris Karloff.'

'Highly amusing. Come on.'

'Don't you have to rest? They shot you full of drugs, didn't they?'

Mavros nodded. 'See, I can move my head without it falling off.' He touched the dressing that ran from under one ear to the other. 'For the time being. Which means there's no time to lose.'

'Where are we going?'

'Isn't it obvious?' Mavros said, pointing towards the centre of Chania.

'You're not serious.'

Mavros looked at his watch. 'Coming up to ten. They should be in the Black Eagle by now.'

Mikis opened the door of the Jeep for him. 'They and about twenty others of their species.'

'I take it you've got that Colt with you.'

The Cretan stared at him as he put the key into the ignition. 'You've lost your mind, my friend. I can't go into a bar in the centre of Chania waving it around.'

Mavros smiled. 'No, of course not.' He waited till Mikis had driven away from the clinic. 'But I can.'

There was a squeal of burning rubber as Mikis hit the brakes. There was a loud horn blast from the car behind. He drove on, shaking his head.

'I'm not giving you it, Alex. You're so doped up you'll hardly be able to lift it.'

'Too bad. I'm serious, Miki. How do you feel about what those wankers did to me?'

That hit the spot. Cretans took hospitality and the safety of those under their protection very seriously.

'All right,' the driver said, 'but I'm doing the shooting.'

'Who knows?' Mavros said, with a smile. 'Maybe it won't even come to that.'

Mikis glanced at him. 'You want a bet?'

SEVENTEEN

Hildegard Kersten was at her husband's desk in their apartment, papers and memorabilia all over it. Rudi had destroyed most of his wartime documentation, though he had kept his paratrooper's jump badge, with the gilt eagle diving earthwards over a silvered oak leaf and acorn wreath. He'd never told her why he would often look at it, though she was sure he felt no residual loyalty to the unit – at the memorial services in the official cemetery, he kept away from the other survivors. Having read *The Descent of Icarus*, she was sure it reminded him of the woman he had been obsessed by. She'd never been jealous of that obsession, which dated from long before she knew Rudi and was not in any way erotic or sexual. He admired the woman, seeing her as a heroine who died for her homeland rather than allow it to be overrun by the invader; he wished that he could have been a defender of his homeland too, though not the ruined Germany he had fought in during the last months of the war. The false dream of the paratroopers had long vanished by then, as had most of the men.

She supposed she would have to get all Rudi's things in some sort of order for the lawyer who would execute the will. There would be a pension and the use of the apartment till she died, but there was little of monetary value apart from the jump badge, which she would never sell, and his coin collection, which was to be donated to various museums in Crete and mainland Greece. Oskar would soon find that out – or perhaps Rudi had already told him, prompting his stealing of the thirty coins. No, Rudi would never have done that without telling her first. They didn't have secrets. Those coins were only a small part of the total, which numbered over six hundred. Some were badly worn Roman *sestertii* of negligible value, but others – the magnificent Syracusan *dekadrachms*, the perfect Athenian 'owls', the Venetian ducats and *scudos* – were worth a lot of money. But that was of no concern to her. She would hand them over to the museums Rudi had indicated after his funeral.

Ah, the funeral, she thought, struggling to find the energy to proceed with the arrangements. Several of the hotel staff had offered to help. Rudi had always said that he wanted to be cremated and his ashes thrown to the winds, but that was not done in Greece and she didn't want either the expense or the trouble involved in shipping his body to the nearest crematorium in Bulgaria, a country neither of them had ever visited. She wondered whether to ask the priest at Makrymari if her husband could be buried outside the cemetery wall. He had given plenty of money to the village over the years, even helped to rebuild the church, but she wasn't sure if she wanted to impose on the descendants of the massacre. It didn't seem right. The easiest thing would be to bury Rudi in the grounds of the Heavenly Blue, but she had a feeling the new owners would not like that.

The phone started to ring. For a while she left it untouched, then picked it up and murmured her name.

'Grandma?' came Oskar's voice. 'I'm so sorry. I've been out of town. I only heard a few minutes ago. I'm on my way.'

'No!' Hildegard said, surprising herself by the strength of her voice. 'No, Oskar, not tonight. I am . . . I am very tired.'

'You don't sound tired.'

'What's that? I can hardly hear you. Where are you?'

'In a bar,' her grandson shouted. 'Raising a glass to Grandpa's memory.'

As if you ever cared about your grandfather, Hildegard thought.

'I'll come tomorrow and help you sort out the coin collection,' he continued, making no effort to conceal his interest it. 'You know Grandpa would have wanted me to have it.'

'I know no such thing, Oskar. The collection is to be split between various museums.'

All she could hear was shouting and the thump of loud music.

'That . . . that cannot be,' her grandson said, his voice cracking. 'The coins are for me.'

'Come over tomorrow and I'll show you the will,' Hildegard said firmly. 'Goodnight.'

After she had replaced the handset, it struck her that she had put herself in a difficult, even dangerous position with Oskar. She would tell Mr Capaldi to let her know when Oskar entered the resort.

It was only when she kicked the bottom of the desk by mistake that a narrow drawer she had never seen before slipped silently open. Inside was a long knife in a canvas and steel sheath. Slowly she bent forward and picked it up, then pulled the silvery blade out. The pommel was in the rough shape of an eagle's head and the grip was dark wood.

Hildegard Kirsten shivered. She had no idea why her husband had kept the fearsome Wehrmacht bayonet, nor why its blade was so brightly polished. Then she noticed something else in the drawer – a silver double axe head about ten centimetres across. She recognized it as a Minoan *labrys* and was aware that Rudi had donated several to museums of Crete and the mainland. She also knew that it had religious significance related to the moon and the mother goddess. But why had her husband kept this one? She was almost certain it was because of his obsession with the woman in the war. That made her feel small and insignificant.

Mavros and Mikis looked round the corner towards the Black Eagle. There were a few misguided tourists sitting outside the bar, but no skinheads.

'Clear about what we're going to do?' Mavros asked, his mouth suddenly dry.

The Cretan nodded, the large pistol under his shirt, which hung loosely over his jeans.

'All right . . . action!'

They walked down the narrow street, keeping close to the walls on the same side as the Black Eagle. When they got to the edge of the bar, Mikis took a cautious look inside.

'They're here,' he said. 'All three of the bastards who wrapped you up plus that German tosser we took the coins from.'

'Any other neo-Nazi types?'

'Not as many as last time. Maybe ten.'

'So it's fourteen to two,' Mavros said, his blood up. 'Or rather three, including Mr Colt.'

'Mr Colt has an eight-round clip,' Mikis said, smiling wickedly.

'Fourteen to ten, then. Piece of piss. Your move.'

The Cretan steeled himself, and then marched quickly into the bar. Mavros kept close behind him. The three men were seated round a metal table, bottles of lager in front of them. Mikis reached the shortest of them before anyone noticed and stuck the pistol's muzzle in his ribs.

'Outside,' he shouted, above the din of the music. 'Only you.'

The other two had started to get up, but they sat down again when they saw the Colt. Meanwhile, Mavros leaned over Oskar Mesner, who was at another table, and spoke into his ear loudly.

'You see the pistol my friend's holding on that fucker over there?'

Mesner nodded rapidly.

'Well, I've got another one,' Mavros said, patting his waist. 'Get up and walk slowly to the street.'

The German obeyed, but as they reached the gaping French windows, he squealed for help in his own language. Mavros pushed him out, while Mikis turned back to the occupants of the Black Eagle, left arm wrapped round his captive's neck.

'Come on, if you've got the balls!' he challenged, holding up the pistol.

One of the Greek skinheads stood up, shouting, 'At them, boys, there are only two—'

The blast of the Colt was thunderous, despite the death metal that had been playing and which abruptly stopped. The skinhead looked at the large hole that had appeared in the plaster behind him and crashed back down on his chair.

'Seven more rounds,' Mikis said. 'Anyone fancy his chances?' He looked around at the cowed young men. 'What a surprise. And don't even think about coming after us.'

Mavros had stuffed a handkerchief into Mesner's mouth as the tourists outside the Black Eagle scurried away down the street. He and Mikis, who had gagged the other man, went the other way. The Jeep had been left as close as possible and they were soon there, with no one on their tails.

'Put your hands out,' Mavros ordered the two men. 'Remember this?' he said to the Greek. He wrapped duct tape around the proffered wrists as Mikis did the same with Oskar Mesner. Then the two men were shoved into the back of the Jeep.

'Here,' Mikis said, handing the Colt to Mavros. 'If they move, shoot them in the knee. At this range, they'll lose a leg, but they'll still have time to spill their guts.'

Mesner and the shaven-headed Cretan sat stiller than statues, even when Mikis went round corners. Ten minutes later they were out of the urban sprawl and in another ten were bumping over a rough track between lines of olive trees. Mikis stopped the Jeep in a small clearing and went to the back of the vehicle. He returned with two spades.

'Out!' he said, hauling the Greek from the back seat.

Mesner followed meekly, his eyes bulging.

Mikis led them into the beam of the headlights and cut the tape from their wrists, laughing as they winced when he ripped the strips off. Mavros was to the rear, covering them with the pistol. Mikis gave each of the captives a spade and stepped back.

'Start digging,' he ordered, and then made the appropriate movement to enlighten Mesner. 'Don't look so surprised,' he said, in English. 'Your fucking soldiers made resistance fighters and civilians do this often enough in the war.'

Mesner looked at Mavros for help, but all he got was a stony stare. He couldn't speak as the gags were still in their mouths, but the sounds he made were piteous.

'Dig!' Mikis said, examining the clasp knife he had just opened. 'Or I'll cut your eyelids off.'

They dug, flinging up spadefuls of dusty earth and small stones. After ten minutes, Mavros nodded to Mikis, who told the skinhead to stop.

'You keep going,' he said to the German. 'That grave isn't nearly deep enough for two.'

A dark stain appeared in Mesner's groin and he sobbed through the gag as he dug on, Mikis standing near him with the second spade in his hands.

'On your knees,' Mavros ordered the other man, lowering the pistol till it was pointed at his face. Then he leaned forward and pulled out the handkerchief.

'Please,' the Cretan gasped, 'please, I'll tell you . . . anything you want to know.'

'I have no doubt about that,' Mavros said. 'The question is, will it be enough to keep you out of that hole?'

The skinhead looked over his shoulder at Mesner, who was up to his knees in the earth. 'Anything,' he pleaded. 'Ask me anything.'

'Name?'

'Petros Lagoudhakis.'

'Who told you to cut me?'

The man's head dropped. 'They'll kill me,' he mumbled. 'And then they'll kill you.'

'Wrong. *I'll* kill you and then take my chances.' He paused and looked over at Mikis. 'Actually, we won't kill you.'

Relief flooded the skinhead's face.

'The weight of the sweet Cretan earth will.'

The man's head dropped again. 'Roufos,' he muttered. 'Tryfon Roufos.'

Mavros hadn't been expecting the antiquities dealer to be so directly involved. 'No one else?' he asked, thinking of David Waggoner.

'No.'

'How did Roufos find you?'

'He . . . he's involved in our organization. He gives money.'

That was less of a surprise. Tryfon Roufos was exactly the kind of slimeball who would use far-right crazies to do his dirty work – he probably agreed with their vile ideology as well.

'And did he give you a reason?'

The skinhead looked up. 'Didn't need one. I was in the Black Eagle when you and your heavy caused chaos the other night. We've been looking for you ever since.'

'Where's Roufos staying?'

'Don't know.' The defeated tone convinced Mavros he was telling the truth.

'How does he contact you?'

'From public phones.'

The sleazy Athenian knew how to handle himself, Mavros thought. Then he wondered about his captive's background.

'Where are you from?'

'What?'

'You heard me.'

'Tavronitis.'

Mikis looked over. 'It's a village near Maleme.'

'Know anyone from Kornaria?'

The man's eyes widened. 'You must be joking. I've never been near the place. Those people are fucking insane.'

'Even by your standards, eh?'

'Hey, they kill people.'

Mavros leaned close. 'While what you do is get your goons

to run a knife across my throat. Miki, this piece of shit is ready to start digging again. Bring the German over here.'

Mesner was dragged across and his gag removed, while the other sodden handkerchief was reinserted into the skinhead's mouth.

'So, Oskar,' Mavros said to the kneeling man, in English. 'What have you got to say for yourself?'

'Please, I don't know anything about what they did to you.'

Mavros brought the Colt's muzzle up to the German's forehead. 'Are you sure about that?'

'Well . . . well, I heard someone was going to teach you a lesson, but I wasn't involved.'

'Uh-huh. And who was that someone?'

'The person Petros named.'

'Tryfon Roufos the antiquities dealer?'

Mesner was shaking. 'I . . . I know who he is, but I've never met him.'

'You haven't talked to him about your grandfather's coin collection on the telephone, by any chance?'

'I . . . yes, I have.'

'When?'

'Last week.'

'You know he's on Crete?'

'Ye . . . yes.'

Mavros reckoned he was being told the truth.

'So the thirty coins you stole weren't anything to do with your grandfather's actions, but a taster for Roufos?'

Mesner scowled. 'You screwed that up.'

'Had a visit from Inspector Margaritis yet?'

'What?'

'There's a chance your grandfather was murdered. Where were you this afternoon?'

Oskar Mesner shook his head violently. 'I . . . I didn't do it. I was in Rethymno.'

'Hope you've got some witnesses.'

'Yes, yes, I have. I was with some of the German boys.'

Mavros laughed. 'They'll be convincing.'

'But I thought my grandfather killed himself.'

'I don't think so, though having a grandson like you could have driven him to it. Three more questions. Do you know David Waggoner?'

'Of course not. I read one of his books. That man hates Germans.'

Mavros believed him. 'How about Maria Kondos?'

'From the film crew? I saw a missing person sign about her.'

Again, Mavros didn't catch any hint of a lie. 'And, last but not least, have you ever been to Kornaria?'

'The drug-growing village? No. I heard they're all madmen up there.'

Mavros nodded. 'Miki,' he called, 'give this shithead his spade back.'

'No, please,' Mesner stammered. 'There's something else I can tell you. The film director, Luke Jannet. A friend of mine buys dope from a guy from Kornaria. He told him that Jannet's family was originally from the village.'

Mavros took a step back and lowered the pistol. That *was* a surprise. Could it be that the director's interest in Maria Kondos was more complicated than he had assumed? After all, he had come to Athens in person to hire him.

'Can we stop now?' Lagoudhakis asked, breathing heavily. He was up to his thighs in the hole.

'Tape up their hands,' Mavros said to Mikis, then gave the skinhead a tight smile. 'And that asshole's mouth. I want their mobiles as well.'

Mikis came back with the spades and phones.

'How long will it take them to get back to civilization?' Mavros asked as the Jeep was turned round.

'If they follow us, an hour or so.'

'Maybe we should have tied them to a tree.'

'Showing mercy often has its own rewards,' the Cretan said. 'That's what my grandfather said.'

'The shepherd?'

'No, the one on my mother's side, but I don't think he followed his own advice very often – he was an *andartis*.'

Mavros shrank down in his seat as the adrenaline ebbed away. He wasn't a violent man, but Crete seemed to be turning him into one. Where would it end?

He decided to spend the night in Nondas's place in Chania. Although he didn't have his laptop with him, there was a desktop computer in the flat.

'You want me to stay with you?' Mikis asked, as he pulled up at the end of the street.

'Haven't you got a woman waiting?'

The Cretan smiled. 'Possibly.'

'All right, so go and do your thing. I'll call you in the morning.'

'Don't open the door to any strange people. Sure you don't want to take the Colt?'

'Definitely not. There's a decent selection of kitchen knives up there. Goodnight – and thanks for your help.'

'A pleasure. Pity we didn't bury those scumbags though.' Mikis waited until Mavros opened the street door and then waved as he drove off.

Logging on, Mavros reflected on how lucky he had been to find Mikis – he had local knowledge and connections, as well as the local propensity for strong arm tactics. He'd have to make sure he was suitably recompensed when it was all over. Not that he was at all clear where the latest information was going to lead.

He found numerous sites with information about Luke Jannet – his films, his brief affairs with actresses, his ranch in northern California, but nothing about a Greek family background. He thought about the surname. There was no single letter corresponding to the 'j' sound in Greek – it was formed by the pairing of 't' and 'z'. He tried to think of names beginning 'Tzannet' and one immediately came to mind: there had been a politician who briefly served as prime minister in the late 80s called Tzanis Tzannetakis, although he hadn't been a Cretan. The '–akis' suffix was, however, a standard one on the island.

He typed the surname into a search engine, ignoring all the references to the politician, who had been imprisoned by the Junta and was not the standard money-and-headline-grabbing piece of shit. There was nothing relevant in the first ten pages, after which more random information started to appear. He added the first name 'Luke' to the surname and immediately got a hit – as well as a frisson that ran all the way up his spine.

The site was that of the Sons of Daedalus, Florida Division, a registered charity run by Americans of Cretan origin. On the page recording events in 1991, there was a photograph of major benefactors, the Tzannetakis family – father Eugene – 'owner of a well-known automobile parts supply chain' – mother Koula,

son Luke – 'an up-and-coming film director' – and daughter
Rosa. Luke Jannet was a younger version of his current self, his
hair in a ponytail even then. It was Rosa who drew his attention
most. Although her face was less hard and her body less fleshy,
there was no question that she was the woman who was now
known as Rosie Yellenberg. Another search revealed that she had
married a Hollywood producer called Pete and that the marriage
had ended in divorce four years ago; there had been no
children.

Mavros sat back in his chair. So Luke and his producer were
siblings. Was that significant? It was certainly suggestive that
they hadn't made their family status clear to him, though maybe
some of the film crew knew – as it was that they hadn't declared
their Cretan background, though it was quite possible they didn't
speak the language and had no particular interest in their heritage.
Then again, they had chosen to make a film on the island.

He typed in Eugene Tzannetakis and hit the motherlode on
the first page. According to the *Florida Sun-Times*, the car parts
dealer had been arrested in 1998 on suspicion of using his chain
of stores to facilitate the trafficking of drugs. His family was said
to be from a mountain village in Crete called Kornaria, and
Michael 'the Bat' Kondoyannis was cited as one of his associates. The lawyers had fought hard, citing his charitable work and
donations, and he was sentenced to only eight years, partly
because the FBI had mishandled some of the evidence.

So what exactly was going on here? Luke Jannet and his sister
were descended from a Kornaria family and their father was a
jailed drug trafficker. Maria Kondos's father, who was also from
Kornaria, had been a full-on mobster based in Florida before
being convicted of involvement in the drugs trade. Why had
Maria been in the village and what had happened to her? And
where was she now?

Mavros called the Fat Man.

'What time do you call this, demi-Scot?'

'Time for you to tell me what you found out about Kondoyannis.'

'Oh, that,' Yiorgos said, dismissively. 'I sent you an email.
Remember those?'

Mavros kicked himself for not having checked. Now the Fat
Man was one up on him. He went to his inbox.

'I don't know, I do the work but he just ignores it.'

'Shut up, Yiorgo, I'm reading.' He ran his eye down the page, which was a series of extracts from Cretan and Athenian newspapers, mostly dated from the time of the gangster's arrest.

'He's reading, is he?' the Fat Man continued. 'There was me thinking he was running around the Great Island waving a huge great pistol.'

'I was actually.'

'Really?' Yiorgos's tone changed instantly. 'Did you shoot someone? What kind is it?'

'No, and a Colt Double Eagle.'

'A forty-five?' The Fat Man had always been fascinated by firearms, mainly because he'd never been allowed to use one by the Party.

'Yes, a forty-five. Will you let me read this?'

'I'll save you the bother. The only thing linking "the Bat" to Crete is a trip he made there in 1995. He was given a hero's welcome in Kornaria.'

'What a surprise.'

'During which he met that well-known agent of imperialism David Waggoner.' The Fat Man mangled the Englishman's surname with relish.

Mavros stared at the extract, which said that Kondoyannis had visited the house of the 'wartime British commander', along with the Mayor, Vasilios Dhrakakis.

'Are you still awake?' Yiorgos demanded.

'What? Of course I'm awake. Thanks, Fat Man, this is useful.'

'No chance of you telling me in what way?'

'Er, no. Talk to you tomorrow.' He knew his reticence would drive his friend to distraction.

Too bad. He was even more convinced that everything he was doing on Crete was linked, but he couldn't see exactly how. The idea that the highly decorated former SOE man had got involved in the international drugs trade was surprisingly easy to swallow.

Then his mobile rang. Niki's number was on the screen. He answered with apprehension.

EIGHTEEN

As it turned out, Niki didn't give him a hard time.

'Still busy?' she asked pleasantly.

'Even more than before,' Mavros replied, fingering the dressing on his neck. When she saw that, he'd get several earfuls. 'But I hope to be home in a day or two.'

'Don't worry,' Niki said. 'I'm busy too.'

'Everything all right?' he asked, remembering how disaffected she'd been.

'Oh, the usual stuff, but I can cope. See you soon, my love.'

To his surprise, she rang off. He looked at the phone and tried to work out what lay beneath her strangely buoyant tone, then gave up. He swallowed a couple more of the painkillers, had a shower with a towel round his neck, and collapsed into a dreamless sleep . . .

. . . until the early dawn, when he heard the bell of a nearby church and found himself in the limbo between wakefulness and oblivion. Faces flickered before him – David Waggoner's with its craggy features; Rudolf Kersten's contorted death mask; Hildegard's soft skin; and his father, eyes flashing and lips set in an unmoving smile. Then Waggoner reappeared, leaning forward avidly as he had been when he was with Tryfon Roufos in the taverna. Waggoner, that was what Spyros was telling him – concentrate on the SOE man, who spread lies about me . . .

Mavros sat up with a start. Waggoner had told him he had a place in Chania. With the filming in progress, it seemed likely he would be staying there. Early morning would be the perfect time to catch him unawares. But how to find where he was? The obvious thing would have been to call Rosie Yellenberg, aka Tzannetaki, but he couldn't trust her. There was one person on the production crew he thought was reliable.

'Alice Quincy.' The voice was faint and full of sleep.

'Alex Mavros. Sorry it's so early, but I really need to find David Waggoner.'

'What?' the young woman mumbled. 'I don't understand.'

'You don't have to understand, Alice. It's to do with Maria Kondos going missing again. He may have seen her.' Phrasing the untruth that way reduced his guilt.

'Ah, right. Hang on.' He heard her fingers fly across a keyboard.

'Sarpaki Fourteen,' she said. 'Do you want the phone number?'

'Yes.' He entered it into his mobile's memory. 'Thanks, Alice. Could you do me a favour? My talking to him is a bit sensitive. Could you keep this between us?'

'Oh. OK.'

He cut the connection before she could ask more, then dressed quickly, pulling on a classy striped shirt of his brother-in-law's that flapped about his thin frame.

Odhos Sarpaki was only a few minutes' walk away. Mavros thought about calling Mikis in as back-up, but decided he could handle the old soldier on his own. He'd also borrowed one of Nondas's kitchen knives, one with a worn handle but a very keen edge. He reconsidered ringing Waggoner first, but decided warning him wasn't a good idea. Not for nothing did the police make house raids in the early morning – catch the bad people at their most befuddled.

A seagull took off from the deserted street when he turned the corner, leaving behind a partially consumed chicken carcass. The scent from the flowers on the plants hanging from the wooden balconies covered the whiff of decay. Mavros found number fourteen, which had Waggoner's name neatly printed on a card, and pressed the bell for over half a minute. Then he started pounding on the door.

'Who is it?' came a shocked voice from behind the door, in Greek.

Mavros kept thumping away.

The door opened to reveal David Waggoner in a striped silk dressing gown and leather slippers.

'Morning,' Mavros said, brushing past him. 'You and I need to have a chat.'

'What do you mean coming—'

'What do you mean consorting with known drug traffickers and antiquities thieves?'

That put a stop to the old man's protestations.

'You'd better come up,' he said, heading for the wooden staircase.

The house contained floor tiles and ornate ceilings that suggested it was several hundred years old. On the first floor, a double door led into a large open space, furnished at one end as a *saloni* and the other as a dining room, both full of antique pieces. There were several vases of cut flowers.

'Do you own this place?'

Waggoner nodded.

'And the house at Kornaria? Your army pension must be very generous.'

The old man looked at him combatively. 'I went into business after I left the forces.'

'Yes, that's one of the things I want to talk to you about.'

'What makes you think I'll take part in any conversation?'

'This,' Mavros said, pulling the knife out from under his shirt.

Alarm flashed across Waggoner's face. 'You . . . you wouldn't . . .'

'Strange you haven't asked about this,' Mavros said, pointing at the dressing on his neck.

'What . . . what happened?'

It was clear he was prevaricating. 'You know exactly what your friend Tryfon Roufos ordered.'

Waggoner's head dropped. 'He's not my friend.'

'Business associate, then. You know how untrustworthy he is, don't you?'

'I . . . I've heard things, yes.'

Mavros plunged the knife into the wooden table between them and left it vibrating to and fro. The former SOE man's eyes followed it like those of a small jungle creature being hypnotized by a snake.

'I'm not leaving till I find out what you're doing,' Mavros said, glancing at the knife. 'If you don't want your throat to end up with a deeper cut than mine, start talking. Now!' His anger surprised him – the Cretan urge to violence had taken him over again. Then he remembered that Waggoner had killed many times in the past and watched him even more closely.

'I . . . Roufos made me a proposition.' He hesitated, but continued when he saw the intensity in Mavros's eyes.

'He knew I had free access to the Heavenly Blue – and he found out what I thought about Rudolf Kersten.'

'What was the proposition?'

'That I – what's the expression? – case the joint to see how Kersten's coin collection could be stolen.'

'Uh-huh.' Mavros smiled tightly. 'You know that Roufos was using Rudi Kersten's grandson for the same purpose?'

Waggoner's jaw headed floorwards. 'What? I wasn't aware there was a grandson.'

'Oskar Mesner. He's here in Chania. Coincidentally, he knows the neo-fascist shit-heads Roufos got to tickle my throat. In fact, your pal Roufos contributes to an organization of far-right head-bangers who go around goose-stepping and giving Nazi salutes as they beat up immigrants. What do you feel about that?'

Waggoner was clearly taken aback. 'I don't know anything about it.'

'I always find it's a good idea to do basic research on people before you go into business with them.' The words rung hollow in Mavros's ears – he'd only recently discovered essential information about Luke Jannet and his sister. 'Anyway, what was your interest? You've been blackmailing Kersten for years. Did you want to take every single thing of his, even via a bastard like Roufos?'

'The man was a hypocrite and a murderer. He deserved to die on the street.'

'As opposed to an orange grove not far from where you were watching the massacre shoot.'

Waggoner glared at him. 'What are you implying? I had nothing to do with his death.'

'Don't worry, I saw where you were sitting. But maybe you got one of your bandits from Kornaria to do the deed.'

'That's ridiculous,' the Englishman blustered, but he lowered his gaze again.

'Or maybe Roufos used your inside knowledge of the set to send one of his heavies in. I saw you speaking on your phone while you were on the platform.'

There were beads of sweat on Waggoner's forehead. 'That's all speculation, Mavros. Kindly leave.'

'I'm not finished. Besides, Inspector Margaritis will get to you and your phone records soon enough.' Mavros doubted that, given the official feeling that it was suicide, but even imaginary leverage was useful.

'Now,' he continued, 'let's talk about Kornaria. I know you used the village as one of your bases during the war.' He waited till the old man confirmed that with a nod. 'So it's perfectly reasonable that you built a house there – even if the money you used to do so resulted from blackmail, which is a crime even in Crete.'

'Get to the point.'

Mavros smiled. 'I was hoping *you* would. No? Well, allow me.' He leaned forward and pulled the knife from the table.

Waggoner stood up unsteadily. 'Now look here, you can't—'

'I can!' Mavros yelled, stepping round the table and pushing the old man on to the sofa. 'I can do anything I fucking well like, you murdering, thieving, lying piece of empire detritus. You want to know something? The EAM man Kanellos you said betrayed you to the Germans, he was my father.'

'What?' Waggoner gasped. 'Your father?'

'And, as you know very well, he had nothing to do with the betrayal of your band. You executed that man yourself.'

Waggoner's face was now slicked with sweat and his thick-veined hands were trembling. 'Your father?' he repeated. 'How can that be?'

'It's a small country,' Mavros replied. 'Sooner or later, everyone knows everyone else.' He raised the knife. 'As you can imagine, I'm seriously pissed off about the lies you spread. There's only one way I'm leaving this house with you still breathing – tell me everything I ask.'

'I have nothing to say,' the Englishman said, his lower jaw protruding like the bow of a battleship.

Eventually Mavros turned on his heel and left.

Mikis drove Mavros to the Heavenly Blue.

'Are you sure this is a good idea?' he asked. 'They are your employers, after all. And mine.'

Mavros shrugged. 'You can leave me at the gate if you want.'

'What? Like they don't know I was with you in Kornaria and in the fight afterwards? No, fuck 'em. I'm coming with you.'

'Thanks.' Mavros was relieved, but he would have gone through with his plan on his own. As they approached the resort, he made a call.

'Hi, Cara, good morning.'

'Same to you, Alex.' The actress sounded like she was ready to take on the world. Then she remembered his raison d'être. 'Any news about Maria?'

'I'm working on it. Can you do me a favour?'

'Anything.' She laughed. 'Within reason.'

'Let Luke Jannet and Rosie Yellenberg know that I need to talk to them in your suite.'

'OK. When?'

'Ten minutes?'

'Consider it done. I'll offer them breakfast. If that doesn't work, I'll threaten to stop working again.'

'You're good,' he said, in admiration. 'Really good.'

'Why, thank you, sir.'

Mikis parked as near the hotel entrance as he could. 'Am I bringing hardware?'

'I don't think that'll be necessary.'

'What about that knife you're carrying?'

'I may need to cut some fruit.'

As they crossed the reception area, Renzo Capaldi stepped forward from the door to the Kerstens' apartment.

'Mr Mavros,' he said, smiling ingratiatingly. 'Everything is fine. I had a man patrolling outside all night. I spoke to Mrs Kersten a few minutes ago.'

'How is she?'

'Calm, I would say.'

'I'll call in to see her soon.' Mavros led Mikis to the stairs.

'Race you,' the Cretan said, disappearing round the first corner.

Mavros, worried about stretching the stitches in his neck, let him go and took the lift from the first floor. He found Mikis on the fifth with his chest expanding at a normal rate.

'Is that natural fitness or do you work out?'

'Both.'

'Arrogant Cretan shit,' Mavros said, nodding at the gorilla outside Cara's suite. They were allowed in.

'Alex!' the actress said, when she saw the dressing on his neck. 'What happened to you?'

'Yeah,' Jannet added, from the armchair he was slouching in. 'Cut yourself shaving?'

'Something like that.' Mavros looked around. Alice Quincy

was sitting behind her boss, but there was no sign of the producer.

'Don't worry,' Cara said, giving him a cup of coffee, 'Rosie's on her way. Who's your friend?'

'Mikis Tsifakis,' the Cretan said. 'Driver.'

'You brought the hired help?' Jannet asked contemptuously.

'Why not?' Mavros replied. 'That's what *I* am, isn't it?'

Mikis smiled and went over to one of the windows. Shortly afterwards, the external door opened and Rosie Yellenberg came down the hall. She looked at Mavros, but made no comment. He watched as she cast an expressionless glance at her brother and then caught Cara's eye.

'What's this about? Some of us have got work to do.'

'Aw, chill out, will you, Rosie?' Jannet said, looking up from his phone.

'Was she always like this?' Mavros asked. 'I mean when you were kids.'

There was silence while people exchanged surprised looks.

'Well, lookee here,' the director said, his eyes narrowing. 'We've got ourselves a dick who knows how to dig.'

Mavros wondered if that was a reference to what he had put Oskar Mesner and Roufos's skinhead through last night. It seemed unlikely as even Waggoner hadn't seemed to know about it.

'You and Rosie are brother and sister?' Cara said, in astonishment.

The producer directed an icy glare at her. 'Something wrong with that?'

'Well, yes, actually,' the actress replied. 'Like why you've kept it secret.'

Jannet looked at his sister. 'Any reason why we shouldn't? That is, any reason we have to share personal stuff with you?'

'It's weird,' Cara said.

'Like everything else in the movie business isn't?' the director returned.

'It's more than weird,' Mavros said. 'What they've also failed to mention is that their father, Eugene Tzannetakis, came from the notorious drug-producing village of Kornaria and that he was jailed for drug trafficking in the States.'

'Kornaria?' the actress said. 'That's where Maria was held,

isn't it?' She moved towards Jannet. 'What have you done to her, you animal?' she demanded, her voice rising.

'Whoah.' The director raised his arms. 'I haven't done anything to that bitch.'

Cara kicked him on the shin. Given that she was wearing pointed boots, he must have been in pain, but his face didn't show it.

'Sit down,' Rosie said, with authority. 'And calm down as well.'

Mavros took Cara back to her place at the end of the sofa. 'Leave this to me,' he said quietly. He went back to centre of the room. 'Let's be clear about this, Mr Jannet,' he said formally. 'When you hired me, did you or your sister know where Maria Kondos was?'

The siblings exchanged glances.

'No,' they said, in unison. The effect was reasonably convincing.

'OK,' Mavros continued. 'Are either of you involved in the drugs business?'

Again, they looked at each other.

'Not exactly,' Jannet said.

'What the hell does that mean?'

'Cool it, man,' the director said, with a wry smile. 'Here's how it is. Yes, our old man was sent down for trafficking. That's one reason why I changed my name – as well as the fact that no fucker could pronounce the full version.' He looked around but received only stony stares. 'Anyway, when we came to Crete, we decided to keep away from the village in case any weasel journalist picked up a scent.'

'If you're not involved in anything illegal, why would that have been a problem?' Mavros asked.

'Now your naivety is showing like a pole dancer's tits,' Jannet said. 'You any idea how hard it is to raise money for pictures these days, especially ones with foreign locations? Tell him, Rosie.'

The producer nodded. 'Everything in Hollywood is about surface appearance, from Cara's pretty face and beautiful . . . chest, to the people with the money. As long as investors can say to their shareholders that everything looks all right, we can do business.'

'Obviously you knew that Maria Kondos's father was a mobster,' Mavros said, glancing at Cara.

'What?' she shrieked. 'What the fuck is going on here?'

'Michael "the Bat" Kondoyannis,' Jannet said. 'He's some piece of work. I heard he had a snitch sliced up in front of the guy's wife and kids. They never went to the cops.'

Cara was staring at him, her eyes damp. 'I don't understand any of this,' she said, with a sob. 'Are you saying Maria's some kind of criminal?'

'Oh yeah,' the director confirmed.

'We weren't sure what she was doing,' Rosie Yellenberg put in, 'but in the first week here we saw her with a man we later discovered was the mayor of Kornaria. Then she disappeared.'

Mavros held up a hand. 'Hang on. If she was tied to the village, maybe as her father's representative, why was she held captive there? And where is she now?'

'Fucked if I know,' the director said. 'You still on the job or what?'

Mavros walked over to him and let the knife handle appear between the flaps of his shirt. 'I told you at the beginning that I've never failed to find a missing person and I don't plan on letting you screw up that record. Why didn't you tell me all this upfront?'

Luke Jannet smiled. 'Would you have come running, even at that fee? Anyway, you managed to get her back the first time.'

'At the risk of her life and my friend's here, let alone my own. Before I try again, is there anything else you'd like to tell me?'

The director looked at his sister.

'Let me make one thing crystal clear,' Cara Parks interjected. 'You can forget about me working until Maria's back. *Capisce*?'

Rosie Yellenberg rolled her eyes. 'Mr Mavros, you see the urgency of the situation. The only other thing I know is that Maria has a cousin living in Galatsi. Naturally, we checked she wasn't there before calling you in.'

'And have you checked again this time?'

'No. That's your job.'

'You don't really want her back, do you?' he said, stepping towards the producer. 'Except Cara's made that impossible for you now.'

'I don't know what Maria's doing, but if she's involved with the drugs trade, she could screw this project into the ground,' Rosie said.

'Give me the cousin's name and address,' Mavros said, taking the piece of paper she scribbled on. 'All right, Miki, let's get out of here. The stink of bullshit is really getting to me.'

Cara came with them to the door. 'I can't believe this,' she said.

'I know those unlikely siblings are holding out on us,' Mavros told her. 'Don't believe anything until further notice.'

'Except that you'll find her, won't you, Alex?' Cara put her hand on his arm.

'I'll find her,' he repeated.

She kissed him on the cheek, not far from his lips.

Mikis got them to Galatsi in a few minutes. The cousin, Yiota Prevelaki, lived on the main street, a short distance from the square, in which there was a marble statue of an ancient goddess cradling a dead soldier in her arms.

'There was a hell of a battle during the war,' Mikis said.

'I know. My father was here.'

The Cretan almost drove into a tree. 'What?'

'He was in EAM. He tried to convince the locals not to take part in the charge.' Mavros told him what else he had found out about Kanellos.

'Good for him. Dozens of them were killed.' Mikis glanced at Mavros before he drove on. 'Those Hollywood assholes aren't the only people who've been keeping secrets.'

'Sorry, I've been struggling to come to terms with it. You see, I didn't know anything about what he did in Crete until a few days ago, and then there were Waggoner's lies.'

'Yes, that must be tough.' Mikis stopped outside a small but neatly maintained house, the garden out front full of flowers. 'Uh-oh.'

Mavros followed his gaze. There was a wheelchair lying on its side at the bottom of the steps that led to the terrace around the house.

NINETEEN

Mavros looked up and down the main street. There were cars parked on both sides, including a large black pickup with tinted windows.

'You'd better get your pistol,' he said to Mikis. 'And your meat cleaver.'

The Cretan came back with the weapons covered by a jacket. 'How do you want to do this?'

'Let's get up to the terrace. You go left and I'll go right.'

'Thought your old man was a Commie.'

Mavros smiled as the adrenaline began to flow. They went up the steps as quietly as they could, obscured from view by tall bushes. When Mikis moved away, Mavros took out the kitchen knife and put his ear against the bright blue door. Nothing. He walked to the nearest window and slowly put his head round. He saw a tidy sitting room, but there was no one in it. Then he heard a high-pitched wail that could have been a cat, but he was sure was human. It came from the rear of the building. Stepping less cautiously, he rounded the corner and went along the side wall. A window towards the rear showed the kitchen. There was a pair of bare legs lying inside, while the rest of the person was on the back terrace.

By the time he got there, Mikis was crouching over a women in a short skirt and white blouse, who was on her front. There was blood on her arms.

Mavros joined him and they rolled the woman on to her side. Blood came from her mouth, as well as a couple of teeth.

'Bastards,' Mikis hissed.

The woman moaned and opened her eyes, looking at them blearily as she spat out more blood.

'Yiota?' Mavros asked. 'Yiota Prevelaki?'

'Yes,' she said weakly.

'Where's Maria?'

The woman tried to focus. 'Maria? She's . . . she's inside.'

'Shit,' Mikis said. 'Stay with her.' He stepped over her

legs and headed inside. A few seconds later, there was a loud crash and the sound of subdued male voices.

'Stay on your side,' Mavros said, getting up and going into the kitchen.

By the time he made it to the hall, the front door was open. Mikis was lying motionless a metre inside. Two men in black, caps drawn low over their faces, were carrying a woman out of the gate, her long black hair hanging down.

'Stop!' Mavros said, looking for Mikis's pistol. It was nowhere to be seen. He ran down the steps, brandishing the kitchen knife. 'Stop thieves!' He hoped that would attract attention from passers-by.

The men were pulling shut the doors of the pickup when he got to the street. The engine roared and it veered out into the street, provoking vigorous horn blowing from an old man in an ancient Fiat. Mavros squinted into the late morning sun and tried unsuccessfully to make out the number plate. He cursed himself for not taking it earlier – the vehicle was the kind that men from Kornaria drove.

Running back to the house, he turned Mikis on to his side and made sure his airway was clear. There was a nasty wound on the side of his temple, blood welling from it.

Mavros called for an ambulance as he headed back to the woman. She had pulled herself up and was sitting against the doorframe, her head back.

'Did you recognize the men, Yiota?' he asked, checking that she was breathing without obstruction.

'No . . . one . . . one of them knocked on the door and they . . . they just pushed in, grabbed me by the hair. I managed . . . to pull away and run this way, but one of the pigs caught up with me and punched me . . .'

He found a cloth and soaked it in water. 'Here, hold this against your mouth.'

He looked back at Mikis. He hadn't changed position, but his chest was moving.

The paramedics arrived quickly and looked the casualties over. One of them led Yiota to the ambulance and then returned to help his colleague with the still unconscious Mikis.

'I don't like the look of that wound,' he said, turning to Mavros. 'What happened?'

'He was hit, I don't know what with. Maybe a pistol butt.'

The men exchanged glances and started to move Mikis on to a stretcher.

'Take them to the West Crete Clinic, please,' he said, slipping the Cretan's phone and car keys out of his pocket. His large knife must have been removed along with the Colt.

Before he went to the Jeep, Mavros scrolled down the phone book and found the entry for 'Dad'. Inhaling deeply, he called Mr Tsifakis and explained what had happened.

'We'll see you at the clinic,' Mikis's father said, with impressive composure. 'Don't call the police.'

I wasn't thinking of it, Mavros said to himself, as he walked past the overturned wheelchair.

But the police, in the form of Inspector Margaritis and a bull-chested sidekick, were waiting for him at the clinic.

'Alex Mavro,' the inspector said, with a thin smile. 'You've been poking your nose in all sorts of places.' He pointed at the dressing on Mavros's neck. 'You should be more careful.'

'You should be looking for Rudolf Kersten's killer.'

'Rudolf Kersten killed Rudolf Kersten,' was Margaritis's riposte. 'The forensic examiner's report is in.'

'That was very quick.'

'We don't have as many suspicious deaths as you do in the big city.'

Mavros made to move past them. 'If you don't mind, I'd like to see how my friend is.'

'This won't take a minute,' the inspector said, grabbing his arm and pressing long nails through Mavros's shirt. 'Get off the island, you meddling piece of shit. There's nothing to keep you here.'

Mavros said nothing about Maria Kondos's abduction. 'You're not the first person to say that. Who's paying you?' He leaned close to the thin man's sparsely covered head. In the background he saw a large man with grey hair and a face that was a heavier version of Mikis's. The woman next to him was almost as bulky and her face was set hard as she looked at the policemen. He reckoned he could go put the boot in. 'Waggoner? Roufos? Or the wankers up in Kornaria?'

Margaritis dropped his arm like it was a piece of carrion. 'You—'

'*You* fuck off,' Mavros said, glaring. 'If you want to arrest me, go ahead.' The inspector stood motionless. 'Thought not.'

'What happened to the woman and young Tsifakis?'

'Slipped on a step.'

Margaritis snorted. 'Both of them? Anyway, that's not what we heard. There was another woman.'

Some citizen of Galatsi had obviously become suspicious when Maria was carried out of the house.

Mikis's parents came over.

'What's going on, Inspector?' his father demanded.

'Nothing,' Margaritis said, with an unctuous bow. 'We're finished.' He departed.

'Haris Tsifakis,' the big man said, extending a thick-fingered hand. 'My wife, Eleni. Pleased to finally meet you, Mr Mavro.'

'Alex, please.' Mavros shook their hands. 'I'm very sorry about—'

'No need for that,' Tsifakis said brusquely. 'Mikis can look after himself.'

'Not this time,' his wife said, looking into Mavros's eyes. 'We know you and Mikis have put yourselves up against some of the island's most dangerous people. That shows courage. But tell me that you didn't lead my son into unnecessary danger.'

'To be honest, he's been the one leading me most of the time,' Mavros said, provoking a grin from Mikis's father.

'That's my boy. Let's go and see how he is.'

Mavros led them to the lifts and they went up to the fourth floor.

'You again,' said Doctor Stavrakakis to Mavros. 'Do you like this place so much you're going to take up residence?'

'How is my son?' Eleni put in.

'Excuse me, Mrs Tsifaki.' The family was obviously well known. 'I'm afraid he's still unconscious. We're carrying out various tests, but there's little I can tell you now.' He glanced at Mavros. 'As our Athenian friend knows, head wounds are unpredictable. How is Ms Kondos?'

'She was kidnapped this morning.'

The neurologist looked less taken aback than he might have done.

'The woman that came in with Mikis, how is she?'

'Mrs Prevelaki? I checked her. There's no significant head

trauma, though she'll have to be wary of concussion. She's downstairs having her lip stitched. I think you know the way. You might take the opportunity to have that dressing changed.'

The doctor nodded to Mikis's parents and walked away.

'This is connected with those drug-dealing bastards in Kornaria, isn't it?' Haris said. 'Don't worry about the vendetta. We can come back at them with plenty of firepower.'

His wife nodded avidly, making Mavros glad he was on their side.

'In the meantime, we'll stay to see how Mikis gets on,' she said. 'Let us know when you need help.'

Mavros nodded and walked to the stairs, noting that she had said 'when' rather than 'if'. That didn't make him feel great, though he appreciated their support. He'd much rather have had the gun-wielding Mikis by his side.

Yiota Prevelaki was sitting outside the treatment room on the ground floor, with a dressing around her mouth.

Mavros took the seat next to her. 'How are you feeling?'

'They gave me a local anaesthetic,' she said, lisping. 'I'll be all right until it wears off.'

'Then you just take painkillers.'

The woman looked at him. 'Maria told me about you. How you saved her from those animals in Kornaria.'

'That was my friend upstairs more than me.'

'There was something about a rock in an armed man's face?'

'Ah, that. I got lucky.'

She smiled with difficulty. 'You're too modest, Mr Mavro.'

'Alex, please. Are you waiting for someone?'

'No, my husband's on a ship in the Pacific. I was summoning up strength to call a taxi.'

'I'll take you home.'

When they were in the Jeep, Mavros made a mess of engaging first gear.

'Your friend's a driver, isn't he?' Yiota said. 'The Tsifakis family is an important one in Chania.'

He nodded. 'I hope he pulls through.'

'So do I. What are you going to do now? Maria must be back in Kornaria now. You can't go up there. They'll use you for target practice.'

'I'll deal with that when I have to. First, I need to know more about your cousin.' He pulled on to the main road heading west.

'I can't tell you much—ow!'

'Careful,' Mavros said, touching his own dressing, which he'd forgotten to get changed. 'That spray will be wearing off.'

Yiota nodded slowly. 'There isn't much I can tell you about Maria, Alex. We exchange emails from time to time, but we've never been close. I didn't even see her when the film crew arrived – until she called me yesterday afternoon.'

'Did you go to pick her up from the Heavenly Blue?'

'I don't drive. No, she came in a taxi – not one of the Tsifakis cars. She got the driver to pick her up from the back of the hotel.'

'So she told you she'd been in Kornaria.'

'Yes, she said she'd gone for a walk outside the resort on Sunday evening – something about being sick of being cooped up – and that a car stopped and the driver offered her a lift.'

'Did she know the driver – was it a man or a woman?'

'A man, I think, but she didn't say whether she knew him. Someone was hiding in the back seat and suddenly a hood was over her head and a rope round her neck. She was pushed forward so that she was out of sight.'

'Sounds like the guys who grabbed her today – or equally proficient hard men.'

Yiota Prevelaki turned to him. 'Not everyone in our family is worthy of approbation, Alex.' She stared at his expression. 'What? A village woman isn't allowed to use learned vocabulary? I trained as a teacher, but my husband's family doesn't allow me to work.' There was a weight of pain in her voice.

'I'm sorry,' he said, embarrassed both by underestimating her and at the plight of an educated woman in a Cretan village. 'Don't worry, I know about the Kondoyannis family in Florida and the delightful Michael "the Bat".'

'Oh,' she said, surprised. 'Well, I have nothing to do with them.'

They drove past the gate to the resort, which was now besieged by even more journalists and reporters.

'Rudolf Kersten was a hero to many people here,' Yiota said.

Mavros made no comment, still unsure what to believe about the old German's activities.

'I don't know much about the film Maria is working on, though,' Yiota said. 'Have you met Cara Parks?'

'I have.'

'What's she like? She doesn't strike me as the most likely Cretan resistance hero.'

Mavros got the feeling she was leading the conversation in another direction.

'Listen, Yiota, your cousin is in serious danger. I don't know if she told you, but she didn't say anything to us about what happened to her in Kornaria. If I'm going to have any chance of rescuing her again, I need to know everything about her.'

His passenger lowered her head. 'I can't, Alex. She's family.'

'She'll be dead family soon!' he shouted, making her jolt upright. 'Is that what you want?'

Yiota Prevelaki was quiet until he drew up outside her house. Then she turned to him and spoke in a low voice.

'The only thing Maria told me was that another Greek-American family has muscled in on the Kondoyannis business, including her father's links with the Kornaria producers. They seem to think she has something to do with the drugs trade.'

'And she doesn't?'

'No!' Yiota exclaimed.

'Are you sure of that?'

Her gaze dropped. 'No,' she answered.

Mavros got out and walked her to the front door.

'Please try to get her back,' the woman said softly.

'I will,' Mavros said, squeezing her hand.

As he walked back to the Jeep, he wondered if the other Greek-American family was that of Luke Jannet and Rosie Yellenberg. Despite their assurances that they had nothing to do with their father's activities, had they been playing him for a fool from the start?

Cara Parks called as Mavros was approaching the Heavenly Blue. He told her he'd be with her shortly. First, he intended to talk to Hildegard Kersten. Though he had little to tell her, he had some questions.

The widow expressed shock when she saw his neck and was patently unconvinced when he said his razor had slipped. She welcomed him into the apartment, which was the same as it had been when her husband was alive, apart from orderly piles of paper on the desk. She brought coffee and sat down on the sofa next to him.

'So, Alex, have you found anything out about my Rudi?'

'I presume you've heard from the police that his death has been classified as suicide by the medical examiner?'

She nodded slowly, her lips tightly pressed together. 'You know as well as I do how unreliable those people are. All they want is a quiet life.'

Don't we all, Mavros thought, taking a deep breath. 'Hildegard, I'm getting conflicting stories about your husband.'

'What do you mean?' she asked, eyebrows rising.

'According to David Waggoner, Rudolf *did* take part in the massacre in Makrymari. A witness told him so.'

'Waggoner!' the widow scoffed. 'You can't believe anything that man says.'

'If your husband didn't shoot any civilians, why did he pay blackmail for all those years?'

Hildegard sighed and put down her cup. 'Alex, you must understand. Coming to Crete to live in the Sixties was very difficult for us, but Rudi felt it was his duty to put back as much as he could into the local economy to make up for what happened during the war. As you can imagine, many people didn't want us and they particularly didn't want us to build the resort. Rudi eventually convinced the Cretans he was serious by funding village regeneration projects, by setting up scholarships for poor students and so on. But in order to get the permits to start building here, he had to be seen to be cleaner than clean.'

It struck Mavros that there were similarities between the appearance Kersten had to project and the appearances necessary to get funding in Hollywood that Rosie Yellenberg had described.

'I still don't understand why he felt he had to pay David Waggoner off.'

The widow looked beyond him towards the sea, which was a mid-afternoon pale-blue, only a few white horses whipped up by the breeze. 'Alex, I can't be sure what Rudi did at Makrymari. I'm not sure he knew himself, no matter what he wrote in his diary. He'd received a severe head wound. It may be that, deep down, he saw himself as a cold-blooded murderer of women, boys and old men.'

From what Mavros had seen of the soft-spoken Kersten with his life-worn eyes, that possibility couldn't be ruled out. But he was sure there was more.

'What about Kornaria?' he asked, his tone hardening.

Hildegard regarded him cautiously. 'The drugs village? What about it?'

Mavros slumped back. 'If you want me to find out what happened to Rudi – and I *know* it was murder – you'll have to help me. Were the Kornariates blackmailing him too?'

'No, no,' the old woman said, her eyes holding his. 'Waggoner was earning enough for all of them.'

'What do you mean?'

She looked down. 'The Englishman wasn't simply black-mailing us because of Rudi's wartime deeds, whether he took part in the massacre or not. He was extracting protection money. On this island, especially back in the Sixties, you needed someone to look after your property. I don't think Kornaria was producing many drugs back then. The mountain men watched over us when the resort was being built. They invested those earnings in mari-juana cultivation sheds, from what I've heard.'

'And Waggoner was their intermediary?'

'That's right. When Rudi told him we had no more money, he started asking about the coin collection. Rudi couldn't counte-nance him getting that and said so.'

'When?'

'More than once, but the last time was only a few days ago – on Saturday.' Hildegard went over to the desk and took some papers from one of the piles. 'I found these when I was going through the drawers here.' She handed them to Mavros.

He ran his eyes down the sheets. They were copies of emails that Rudolf Kersten had sent to Waggoner in the days before his death. In them, he threatened to expose the former SOE man as a blackmailer if he didn't leave him alone. They could certainly be construed as a motive for murder.

'My God,' he said. 'Why didn't you tell me about these before?'

'I only found them today.' Hildegard looked at him gravely. 'They mean he arranged for Rudi's death, don't they?'

'It certainly looks that way. You have to give them to the police.'

She shook her head. 'No. I told you, they are worthless. It

wouldn't surprise me if Inspector Margaritis was in the pay of
Waggoner and the Kornariates – many of the local politicians
and officials are.'

Mavros glanced around the room. 'Where are the coins?'

'In a safe place,' the widow replied. 'Not in the resort.'

'Better you don't tell me.'

'Very well. What do you intend to do?'

'Take down David Waggoner.'

'Yes, but how?'

'Better I don't tell *you* that.' He got to his feet. 'Make sure
you keep all the windows and doors locked. Short of putting up
signs saying the coins are no longer here – which no one would
believe – there isn't anything to do apart from ensuring the
security is as high as it can be. I'll talk to Capaldi again.'

'He's a good man. Rudi trusted him and he's never let us
down.'

'Apart from the night your grandson got in and took the thirty
coins.'

Hildegard nodded. 'True. I much appreciate what you're doing,
Alex. Rudi said you were an honourable man and a dogged
investigator. He looked you up on the Internet.'

Mavros was strangely moved by that. 'You shouldn't stay here,
you know. Even another room in the hotel would be better.'

'This was our home. I'm not leaving, especially when Rudi
is still not buried.'

'I understand. Keep your phone close at all times and call me
if anything worries you.'

They said their goodbyes and he left for the actress's suite.

TWENTY

'What happened?' Cara Parks demanded. 'Rosie told me that Maria was kidnapped.'

Mavros wondered how the producer knew that – had the police or paramedics blabbed to the local radio station, or was she in with the men who'd taken Maria?

He told the actress what had happened to Maria at Yiota Prevelaki's house and about Mikis's head wound. That reminded him to call the hospital. Doctor Stavrakakis told him that the driver was still unconscious and that there was swelling inside his cranium – if it continued to expand, he would have to operate.

'Did you believe Rosie and her brother?' he asked. 'I mean, when they said they had nothing to do with their father's drug trafficking?'

'I don't know what to believe. Thinking of them as brother and sister is hard enough. But dope-dealers?'

'Hm.' Mavros gave her a potted version of what he had learned from Maria's cousin and from Hildegard Kersten.

'Hold up,' the actress said. 'Where are you going with this? Are you suggesting Maria's in the drug business as well?'

He shrugged. 'I'm having trouble understanding why she's been kidnapped twice. And why she refused to tell anyone – even you – about what happened to her after we got her back from Kornaria.'

'She had a head injury,' Cara said, but she wasn't even convincing herself. 'Jesus. This is the kind of shit that'll fuck the movie up big time.'

Mavros wasn't impressed. 'Well, fuck *Freedom or Death* then. Do you know what really happened at Makrymari? The woman your character is based on didn't get away while her fellow villagers bravely took the bullets for her. She was shot down like the rest of them. That's what happens on this island, in case you haven't noticed. People live and die violently.' Suddenly he thought of the black youth Cara had driven into. 'Like on Mulholland Drive.'

Cara's head went down. 'Old Mr Kersten didn't commit suicide, did he?' she said, in a small voice.

'The authorities are saying he did, but I'm certain he was murdered. As well as looking for Maria, I'm trying to find his killer.'

The actress looked up. 'I'll help you.'

'By doing what, exactly? Can you fire a gun?'

'Rifle, shotgun, pistol and revolver,' she said, with a smile. 'My daddy made sure I could handle firearms before I turned sixteen.'

'Right,' Mavros said, taken aback. 'I suppose you can fight as well.'

'Kick-boxing, judo and karate – state champion at high school.'

He took an involuntary step back. 'Uh-huh. So, Ms Parks, what do you think you can personally bring to this role?'

She laughed. 'I might be able to save your ass, Alex – not just in a brawl with those crazy villagers, but with Maria. If she really is her mobster father's daughter, she might cut up rough – but not with me. She loves me, for Christ's sake.'

'What makes you think Maria's not being held captive up in Kornaria? She'd been mistreated when she came down the hillside the last time.'

Cara thought about that. 'It's hard to put my finger on. She was different when she was in the clinic. Sure, she'd been through some shit – like you guys on the road back down – but she didn't seem particularly affected by it. I'm beginning to think she might be a better actor than me. I mean, you saw her when she said she was coming back to work. She didn't exactly look trauma-tized, did she?'

'No,' he replied, remembering the Greek-American's demeanour. 'More like traumatizing.'

Cara laughed. 'Give me a moment. I've got to change.'

She reappeared in a dark-blue tracksuit that emphasized her curves. Her trainers were pristine but thick-soled, and she'd gathered her hair back.

'Charlie's Angel?' Mavros asked.

'And Frankenstein's monster.' She offered her arm. 'Let's knock 'em out, Boris.'

The big man on the door stared at them as they brushed past him. Cara told him not to follow them.

'Take the stairs,' Mavros said. 'I'll race you.'

Despite the start he'd given himself, she overtook him one flight down and was waiting on the ground floor when he got there, panting. He missed his footing on the bottom step and toppled forward. Cara moved quickly towards him and caught him in surprisingly strong arms.

'Shit,' he grunted and they both started to laugh hysterically, holding on to each other like kids who'd taken their first toke.

'What's the joke?' came a voice that silenced Mavros instantly.

He looked over the actress's shoulder and saw Niki a few metres away, an overnight bag between her bare legs and her face set hard.

'My woman,' Mavros whispered to Cara. 'Cover for me. Please.'

'Don't sweat it,' she returned, taking her arms away and stepping back. 'My, my, Alex, you need to be more careful. If I hadn't caught you, you'd have done some serious damage to that magnificent nose.'

'Thanks for nothing,' he muttered, going towards the seething Niki. 'My love,' he said, in Greek. 'What are you doing here?'

Niki stared at the bandage on his neck. 'Let's stick to English. I'd like your friend to hear.' She pronounced the 'f' word as if it were a curse. 'And you are?' she said, moving forward and extending her hand.

'Cara Parks,' the actress said, smiling broadly. 'It's so nice to meet you. Alex has told me *so* much about you.'

Mavros glared at her, aware that he hadn't mentioned Niki's existence.

'I'm Alex's other, better half,' Niki said acidly. 'What was so funny?'

'Oh, nothing,' Cara said, waving her hand loosely. 'We were just horsing around.'

Niki turned her frozen gaze on Mavros and then looked back at the actress.

'Cara Parks? The star? Oh my God.' She put her hand out again. 'It's a real pleasure to meet you. I love your work.'

Mavros knew he wasn't off the hook, but Niki's transformation from ice queen to quivering fan was an eye-opener.

While the women were building bridges, Mavros went over to reception and asked for Renzo Capaldi. The security manager arrived hotfoot.

'Ah, Mr Mavros. I have been looking for you. How is the throat?'

'Painful. Why did you want me?'

'To tell you that I am going to look after Mrs Kersten personally. I will patrol outside her windows all night.' The Italian raised his massive shoulders. 'Of course, my staff will be doing their usual rounds, but I will provide extra protection.'

'That's very good of you.'

'It's nothing. Mr Kersten was a great man and a very kind employer. I . . . I would do anything to bring him back.' Tears appeared in his eyes and he wiped them away with the arm of his suit.

Mavros nodded to him and went over to the women.

Niki's gaze was slightly less frosty. 'Cara tells me you're going out on a job.'

The actress smiled at him, despite the look she got in return.

'Job?' he repeated. 'I'd hardly call it that.'

'Oh?' Niki said. 'And how would you describe going to rescue Cara's assistant from a village full of criminals?' She raised an eyebrow. 'I'm coming too.'

Mavros's joy was confined.

'Where are we going?' Niki asked. She was squeezed between Cara Parks and Mavros in the Jeep, having left her bag at the hotel. He had explained about his neck wound without going into too much detail.

'Chania,' he replied.

'Not the village?' Niki smiled crookedly. 'You don't think we're up to it, do you?'

'Three of us taking on a horde of heavily armed Cretan mountain men who have proclaimed a vendetta . . .' He stopped himself too late.

'A vendetta?' Niki said. 'Against who?'

'Um, me,' Mavros mumbled. 'And the guy who was driving

this.' He had no choice but to recount the story, without going into Mikis's use of the Colt.

'You threw a rock into the face of an armed man from the most dangerous village in Crete?' Niki said, her voicing rising to a shriek. 'Are you completely insane?'

'He was only knocked out,' Cara said, trying to calm her. 'And Alex got my friend Maria back.'

'Who's since been kidnapped – again.' Niki turned and gave her an appraising look. 'I can see why they call you "Twin Peaks". Are they real?'

Mavros restrained himself from smashing his head against the steering wheel. 'For Christ's sake, Niki, get a grip. Cara isn't the enemy.'

'Is that right?' Niki took a deep breath. 'OK, I'm sorry, that was rude. I'm . . . I'm worried.' She looked through the windscreen. 'This island is like a foreign country – one with extremely restless natives.'

'They're not all bad,' Mavros said. 'Behave yourself, please. We're about to meet some of the good ones.'

He had looked at the map before they left the Heavenly Blue and now found the Tsifakis depot without trouble. There was a fenced enclosure with numerous cars and small buses beyond a wide gate. The offices were in what looked like an old factory. A lot of money had clearly been spent on its renovation.

Haris Tsifakis met them in the stone-flagged reception area.

'Alex,' he said, nodding. 'Ms Parks.' He waited to be introduced to Niki.

'Oh, this is my . . . partner from Athens,' Mavros said awkwardly.

'Niki Glezou.' When she wanted, Niki could be very user-friendly. She gave the Cretan a broad smile and shook his hand vigorously.

'What news of Mikis?' Mavros asked.

'My wife is at the clinic,' he said, his face falling. 'Our son is still unconscious. It seems he will need an operation, but the doctors want to wait until this evening to decide. Please, come to my office.' He led them into a large room with two mahogany desks, both equipped with computers and several telephones. 'Eleni and I have always worked together. We set up the car-hire business in 1966 and grew it very quickly, largely thanks to Mr

Kersten. He used us for guest tours and transfers.' He shook his head. 'His death is a tragedy.'

Mavros was interested by the Cretan's response. He wasn't old enough to have fought in the war, but his parents' generation would have lived through the horrors of the German occupation. He still revered a man who had landed by parachute on the first day of the invasion.

'Can I use one of the computers?' he asked.

Haris went behind the nearer desk and booted up the machine. Mavros found what he wanted in under a minute and printed out the image.

'We urgently need to find this man,' he said, handing over the picture. 'I know he's in Chania or the environs.'

'That's the antiquities dealer who's always walking out of court with a sick smile on his face,' the Cretan said.

'Tryfon Roufos,' Mavros confirmed. 'Can you find where's he's staying?'

'Easily – if he's in a hotel or pension.' Haris picked up a phone and gave instructions to an employee. 'If he's in a private house, it'll take a bit longer, but I can circulate his photo.'

'I saw him in a taverna in the old town a few nights ago,' Mavros said. He described the location.

'Tou Philippou. Good, the owner is a friend.'

'He was with David Waggoner.'

'Was he now? I've never thought much of Mr Waggoner. He made much of his exploits here during the war, but the truth is that the local resistance leaders were much more important in the fight against the occupiers.'

Mavros didn't need much more convincing that the former SOE man had feet of clay. The question was, had he orchestrated Rudolf Kersten's death?

'Leave this with me,' Haris said. 'I'll call you as soon as I get anything. I presume you want to keep the Jeep?'

'Is that all right?'

'Of course.' The Cretan beamed at Cara. 'It's on the film's account.'

Mavros thanked him and led the women out.

'You didn't tell me Roufos was on Crete,' Niki said, as they headed for the vehicle. 'Then again, there are a lot of things you haven't told me.'

'This Roufos,' Cara said, as she opened the Jeep's door. 'What's he supposed to have done?'

'A lot,' Mavros said.

Two pairs of eyes bored into him as he started the engine.

'All right, I'll tell you.' Mavros ran through Roufos's interest in Kersten's coin collection, his attempt to scare him off by sending round the three skinheads, and his connection with Waggoner. 'The Englishman has a house on the outskirts of Kornaria—'

'The village where Maria was held,' the actress put in. 'So what is it you think, Alex? That Roufos is involved in her kidnapping?'

He shrugged. 'That's one of several things I want to ask him. I'd also like to . . . shit!'

A large pickup cut in front of him as he tried to turn out of the Tsifakis depot. Three muscle-pumped men got out and walked slowly towards the Jeep, their faces set in stone.

Hildegard Kirsten had been going through her husband's clothes and wardrobe. She didn't know why, but she felt compelled to check the pockets of his jackets and shirts, even though they had almost all been laundered. She found a single euro in one of the jackets he had worn recently, perhaps that evening they had met Alex Mavros and the beautiful actress at the beachside bar. She put the coin against her cheek and tried to transfer the touch of Rudi's fingers on it to her skin.

Blinking back tears, she slipped the euro into the pocket of her skirt, where she had also put the *labrys*, and continued running her hands over his clothes. Many of them were old, but their experiences of the war and its aftermath in Germany had made them reluctant to discard anything that might be useful – and relative poverty had recently been threatening them.

Then she found it. Tucked away in the back pocket of a pair of slacks Rudi had worn a week ago was a single sheet of A4 paper, folded twice. She had a strong feeling of foreboding as, fingers trembling, she knelt on the floor and spread out the page. The writing, in German, was Rudi's, his well-formed and spaced letters as legible as they had been in his love letters to her all those years ago. But this was very far from being one of them. The blue ink from the fountain pen he always used was unfaded and looked to have been written recently. She read:

Waggoner – Oskar to dispose of with contacts. Coins value 100K
Roufos – sell half remaining coins for H
Mavros – send to Kornaria

Hildegard rocked back on her heels, struggling to fathom what the words meant. Did 'dispose of' mean kill, using their grandson's awful shaven-headed, neo-Nazi friends? Had Rudi gone back on his anti-Nazi principles of decades and considered using the new generation of far-right thugs to get rid of the man who had bled them dry? Could he have seriously considered breaking up his precious collection, even if 'H' referred to her? But worst of all was the last line. Alex Mavros had been a good friend to them and was trying to find out what had happened to Rudi. Why had he been planning to send him to the drug-producing village? She and Rudi had never been up there – Germans were not welcome, even benefactors – but, from what she'd understood, going there would be highly dangerous for the investigator, especially after his involvement in the return of the actress's assistant.

Confused and suddenly feeling very old, Hildegard stood up slowly and went over to the desk. The least she could do was warn Alex Mavros about Kornaria.

Mavros's first reaction was to reach beneath the driving seat for any other weapons Mikis might have stashed there. All he found was a long spanner. He grabbed it and put his shoulder to the door.

'Wait! Wait!' said the closest of the hulking men. 'We're on your side. Mr Tsifakis told us to keep a look out for you.'

Mavros ran an eye over them. Now he recognized one of Mikis's friends, who had been on guard duty outside the clinic when Maria Kondos was there.

'Shit, you gave me a fright!'

'Sorry about that. The old man must have screwed up your number.'

Mavros gave him the correct number. 'And you are?'

'Yannis.' He looked over his shoulder. 'And these are Christos and the Pig.'

The latter was marginally larger than his companions, but certainly not overweight. 'You should see his flat,' Yannis explained, with a laugh. He looked into the Jeep. 'Who are these lovely ladies?'

Cara smiled sweetly at him, while Niki ratcheted up her stare to high frost.

'Anyway,' Yannis continued, 'what can we do for you? Mr Tsifakis doesn't want anything nasty to happen.'

'That's comforting. Have you got any weapons?'

'What do you need?'

Mavros smiled. 'In the middle of the city, nothing. Later, who knows?'

'Put it this way,' said the big man. 'This pickup has enough arms to keep a small army at bay.'

'Let's hope we don't need them,' Mavros said, thinking of the mountain men who were on his case and realizing how small that hope was. 'Listen, Yanni, give me your phone numbers and I'll call you if I need you.'

The Cretan looked in at the women again. 'You sure you don't want us to cover your . . . backsides?'

'Ha. Not right now.' Mavros input the numbers into his mobile's memory.

'OK, happy travels,' Yannis said, waving into the Jeep.

'Who were those madmen?' Niki asked, when they set off again.

'Our guardian angels,' Mavros said. 'But we don't need them now. It's time for an early dinner.' He headed into the centre of Chania, keeping an eye on his mirror. There were no macho-man pickups to be seen.

Then his phone rang. He listened to what Hildegard Kersten had to say, struggling to make sense of it. 'You mean your husband was doing business with Roufos?'

'At least thinking about it. Alex, you must be very careful. Whatever you do, stay away from Kornaria.'

'I'm working on that,' he replied, not telling her that he was sure he'd have to go to the village to get to the bottom of Maria Kondos's kidnapping and of her husband's death.

'If you see Oskar, tell him to stay away from Waggoner. And to come and visit me. I have things to tell him.'

Mavros agreed to that and cut the connection. If he saw Oskar, it would probably be in the company of numerous unfriendly skinheads, and he had the feeling the Kerstens' grandson would not have forgotten his humiliation in the orange groves.

Then his phone rang again. It was Haris Tsifakis.

'I've found Roufos.'

'Wow, that was quick.'

'You'd better get over there as soon as you can. My contact says he's been looking jumpy.'

'I'll bet he has.'

'Do you want Mikis's friends to come along?'

'No, thanks. I can handle that sleazy beanpole.'

'What about your women?'

Mavros hoped Niki didn't hear that characterization of her and Cara. 'You think I can get rid of them? Besides, they might distract the tosser.'

The Cretan laughed. 'Make sure they don't distract you, my friend.'

Mavros glanced at them. Cara was looking out of the side window, while Niki's eyes were fixed straight ahead. For a second, he wished the Jeep was fitted with passenger ejector seats.

TWENTY-ONE

Mavros parked the Jeep as close as he could to the harbour and led the women down a narrow street.

'Nice,' Niki said. 'I wish Athens was so quiet.'

Mavros glanced at her. She seemed to be genuinely enjoying the surroundings – old walls, balconies, flourishing plants cascading to the paving stones. A kid on a bike came past like a rocket, honking his horn. Even that only raised a smile from her. For the umpteenth time, he was amazed how quickly her mood could swing.

They came out on the restaurant-lined front with the dome at the eastern end and Cara drew her cap down lower. There weren't many people around in the early evening, the sun sinking slowly and casting its reddening light on the island of Ayii Theodhori.

'That's the bastion of St Nicholas,' the actress said, pointing to the low fortification on the long jetty that almost enclosed the harbour. The lighthouse that was a well-known local feature was at its end. 'Venetian, but much of the other building work was carried out during the Ottoman Empire.'

Niki looked at Cara in surprise. 'You've been reading up on the city.'

The actress laughed and stuck her chest out. 'Not just a pretty pair of peaks.'

Mavros had to bite his tongue. 'Erm, right. Why don't you two go to that café while I talk to Roufos?'

'No,' they said, laughing at their unintentionally perfect timing.

'Forget it, Alex,' Niki said. 'I've come all the way to Athens to see you. Besides, we can guarantee your safety.'

'Exactly,' Cara agreed. 'He's hardly going to hold a Hollywood star at gunpoint, is he?'

'Probably not,' Mavros admitted, though he didn't discount that Roufos might have other scumbags on hand to do his dirty work. 'All right. But at the first sign of trouble, you do exactly what I say.'

The women looked at him dubiously and then nodded.

Mavros led them to the five-star Kydhonia Palace hotel at the far end of the front. It had been formed by knocking together several Venetian buildings that had escaped the German bombing and had a distinct look of opulence. The sunshade stands were painted gold and the chairs were several leagues above the arse-racking furniture of a *kafeneion*.

A young woman in a figure-hugging dress that was someone's idea of a Minoan priestess – without the breasts entirely bare – gave them a wide smile.

'We're here to see Mr Tryfon Roufos,' Mavros said, carefully keeping his eyes level with her face, as Niki was right behind him.

'Certainly, I'll let him know, Mr . . . ?'

Mavros gave what he hoped was a complicity-inducing smile. 'The thing is, these ladies are a surprise for his birthday. Do you think you could send us up unannounced?'

The receptionist gave Cara and Niki the once-over and then turned back to Mavros. 'I understand. Mr Roufos often has . . . lady friends.' She gave a moue of distaste. 'It's suite 513 on the top floor.'

Mavros nodded his thanks and headed for the stairs.

'Excuse me,' Niki said. 'Some of us have been up since dawn. I'm taking the lift.'

'See you up there,' Cara said, setting off rapidly.

In the lift, Niki gave Mavros a soft smile. 'I like her. I even believe you haven't laid a finger on her.'

'Oh, thanks.' He gave her a weak smile. 'She's way out of your, I mean, my league.'

That earned him a kick on the shin, but he'd had worse.

'Listen, Niki, it really isn't a good idea, your being here. This could turn nasty any minute.'

'All the more reason for me to protect my man,' she said, taking his arm.

'With what?' he demanded. 'Have you got an Uzi in your bag?'

'Bastard.' Her eyes filled with tears.

'Oh, shit,' he said, putting his arm around her. 'I'm sorry.' The previous year, they had been sprayed with machine-pistol fire by Athenian gangsters and Niki had ended up in hospital.

There was a loud ping and the doors slid apart.

Cara was leaning against the wall, her breath under control. 'Sweet,' she said, then noticed Niki's eyes. 'Hey, what's up, hon?' She gave Mavros a fierce look. 'What have you done?'

'Nothing,' he said hastily, leading Niki out of the lift.

After a moment, she came back to herself and smiled at Cara. 'Don't worry, I'm fine.' It was clear that she appreciated the support. 'Let's go and sort this old pervert out.'

Cara nodded, pulling down the zip of her top. Niki laughed and undid several of her buttons.

Mavros stood, shaking his head. 'Shall I undo my flies? The story is that Roufos will screw anything, though he prefers underage bodies.'

'That's all right,' Cara said, stepping down the corridor. 'I can do teen.'

They got to 513 and Mavros knocked on the door, letting Cara stand in front of the spyhole. The chain rattled and then the door opened.

'Oh, gross,' the actress said, sidestepping Tryfon Roufos. She went into the room, found the TV handset and turned off the porn movie that was playing.

The antiquities dealer was wearing nothing but a pair of sagging underpants. His thighs were skinny and his chest covered in thick white hair. He stared at Mavros after running a lascivious eye over the women.

'Alex Mavro,' he said, focussing on the dressing on his neck. 'What are you doing here?'

The punch to the belly wasn't particularly hard, but it doubled Roufos up and left him gasping. Mavros grabbed him by the scruff of the neck and hauled him over to a newspaper-strewn sofa.

'What I'm doing is paying you back for what your goons did to me. Not that I've finished. But I'd also like the answers to some questions.'

'Fuck . . . off,' Roufos said, arms cradling his belly. 'It'll only take one phone call for me to finish you for good.'

'Careful,' Mavros said. 'There are witnesses.'

Cara had taken off her cap. It was clear that the antiquities dealer recognized her. 'You gonna have me finished too, tough guy?' she asked, giving him a look that Bette Davis would have been proud of.

'And me?' Niki demanded, taking her hand out of her bag.

She had slipped a key from her ring between each finger, the longest being that to her flat. It could easily put an eye out.

Mavros was taken aback, both by the women's lack of surprise at his resort to violence and by their apparent willingness to indulge in the same. It seemed Crete really did get to people, even within hours of their arrival. He went over and put the chain and double lock on the door, then looked around the suite. He didn't find any weapons, but he did gather up three mobile phones, as well as a cardboard folder from a worn briefcase.

'All right, you piece of shit,' he said, sitting down beside Roufos. 'Start talking, first about Rudolf Kersten's coin collection.'

'What about it?'

Mavros slapped him on the cheek. He didn't usually treat people like that, but he'd had dealings with the antiquities dealer in the past and he knew how devious he was.

'You've been trying to steal it.'

'You can't prove that,' Roufos muttered, head down to avoid more blows.

Mavros laughed. 'I don't have to. I just have to go on hitting you till you come clean. Toss over those keys, will you, Niki?' He caught them and threaded them through his fingers, then ran the metallic tips along the dealer's balding head. 'You sent Oskar Mesner to steal some coins in order to scare the Kerstens, after getting David Waggoner to case the building.'

'I don't know any Oskar Mesner,' Roufos said sullenly.

'Liar,' Mavros said, pressing the keys harder into his skull.

'All right, I admit I used him,' the dealer said. 'What of it? You and your heavy took the coins back.'

'So then you got in touch with Kersten and got him to agree to sell you half the collection.'

Tryfon Roufos raised his head and stared at Mavros. 'How do you know that?'

'Never mind.' He opened the folder and started flicking through papers. 'Oh, what's this? A draft bill of sale for two-hundred-and-sixty coins, description as per addendum "A", price four hundred thousand euros. Interesting. What are they really worth?'

'What? I don't know. It depends on specific market considerations and—'

'Bullshit. You must have a sum in mind, a calculating snake like you.' He drew the key points towards Roufos's left eye.

'I . . . oh, all right . . . at least a million.' The dealer's chin fell to his chest again.

'A decent profit even in your dirty line. Then again, you could have the whole collection, couldn't you?'

The dealer stared at him. 'What do you mean?'

'Mrs Kersten is all on her own. No doubt you could bribe the security staff.' Mavros wasn't worried about putting Hildegard in danger because he trusted Renzo Capaldi to look after her. Telling Roufos that the collection had been removed would have guaranteed her safety, but he wanted to see how the dealer responded to the temptation.

'Or you could use Oskar Mesner to slither his way in and sweet talk his grandmother.'

Roufos was clearly trying to work out where Mavros was trying to go with this angle of attack, but he wasn't allowed any more time.

'David Waggoner. What's the nature of your business with him?'

'Waggoner?' the dealer asked, making more of a mess of pronouncing the name than was necessary. 'Who's he?'

'I saw you with him the other night in Tou Philippou, you lying shit.' Mavros edged the longest key closer to Roufos's eye. With a rapid movement, he dug the point into the side of his forehead. He heard Cara's intake of breath, though Niki didn't seem to be disturbed. 'Last time. What are you scheming with Waggoner about?'

'I . . . we . . . we have some interests in . . . in Kornaria.'

Mavros laughed. 'What a surprise! They wouldn't by any chance be illegal interests, would they? I seem to remember you deal in Byzantine icons. They wouldn't be being packed up with drugs shipments to the US, would they?'

Roufos's failure to answer confirmed Mavros had hit the spot.

'And Minoan remains?' he added. 'There aren't so many at this end of Crete.'

'A . . . a few,' the dealer confirmed.

'Chania is built over a Minoan city called Kydhonia,' Cara said, prompting a raised eyebrow from Niki.

'Quite,' said Mavros. 'So you reckoned that scaring me off would give you a free run to infinite riches.' He leaned closer. 'Big mistake.'

'You won't leave the Great Island alive,' Roufos said, closing his eyes as the keys moved closer. 'The Kornariates have already beaten your driver into a coma. It's only a matter of time till they catch up with you.'

'Now that's helpful,' Mavros said. 'You've moved the conversation on to my next topic. Why was Maria Kondos kidnapped?'

'Maria who?'

'Oh, I'm sorry, I mean Maria Kondoyanni. Daughter of Michael "the Bat", that well known Florida mobster who I'm sure you've had dealings with.'

'Haven't,' Roufos whispered.

'Now I come to think of it, you've probably had dealings with Eugene Tzannetakis too.'

'Who?' The antiquities dealer's voice was almost inaudible.

'You heard. As it happens, he's the father of Luke Tzannetakis, also known as Luke Jannet, director of Cara here's movie.' Mavros moved the key up to Roufos's right eye and pressed it against the closed lid.

'All right!' the dealer squealed. 'I've sent shipments to them both in containers, along with the drugs.'

There was a loud knock at the door.

Cara was up quickly and on her way to look through the spyhole. She stepped back with a wide smile on her face. 'Speak of the devil,' she said, in a loud whisper.

'Jannet?' Mavros returned. 'Is he on his own?'

'Looks like it.'

'Let him in.'

Cara undid the chain and lock, then pulled the door open. As Jannet entered, a slack smile on his face, she kneed him hard in the groin. He went down on one knee, then gradually hauled himself up.

'What the fuck was that for, bitch?' he asked, pulling a pistol from above his backside and pointing it in her face.

'Behind the sofa!' Mavros yelled at Niki, heaving Roufos up and using him as a shield.

Stalemate.

David Waggoner stood on the terrace of his house to the west of Kornaria and watched the last of the sun ebb away from the mountainsides into the distant sea. He had seen the same sight in his twenties, when his group of *andartes* came down from the high caves to stock up on supplies. There was always a *glendi*, a feast with sheep being killed and roasted, and barrels of wine broached. Scouts were posted on the almost impassable tracks, but the Germans knew better than to send patrols up there, especially at night. He took a sip of the *raki* that had been distilled from the stems of his own vines and tried to set what was left of his life in order.

The former SOE man knew that he'd made several mistakes recently. The first of those was trusting Tryfon Roufos. Contacts in Athens had told him that the antiquities dealer was a snake with only his own interests at heart, but the temptation to prise Rudolf Kersten's precious coins from him was overwhelming. And the truth was that the coins should have been sent to Egypt by submarine and never fallen into the German's hands after the war. He thought about the lies he had written in his memoirs. Why had he accused the EAM man known as Kanellos of betraying them? With hindsight, the reason didn't make him proud, but he had always been headstrong. The idea of admitting in public that one of his own men had been a traitor was abhorrent, even though he had personally put a bullet in the bastard's head and made sure his wife and children were driven from the village. He was an uncle of the Kondoyannis who was now in jail in Florida.

Waggoner shook his head to dislodge those images. His second mistake had been to underestimate Alex Mavros. The same Athenian contacts had told him to be careful – the investigator had a reputation for doggedness. That was why he had approached the long-haired, unshaven man in Kersten's hotel and told him not to trust the German. That scheme had backfired spectacularly. Now Mavros was trying to find out what happened to Kersten, even though the local authorities had been bribed to declare his death suicide. The reach of Kornaria was long and well established.

'You are worried, my friend.'

The Englishman looked down and saw the mayor, Dhrakakis, standing beneath the terrace. 'Good evening to you, Vasili,' he replied. 'Worried, no. Concerned, of course.'

When the black-clad figure had come up the steps, he handed him a glass of the spirit.

'To our health,' the mayor said. 'Ours and Kornaria's.'

Waggoner led him to the table, where his housekeeper had laid out an array of *mezedhes* – small plates of cucumber, tomato, cheese and cured pork. Dhrakakis speared a piece of the latter with a toothpick and drained his glass.

'You have been greedy,' the Englishman said. 'Establishing links with the Kondoyannis family in Florida was a bad move.'

The mayor raised his heavy shoulders. 'We made a lot of money. And what else were we to do with our products? They were far too much for the Greek market.'

'Michael Kondoyannis has no self control,' Waggoner countered. 'You saw that when he came here. That poor girl almost died.'

'Her family was paid well.'

'But now they want to do worse to "the Bat's" daughter, Maria. How do you think he will react to that, especially if he finds out you tricked her to come up here and then had her kidnapped? He still runs his business from prison, you know.'

Dhrakakis laughed harshly. 'He may think he does, but he has serious competition.'

'You mean the Tzannetakis family? How can they control a drugs operation across the American South when they're holding down high-profile jobs in Hollywood?'

'Ach, Lambi,' the mayor said, using the Englishman's old cover name, 'you forget that Greek families raise many children. Luke and Rosa have three younger brothers and they all learned the business from their father.'

'So you intend to switch to them?'

Dhrakakis stared at him. 'Do not forget that you are a guest here, Lambi. You have no say in how we make our living. You used to facilitate our dealings with the bureaucrats on the coast and with the Germans, but those days are over.'

Despite the burning of the spirit, Waggoner felt a chill run through his body. What the mayor said was true. His wartime heroics meant nothing any more. He was an old man who had connived at the villagers' illegal drug production and trading for years, and now there was nothing he could do about it.

'Do not do anything that could endanger us,' Dhrakakis said, the soles of his boots clicking across tiles. 'Good evening.'

David Waggoner watched him strut down the path that led to

Kornaria. The mayor was too young to have experienced the fight against the Germans, but he had survived many vendettas and attempts to oust him. His soul was tainted by the violence that lay beneath the surface in mountain villages. The Englishman knew himself well enough to see that his character too had been blemished by the sordid reality of the war – shooting wounded prisoners, driving pathetically equipped gendarmes and ordinary citizens into the fire of the paratroopers, countering the communists' scheming with summary justice. He was ashamed of it all, but it was far too late to change the way he was.

The former SOE man went into his house and opened a wooden trunk in his study. Among the contents were things that he knew would keep Alex Mavros off his back for the rest of his life.

A sudden rush of blood to the head forced him to stagger to an armchair. Was this it, the end he had seen overtake so many comrades and enemies? The doctors had told him he had anything between a month and six months. He wanted to die in peace, as the sun rose over the east and flooded his terrace for the last time. If throwing Mavros into the pit was the only way to achieve that, he was ready.

TWENTY-TWO

L uke Jannet had one arm round Cara Parks' neck.
  'Nice to feel your ass against my dick at last,' he said,
  grunting. 'Even if my dick is in agony. I say again, why
the fuck did you knee me, Twin Peaks?'

Mavros glanced to the side, checking that Niki was completely
out of sight. Roufos struggled in his grip, but with little strength.

'Whatcha gonna do now, tough guy?' Cara asked. 'Cop a feel
of my tits?'

'Tempting, but I've got to hold this fine weapon on your friend
Mavros.' He looked over her head. 'Hey, Scotsman, Greekman,
whatever the fuck you are? This here's a Sig Sauer P239. It's
carrying nine .357 Parabellum rounds. You think that beanpole
will stop them blowing you apart?'

Mavros considered that and didn't feel optimistic. He needed
to buy some time. 'You're going to shoot Tryfon Roufos to get
me? You came up here to see him, didn't you?'

'Oh yeah?' Jannet said, tightening his grip on Cara. 'What
makes you think I wasn't going to send him straight to hell?'

Mavros felt Roufos stiffen, but he wasn't convinced the director
had come with that in mind. The dealer had seemed to slump in
relief when Jannet appeared.

'Interesting,' Mavros said enigmatically.

'What the fuck's that supposed to mean?'

'That a drug trafficker's also concerned with antiquities
smuggling.'

Jannet glared at Roufos. 'You been talking, you piece of snake
shit?'

The dealer shook his head frantically. 'No, Luke, no, I—' He
shut up when he saw the even fiercer look on the gunman's face.

'Clever,' Jannet said, grinning at Mavros. 'Except you've now
signed everyone else in here's death warrant. How do you feel
about that, dick?'

Mavros smiled as credibly as he could. 'You think we came

here without protection?' He was hoping Niki would get on her phone and search for Tsifakis's number, then text for help.

'Bullshit,' the director said, squeezing Cara's left breast. 'If you had backup, they'd already be here.'

'You planning on killing the star of your movie, asshole?' Cara demanded, trying to shake him off.

'It won't look like that, darlin'. It'll look like Mavros here went crazy and took all of you out before he plugged himself.' Jannet laughed. 'One of my better storylines. And before you get all uppity, TP, consider this – pumped-up lookers like you are ten a dollar in LA. What, you think you got the job because you can act?'

Mavros kept on with the time-gaining tactic. 'You into silver coins, Luke?'

The director stared at him blankly. 'Hell, no. I got enough of those. I'm interested in the really old shit – Minoan axe heads, clay figures, bull's heads, like in the Iraklion museum. People pay serious top dollar for that.'

'And our slimy friend here has been helping you get your hands on it.' He pressed the key against Roufos's forehead again. 'He won't be much use to you without eyes.'

Tryfon Roufos let out a petrified yelp. 'Please,' he gasped, 'do something, Luke. I can get you more Minoan objects, many more.'

The pistol in Jannet's hand moved around as he tried to lock on to Mavros's body. 'You so much as twitch, TP, and you'll be next,' he said, his other arm tightening round her neck.

The noise of the door being smashed in was deafening. The top of it caught the director on the shoulder and made him let Cara go. She fell forwards, sprawling on the floor as Mikis's friends Yannis and Christos forced their way into the suite, the former carrying a thick metal cylinder with handles that he had obviously used as a battering ram. Luke Jannet scrambled to his feet and dived towards the corridor, the pistol still in his hand. The Pig was waiting for him and relieved him of the weapon with a sharp downward movement of his hand.

'Agh!' the director screamed. 'You broke my fucking arm!'

The Cretan grabbed him by the scruff of his neck and dragged him back into the suite. This time Cara Parks landed her foot between Jannet's legs, extracting an even higher pitched squeal.

'Dope-dealing fucker,' she said, leaning over him, her face suffused with joy. 'Happy you rubbed up against my ass now?'

Christos put down the ram and pulled her back gently.

Mavros handed Roufos over to Yannis and went to Niki, who was standing behind the sofa.

'You were on your phone long before I dropped that hint, weren't you?' he said, kissing her.

'I'm not a complete idiot, Alex.' She looked over his shoulder. 'What next?'

'Good question.' Mavros looked at Yannis. 'We need to get out of here.'

The burly young man nodded. 'Mr Tsifakis is talking to the hotel owner.' He sat Roufos down in the armchair as if he was a rag doll. 'This wanker will be paying for the damages.'

'Agreed?' Mavros asked the antiquities dealer.

'If you leave me alone, agreed.'

'Oh, I'll leave you alone – as long as you're on the night boat to Piraeus.'

Roufos signalled his agreement with a sullen nod.

'What about this piece of shit?' Cara demanded, glaring at Luke Jannet.

'Another customer for the clinic,' Mavros replied, then switched to Greek. 'One of you guys can keep an eye on him. I don't trust the police, at least not till I've got to the bottom of his ties with Kornaria.'

They left Tryfon Roufos in his now less-than-private suite, Mavros taking the cardboard file with him. That would slow his business dealings down, though he had no doubt he'd be back to work as soon as he got back to his office in Athens. He also relived him of his mobile phones, as he did with Jannet. Holding people incommunicado was a useful way of finding which rats came out of the sewers to help them, although in the director's case it was obvious who the first one would be – his sister, Rosie Yellenberg.

'Where to now, Saint Peter?' Cara asked as they walked back to the Jeep, the Cretans having headed off to their pickup with Jannet, to take him to the clinic.

'You like early Elton John?' Mavros said, impressed. 'You must have been about minus five when *Tumbleweed Connection* came out.'

'Good music is good . . . what the hell?'

Mavros looked ahead and his gut performed a somersault. A crowd of skinheads was moving rapidly towards them down the narrow backstreet.

'Don't think that bunch of keys is going to work this time,' Cara said.

'Back to the harbour,' Mavros said, taking her and Niki by the hand and running.

Before they got there another line of far-right scumbags blocked the way.

Petros Lagoudhakis, the Cretan Renaissance leader forced to dig his own grave by Mavros and Mikis, was in the centre.

'Roufos,' Mavros said under his breath. 'The bastard must have called in the troops on a landline.'

Then the punches started raining down on his head. He ducked as low as he could and kept driving forward. He had no idea how long the uneven contest lasted, but suddenly he found himself round the corner, the harbour and its busy cafés only a few yards away. Cara was on one knee, her chest heaving and her hair loose.

Of Niki and their attackers, after he had cleared the blood from his eyes, there was no sign at all.

Hildegard Kersten looked through the spyhole and saw her grandson outside the apartment. She undid the chain and opened the door.

'Hallo, Grandma,' the young man said, embracing her. 'I'm so sorry about Grandpa.'

Hildegard held him close, unsure how real the display of emotion was. Oskar had never been demonstrative, even as a small boy.

'Come in, child,' she said, pushing him gently away and closing the door. 'Did Alex Mavros give you the message to come?'

'Mavros?' Mesner recoiled as if he'd been jabbed with a cattle prod. 'Why would I have seen him?'

'He's looking into your grandfather's death. It wasn't suicide, you know.'

Oskar stared at her. 'But the police . . .'

'The police are controlled by other interests. You're not in Germany now.'

'What other interests?' he said, wiping the sweat from his forehead with a handkerchief.

'Never mind. You won't be here for long. It doesn't concern you.' Hildegard busied herself with preparing coffee.

Her grandson followed her into the kitchen. 'Who said I wouldn't be staying? With Grandpa gone, I thought I could look after you.'

Hildegard smiled. 'I can look after myself. It's time you went back to work. I know about the people you spend your time with. Fortunately for you, I didn't tell your grandfather. He had no time for Nazis and even less for their modern followers.'

'The war made Grandpa crazy,' Oskar said, in a low voice.

'Wrong!' Hildegard said shrilly, trying to convince herself as much as Oskar. 'The war made him a true human being, one who understood the sufferings and plight of others. It is you who betrayed his values.' She bustled through to the living room with a full tray.

Oskar sat opposite her, his head hanging. 'I can't find work in Germany, Grandma. I'm not cut out for the way people work today.'

'You're not cut out to work at all, you mean,' she replied tartly. 'Well, I hope you aren't expecting anything from your grandfather's will.'

He lifted his head, his face white. 'What do you mean?'

'There's nothing apart from the coins – and they are going to museums.'

Hildegard took out the paper she'd found in her husband's pocket. 'Explain this to me, Oskar. "Waggoner – Oskar to dispose of with contacts. Coins value 100K". And don't tell me Rudi didn't write it – I know his hand like my own.'

'I . . . will I still get the one hundred thousand euros' worth of coins?'

'I might consider it,' she replied. 'If you tell me what happened.'

Oskar suddenly looked less pale. 'It was after I stole the thirty coins. He called me and told me he'd give me more, but I had to arrange for the Englishman to . . . to have an accident.' He smiled weakly. 'A fatal one.'

Hildegard put her hand to her heart. It was as she had feared. Rudi had crossed the line from victim to killer as regards their long-term tormentor. She felt sick, but managed to conceal that from her grandson.

'And how was that to be achieved?' she asked.

'Well, I have some pretty dangerous friends. The plan was to burst into his place in Chania and rip it up, so it looked like a burglary that had gone wrong. But we got distracted.'

'And were you the one who was going to kill the Englishman?'

'I . . .' He looked away. 'No. One of my friends from Rostock has finished off more than one ni— I mean immigrant. He likes killing.'

The widow was struggling to keep her breathing regular. 'I see. Have you ever met this man Waggoner?'

'No. Grandpa showed me a picture of him.'

'Ah.' She paused. 'How about a man called Roufos?'

Oskar kept his eyes her. 'No. I've heard of him. Your friend Mavros knows him.'

'Indeed? Did your grandfather ever say anything to you about Alex Mavros and Kornaria?'

Oskar looked at her through narrowed eyes. 'Only that he thought it was a pity Mavros came back from the village in one piece. He said there were people up there who would stop his interfering permanently.'

Hildegard stood up and walked slowly over to the desk. The object she wanted was in the top drawer now. She picked it up and moved back to her grandson, who was facing away from her.

'Get up!' she said, firmly.

Oskar Mesner turned his head and was confronted by the gleaming blade of the Wehrmacht bayonet.

'Out, now!' his grandmother screamed. 'I never want to see you again!'

Oskar stood up and edged away from her, then ran for the door, slamming it behind him.

Hildegard Kersten sank to her knees, the bayonet falling from her hand. Everything she had believed about Rudi – his determination to make reparations, his generosity to the Cretans, his essential humanity – had been completely destroyed. He had conspired with far-right thugs to kill David Waggoner; he had planned to sell half his coins to Roufos – the fact that the proceeds were apparently destined for her made her feel even worse; and he had plotted the death of the very man who was investigating his murder, using violent men from the drugs village he had always purported to despise.

To her horror, she found she couldn't weep. It had dawned on her that Rudi had deserved to be murdered. She picked up the long blade again and held it to her chest, hoping that, wherever she went, he would not be there.

Mavros called Yannis and told him what had happened. The Cretan promised to round up as many 'helpers' as he could find to track down the skinheads.

'Are you all right?' Mavros asked Cara.

She nodded. 'They hurt worse than I do. What about you? That eye doesn't look too good.' She found a tissue in her pocket and held it above his right eye. 'Needs stitches.'

'Forget it,' he said, moving as quickly as he could to Roufos's hotel.

The statuesque receptionist stared at him as they went to the lift. It took only a few seconds in his suite to establish that Roufos had left – all his clothes and personal items were gone.

'He checked out, I presume,' Mavros said, on their way out.

'Yes,' replied the bewildered Minoan. 'He took a taxi to the ferry port.'

'Shall we go after him?' Cara asked.

'Forget it,' he replied. 'He'll be onboard in Suda by now.'

'What if he's got Niki with him?'

Mavros thought about that, then was interrupted by his phone.

'We've got some of them,' Yannis said. 'But not your friend.'

'Can you find out where she's been taken?'

'Already done that. Kornaria, I'm afraid. They were hired by someone from the village. I don't think they know his name.'

'Shit!' Mavros said, glancing at Cara. For all her poise, she didn't look like a movie star right now. 'All right, meet me at the clinic.' He led her to the Jeep by a roundabout route, in case there were any more headbangers lying in wait. 'You know,' he said, as they got into the vehicle, Cara on the driver's side, 'I've got a family place round the corner from here. You could hole up there.'

'What, you think I don't want to be in at the end of this?' she countered.

'Those fuckers have got Maria, remember?'

Who was probably also in Kornaria, Mavros thought – the very place he couldn't go if he wanted to stay alive.

He directed the actress to the clinic, asking her what she thought Luke Jannet would do if they released him.

'Go back to the set,' she said bitterly. 'He's brazen enough to deny anything we say.'

'But how can he expect you to finish the movie after the way he treated you in Roufos's suite?'

She laughed. 'He's right about there being plenty of young actresses who would do anything – and I mean anything – to take over from me. Rosie being the producer makes that even easier.'

'What about the cost?'

She glanced at him. 'You get the idea they're short of money? Besides, there's insurance if performers have breakdowns, which is no doubt what they'll say about me. Bye bye career.'

'Screw that. I'm not letting a bunch of dope-dealers trample over everything that's decent on this island. Plus, your career's worth a lot.'

'Why, thank you!' Cara said, her teeth shining in the glow from the street lamps. 'Don't worry, I can look after myself.'

'I noticed.'

She pulled up outside the clinic. They met Yannis and the Pig in the foyer, and then Mikis's parents.

'He's awake!' Eleni said, with a broad smile. 'They don't think he's going to need an operation after all.'

'That's wonderful,' Mavros said, shaking their hands.

'We heard about your Niki,' Haris said. 'Don't worry, we'll get her back.'

Mavros wasn't clear about how that would be achieved but, before he could ask, Cara steered him away to a treatment room. Doctor Stavrakakis was in the corridor.

'I don't believe it,' he said. 'What is it with you, Mr Mavro? Maybe I should check you for head injuries, and I don't just mean recent ones.'

'No time, Doc,' Mavros said. 'This is a matter of life or death.'

'All right, my friend. Get yourself cleaned up.'

A nurse duly did that, telling him to close his eye as she sprayed anaesthetic on his lower forehead. He felt all four stitches going in, but he didn't shed tears in front of Cara – for some reason that was important to him.

'Any idea where Rosie might be?' he asked the actress, as the dressing on his neck was changed.

She looked at her watch. 'Nearly dinner time. She could well be in the hotel. Or on her way to a restaurant in town'

Mavros took out his phone and asked Renzo Capaldi. The security chief called back shortly and said that Ms Yellenberg had been seen leaving with an unknown man half an hour earlier. They hadn't used a Tsifakis vehicle. He told Cara.

'You think she's gone to Kornaria?'

'I'd say it's pretty likely,' he replied. 'Thanks,' he said to the nurse, taking the painkillers she handed him. 'I'm going to get addicted to these soon.'

'If you live long enough,' Cara said.

'Very funny,' he said, suddenly realizing the magnitude of what he was up against. Niki had been foolish to come to Crete, but he loved her and he wasn't going to let her be abused or worse in the mountain village.

The Tsifakises were still in the reception area, in a huddle with Yannis and the Pig.

Eleni peered at his eye. 'That looks painful.'

He held up painkillers, two of which he had dry-swallowed.

'Where's Luke Jannet?' he asked.

'They're putting a cast on his forearm,' Haris said. 'Christos is keeping watch.'

'Any thoughts about what we do next?' Mavros asked the Cretan. 'Preferably ones that don't involve my or anyone else's death or serious injury.'

Mikis's father nodded solemnly. 'We've been talking about that and we think we have a solution.'

'All right,' Mavros said, heading for a line of chairs. 'I may be half blind, but I'm all ears.'

TWENTY-THREE

Mavros agreed with Haris Tsifakis that the main convoy of vehicles would aim to reach Kornaria at four a.m., when most people would still be asleep. Scout groups led by Yannis, Christos, and the Pig set off earlier, using little known tracks that would enable them to approach the village from the eastern side. The men would have to carry heavy loads over rough ground at the end, but when he saw the crowd in the Tsifakis depot, Mavros had no doubt they were up to the job. Luke Jannet had been locked in a windowless storeroom with a man on the door.

'What about the sentries on the main road?' he asked.

'Don't worry about them,' Haris said, with a broad smile. 'Need to know basis.'

Mavros didn't argue the point. The only chance he had of getting Niki back was in the hands of the Cretan. Besides, he had other things on his mind. Hildegard Kersten had called him half an hour before.

'Alex,' she said, her voice wavering, 'I want you to give up the case.'

'What?' He was instantly guilty about not having devoted more time to Rudolf Kersten's murder. 'I've been delayed, but don't worry, I'm getting to the bottom of it.'

'No,' the widow said, her voice now firm. 'I forbid you to investigate any further. And Alex, you must promise me one more thing. Whatever you do, don't go to Kornaria. There's . . . there's nothing for you in that accursed place but death. Do you hear me? Don't go anywhere near it.'

'What's happened, Hildegard? You don't sound well.'

'Well?' she said, with a tremulous laugh. 'Soon I will be burying my husband, the hero who helped rebuild this part of Crete. Soon . . . oh, never mind. Go to the good, Alex.'

Mavros had been puzzled by the call. Hildegard didn't sound like the calm and controlled woman she had been even in recent days. What had the widow found out to change her mind so radically about her husband's death? And why was she so adamant about Kornaria? As far as he knew, the couple's only connection with the village was that their tormentor, David Waggoner, lived there.

Not long afterwards, he received a call from Niki's mobile. Heart thundering, he answered it, speaking her name.

'Your Niki is safe, Mavro,' came a voice he recognized – it was that of Dhrakakis, the mayor. 'For the time being. I propose a trade. Luke Jannet for her. But you, and only you, must come with him.'

'How do I know you'll keep the bargain?' he asked hoarsely.

Dhrakakis laughed. 'You have to trust me. We Cretans have a deep-rooted sense of honour.' His tone hardened. 'Be here by midday or you'll hear the woman die on your phone.' The connection was cut.

'What is it, Alex?' Cara asked, taking in his expression.

He told her what had been proposed.

'You can't do that!' she exclaimed. 'They'll kill you and Niki as soon as you give them that shithead Luke.'

'It's possible,' Mavros said, going to Haris and speaking to him in a low voice. Shortly afterwards, the Cretan slapped him on the shoulder and called over one of his associates.

Mavros spent the next fifteen minutes on the phone to Athens police commander Nikos Kriaras, the man who had recommended him to Luke Jannet. Kriaras was unimpressed at being called so late, but he was soon hooked. He agreed to give Mavros's idea consideration and talk to his contacts in the Ministry of Public Order. The sting in the tail was that Mavros gave him six hours to come up with the goods, or word would be passed to the press that the authorities had refused to take action in a double kidnap by the most notorious villagers in Crete.

'Why are you looking so pleased?' Cara asked.

'Never mind. You realize there's no way you can come with us?'

The actress gave him a foxy smile. 'I've already talked to Haris about that. He said his wife was coming and I could hang with her.'

Mavros swore under his breath. It wasn't only Cretan men who were one step away from violence. He wouldn't fancy taking

Eleni on in a fight. And the same went for the deceptively dangerous, non-Cretan Cara Parks.

'It's your neck,' he said, shaking his head.

Then his phone rang again. He didn't recognize the number.

'This is David Waggoner.' The former SOE man sounded faint. 'Listen carefully. I know your woman is in the village, but you must *not* come up here. They will eventually let her go, believe me. Perhaps your friend Tsifakis can broker a deal. If you appear, you'll be committing suicide.'

Mavros tried to keep his voice steady. 'Why the sudden interest in my safety? You and Roufos set those neo-Nazi attack dogs on me.'

'I had nothing to do with that. My only connection with that repugnant man was over Kersten's coin collection. I have cut all ties with him.'

'And you still say you had nothing to do with the German's death?'

'I certainly do.' Waggoner paused. 'Listen, Mavros, you've got the wrong end of the stick about me. I may have overstepped the mark by obtaining payments from Kersten over the years, but the man was a cold-blooded killer in the war and a hypocrite for the rest of his life.'

'You also overstepped the mark, not to say the law, by aiding and abetting the Kornariates in their protection rackets and other activities for decades. For all I know, you're the mastermind behind the village's drug production.'

'Don't be ridiculous, man!' the Englishman barked. 'I facilitated their dealings on the coastal strip, nothing more.' He sighed, as if in pain. 'Look here. It's as simple as this. If you stay away from Kornaria, I will give you certain papers and memorabilia that I took from the EAM man known as Kanellos in 1943.'

Mavros felt a blow to his heart. 'You have things belonging to my father?'

'To him or his beloved party, yes. Do you want them?'

Of course I fucking want them, Mavros said to himself, trying to keep afloat in the maelstrom of emotion that was suddenly sucking him down. 'How . . . how do I take delivery?'

'You know where my place in Chania is. Be there tonight at nine o'clock. But bear in mind, I will know if you've been in

Kornaria, even if by some miracle you escape. I will destroy everything immediately, be sure of that.'

'Why do you care if I go to the village?' Mavros asked, trying to keep the old soldier on the line.

'That's my affair,' Waggoner said, breaking the connection.

Mavros called back, but there was no answer. He slumped in his chair.

'What is it?' Cara asked, putting her arm around his shoulders. 'Those blows to your head playing up?'

'Yeah,' he replied, gradually getting a grip. It wasn't the first time he had been tempted by information relating to his family, though in the past it had been about his brother, Andonis. In almost every case, people had invented things to distract him from the case in hand. It was very likely that David Waggoner was doing the same thing – but why? What interest could he have in Mavros and Niki?

He looked up to see Haris standing in front of them.

'All will be well, Alex,' the Cretan said. 'We have the equipment you asked for and my technicians are working on it.'

'What equipment?' Cara asked.

'Need to know basis,' Mavros said, tapping his nose.

Hildegard was sitting in front of the fire, watching the last blackened wisps of the papers she had burned disappear up the chimney. All the photographs of her and Rudi had gone up in smoke earlier. There were only two things left, and she would be making use of them soon. The *labrys* she had placed on the mantelpiece, no longer needing whatever power it might have bestowed on her as a woman. Oskar had called earlier, trying to make peace, but she had told him not to bother her again. That was the last time she would speak to him.

It was impossible not to think of the distant past – the ruins of Berlin, the horrors of the Russian occupation, the rapes she had suffered. For decades, their life in Crete had provided a refuge from those terrible memories, but no longer. Rudi's life had been a sham, he had been the hypocrite that Waggoner always said he was. Which meant their life together had also been a sham – no, worse than that, a perversion of the good. Oskar's revolting beliefs proved that, but the idea that Rudi had tried to take advantage of them was almost the last straw.

The only saving grace in the last few days had been Alex Mavros. He had been taken in by Rudi, but so had she and for much longer. At least Alex had tried to get to the truth. She only hoped he would take her advice about not going to Kornaria. That place was evil, her husband had always said so – but at the last he had been prepared to use it to dispose of the very man who had helped them. Why had Rudi been so keen to hire Mavros to get the thirty coins back? Of course, he hadn't wanted them back at all, employing Mavros only to prove to the insurance company that he had taken every possible step to secure their return. He had wanted to pay a deposit to Oskar for God knows what services, and the burglary must have been a set-up. He would never have expected Mavros to succeed against the ranks of skinhead swine. Getting the coins and the money back must have been a terrible shock to him. The paper she had found in his pocket was obviously written after that – when he had truly lost control of himself.

Hildegard looked down at the objects on the rug between her and the fire. Her plan was simple, but needed a steady hand and much determination. She intended to push her husband's para-trooper's jump badge as far down her throat as she could and then force the point of the silver-shining Wehrmacht bayonet between her ribs and into her heart. She had made all the necessary arrangements about what was left of their estate with the lawyer – small sums were to be given to hotel employees who had been with them for many years, as well as to Alex Mavros, in recognition of what he had tried to do for them. The jump badge and bayonet were to be dropped in the sea off Maleme in a weighted bag once they had been returned by the police and medical examiner. She was ready.

The badge was in her hand when she heard a noise at the French window at the far end of the living room. For a few seconds, she wanted to continue with her plan, but the thought of being discovered when she was still warm and being rushed to hospital, even the faint chance that she might be saved, made her drop the badge and pick up the bayonet.

'Who's there?' she called, getting to her feet.

The door slid open and a large figure slipped into the dimly lit area. As it came closer, she saw who it was.

'Mr Capaldi? What are you doing?' she said, then caught sight of the silenced pistol the security manager was pointing at her. She moved the hand holding the bayonet behind her back.

'The coins,' the Italian said. 'Tell me where they are.'

'How dare you? Get out of here now!'

The spit of the shot was scarcely audible. She crashed to the ground, a searing pain in her lower leg. In a second, Capaldi was beside her, his lips near hers.

'Be quiet, you German bitch, or I'll put a round in your thigh.' He grinned. 'Which will quickly be fatal. The coins – where are they? I want the keys and combination numbers.'

'Did . . . did Roufos put you up to this?' Hildegard asked, blinking as the pain flared even more.

'You are still sharp. But not sharp enough to see something more important.' The look on his face changed and Hildegard realized that he was going to kill her. That thought brought enlightenment.

'You . . . you killed Rudi.'

'Ah, that was a mistake. Mr Roufos told me to put as much pressure as I could on your husband to hand over the collection. Unfortunately, your husband's neck snapped like a twig.' The Italian showed no sign of regret. 'Stringing him up got the cops off our back.'

'Go to hell, Capaldi.' Hildegard bit her lip and swung the bayonet round as hard as she could. The point slipped into the soft flesh of her attacker's lower back. He gasped and then toppled forward on to the rug beside her. He stopped breathing soon afterwards.

Hildegard Kersten saw the slick of his blood join with that pumping from her leg wound. The heat was disappearing from her body and she slipped away from consciousness, happy that her mind was filled with the glinting snow peaks of the mountains she had looked up at for so many years.

Mavros had a bad feeling about Hildegard Kersten's call. He rang the Heavenly Blue and asked for the widow, but heard she had told reception that no calls should be put through. Then he asked for Renzo Capaldi, only to hear, after a while on hold, that he couldn't be located. That made him even more worried.

'Listen, this is Alex Mavros, the investigator. I think Mrs

Kersten is in danger. Break the door down to her apartment if she doesn't answer. Do it now!'

There was a muffled conversation and then he was asked to stay on the line. Shortly afterwards he heard screams and his stomach somersaulted. Eventually one of the staff came back on.

'Thank God you called, Mr Mavro,' the man said, shocked. 'Mrs Kersten has been shot in the leg and Mr Capaldi is . . . is dead. It looks like she stabbed him.'

'Don't touch anything in the apartment, do you hear? Call an ambulance and then the police. I can't come to the hotel now.'

'The ambulance is already on its way.'

'Good. If she's conscious, tell her I expect to see her tomorrow.' He rang off.

'Expect to see who?' Cara asked.

Mavros ran his hand through his hair. 'What?' he said distractedly, then told her what had happened.

He had been a major idiot. Waggoner and Oskar hadn't been the only people the scheming Roufos had put up to laying hands on Kersten's coin collection. And Mavros had entrusted the widow's safety to the former elite soldier. He could only hope he hadn't been too late. Then he had another thought. He had seen Renzo Capaldi on the massacre set, but had paid no attention as he assumed he'd been escorting Rudolf Kersten. Now he wondered if Capaldi had actually killed the old man. If so, had he been acting on Roufos's orders? He made another call to Nikos Kriaras in Athens, asking him to ensure that the antiquities dealer was picked up when the night boat docked in Piraeus, even though he was pretty sure Tryfon Roufos would never crack under interrogation.

'Jesus freakin' Christ,' Cara said, standing up rapidly.

Eleni Tsifaki had appeared, wearing a camouflage jacket and trousers, with belts full of shotgun shells crisscrossing her chest and a large hunting knife in her belt.

'Come with me, Cara,' Mikis's mother said. 'I have the same for you.'

Mavros sat with his chin in his hands before he was joined by Haris.

'It's time for you to check your equipment, Alex,' he said. 'The advance teams have already set out.'

'Are you sure there's no other way of doing this?'

The Cretan raised his broad shoulders. 'Kornaria has been a cancer in this island for too long. Besides, they won't hand over your woman or the other one, even if the man who calls himself Jannet is returned to them. I know how Dhrakakis works.'

Mavros thought for a few moments. 'What about Waggoner?'

'Ach, Waggoner. My father told me he was a fierce fighter in the war, but men like him often do not do so well in peacetime. I don't know if he's involved in the drug trade, but he's had his snout in many other dirty deals over the years.'

'He told me he has some things that belonged to my father, and that he'll only give them to me if I don't go to the village.'

Haris sat down beside him. 'Alex *mou*, this I cannot help you with. But I know what I would do – put the living before the dead, God rest your brave father's soul.'

Not that Spyros, as a good communist, thought he had one of those, at least not currently residing in heaven. Mavros nodded. 'You're right. Let's do it.'

He followed Haris into the depths of the old building.

TWENTY-FOUR

Luke Jannet was removed from his makeshift cell, allowed to use the toilet with the guard present and then handcuffed by his unplastered wrist to the same solid Cretan.

Mavros, wearing a loose green cotton combat jacket, came up to the pair.

'Guess what?' he said. 'We're taking you to Kornaria to swap you for my other half and Maria Kondos.'

'Are you fuckin' kidding?' the director said, his eyes wide. 'I don't want to go anywhere near that place.'

'Really? And there I was, thinking you were their new best friend.'

'Yeah, well, that depended on me bringing a large amount of cash to the table.' He glared at Mavros. 'Cash I'd have got if you'd let Roufos do his job.'

Mavros held his gaze. 'So you were going to take the proceeds of the coin collection. In return for what? Cutting Roufos in on the drug trafficking?'

'The two things go together – in the same containers, I mean. It's a perfect fit.'

'A perfect fit that's about to get too tight for comfort.' Mavros laughed. 'Don't worry, they're very hospitable up there. Or so Maria Kondos didn't say.' He turned on his heel and left the American moaning. Suddenly that stopped. He looked over his shoulder and saw that the guard had placed his very large fist in front of Jannet's face as a warning. Scene over.

His phone rang shortly afterwards.

'Oh, he lives and breathes,' the Fat Man said, with heavy irony. 'I've been trying you for hours. You turned yourself into a telephone exchange?'

'Busy-busy, Yiorgo. About to go into action.'

'Cinematic or vendetta?'

'Primarily the latter.'

There was a pause. 'You're serious, aren't you?'

'Very. Niki's been kidnapped. I've got plenty of help, but so have the opposition.'

'Those drug-producing tossers?'

'Correct. If . . . if I don't get out of this alive, you'll have to tell my family.'

'What? Alex, you're hereby banned from doing anything dangerous, you hear?' The Fat Man's voice had gone up several octaves.

'Too late for that, Yiorgo. Whatever happens, it'll be on the news tomorrow. Kriaras is handling things in Athens.'

'Oh, great. So why have you got to take any risks?'

Mavros sighed. 'I told you, Fat Man, they've got Niki. But don't worry, we've got some tricks up our sleeves.'

'So now you're Prince Charming, going off to rescue a fair damsel?'

'I might also get back some stuff that belonged to my old man during the war.'

That shut Yiorgos up, but not for long.

'Call the cops in Chania. They can take charge till Kriaras's people arrive.'

Mavros laughed. 'Listen to yourself, Yiorgo. The cops down here have been living off Kornaria for decades. Look, I've got to go. I'll talk to you tomorrow. Love you, Fat Man.' He cut the connection before he heard his friend's reaction to that. Communists weren't supposed to be emotional and Mavros had never said those words to Yiorgos before.

Cara came over, dressed like Eleni and carrying a pump-action shotgun.

'Reminds me of my second picture,' she said. 'Country girl who got raped and took out a whole village of freaks.' She racked the slide. 'Good to be carrying live rounds for a change.' She peered at him. 'What's up?'

'Nothing,' he said. 'Something in my eye.'

'Uh-huh.'

'Look, will you try to keep your head down? I've grown quite fond of you and I wouldn't like you to get hurt.'

'Aw, sweet.' She kissed him, taking care not to touch his abdomen. 'Haven't you noticed?' She unzipped her jacket to reveal a Kevlar vest. 'Tightly constricted twin peaks.'

He laughed and they headed for the exit. In the parking lot, two long wheelbase Land Rovers and two large pickups were being loaded with various supplies.

'There will be twelve armed men in the convoy,' Haris said, glancing at his wife and Cara. 'Plus two armed women.'

'Keep them all out of sight for as long as you can,' Mavros said. 'It may be I can finish this on my own.'

'And maybe I can sing *Tosca*,' Eleni said, with a sardonic laugh. 'This is a fight to the finish, Alex, and you know it.'

He nodded. 'Let's hope that Niki and Maria aren't among the casualties.'

'You forgot someone,' Cara said. 'Yourself.'

'Leave him be,' Haris said, pulling her back. 'He's getting his thoughts in order. He's going into the village alone apart from that wanker of a director. The adrenaline has to be controlled.'

Mavros got into the second vehicle, a Land Rover, with Haris, while the women went in the third. The lead pickup was filled with four young Cretans, to deal with the expected road block. Jannet was with his escort in the last vehicle.

As they headed through the dark orange and olive groves, he looked up at the night. The snow on the mountains was visible, an almost full moon casting its pallid light over the line of ridges and summits.

'Are you sure about the timing?' Mavros asked Haris.

'The sooner you walk up there the better. They'll all be awake from sunrise, but the longer we wait, the more likely that one or other of our people will be spotted.' He gave a guttural laugh. 'It's always best to take your enemy by surprise. Dhrakakis will assume you'll leave it till the last minute to show up, having wasted your time trying to get the police interested.'

'You sure your men will be able to extract the walkie-talkie passwords from the sentries?'

'You've obviously never had a hunting knife in the immediate vicinity of your balls.'

'Erm, not yet.'

Haris slapped him on the thigh. 'Don't worry, they won't come near you.'

'Best you observe the same principle.'

The Cretan glanced at him and then nodded. 'Sorry, that was stupid.'

'I appreciate the sentiment though,' Mavros said. Then he slipped into a zone where the people he would be trying to save flashed before him – Niki, smiling bravely; Maria Kondos, as haughty as ever. Then his father appeared, his face younger and less care-worn than in the photos that Mavros's mother had on display. Suddenly he understood. Although Spyros's experiences on Crete – the paratroop landings, the Battle of Galatsi, the years on the run – had been terrible, it had been on the island that he learned the truth about violence: that it led to more brutality and heartbreak, and that no political system, even a communist one, could be built on blood-drenched foundations. Whatever happened in Kornaria, Mavros had to remain true to those principles. The rock that he had thrown into the Kornariate's face had to be his last violent act.

The sky in the east was lightening to grey and the vehicles in the convoy turned off their headlights, following an order from Haris, relayed by walkie-talkie.

'Roadblock in sight,' said one of the men from the Land Rover in the lead. 'Approaching on foot.'

That meant the men were splitting up and heading in a wide circling movement towards the pickup that had been parked across the road. Haris stopped the Land Rover and waited. Tension in the cab rose and Mavros struggled to keep his breathing regular. If they couldn't get beyond this first barrier, the whole plan would be compromised – although Haris had told him he had reserve options.

'How often have you done this kind of thing?' Mavros asked, in a low voice.

Haris smiled. 'You aren't taping *this*, I hope. Not so often, and never on as large a scale as this. Crete isn't like the rest of Greece, my friend. We have our own ways of justice. I don't only mean vendettas. If someone persists in anti-social and damaging behaviour, he is taught a lesson. That is not a bad thing.'

'Unless it gets out of control.'

'You are worried this operation will go that way? I can understand that. But you must trust me, Alex, as I trust you. That is how the Turks and the Germans were driven out – we acted in unison.'

'Freedom or death,' Mavros said. 'But this time you'll be fighting against your fellow Cretans.'

Haris shrugged. 'Criminals and bullies are the same the world over. Someone must stand up to them.'

There was a burst of sound from his walkie-talkie.

'Road block neutralized. WT codes obtained. No serious injuries.'

'You see?' Haris said. 'Now all we need is confirmation from the advance units.'

That came in three separate messages over the next ten minutes.

'All is ready, Alex. Are you?'

Mavros nodded. His heart was beating at a normal rate and his breathing was regular. He got out of the Land Rover and checked his equipment, then watched as the pickup containing Luke Jannet came slowly alongside. The director had been gagged with duct tape. His guard unlocked the cuff on his wrist and attached it gingerly to Mavros's belt.

'Is everything that needs to be turned on?' Haris asked.

'Yup. Thanks for everything. I'm only sorry Mikis couldn't be here to see this.'

The Cretan nodded solemnly. 'He would have enjoyed it, but he's better off in his bed. Now, Alex, bring your woman and the other one back.' He stopped himself slapping Mavros's back just in time.

Mavros dragged Jannet into the pickup and took the wheel.

'Keep still if you want to stay alive,' Mavros said.

The director, who had been told what Mavros was carrying, nodded vigorously.

The pickup moved slowly up the road, past the vehicle which had been moved out of the way. Mavros saw in the mirror that Haris's men had taken the villagers' *mandilia*, jackets and shotguns. He continued at low speed, avoiding the worst potholes and ridges, until they passed the sign announcing Kornaria. It had been riddled with pellets.

'Welcome to Hell,' Mavros said, glancing at Jannet. 'This is going to be better than any film you've shot, asshole.' The director's face was white around the strip of black tape.

Mavros drove up the narrow street between the white houses. The shutters on some had been thrown open to take in the early morning light, but there were no people to be seen. He pulled up in the square and hauled Jannet out, then put his hand on the pickup's horn. It wasn't long before heads appeared at windows and men started coming out of doors, some of them carrying shotguns.

Mavros took his captive towards the *kafeneion* where he and Mikis had talked to the mayor. It wasn't open yet. Then a metal door a few yards down the square swung open and Dhrakakis came out, rubbing his eyes. He was wearing a singlet, blue pyjama trousers and slippers.

'You don't look like the man behind a multinational drugs business,' Mavros said. 'More like a grandfather who's just wet himself.'

As he'd expected, the words stung the mayor. Mavros held Jannet in front of him as the Cretan approached, his cheeks red. The next few seconds were decisive.

'You'll pay for insulting me, you Athenian arse-bandit,' Dhrakakis said, as he came closer. 'Look at you, hiding behind your hostage.'

'Come and get him then, Grandpa,' Mavros said, with a sharp smile.

'*Ela*, Louka,' the mayor said, his arm extended towards Jannet.

Mavros waited as long as he could, and then pulled out the other handcuff attached to his belt and snapped it shut around Dhrakakis's wrist. He unzipped his jacket and took out the detonator that was wired to the explosives on his chest, his thumb over the short plunger.

'Tell your men to keep their distance,' he said calmly to the Cretan. 'If any of them comes within range, we three will turn into very small pieces. If you try to take the detonator from me, ditto.' He laughed like a madman. 'I know what you'll have done to my woman and to Maria Kondos. I don't give a shit what happens to me.'

This was another critical moment. If Dhrakakis thought he was bluffing, there would be no way out.

'No, no,' the mayor stammered. 'Nobody has touched your woman. I swear it.'

'Why should I believe you?' Mavros demanded. 'You run the most lawless village in Crete. You've bribed the police, the local authorities, the politicians, the bankers, anyone you could, to keep this place in business. What I want from you is a confession. Then I'll let you go.'

It wasn't obvious that he was wearing a wire, but Dhrakakis was the kind of scheming bastard who would immediately think of that. Mavros was hoping that he would talk, assuming he would subsequently be able to kill Mavros and destroy any recording device before others arrived.

There was a pause, and then the Cretan started to blab. With prompting from Mavros, he started to name every person who had received money from Kornaria. Some of them were a surprise – a television channel and newspaper owner, the director of a reforestation charity, a famous actress who had slept with various politicians. Other names were to be expected: government ministers; members of parliament; local officials and policemen, including Inspector Margaritis; the owners of hotels on the coastal strip, doctors, lawyers, customs officials – all had gained benefits of various kinds from their links to the village. Mavros also extracted the names of the Greek-Americans who were involved in the drug trafficking. The Tzannetakis family was conspicuous by its presence, as was the Kondoyannis clan.

'Have you heard enough?' Dhrakakis demanded.

Mavros nodded. 'Now produce the women.'

The mayor gave the order to one of his henchmen, who had a bandage round his head – Mavros recognized him as the man he had hit with the stone. Soon after, Niki and Maria Kondos appeared round the corner. They were both pale and the Greek-American was limping, but otherwise they looked uninjured.

Mavros raised a hand. 'Stop there!' he shouted, when they reached the middle of the square.

'You said you'd let us go,' Dhrakakis said impatiently.

Mavros nodded, then took out his walkie-talkie. 'Codeword "Maleme", repeat "Maleme".'

'Received,' came Haris's voice.

'Now what?' the mayor asked.

'Hold on a minute,' Mavros said, waiting for the first smoke to rise above the houses to the east. 'Oh, what's that? Even though there are no trees up here, there seems to be a forest fire.'

Dhrakakis followed the direction of his gaze. 'What have you done, you fucking bastard? To the cultivation sheds and warehouses, all of you!'

The booted men in the square ran towards the smoke, which was now thick black and roiling.

'You bastard,' repeated the mayor. 'You—' He broke off as Haris's Land Rover and the other vehicles roared into the square and armed men jumped out. Only a couple of shots were fired in the air to clear out the last of the villagers.

Haris and three of his men surrounded Mavros and his captives and unlocked the cuffs from his belt, before cuffing the pair together. Dhrakakis groaned as he saw smoke to the north of the village as well.

Mavros ripped the tape from Jannet's mouth. 'Sorry, did that hurt? Well, it's a hard life being a criminal. If you're lucky the FBI will take you home – you really don't want to spend time in a Greek prison.'

Luke Jannet lowered his head. Then Maria Kondos came up to the American-Greek and slapped the side of his head hard.

'Let him go!' came a shrill voice from the centre of the square.

They all looked round and saw Rosie Yellenberg with her arm round Niki's neck and a pistol jammed in her ribs. 'Get over here, Luke!' she screamed, dragging Niki to the last of the pickups.

Haris nodded and the director's cuffs were loosed. He ran to his sister.

Mavros made to follow him, but Haris grabbed his arm.

'Wait,' the Cretan said.

They didn't have to do so for long. As Rosie and Luke manoeuvred Niki to the vehicle, Eleni Tsifaki and Cara Parks appeared from behind it. The former smashed her elbow into Jannet's face and flattened him with a punch from the other hand. Cara kicked the pistol out of Rosie's hand and then swung round on her other foot before delivering a knockout blow to the producer's jaw. Niki sank to her knees and wailed Mavros's first name.

'Excuse me,' he said to Haris. 'She's been through a lot.'

'Excuse *me*,' the Cretan said, removing the detonator from the charges. 'You don't want to go up in a cloud of fireworks.'

'I think that's going to happen anyway,' Mavros said, then ran to his beloved.

TWENTY-FIVE

There could never have been so many vehicles on the unmetalled road leading to Kornaria before: police cars, marked and unmarked, TV vans, press personnel on motorbikes and in 4 x 4s. They were forced to the side by the fire engines that rumbled up to deal with the blazes in the drug sheds and warehouses. By the time they got there, only smoking remains were left and the firemen busied themselves ensuring that the flames didn't spread to the village or to the sparse shrubs on the surrounding slopes. A helicopter hovered above the village and eventually set down on an old threshing floor. One of the men who climbed out was police commander Nikos Kriaras.

'You didn't leave us much to do,' he said sourly, as paramilitary policemen spread though the village.

Mavros shrugged. 'We couldn't wait. I didn't set the press dogs loose – one of the villagers must have. Look, Niko, this place has been screwing the western end of the island for decades. Someone had to do something and I couldn't wait.'

There were a few shots in the distance, but the crowd of disarmed male villagers in the square was growing by the minute. They were surrounded by armed police.

Kriaras glowered at him. 'And that person had to be you, eh?'

'They had Niki. Would you have left your wife to these lunatics?'

The look on the policeman's face was inscrutable. Mavros reckoned he might have, but he kept that to himself.

'What about Roufos? Did you get him?'

Kriaras looked away. 'Not yet. He seems to have bribed an engineer on the ship for his uniform.'

'See what I mean about having to do things myself?' Mavros said, shaking his head. 'The *kafeneion* owner. Go easy on him. He gave me the lead to the Kondoyannis family. Don't know why, probably in a feud with them. And Maria Kondos – I'm not sure if she's a victim or if she's involved in the dope trade.

Make sure you take her into custody.' Then he had another thought: David Waggoner.

'Excuse me,' he said, going over to one of the local women who had gathered to support their men folk and asking where the Englishman's house was. He followed her directions to the west.

'Do you want us to come with you?' Haris called. He was with his wife, while Niki was talking animatedly to Cara Parks. Maria Kondos was standing alone a few metres away.

'I'll be all right,' Mavros answered, hurrying down the lane. Suddenly he had a bad feeling about Waggoner. How would he be reacting to the events in the village he'd lived in and helped for decades?

A narrow track led to a two-storey stone house a couple of hundred metres beyond the edge of the village. The blue shutters were open and the terrace was covered in floods of bougainvillea and oleander blossom.

'Waggoner!' Mavros shouted, as he approached. 'Are you there?'

There was no reply. He climbed the steps and looked to each side. There were a table and chairs on his right, a tray containing a small coffee cup and a half-drunk glass of water on the former.

'Waggoner!' He stepped through the bead curtain and into the cool house. The living area to the right had dull-coloured floors and was sparsely furnished with antique dark-wood pieces. Animal heads and regimental shields hung on the walls.

'The hands go up, fucker.'

He recognized the voice and turned to see the shaven-headed Petros Lagoudhakis, leader of the far-right Cretan Renaissance, shove David Waggoner into the room, a pistol pointing at Mavros.

'Well, this is a pleasant surprise,' the Cretan said. 'Two shitbags instead of one.'

Mavros glanced at the Englishman. His face was pale and beaded with sweat and he looked diminished from the last time they'd met.

'You realize the village is teeming with police?' Mavros said.

'Won't take me long to finish you two.'

'I suppose I'm in your sights because I made you dig your own grave the other night.'

Lagoudhakis glared at him. 'You don't get over something like that easily. Besides, I heard what you did to Mr Roufos.'

Mavros sighed. He was about to die because he hadn't kept hold of the antiquities dealer. Phoning the Cretan from the ship would have been easy.

'And him?' he said, inclining his head towards Waggoner.

'Him? He persecuted Herr Kersten for years, never mind all the Germans he killed in the war.'

Mavros stared at him. 'Rudolf Kersten told you to kill him?'

'Who else? Herr Kersten supported my organization in many ways.'

'Was Oskar Mesner involved?'

'Leave him out of it.'

Which meant 'yes', as far as Mavros was concerned.

Lagoudhakis raised the pistol towards Waggoner. 'And let's not forget that the British blocked the union of Crete for years in the nineteenth century and screwed up Cyprus permanently. This piece of shit was responsible for the death of several Cypriot freedom fighters. So go to meet them, murderer.'

Then Lagoudhakis went flying forward, smothered by a heavily-built figure with a bandage on his head. The weapon skittered across the floor as the neo-Nazi's hand was smashed against the tiles.

'Miki?' Mavros said, his heart halfway towards his mouth. 'What the—'

The Cretan dragged the now cowering Lagoudhakis to his feet and then planted a heavy fist in his belly. He hit the floor again and started writhing.

David Waggoner limped forwards and handed the pistol that he'd picked up to Mavros. He looked like he was already in another dimension.

'What's the matter?' Mavros asked.

'Pancreatic cancer. I've got a few weeks if I'm lucky.' The former SOE man grimaced. 'Or less – the pain is terrible.' He looked at Mavros curiously. 'Why did you come?'

'I had a feeling you'd do something . . . foolish.'

'You were behind what's happened to the village?'

'Not on my own.' Mavros glanced at Mikis. 'What are you doing out of hospital?'

The driver grinned. 'Watching your back.'

'Thanks, but aren't you supposed to be resting?'

'Nah. Anyway, some fuckers from Dopetown took my Colt, remember? I want it back.'

Mavros smiled. 'You might have a job talking the cops into handing it over.'

'I have several friends in the police force.'

'What a surprise.' Mavros looked back at Waggoner. The old man was picking something up from his desk.

'I was trying to protect you when I told . . . told you to stay away.'

'Guilty conscience?' Mavros asked, not prepared to let him off the hook.

'Something like that.' Waggoner stepped closer. 'Here, these are for you. There are photographs, a pen and some papers.'

'You took them from my father?'

'From Kanellos, yes.' The Englishman hung his head. 'We . . . we beat him to find out if he was the traitor. He didn't say a word. Then we found out who the real rat was and Kanellos was taken back to the city at night. His possessions remained with me by mistake.'

'Why did you keep them?'

Waggoner shrugged. 'I don't know. I suppose I thought he deserved that. He was . . . he was a very brave man. I should never have written what I did about him.'

Mavros looked at the photos. They showed a young Spyros, his moustache even thicker than it was later, surrounded by men in incomplete military uniforms, some wearing the Cretan *mandili* and *vraka*. Their boots were in tatters and their weapons a mixture of elderly rifles and plundered German machine-pistols. But most striking were the smiles on their faces – they looked as if they truly believed they could defeat this and any other oppressor. The writing instrument was an old fountain pen made of dark-blue celluloid. He didn't risk unscrewing it in case it was fragile. As for the writing, it was pages of text in a code he knew he would never be able to read – messages from the father he had scarcely known in a language legible only to long dead communist cipher clerks. At least, he thought, blinking back tears, Spyros had left a pen and not a weapon.

'Thank you,' he said to Waggoner. He couldn't bring himself to shake the hand that had dealt pain to his father, but he gave him a restrained smile.

Mavros and the Cretan dragged Lagoudhakis on to the terrace, the former calling Kriaras to have the neo-Nazi picked up.

'Right, Miki, let's get you back to the bosom of your family.'

'Speaking of bosoms, I heard your girlfriend was here. That means the delectable Cara Parks is up for grabs.'

'I guess so. But bear in mind she's a champion at kickboxing, karate and various other martial arts.'

Mikis grinned. 'Some like them hot.'

Back in the village square, Mavros handed over the recording device to Kriaras. Haris had got one of his men to make a copy of the disk on a laptop, so they were covered.

'Every single name Dhrakakis spouted better be arrested, Niko,' Mavros said, 'or I'm giving the disk to the press.'

'What country do you think you're living in?' the policeman said, in a long-suffering voice. 'Strings will be pulled, money will move between accounts, people will disappear. But don't worry – there'll be a big enough scandal.' He caught Mavros's eye. 'Be thankful you haven't been arrested for taking the law into your hands.'

Mavros laughed. 'Hey, Hari,' he called, 'the commander wants to charge your men with damaging the Kornariates' crops.'

The Cretan waved a hand in the air and went on talking to his wife and son.

'The Tsifakis family is well connected, Niko.'

'I'm well aware of that,' Kriaras snapped. 'Want a lift back to Chania in the helicopter?'

That may have a form of olive branch, but Mavros wasn't interested. The less he was seen with the commander the better.

'No, thanks. I've got some loose ends to tie up.'

'Loose and legal, I hope.'

Mavros gave him a crooked smile. 'Thanks for helping out – not that you won't be using this success to further your career.'

That ended the conversation.

Later, the village began to empty as the men who had been arrested were packed into police vehicles. Mavros had given a provisional statement to a cop from Chania, who was on good terms with Haris.

'At last,' Niki said, seizing his arm. 'My saviour has time for me.' She kissed him long and hard on the lips. 'Thank you, Alex. I knew I could rely on you.'

'How did they treat you?'

'Fine, really. I had food and drink. I think they were nastier to Maria.'

Mavros watched as Cara Parks cradled her assistant's head in her arms outside the *kafeneion*. The actress saw his look and nodded slowly to him. The fact that Maria hadn't asked for a doctor was encouraging. Two policemen were standing close by.

'Let's go,' Mikis said, beckoning from the Land Rover.

'Only if you aren't driving,' Mavros replied.

'I'm driving,' Haris said firmly. 'In the back, Miki, and lie down.'

Mavros and Niki got in the front with him. They jolted down the track and, as it turned to the west, Mavros caught a glimpse of smoke rising from the area of Waggoner's house. The fire engines had already left, but he didn't intend to call them back. Let him go the way he wanted.

Niki sat up, startled. A medium-sized brown and black bird had flown up in front of the Land Rover and was flying at low altitude ahead of them, moving up and down as if it was surfing.

'Hoopoe,' said Haris. 'They are beautiful.'

'Oh, yes,' said Niki, smiling in pleasure.

The Cretan slowed as the bird swerved and perched on a wall. It wiped its long beak against an upper wing and then opened the crest on its head, the tall feathers quivering in the breeze. Its beauty was in stark contrast to the barren slopes, as well as to the horrors brought to the island by men who had jumped into the air from ugly aircraft during the war – horrors whose effects could still be felt.

Mavros felt the stain of violence that had come over him since he'd arrived in Crete finally begin to recede. His father's face flashed before him and smiled in what he took to be encouragement. Mavros squeezed Niki's thigh and huddled against her. Hoopoes were good and so was life.

As they wound down the mountainside, Haris Tsifakis began to sing: 'Oh Crete, your earth is silver and your rocks diamonds . . .'

EPILOGUE

S everal days later, Mavros and Niki were back in his mother's flat on the flank of Lykavitoss in central Athens. They had made love often and slept deeply, but that morning he woke early and watched the pale light of dawn spread over the city's concrete blocks from the balcony.

The loose ends he'd had to tie up on the Great Island turned out to be few. Oskar Mesner had gone back to Germany and no one in the police seemed very interested in questioning him. Compared with the crimes of Dhrakakis and the others, his were insignificant and had been motivated by Tryfon Roufos – who was still at large – and Rudolf Kersten. It was the dead German who troubled Mavros most. He had seen Hildegard in the clinic, where she'd had surgery on her leg. She wouldn't accept any apologies because of his failure to identify Renzo Capaldi as one of Roufos's men. Nor would she talk about her husband, but Mavros got the impression that she'd learned the same awful truth that he had from Petros Lagoudhakis – that Kersten had secretly been faithful to his Nazi beliefs and that David Waggoner, while wrong to blackmail him, had been right about the depth of his hypocrisy.

As for the former SOE man, he died before the fire brigade could return to the village, having barricaded himself in his house and ignited the petrol that he had sluiced around. Mavros was sure he had deliberately copied the method used by Haris's men to destroy the cannabis plants. Unlike Kersten's death, it was a symbolic suicide.

Mikis had recovered from his head injury in every way, though he was still having checks at the clinic. He managed to charm his way into Cara Parks' bed within twenty-four hours and sent Mavros a triumphant text message, containing several translations of 'twin peaks' into Greek. Cara sent him one too, rather less demonstrative. Before he and Niki had left Crete on the production's Learjet, the actress had promised to meet them in Athens before she went back to the US. As it happened, that wouldn't be for some time as, considering the money that had already been spent, a new production team had been put together, a new director brought on board and filming resumed with only a few days' break. Maria Kondos had been questioned by police and released on bail. She was walking with a stick and telling everyone on the crew what they could and couldn't do. He was sure she'd been feigning amnesia after her first visit to Kornaria, keeping her family's business to herself, but there was no way of proving it. Luke Jannet and his sister were in prison in Athens, soon to be extradited to their home country.

The front door opened as far as the chain allowed.

'Hey, Alex,' said the Fat Man in a stage whisper. 'Let me in.'

Mavros closed the bedroom door on the sleeping Niki and took off the chain.

'What the hell is that?' he demanded, staring at the huge package his friend was carrying.

'Double-layer *galaktoboureko*,' Yiorgos replied. 'I found a recipe of the old woman's. Don't know if I've cracked it, though.'

In the kitchen, they carefully removed the paper covering.

'Christ and the Holy Mother,' Mavros said, 'one bite of that will bring instant death.'

'Right,' the Fat Man said, laying out two plates. 'We'd better make a suicide pact.'

'What?' Niki said from the door, rubbing her eyes and peering at the great mound of custard-filled filo pastry. 'Count me in.'

They ate, drank chilled water and moved on to Yiorgos's superlative coffee. Mavros watched the pair of them, surprised that no sparks had started to fly.

Then the Fat Man went too far. 'So, Alex, that Cara Parks? Is she really as well endowed as she looks on the screen?'

There was a brief pause and then Niki launched into a loud anti-male tirade.

Mavros laughed and left them to it. On the balcony, he looked southwards towards the light-blue Aegean, wishing for a few moments that he was back on Crete. Then he came to his senses and re-entered the domestic combat zone.

AFTERWORD

Further background to this novel, in particular regarding the Battle of Crete, can be found on my website, www.pauljohnston.co.uk. All the characters are composites, enhanced by my novelist's imagination, and are not based on individual participants in the fighting.

Some readers might wonder why I have changed the names of certain crucial wartime locations. The simple answer is that it felt right to do so. The sufferings of those involved, especially the Cretans, deserve the utmost respect and sympathy, and I did not want to use actual places of sacrifice in a work of fiction. However, as I describe the horror of the events in detail, it might appear that I am both in possession of my *galaktoboureko* and consuming it. Readers can make their own judgements. As for the drug-producing village of Kornaria, there is a real equivalent but I pusillanimously changed the name to avoid – I hope – a vendetta.

Crete, the Great Island, is a complex and fascinating place. There are plenty of good books for visitors. I particularly recommend the *Rough* and the *Blue Guides* for general information. Christopher Somerville's *The Golden Step*, *Across Crete: Part One* (compiled by Johan de Bakker), and *The Poetics of Manhood* by Michael Herzfeld provide illuminating details.

Many thanks to Crème de la Crime and Kate Lyall Grant for enabling me to exhume Mavros. And, as ever, I raise a large glass of vintage wine to my agent Broo Doherty of Wade and Doherty, whose critique of this book's first draft was astute.